# ORDER OF ROYALS

JUDE DEVERAUX

# ORDER OF ROYALS

MIRA

/||MIRA™

ISBN-13: 978-0-7783-0579-8

Recycling programs for this product may not exist in your area.

Order of Royals



All Illustrations by Imogen Oh



For questions and comments about the quality of this book, please contact us at CustomerService@Harlequin.com.

TM is a trademark of Harlequin Enterprises ULC.

MIRA
22 Adelaide St. West, 41st Floor
Toronto, Ontario M5H 4E3, Canada
MIRABooks.com

HarperCollins Publishers
Macken House, 39/40 Mayor Street Upper,
Dublin 1, D01 C9W8, Ireland
www.HarperCollins.com

**Printed in U.S.A.**

**Also by Jude Deveraux**

***Blue Swan***

ORDER OF SWANS

***Medlar Mysteries***

AN UNFINISHED MURDER
A RELATIVE MURDER
A WILLING MURDER
A JUSTIFIED MURDER
A FORGOTTEN MURDER

AS YOU WISH
MET HER MATCH
MEANT TO BE
MY HEART WILL FIND YOU

***Providence Falls***

CHANCE OF A LIFETIME
AN IMPOSSIBLE PROMISE
THIEF OF FATE

Look for Jude Deveraux's next novel
available soon from MIRA.

For additional books by Jude Deveraux,
visit her website, judedeveraux.com.

# PRINCESS ARADELLA

## CROWN PRINCESS OF PITHAN ISLAND ON THE PLANET OF BELLIS

"They are coming for you," Hale said. She was a large, muscular woman, and it wasn't easy for her to get through the small doorway that led into Princess Aradella's secret library. Hale waited for the young woman to look up. Open on her lap was one of the many books from Earth that had been illegally sent to her. Hale thought that since the books were in the incomprehensible English language, they should be allowed—but she didn't voice that opinion.

"My aunt-queen?" the princess asked, keeping her head down. When Hale didn't reply, Aradella looked up at her. "Not her witchy mother?" There was exasperation in her voice. When Hale still didn't answer, Aradella said, "My three spies?"

One side of Hale's mouth twitched. It was the closest she came to a smile. "No, but they did order new clothes. Larger ones."

Since she and Hale had engineered the plan to keep those snooping women occupied, Aradella smiled at the image. No one would think of the crown princess as "pretty," but when her colorless brows and lashes joined her smile, she was passable. Her blue eyes lit up—something few people saw. "Is Jobi here?"

With a grimace, Hale shook her head and said, "It's the worst of them all."

Aradella groaned. "Please no. Not my cousins! What did I do this time to deserve them? Did I read something that's not approved by the ever-watchful Queen Olina?" She gasped. "Did I dare look at a person not of royal blood?"

Hale was used to her charge's sense of humor. Usually, truth was the basis for it. She moved her hand to indicate the narrow room, letting Aradella know that she needed to leave. They had to prepare for her cousins' unexpected and unwanted visit.

Reluctantly, Aradella stood up. The room had once been a hallway that led to a private door into the palace. But immediately after Aradella was orphaned and Olina was crowned queen, the princess was moved into the small apartment and access was sealed off. "It's to protect the princess," the queen told people. Olina wanted to look good to her subjects. The truth was that she didn't want the residents of Pithan seeing the young woman who was often called "the true princess." Too many people believed that Aradella should be sitting on the throne. Also, Olina didn't want her niece-by-marriage snooping around and hearing what she shouldn't. Or worse, befriending people who might be amenable to a regime change. In the end, the young princess was "protected" to the point that she was allowed few visitors and watched at all times. There were some who said Princess Aradella had been imprisoned—but they didn't say that too loudly.

In spite of the adversity, Aradella had used the isolation to create something good. She'd worked with one of her few friends, Jobi, to make the sealed-off hall space into a library. Under cover of darkness, shelving had been put in, and Jobi sent her books from Earth to fill them. To protect Aradella in case she was discovered, all the books were about plants on the faraway planet. There was certainly nothing like *How to Overthrow an Evil Usurper Queen*. Others might have found the nonfiction books boring, but Aradella was so starved for knowledge that any books were worth the danger they put her in.

Aradella gave a wistful look to the book she'd been studying. It was one of several about poisonous plants. Jobi had told her that she might someday need that knowledge. Since he was one of the three people in the Order of Sight, meaning he could see into the future, she took his advice seriously. She often had Hale quiz her on what to look for in the plants that were not for consumption. Aradella didn't say so, but she wanted to recognize them in case her aunt-queen decided to use one.

Hale crouched through the door and held it open for Aradella, then carefully closed it and checked that nothing was showing. It looked like a wall panel, not hinting that it would open to the little library.

They went to Aradella's bedroom. Since her apartment had once been the housekeeper's quarters, it was very plain. Originally, there had been just two bedrooms, but after the death of Aradella's royal parents, another suite had been tacked onto the side. Installed in it were three women who reported to Queen Olina every day on whatever Aradella did.

The original two bedrooms and bath were for Aradella and her guard, Hale. It wasn't easy to hide that the women had become friends. "My savior," as Aradella called her since Hale had changed her life.

Spread out on the bed were the pads that Hale had made, with a big, flowing dress beside them. Aradella groaned.

"They won't stay long," Hale said. "I'll insist they have something to eat and that'll make them leave."

Aradella gave a smirk of agreement. "I hope it's those cherry pies. I know Shay likes them. It will hurt her to turn them down." She picked up the hip roll pad, tied it about her waist, then lifted her arms for Hale to tie on the upper pad. Over this went the big dress with voluminous sleeves. When they were done, Aradella looked at herself in the full-length mirror. She was nearly as wide as she was tall. "This should please them," she whispered, then looked back at Hale. "So help me, if Shay says how good I look, I'll . . . I'll . . ." She couldn't finish because they both knew she couldn't expose herself to anyone. If Olina found out that Aradella was lying about anything at all, her life would be in jeopardy. She motioned to the side. "They're out of the way?" She meant the spies that Olina had put in the house with the princess.

"Dead to the world," Hale assured her. Over a year ago, Hale had asked Queen Olina for a medicine that would calm the princess down. It was quickly given to her. That it was fed to the spies was never known, and the women didn't dare tell the queen that they spent their days drowsy, if not fully asleep. Olina's rage was so quickly aroused that the women might forfeit their lives.

Aradella, now fully disguised with her padding, waddled out to the large room at the front. The sprawling palace with its many smaller buildings for workers was in a cold volcanic crater called the Cauldron. The high protrusions that had once been molten lava encircled the space, making an excellent barrier to keep out intruders.

Most of the windows that looked out the front of the quarters had been covered. Olina said it was to give the princess "privacy." Everyone knew it was to keep people in the compound from seeing her. But the side windows that opened to a walled courtyard were still there. Aradella stretched to look through a slit in the wall and she could see her cousins coming toward them.

Princesses Shay and Bree Varlon were beautiful. *Like a princess should look*, Aradella thought yet again. Their father, a soldier, Sojee, had married the king's sister, Aradella's aunt, and they'd produced these beautiful young women, identical twins, the year after Aradella was born. The contrast had been noted. Aradella had always been too plump, too plain. The only thing remarkable about her was her brain. "Too bad you can't *see* that," someone said and others agreed. Aradella was sure that *beautiful-princess* was supposed to be one word—and she had never lived up to that ideal.

But the twins fulfilled the requirements lavishly. From birth, they were divine, glorious. They made the silk that was imported from Earth look rough. The way they walked, moved, spoke, was beautiful. They were adored by everyone who met them.

Except Aradella. She couldn't abide either of them, even though their personalities weren't alike. Shay had no heart while Bree's heart bled for everyone. She felt so very sorry for Aradella! When Aradella was younger, she'd let the sisters know what she felt about them, but not now. They were always so very kind to her. On the rare times when the three of them strolled about the Cauldron together and Aradella had trouble keeping up with them, they waited for her. They did it while pretending to fix a shoe or retie a hair ribbon. They complimented everything Aradella wore, said, noticed, anything that she knew. Kindness needed a higher definition to describe the twins.

But Aradella knew it was all fake. She fantasized about slicing off their heads with a sword. In fact, she had Hale set up pumpkins on two straw bodies, one pink, one blue, just so Aradella could whack them off. The plop of the pumpkins, then the explosion when they hit the ground, was deeply satisfying.

"They look like they have news," Hale said from beside her.

"I'm sure they do. Did someone find a new shade of pink for them? Or maybe Shay has decided to wear purple. Wouldn't that be monumental news? I can hardly wait to hear what they have to tell me." Aradella drew herself up, shoulders back, preparing to face her cousins. The girls opened the gate, then stopped and talked excitedly, but they kept their voices down.

"I've never seen them like this," Hale said. Like her charge, she was suspicious of everyone. "What are they up to? Has someone sent them?"

Aradella was much less interested in what they had to say than Hale was. She couldn't imagine anything of importance being entrusted to them.

"They're coming." Hale stepped away from the window.

She'd set a platter full of folded cherry pies on the table. They had to keep up Aradella's false façade about what she ate and wore, and most of all, what she did every day. When the knock came, Hale opened the door, and Aradella looked up from her seat, an embroidery hoop in her hand.

Politely, the twins waited for an invitation to sit down. Their excitement filled the air so strongly that the old, worn furniture seemed to vibrate.

"Would you like something to eat?" Aradella asked, pretending not to notice that they were nearly on fire with whatever they had to tell.

"No, thank you." Bree's voice gave a little jump as they sat down.

Hale was standing by the wall, her guard uniform stiff, unwrinkled. She was formidable looking.

Bree, the quieter, more gentle of the two, turned to her sister. "Go on." She sounded urgent. "Tell her."

Shay looked like a kettle about to blow its top. If she didn't tell immediately, she would explode. She took a deep breath. "Remember five years ago when we went to Eren?" She was referring to an island that was not divided between men and women. "We were guests of King Aramus?"

Aradella bit her tongue to stop a sarcastic retort. Of course she remembered! That trip was the highlight of her life. But she wasn't going to tell them that. "Yes, I do."

Bree leaned forward. "Remember the swan show?"

Aradella's heart did a little skip. "It was a nice display."

"Nice?" Shay said with enthusiasm. "It was magnificent! Those men with their birds were resplendent! I'll never forget it. We—"

Bree put her hand on her sister's arm to keep her from being overcome by the memory. "You know that our father has been gone for some time."

Aradella nodded as though she couldn't be bothered with such unimportant information.

"All this time, he was with Tanek Beyhan," Shay said.

At that name, Aradella's needle jammed against her thumb, but she'd die before she let them see she was affected by anything they had to say. "He was one of the swansmen, wasn't he?"

"Yes!" Shay leaned forward. "It has been revealed that his mother is one of the Seven."

It took all of Aradella's years of hiding what she felt to not show her shock. The Seven lived on the forbidden island of Empyrea and they ruled . . . well, everything. They had much more power than Queen Olina with her little island. "Is that so?" she said blandly.

Shay squinted her eyes at Aradella, trying to ascertain if she was as blasé as she appeared to be. "You danced with him." There was accusation in her voice.

"Did I?" Aradella asked. Like she would forget that night! Soaring with that glorious man. Gliding across the floor. "Yes, I do believe I remember that. Prince Nessa was there."

The twins stared at her in wide-eyed disbelief. How could she remind them of what she said to Nessa that night? And all because of the swansman. In unison, they glanced at Hale standing rigid by the wall. The awful thing Aradella had said to the young man she was to *marry* had changed everything. As punishment for that night, Aradella's beloved nanny was taken from her and the formidable Hale had been assigned in her place. "What you said . . ." Shay whispered.

"We were children," Aradella said in dismissal. "What does it matter now?"

"You were fourteen," Shay said. "Nessa and we were thirteen. That's old enough to—"

Bree spoke up loudly. "You're to marry the swansman Tanek."

Aradella gave up her pretense of sewing, put the hoop down, and stared at her cousins.

Shay was annoyed that her sister had taken over the glory-announcement. "Queen Olina has to agree, but of course she will. She can't go against a Seven."

"But what about King Aramus?" Aradella asked. "I'm to marry his son. It was arranged years ago."

"Not anymore," Shay said. "Too bad, as Prince Nessa was charming." She hesitated. "Well, maybe not to you, but he was to us. Which proves that he can be nice."

"That's not what Papá said about him," Bree muttered, and both young women looked at Aradella, waiting for her to say something.

But she was silent. She put on the face she used when she didn't want anyone to know what she was thinking. The twins looked at Hale. Her chin was up and she was staring straight ahead, her face also unreadable.

When the twins didn't take the silence as a sign that they were to leave, Aradella knew they had more information. She just had to wait for them to get around to telling it.

Shay got a faraway look. "I vividly remember him with the swans. We were sitting by the lake and he was diving with them. The swans wrapped their necks around him in a way that made all of us sigh." She looked at her sister to back her up.

"And then he rose out of the water," Bree said. "His wet shirt was clinging to him. We were so young and we'd never seen anything like it."

"And we haven't since!" Shay said.

At that, the sisters emitted giggles, but Aradella was still staring at them in stony silence.

Bree said, "When we got home, we told Papá how much we admired the man. We made huge hints for him to arrange a meeting."

"Ha!" Shay said. "You wanted him to arrange a marriage. With *you*."

"I was too young then, but now . . ."

The twins looked at Aradella. It was hitting them that *she* was to get the prize man. Not mean-spirited, scrawny Prince Nessa, but an actual *man*.

When it was obvious that Aradella wasn't going to join them

in giggling lust, Shay said, "Papá is with Tanek now. I think your marriage is to be quite soon."

Bree gave an encouraging smile. "I've heard that swansmen are very fertile. You'll be with child the morning after you marry him." There was longing and envy in her voice.

Shay groaned. "That's *your* dream, to have a dozen brats."

"And you don't want children?" Bree shot back.

"Two at most. But I haven't seen anyone who is husband material."

At last, Aradella spoke. "We live on an island that's nearly all women. None of us have seen many men—and certainly none equal to our status. We take what we are given."

When the sisters looked at each other, Aradella braced herself for what more they were to dump on her.

"There's to be a celebration at your wedding." Bree looked at Shay to continue. It seemed that she was stepping back and letting her more aggressive sister tell.

"With men," Shay whispered. "Men." There was so much emotion in her voice that she could hardly speak.

"Men?" Aradella asked and the sisters nodded. Many years ago, the Empyreans had separated men from women. Empyreans called it "The Righting of Ancient Wrongs." The men were sent to the island of Selkan while the women stayed on Pithan. There were some men on Pithan, such as the twins' father, Sojee, but he was needed to head the security of Queen Olina. There was some fraternization as there were a few precious children, but boys were sent to Selkan when they reached seven years old. Young people, like Aradella and the twins, had grown up in a world that was nearly all female. "We are to go to Selkan?" For all Aradella's self-control, she couldn't keep the shock out of her voice.

"No," Shay said. "Men are to come *here*. To us. *Many* men. They'll be here for two days."

"She won't like that," Aradella whispered.

They knew she meant Queen Olina.

"It's not her choice," Bree said. "The Seven have declared it. But you are right. The queen will not like it."

Aradella looked at her sharply. Sometimes Bree seemed to have a brain, but that couldn't be true. "There will be violence."

"Papá will stop it," Shay said confidently. The other women, including Hale, looked at her, seeming to ask how one man could control "many" men. Shay didn't like the way they were looking at her. "Perhaps they're coming here so we can choose husbands. King Aramus's brother has a walled estate on Selkan. We could live there and . . ." She trailed off. It was obvious that she'd thought about this and she appeared to be looking forward to it. She got control of herself and gave Aradella a hard look. "You need to plan what you're going to say to the swansman." Her tone was of warning. "Papá is coming with several people, even an Earth woman, and he's bringing your husband-to-be. They'll be here soon."

Bree said, "There will be a presentation ceremony where you and he will be formally introduced to the people. Then you'll need to—"

Hale stepped forward, cutting her off, and said loudly, "Would you girls like some cherry pies to take with you?"

The girls knew they were being dismissed and they stood up.

Shay didn't hide her disappointment in Aradella's cool reaction to the mass of news she'd been told. Shouldn't she be pleased? Certainly excited. But no, Aradella just sat there, her face unreadable. Several times over the years, Shay had said that Aradella wasn't real, that she was something created by the Empyreans. Shay remembered the time she'd stood behind a big, round barrel, put her arms and a leg out, and waved them. "I am Aradella and I think I am the smartest person on the planet. No one matches even half my brilliance!" Bree had laughed but then covered her mouth because she knew she shouldn't.

When Hale opened the door, the sisters hurried out. She was too big and frightening for them to disobey.

Aradella sat on the wide chair in silence, hearing and seeing nothing.

Hale made sure the girls were out of the courtyard, locked the gate behind them, then went back inside the house. She knew her charge needed time alone so she could digest what she'd been told.

Slowly, Aradella stood up, then began removing her many pounds of clothing. When she fumbled with the ties, Hale helped her, but they didn't speak.

Had she been something other than a royal princess who was destined to inherit a throne, Aradella would have walked about Pithan. She would have passed farms and seen the entrances to the other craters. But she didn't have such freedom. The only place she could go for privacy was her little library. And right now she desperately needed time to reflect on what was about to happen to her.

Hale led her to the room, handed her a ceramic bottle of cool water, then made sure the door was securely closed behind her.

Aradella collapsed into her big chair. It was covered in a blue-and-white fabric that Jobi had brought from Earth. He'd explained that it was Chinese and the buildings in the print were called "pagodas." Right now, such a simple conversation seemed far away.

She closed her eyes and tried to remember every detail of the visit, five years ago, to the island of Eren.

*It had started with a parade. Every guild on Pithan was represented by a wagon and the prettiest girls from each one had graced them.*

*At the end was Queen Olina's long, flat wagon. On it was her old mother, Olina's dazed and drugged husband, and of course the beautiful twin princesses. Their dresses sparkled, their long, thick hair was like sunlight, and they wore jewels of every color. All the residents of Eren and people from other islands came to watch and cheer as they ran after the trinkets that were thrown into the crowds.*

*Very few people noticed that far to the back of the queen's wagon sat a plain-faced girl encased in a heavy robe of colors so dull they could hardly be seen. To counteract the great weight of the robe, it had been nailed to the thick chair. Aradella was put into the garment then the front was sewn shut. She could not get out without the help of other people and the use of scissors. Queen Olina's explanation was that Aradella was "too important" to risk the harm that might come to her if she was too near the crowd.*

*After their flamboyant entry into the city, Aradella was told that she'd be spending time with Prince Nessa, the young man she was to marry.*

*In the afternoon, she was presented to her fiancé in an elaborate ceremony. She peeked around the pretty girls who were to enter ahead of her and saw him sitting in a big gold chair. At thirteen years old, he was short, very thin, and he had bad skin.*

*Aradella had often been told she was no prize when it came to looks, so the match seemed fair. She was told to stand to the back, behind the parade of young women entering, then her cousins, Shay and Bree. Aradella would go last.*

*Scrawny Nessa loved all the attention and the pretty girls, but when he saw Aradella, he stood up, his face showing his dislike of his wife-to-be. At that time she was taller than him and much wider. The women from the Beauty Guild had asked to be allowed to apply makeup to Aradella, but Olina told them no. "He is to see her as she truly is." No one missed the maliciousness in her tone. At the sight of her, Prince Nessa yelled "No! I will not marry her!" so loudly that he'd been ushered from the room. Everyone looked at Aradella in sympathy—but mixed with understanding.*

*After that first unfortunate introduction, Aradella was told she had to stay with Nessa, Bree, and Shay. As they were shown the sights of Eren and introduced to dignitaries, the twins made Nessa laugh. He didn't so much as glance at Aradella. They were often told of a coming water show that would feature three generations of men from the Order of Swans. Afterward, there was to be a dance that was just for the young people.*

*In silence, Aradella dutifully followed her cousins, the prince, and his simpering entourage. She just wanted to get away from them all.*

*On the afternoon of the second day, they were escorted to a beautiful lake where a covered pavilion had been built. Aradella was given a seat of honor to see the swan show. It was the Beyhan men—father, son, and the young grandson. The men were heavenly to look at and the fluidity of their movements with the swans was beyond anything Aradella had ever seen. The men could "soar," meaning lift themselves up, then glide through the air. Someone whispered that the men were descended from swans and used to have wings. She could believe it.*

*When the show was over, Aradella didn't want to leave, but she was pulled away. She had to get ready for the dance. She was to wear a heavy robe with a train, something that befitted a princess. She knew it was too heavy to walk in, let alone dance.*

*In a huge, sparkling room of King Aramus's home, food and beverage and an orchestra had been set up.*

*The pretty girls from Pithan and some locals were invited, but Aradella and Nessa were designated as the most important. For all that the dance was supposed to be for young people, it was heavily chaperoned. The three woman who spied on Aradella were there, eating and drinking in abundance. In the shadows was King Aramus's chief advisor, Fahir, standing to the side and watching everyone. The purpose of the dance was for Nessa and Aradella to become "better acquainted." But he much preferred the company of the beautiful, radiant, twin princesses, Shay and Bree. Even at thirteen, they were a sight to behold. They were dressed in starry colors of silk, with skin and hair that glowed. People were saying that when they smiled, the room became brighter.*

*Aradella found a chair that was as hidden as possible and tried to ignore all of them. She'd thought the parade had been bad, but the days she'd had to spend near Nessa topped that. She did her best to put her mind on the memory of the swan show. It was there that she'd seen* him. *He was like no one she'd ever before seen. His dark hair, the water over his body, the way he moved. All of it. She'd never seen or felt sensations such as ran through her. He—*

*She was pulled back to reality by the loud laughter of Prince Nessa. Her stomach seemed to turn over in revulsion as she reminded herself that Prince Nessa was the man she was to* marry. *The last days she'd spent in his company were more than enough to know what he was like. Others seemed to know his true nature since she'd been threatened to not say or do anything that would upset him. "You better not give a reason for this alliance to be called off!" her aunt Olina had yelled at Aradella. "Do I make myself clear to you? I'll—"*

*"She understands." Olina's old mother, Urah, stared hard at Aradella. Everyone knew that Urah was a witch, so no one dared contradict her, not even her daughter. Aradella had done her best to be humble and subservient to Prince Nessa, but he was stupid and thoroughly unlikable. The very sight of him made her feel sick. She did her best to hide her feelings. But sometimes it seemed that old Urah saw Aradella's true thoughts.*

*Sitting in her chair at the dance, she glanced at the scrawny prince. As usual, he was laughing and flirting with the twins, and they were giggling. It was a sound that Aradella was incapable of making.*

*Fahir, King Aramus's formidable emissary—and some believed he was the real king—left his place in darkness to say something to Nessa. The skinny boy frowned, then dutifully stalked across the room and asked Aradella to dance. She did not want to get too near him, but she couldn't say no. Slowly, she heaved herself up.*

*He was sneering as he led her onto the dance floor, then he held her as far away as his arms could extend. She wished it was farther.*

*"Since you are to be my wife," he said loudly so the princess-cousins could hear him, "you need to be told what you will be allowed to do. First of all, you must ask my permission for everything. At all times, you must remember that you are to be a* wife *to me. You must obey me for I will be the* king*!" The last was said at the volume of a man on a battlefield.*

*Through this list of "musts" Aradella didn't say a word. She clamped her teeth on the sides of her tongue and said nothing.*

*Finally, the music ended, he abruptly dropped her hands and walked away. His walk was one of triumph. He'd won a battle; he was the ruler of all he saw.*

*Trying to keep her dignity, Aradella went back to her chair.*

*To solidify his triumph, Prince Nessa stood close enough to Aradella that she could hear him as he bragged to the twins. "I told her what was expected of her," he said. "She must obey me in all things."*

*"This must stop!" said a man's deep voice.*

*Startled, Aradella looked up to see the swansman Tanek standing near her. He was wearing a long robe that she knew was woven from swan feathers. It looked like he was going to say something to Nessa. "No!" she said loudly.*

*Nessa whipped around to give her a look of chastisement, meaning that she was not to be so loud. As though he was protecting them from her, he escorted the twins away.*

*Tanek didn't move, but looked at Aradella in question.*

*"It's all right. I'm used to it. Besides, my cousins are worse than he is. They feel* sorry *for me." She stood up, meaning to leave. She'd had all of the party she could take. But she stumbled over the long dress her aunt had made her wear. She would have fallen but Tanek caught her arm and held her upright.*

*They heard Nessa say something unintelligible, then the twins laughed in that girly way that was naughty and enticing. Of course the object of their amusement was heavy, clumsy Aradella. She put her chin up, meaning to exit with as much dignity as she could muster.*

*But Tanek stepped in front of her, his back to the others. "Put your hand on my shoulder," he said, "and hold my hand tight."*

*"I'm not good at—"*

*He pulled her forward in a way that made her stop talking. They were on the dance floor, the music was playing, and the beautiful man pulled her closer to him. Aradella's feet entangled themselves. Between the long dress and her inexperience, she was going to fall. But then, something odd happened. She seemed to lift into the air. Not high, but just enough to take the weight off her feet. She felt as light as one of this man's swans. She knew what he was doing. It was the soaring she'd seen that afternoon.*

*They glided about the dance floor. They went slowly, then faster. The musicians, glad to have something other than the previous boring dancers to play for, went fast, slow, and in between. Aradella and Tanek followed every note.*

*"This is wonderful." She was breathless. "I've never felt anything like this." She looked over his shoulder. Prince Nessa and the twins were staring at her in disbelief—and awe. "They think I am doing this." That thought made her smile as she hadn't done in years. "I feel like one of your swans. I've read so much about them, but I never imagined I'd feel like one." Instantly, she knew she'd made an error.*

*His hand tightened on hers. "You* read *about them?"*

*"I didn't mean to say that. My aunt doesn't allow me to read, certainly not Earth books. She will—"*

*"Where did you get the books?"*

*All Aradella could think of was the horror of losing her library, which would happen if her aunt-queen found out about it. She was too fearful to speak.*

*Tanek seemed to know that her problem was secrecy. "I swear on the life of my swans that I won't tell."*

*She knew she was risking a lot by trusting this man, but she did. "A man brings books to me from Earth and he adjusted the translator so I can read them." She hesitated. "They are hidden away."*

*"Was it Jobi who did this?" When she nodded, he said, "I know him well. My father has been to Earth and he has some books. I'll send them to you."*

*"No! I mean, the queen might see them, then . . ." She wasn't going to disparage the queen to anyone. Doing so could mean death.*

*"How does Jobi get them to you?"*

*She was glad for his understanding. "I'm allowed to eat all the cakes there are, so he sends me a big basket of them. The books are underneath."*

*"Then I shall send you pastries that our cook makes and under them will be several Earth books."*

*"That would be wonderful. Thank you!" She smiled broadly.*

*"I'll do most anything if it makes a pretty girl smile at me."*

*He couldn't have said anything that shocked Aradella more. No one had ever come close to calling her "pretty."*

*For a few minutes they danced together in silence and Aradella knew that she'd remember this night for the rest of her life.*

*When the music ceased, they floated to the ground. For Aradella, it felt awful to have her weight back on her feet. Tanek stepped away, then he pressed his lips to her hand. "Are they still smirking?" he asked softly.*

*"No," she said happily. "They're looking at me in shock." She smiled at Tanek. "Thank you."*

*He stood up straight and was about to say something but heard, "Papá!"*

*"You'll have to excuse my son," Tanek said. "He has done a bit of work so now he must eat to equal his weight." He paused. "Would you like to meet him?"*

*Aradella glanced at the others. Everyone was frowning at her. "Perhaps another time."*

*"Then I will leave you and I thank you for a lovely dance." He smiled again, then turned and left.*

*Aradella wanted to go after him, but Nessa leaped in front of her. "How disgusting that you'd make a spectacle of yourself like that! That man is old enough to be your father. I don't know why he was allowed in here. He should stay with his filthy birds."*

*Looking past him, Aradella saw Tanek put his arm around his son's shoulders as they left the room. She looked at ugly, scrawny Nessa. "Tanek Beyhan is more of a man than you will ever be. You are a pompous, strutting, weak fool. You're not worthy of your title or even the space you take up on this planet." With her head held high, she left the room.*

*Minutes later, the spy-maids caught up with her—and as always, they started telling her that she was bad, ungrateful, and full of herself. Aradella knew that everything she did and said was reported to the queen, so she usually kept her mouth shut. But this time, she didn't want these horrible women to ruin her sweet memory. She looked at the first one. "You will keep your silence or I'll tell my aunt that you steal from my clothing allowance." To the second one, she said, "And you take food from the palace." She looked at the third one. "You meet your lover in the night." Aradella stepped back. "Do I make myself clear?" She didn't wait for an answer but walked away, leaving them behind.*

Abruptly, Aradella came back to the present, to sitting alone in her little library. That day when she'd walked away from the spy-maids, she'd thought she'd won. She left feeling as light as though she were still dancing with the swansman.

But her euphoria didn't last long. The next day, she found out that her threats had achieved nothing. It was her friend Jobi who told her what happened. No one knew he was Aradella's friend, so the court felt at ease talking in front of him.

The maids went to Queen Olina and exaggerated everything that had happened at the dance.

"For no reason," one maid said, "she was exceedingly nasty to the lovely Prince Nessa—and to us."

"She has no respect for anyone," the second one said. "I was sickened by what she said to dear Prince Nessa."

Olina frowned. "What did she say?"

They looked at the third maid as she had the best memory. She exactly quoted Aradella's remark about Nessa being "a pompous, strutting, weak fool."

Olina gave a snort of laughter, as what Aradella said was true. But Olina got herself under control. "She will have to be punished." Since *punish* was Olina's absolute favorite word, her eyes gleamed. She turned to her mother, who was always by her side. "Does she *like* anyone?"

Her mother didn't hide her displeasure that her daughter knew so little about a girl who was her competition for the throne. "Her nursemaid has been with her all her life." An hour later, Aradella's beloved companion was taken away and the princess was left truly alone.

Days later, the queen delighted in telling the fawning entourage that always surrounded her the story of how she'd found Aradella's new, formidable caretaker. Jobi listened and later he told the story to Aradella. The queen had been on horseback, inspecting her kingdom. That meant she was making sure that no one was receiving more than her. When she saw a big, muscular woman working in a farmer's field, she halted and watched. The woman easily controlled four heavy horses, then broke up a vicious dogfight. The queen asked the farmer about her. He said the woman was called Hale, no other name given.

"'Everyone is afraid of her,' the farmer told me. 'We stay away from her, but she does the work of six women so we keep her.'" The queen looked at her audience and said, "So I had her brought to me and I asked her if she'd like to take over the care of the ugly princess. I said, 'You're to do nothing with her, just keep her away from others, and don't let her cause trouble.' The big woman gave me a look that I don't usually allow, but then she said, 'You mean you keep her in prison and I'm to be her jailer?' I wanted to punish her insolence, but I could see that she truly understood the job. I told her that yes, that's exactly what I want. She wiped the horse manure off her face, and said, 'When do I start?'"

No matter how many times Olina told this story, her audience obligingly howled with laughter at the queen's great wisdom.

When Hale opened the door to the little library, Aradella looked up at her. For a moment their eyes locked. The two of them had been through a lot in the last years, and they'd shared their deepest thoughts. "She won't approve of this marriage," Aradella said.

"No, she will not," Hale said.

Aradella's eyes were hollow. "You know that I'm as good as dead, don't you?"

Hale didn't bother lying. She just nodded. Yes, she knew that very well.

# QUEEN OLINA

## THE QUEEN OF PITHAN THROUGH HER MARRIAGE TO THE LATE KING'S BROTHER

"I will kill her." Olina's voice was fierce with anger. She and her mother, Urah, were in Olina's most private chamber. It was a big room with walls slathered in gold. Colored gems were embedded in the wooden casements that surrounded the fake windows. Since everything was procured through thievery of the women of Pithan, no one other than the two women was allowed inside. (The three men who had done the work were found at the bottom of a river.) "I will send that vile princess out in a carriage, then plunge it down the side of a crater. She will be a bloody pulp."

Urah was sitting in a chair that had been made for her. Her old body was brittle and racked with pain, but as she looked at her magnificent six-foot-tall daughter, she knew it had been worth it. She'd sacrificed her health and her beauty, plus the two true loves of her life, to create a daughter who would achieve *this*. Only in this opulent room was the full display of what she and her daughter had accomplished allowed to be shown. In the rest of the old palace, they restrained themselves in an homage to that disgusting thing that earthlings called "good taste." Subdued. Quiet. Far from the rich flamboyance of this room.

Urah took a sip of her drink. It was a concoction she and her last remaining sister had prepared to give Urah strength. "You did that to her parents," she said calmly. "People would be suspicious if the same action was repeated."

"Ah, yes, how could I forget that." Olina smiled in memory of the mangled bodies of the king and queen that had been carried away from the bottom of a stony, sharp crater wall. She'd had to stifle a laugh of delight at the sight. After all, she'd worked hard to ensnare the stupid younger brother of the dead king. She'd put up with his contentment, his lack of ambition—and his greedy hands on her body. Yet, even after all that work, after the marriage, her sister-in-law had said that Olina would never be queen. The young queen hadn't meant it maliciously. No, it was said in confusion. Olina had seen something she didn't like and had thoughtlessly said, "When I'm queen I won't allow that." Her sister-in-law, puzzled, said, "But you'll never be queen. Our daughter, Aradella, will inherit the crown."

Olina had wanted to strike the woman. She was always so calm, so smilingly pleasant, that Olina desperately wanted to smash her face. Instead, she said, "Of course. I misspoke. I meant, *if* I were queen." She smiled as much as she could.

Two weeks later, Olina happily gazed down on the mutilated bodies of her in-laws. Since Aradella was only fourteen, Olina's husband was crowned king. Not regent, not a place holder for the princess, but thanks to the cleverness of Olina and her mother, as *king*. Even so, there were some people who protested this.

As the hated princess grew to age, Olina and her mother had frantically tried spells, amulets, virile young men, and gagging down disgusting concoctions in an attempt to make Olina pregnant. But nothing worked. She was barren—which meant that the arrogant, smart-mouthed Aradella was still the heir to the throne. She was just waiting—whether for Olina's death or an overthrow wasn't clear.

In the last few years the talk of the women of Pithan about tossing Olina and her silent husband out had increased. They spoke of Aradella as "the true queen."

Olina looked at her mother—which was something she didn't like to do. The deep, ugly creases on her face and her emaciated body reminded Olina that everyone had a time limit. "She cannot marry the swansman."

Urah took another sip of her bloodred drink. She could feel her daughter's revulsion at her looks, but then Urah felt the same way. There were no mirrors in her own chambers. "Of course she can't."

Olina was too angry to ask if her mother had any ideas about what to do to stop the marriage. But then, Olina liked to think *she* was the power, that *she* made the decisions, that it was *her* intelligent planning that had put her on the throne. "All this because he's the son a Seven!" Olina said. "What right do they have on *my* island?" She glanced at her mother. "The men! They are sending *men* here." As it was, she could barely abide the limited access necessary for procreation. The men couldn't live there!

Urah gave a smile that deepened the crevices on her face. "That will cause chaos. The younger, stronger men have been raised without women. They will attack. Rape. They will terrify the women."

Olina's face brightened at the image. "The men will be allowed no weapons so our guards will go after them. It will be a bloodbath."

"Yes," Urah said. "It will be."

Olina allowed herself to imagine it. Men and women separated for years, then suddenly allowed to mingle together—for just two days. She knew that the men on Selkan had become so savage that they had Cutting Games. They fought one another with swords and knives. Men rated their masculinity by the number of scars on their bodies. Olina envisioned the men being allowed on their island of women. Yes, the violence would be massive.

"But what about *him*? The swansman?" Olina threw up her hands in frustration. "It was all so well planned. That ugly girl would marry that obnoxious Prince Nessa. I'd let the whole island see him, hear him. Absolutely *no one* would want to back that weaselly little creep as a ruler. He'd antagonize the whole island. It was a perfect plan!" She looked back at her mother. "But this swansman has destroyed it! What is to be done? How do I fight this? What do I *do*?" She flopped down in a chair that had a diamond the size of a dodo egg at the top. It had come from Earth, stolen from some long-ago Indian ruler.

Urah gave her daughter time to calm down. When she was this worked up, she couldn't hear anything but her own anger. Finally, Urah said, "Valona."

Olina groaned. "Not now! I have too much to worry about to deal with her."

Urah repressed her own groan. Her daughter didn't grasp concepts quickly. It all had to be explained to her—which was yet another reason why she agreed that Princess Aradella had to be removed. Olina believed she'd thoroughly repressed the girl, but too often Urah saw a light in the girl's eyes that should not have been there. "Do you not remember what time of year it is?"

Olina gave her mother a blank look, not understanding. "Is it another festival in the Lair? I can't keep up with what Valona does."

The Lair was the most remote crater on Pithan and the only one that was still an active volcano. Steam blew up out of the center in a way that made the whole bowl-shaped area a tropical oasis. As for Valona, she ruled the place with an iron fist. The women of the Lair were not allowed to leave without permission. And no one entered. Even Olina's personal guard didn't go to the Lair. There were outrageous stories about what went on there, but as long as the peace was kept, Olina stayed out of it. However, there was one rumor that Olina knew was true. She envied Valona for being able to make it happen.

When her mother didn't reply, Olina said, "At least I don't have to worry about Valona. She'll kill any man who tries to enter her territory."

As always, Urah was annoyed that her daughter didn't see the whole picture. "It is *that* time of year!"

It took Olina a moment to understand what her mother was saying. "That is the perfect solution." Her face fell. "But *I* will be blamed."

Urah drew in her breath to give herself patience. "Yes, someone will need to be blamed. You must marry that man, Tanek, to the princess quickly, but send them to the Lair until the ceremony. And send his pretty son with them. It will be your generous gift to them. Then let Valona do the rest. She'll make sure the two men are held responsible." Urah paused. "And if those Selkan men still come here, when they see the women, they will attack. It will be WAR!" Abruptly, her face hardened. "Whatever is done, I want that man Tanek removed. He *must* be taken out."

Ever since Urah had ordered the murder of Tanek's grandfather and the destruction of his property, she'd feared that Tanek would find out and come after her. She knew the man was too primitive to understand that the deaths—there had been several over time—had been necessary to put her daughter on the throne. Her cause was much more important than caring for his silly birds. "Yes," Urah whispered. "Getting rid of him will solve many problems."

"Then it's settled?" Olina asked.

Urah nodded. "Call that thing so it can tell Valona what we're sending to her."

"You!" Olina said sharply. "Come!"

In a flutter of wings appeared a Never. He was a tiny man, no taller than the palm of a hand, with wings like a dragonfly.

That Olina didn't consider him more than an animal was why he was allowed in their private room. He was the only Never on the island. Olina couldn't imagine what would happen if such vermin were allowed to fly about freely. The women would start communicating between the craters? Guilds would talk to each other? What if—oh horrors!—they spoke with people on other islands?

Olina didn't like the tiny being any more than she liked insects buzzing around her. That it could talk made her detest it even more. "Here! You! Go to Valona and tell her that I'm sending her a royal guest. Say that this girl will be accompanied by two men and she may use *all* of them in her coming celebration. They are my gift to her." She looked at her mother. "Do you think Valona will understand that? Or am I being too subtle?"

Urah smiled. "I think Valona will know exactly what you mean. Send that thing now!"

"Go!" Olina ordered and the little man left in a gust of air so strong that it made her squint her eyes and turn away. "If I didn't need that thing, I'd delight in ripping it apart."

Urah agreed completely.

# KALEY GRACE ARENS

## FROM THE PLANET OF EARTH

Kaley was sitting on a horse, wearing a long, heavy robe that looked like it had come off the set of a Bollywood movie. Underneath, she hadn't had a bath in days and her mind was a mass of turmoil. She wanted to kick her horse forward, run into the forest, and leave all of them. Since that wasn't possible, the question was, *What the hell am I to do?!*

This morning she'd been on an island that was populated almost exclusively by men—although, they'd found out that more females than people knew about had been hiding there.

She was told she had three choices of what to do with her life. One was to go home! Back to Earth. Sleep through the three-year journey back to her father and grandparents, finish her PhD in folklore, and get a job teaching. It's how she'd always thought her life would go.

Second choice was to stay on Bellis and apprentice to a very good-looking warlock named Garen.

At that memory, Kaley shook her head. She'd seen enough on this planet to know that a life of mixing up potions full of lizards' tongues or whatever was quite possible.

The last choice was staying with Tanek. Big, gorgeous, kind, funny, strong, take-care-of-everyone Tanek.

*Gee*, she thought, *which should I choose?* Ha ha. All she knew for absolutely *sure* was that she was in love with Tanek. Deeply. Like as in "can't live without him." His life had become hers. Sometimes she felt that she had been dumped on him the same way his son had been. When Tanek was sixteen, after a one-nighter, a newborn son was handed to him and Tanek had become a single father. He'd taken on the responsibility of his child the way he'd risked his life to protect and care for the earthling that had been thrust onto him.

But before Kaley could say a word about her choice, they—meaning her, with the big protector Sojee, Tanek, and nineteen-year-old Mekos—were hurried onto a little wooden ship and taken to the island of Pithan. Which was mostly women.

So now Kaley was waiting for women to unload packages off the ship, then they were to go see the queen of the island—which would be her second encounter with the odious woman! But right now, it was bothering Kaley that the women who'd come to welcome them were looking at Tanek the way a dieter looked at chocolate.

Kaley very much wanted to loudly declare that her choice was to stay with Tanek. And with Sojee and Mekos and all the other people she'd met during the extraordinary events they'd experienced. She wanted to go to Tanek's family's Homestead, help rebuild it, pop out a kid or three, and live Happily Ever After.

However, there was one itty-bitty problem. This morning they'd been told that Tanek was to marry a princess. It was an arranged marriage meant to unite high rulers with mid-range rulers in the hope that everyone would stop fighting. There was even talk of putting the men and women together. On the same island. Wouldn't that be wild and crazy?

To be fair, the king's sleazy, slimy "advisor," Fahir, had told Kaley she could stay with Tanek and his new, young wife and be a maid. *How kind of him*, she thought.

Right now, Kaley couldn't think past the feelings that were raging through her mind and body. The truth was, being in love had shocked her with how strong the feeling was. No wonder people sang and wrote about it. They died for it. The thought of Tanek with another woman made her heart start to crack—and it gave her murderous thoughts. She couldn't imagine a future without him. The life she'd planned for herself, living in a little stone house and teaching about folktales at the university level, now seemed lonely and empty. It wasn't what she wanted anymore.

So how could she deal with losing him? She couldn't figure out something she couldn't comprehend.

At last, everything was unloaded and put into wagons. Yet again, Kaley thought of how strange the planet was. They had spaceships that had been making trips to Earth for centuries, yet they used horse-drawn carriages and carried swords.

But then, the modern things were all on the forbidden fourth island, the place Tanek and his friends were secretly plotting to overthrow.

Sojee reined in his big horse beside her. He was a huge man, older, bald, with a heavy black beard. He lived on this women-only island and was the head of the Queen's Guard—which had a lot of women and a few men. He also had some connection to the royals, but she wasn't sure what. "Ready?" he asked.

Kaley was too angry to be nice. "Oh? So now you're speaking? You're no longer kneeling in front of the king's hitman and agreeing to sacrifice your friend's life to solve some Lilliputian egg war?"

Sojee was unperturbed by her sniping. "I sense a new story in that and you can tell us later." He nodded toward the front of the waiting people. "Young Tanek doesn't look too bothered."

Tanek, on a large black horse and looking splendid in a silver-and-blue robe, was smiling down at three beautiful young women who were running their hands up his muscular calves.

"What do they think they're doing?" Kaley said through clenched teeth.

"Our Tanek is a ferm."

Kaley looked at Sojee with narrowed eyes. "And what is that?"

"A fertile man. The women of this island are overcome with baby lust."

"Is that why *you* live here?" she snapped.

Laughing, Sojee reined his horse away.

"Great," Kaley muttered. "I'm the only one concerned about this. It's a joke to everyone else." A movement caught her eye. It was Garen, the warlock, his face handsome in spite of the scars. He was looking at her in question. Had she decided yet? Was she going to take him up on his offer to be his apprentice? She gave him a half smile as though to say, *I'm thinking about it.*

To the side was Tanek's tall, beautiful son, Mekos. Kaley had met his mother. She was called a Lely, meaning she was part animal. Mekos was one-quarter fox, which gave him keen senses in eyesight and hearing—as well as cute pointed ears.

Kaley watched as teen girls surrounded Mekos, looking up at him in wonder. But she couldn't blame them. He looked like a dark-haired angel and she was very fond of him.

She looked back at Tanek in time to see a woman run her hand so high up on his leg that she almost reached his behind. Kaley had spent a lot of her life on a horse so it was easy to urge her steed forward.

"Watch out!" a woman shouted at her.

Kaley didn't allow the horse to step on the woman but it was close. She kept her face turned away from Tanek because she knew he was laughing at her. "I hear this is a very pretty island."

Tanek's mouth was twitching with suppressed laughter. "What I've seen of it is beautiful." He was looking at the women who wanted to glue themselves to him.

She turned toward him so quickly the horse did a little dance with its front legs. "Is this a joke to you?"

"Marry a princess? Become king? There are worse things."

All she could do was grit her teeth. This morning when

he'd been told he was to marry the princess he'd been so angry that the king's wizard had put a spell on Tanek and Sojee that made them drop to their knees. Paralyzed. Unable to move or speak. The man had tried the same enchantment on Kaley but it hadn't worked on her. *At least, there are some advantages to being from Earth*, she'd thought.

Kaley started to say more to Tanek, but some women wearing blue uniforms and riding sleek dark horses skillfully separated her from the group. It was like herding cattle—and Kaley was being removed from the herd.

She watched as her friends were led down the gravel road to disappear past the overhanging trees. "Looks like they don't need any more women," she muttered.

"No, they do not."

Garen was on a horse beside her. He had on all black, no gaudy robe that seemed to be necessary to appear before the queen. He was so familiar looking that Kaley had to blink back tears. It seemed that her life was falling apart.

"Shall we cast a spell on them?" he asked. "Turn them into insects so they get trampled on?"

If she were on Earth, she would have laughed, but from Garen, it might be a genuine offer. Either way, he'd made her feel better.

"If we leave, I don't think they'll miss us, do you?" he asked.

Kaley glanced at the trees. Only the last riders, all women, were visible. "I'm not sure they'll remember I exist."

"How I wish that were true," he said with feeling. "Then you'd be free and I'd have a chance." He didn't wait for her reply. "At least you still wear the necklace."

She had on the Truth Necklace. When someone near her told a lie, the half round pendant got warm. The worse the lie, the hotter it got. Unfortunately, there were some types of people it didn't work on, such as those with magic abilities. Since the necklace had been made by Garen's family, he was glad to see her wearing it.

"Come on," he said. "I'll show you some of Pithan before we have to endure a speech by my cousin."

"Who is that?"

"Dear Queen Olina. Her mother and mine are sisters."

"Ah, right." Kaley was trying to piece together what she knew about his family. It certainly wasn't a happy, caring group of people. Incest and patricide were highlights. But then, they were often the building blocks of fairy tales, and this planet was full of fairy tales happening in real life. She followed him down a narrow path that led away from the others.

"Pithan is a cluster of cold volcanos," he began.

She listened as he told of extinct volcanos that had formed high-walled bowls. Inside each one was a village. "But the Lair is different," he said. "It still steams and that makes the whole crater into a secluded, tropical paradise."

"It sounds beautiful."

"I haven't seen the place, but I hear that it is." He said that when the men were ordered off the island the women formed themselves into guilds based on their interests, and each one had its own crater. There was a guild for sports, one for teachers, for art and music, and others. "And there's one managed by my aunt."

"Right," she said. "One of the four sisters." She politely didn't say "witches." One of the sisters had made a gingerbread house that enticed children. Thanks to her and Sojee and Tanek, that hadn't ended well for the odious woman.

Garen told that in one crater was a lake of the purest water. It was where the all-female military lived and guarded. "And then there's the Cauldron." It was the largest and inside it was the royal palace. "It's big and old, cold and drafty." When Garen smiled, one side of his face didn't quite move as the scars held it in place. "There's a rumor that Olina has a room that's covered in gold and jewels, but no one knows for sure."

"From what I've seen of her, it might hold the skins of her enemies," she said and Garen laughed. "It does sound like the women have created an excellent society. Tanek . . ." She hesitated. "I'm sure he'll be very happy here."

They followed a curve in the road and it opened to a town. In front of them, moving slowly, was a long line of people on horses, with Kaley's friends at the head. Women were running along the side, smiling and happy to see the visitors.

Kaley looked around at the town. Since she'd grown up on a farm in Kansas, she was very aware of that expensive terror called "maintenance." Roofs needed constant repair. Tornado-strength winds took down fences, picked up equipment and slammed it into walls. Fires, accidents, and just plain daily use took a toll on everything.

As they rode down the potholed road, Kaley saw what had once been a thriving town. There were shops and homes, and open areas, but now . . .

She looked at Garen, her eyes wide. He gave a shrug of understanding.

The once-pretty buildings were in a sorry state of disrepair. Roofs, walls, windows were broken, falling down, crumbling. There was evidence of attempts at patching but it was flimsy and poorly done.

"My grandfather could . . . My dad could . . ." She didn't need to finish. A sound made her turn. The front window of a shop had fallen out and hit the ground.

She turned to say something to Garen, but then she halted and stared in open-mouthed astonishment. Behind him was a two-story building in pristine condition. It was like a million-dollar house set in the midst of a slum.

"Government House," he said. "Olina brings in men from Selkan to maintain it. Guards keep the women away from the men."

"So there'll be no unplanned children?"

"Yes." He seemed pleased that she understood.

They rode past the high walls of the Cauldron. An iron gate closed the entrance.

"A true fortress," she said.

"More than you know." Garen nodded ahead. "Aradella is—" Considering what was coming with the princess, he thought it best not to mention her.

Standing outside the wall were two very pretty girls. They were identical except that one wore pink and the other one was in blue. "Who are they?"

Again, Garen just nodded. Sojee left the line to stop his big horse next to the girls. In what seemed to be a well-practiced gesture, the girl in blue lifted her arms. Bending, Sojee pulled her up onto the horse in back of him. He repeated the action and the pink girl went in front. It appeared to be a practiced gesture, as though the three of them had done it many times. He reined the horse back into the line.

Kaley looked at Garen.

"You have just seen Princess Shay and Princess Bree, daughters of Sojee and his late wife, who was sister to the king. The latest rumor is that one of them is to marry young Mekos."

"He's too young." She reminded herself that she wasn't on Earth. "Does he close his eyes to make the choice?" She was being sarcastic as the girls looked alike.

"It doesn't matter since neither of them has a brain."

"No!" Kaley said. "That's not good. Mekos is smart and talented. You should hear him sing! He needs someone he can talk to, share things with. He has to have—" She broke off at the way Garen was looking at her, and turned away. What happened to Tanek and his son was going to be none of her business.

Finally, the line stopped and people began to dismount. They were in front of a big wooden platform with stairs leading up to it.

Kaley wanted to inspect the posts that held up the platform to make sure they were strong. "Did the women build that?"

"In this case, the men from Selkan built it," Garen said, laughing at the question.

The area was beginning to fill up with women of all sizes, shapes, and ages. When Kaley heard someone yell "Make way!

Make way!" she turned. The women had formed a protective circle around two women escorting three small children. With great respect, everyone stepped back to let them go through.

"Precious cargo," Kaley said, thinking how she'd seen something similar on the all-male island. In the next moment, some women took the reins of their horses. Garen and Kaley dismounted, then saw that there were already too many people for them to get a clear view of what was happening. Women began to touch Garen's arms.

"Come on," he said as he moved away from them.

Kaley followed him to a tall house that was to the side of the platform. The front door had an X of boards across it, but Garen waved his hand and it opened. He motioned for Kaley to go inside and he followed. It was dark in the house and she heard creatures scurry away. Garen went to the stairs, but Kaley hesitated. She could see that the steps were falling apart.

"You want to hear what the queen has to say or not?"

She followed him up the stairs, skipping rotten treads as best she could.

At the top, he punched open old shutters so they could see the wide, flat platform from the side. There were three big, gilded chairs set close together. In the middle was a young woman cocooned in a thick robe that was more like armor than a garment. They saw her in profile. She had blonde hair and she was looking straight ahead, with no movement. She didn't look real.

On her left side was Prince Nessa, twisting about and waving to the growing crowd. He looked very smug, quite happy. In the last weeks, Kaley had spent enough time with the young man that she knew what he was thinking. He believed that all that was good on the planet should be given to him. Right now he seemed jubilant that he was not going to have to marry Princess Aradella. Kaley knew he'd been promised one of Sojee's beautiful princess daughters. Had someone also hinted that he might be made king? To be king without the bother of Princess Aradella would be the only thing that would make him happy.

On the other side of the princess sat Tanek. He was rigidly upright, looking straight ahead, and not moving. Kaley wondered if he'd again been put under a spell. Standing at the back was Sojee, his eyes searching the crowd for any sign of something that could be a problem. Near him stood his daughters, smiling, and looking happy. A few feet away was Mekos. Like his father, he could keep his face from showing what he was feeling. One of Sojee's pretty daughters kept sneaking glances at him, but Mekos didn't look at her.

"Think they're drawing lots to see who gets the boy?" Garen asked. "And the losing girl gets Nessa?"

Kaley clenched her jaw. It was one thing to read fairy tales that told of arranged marriages, but another to see it in person. Mekos deserved the best, not a dimwit of a bride.

As though she sensed them, Princess Aradella turned her head, looked up to the top of the house, and saw Kaley and Garen watching. As Kaley locked eyes with the princess, she got a feeling of intelligence—but she also sensed the girl's resignation to her fate. Kaley had a deep affinity for animals and this girl's eyes were like an animal caught in a trap. It was almost as though she believed this was the *end.*

Kaley raised her hand, palm exposed, as though to pass hope to the girl. Aradella made no expression, just turned away and looked back at the crowd.

"Are you bonding with your enemy?" Garen asked.

"I doubt if anyone asked her who she wants to marry. That poor, poor girl."

"She certainly doesn't live up to competition from her beautiful cousins."

"Are you kidding?" Kaley snapped. "She's got great bone structure, her features just lack contrast. If I turned Aradella over to one of those YouTube influencers, they'd darken her brows and lashes, smear on brown contouring, and she'd be a knockout."

Garen was looking at her like she was speaking a strange language. "Should I adjust your chip?"

He meant the translator chips that were embedded in the forearms of everyone in this world. Kaley's had been inserted by Jobi when they were on Earth and she was only a day old. The chips allowed them to understand each other in almost any language. She didn't reply to his joke as a great noise came from below. Horns, drums, and high-pitched squeals from the women made a cacophony. It was easy to guess what was happening. The queen was arriving.

Kaley and Garen watched as Queen Olina came up the back stairs. She had on a dress that was so sparkly even people at the back of the crowd blinked against the glare. Behind her came an old man. He was bent over and stumbled up the stairs, looking like he wasn't sure where he was.

"Behold the great and wondrous king," Garen said in sarcasm.

The next person to arrive was a woman so old that she looked like she might go *pouf!* and vanish in a cloud of dust. Kaley looked at Garen.

"She's the oldest of the four sisters. Aunt Reena said she gave up her beauty and youth to make her daughter the queen. Kind of drained it into a vat and stirred." He pantomimed moving a paddle around a big pot, his eyes showing his amusement.

"That sounds like half of the fairy tales. Is your aunt Reena here?"

He leaned forward so his cheek with its stubble of whiskers was very near Kaley's lips. "There."

He pointed to a tall woman with marvelous dark hair and wearing a red dress. She was extraordinary looking! Wherever she went, people must notice her. Kaley had now seen three of the four sister-witches. Only Garen's late mother was missing. "She is beautiful!"

"My mother was better," Garen said as he took his time moving his face away from hers.

When he was again beside her, Kaley was glad to see that Tanek was looking up at them. With the biggest smile she could make, she joyously waved at him. "I wish I had some flowers to toss down to him," she said.

"Something that would give him a rash?" Garen asked. "Or something stronger? Perhaps impotency forever?" When she gave him a look to stop it, Garen laughed.

The last to ascend the platform were half a dozen young women dressed in skimpy clothes, looking a bit like Christmas elves. They formed a half circle behind Queen Olina as she stood at the front of the platform to address her subjects.

"Who are the elves?"

"Mirror girls," Garen said. "They reflect back to Olina what she thinks she looks like."

"Right. Mirror, mirror on the wall," Kaley said. "That fits quite a few stories."

When Queen Olina opened her mouth to speak, an absolute silence came upon the crowd. The people not only didn't speak, they didn't move. Even the few children stood as still as stones. Kaley wanted to ask Garen if the queen had cast a spell on them, but he was staring down, his body so still it was as though he was afraid to move.

The queen's voice was powerful as she announced that in four days, men from Selkan would come to their island. On the fifth day, there would be a celebration of the marriage of Princess Aradella to Tanek Beyhan, a swan herder. She said the last with contempt in her voice.

With that short declaration, she turned in a whirl of iridescent cloth and left the platform. No one moved until she was out of sight—then everyone seemed to explode in loud voices and excited movements.

Kaley's eyes were on Tanek. What would he do now? Help his bride-to-be stand up? The princess looked like she had on about a hundred pounds of clothing. When he didn't move, Kaley's eyes fell on Mekos. He had come out of his trance and was looking to the right. At his father, who was still sitting in the gaudy gold chair? *No,* Kaley thought, *he's looking at something else. At someone else.*

"Are you ready to go?" Garen asked. When Kaley didn't answer, he followed her eyes. "Ah, yes, your mind is on the swansman."

"Actually, I was thinking about birds," she said. "In some birds, the female is quite plain while the male is flamboyantly beautiful. Does that apply in your world?"

"Since many of our creatures have been stolen from Earth, I would imagine so. As for your Tanek, he prefers the great beauty of swans." Garen was looking at Kaley as though he meant her.

Kaley ignored him. She knew she was pretty, but she wasn't a swan. She stepped away from the window. "I think it's time I find out what I'm going to do with my life."

"I agree," Garen said brightly. "We can start your apprenticeship tomorrow."

She didn't reply. Even though she'd made her choice, she didn't know if she could have what she desired. But it sure felt good to be *wanted*!

They went down the rotten stairs and standing outside the rickety front door were three women in blue uniforms. They looked very fit and she wondered if Sojee supervised their training. They said nothing but stepped aside to let Kaley pass, then blocked Garen from joining her. "I guess I'll see you later," she said as she looked back at him.

"I will ready the fires to cast the first spell. Your choice of who and what we use it on." He wiggled his brows in temptation.

"Sounds tempting," she said, but then the women frowned at her. They obviously wanted her to stop talking and go.

The women encircled Kaley, as though they were afraid she'd escape. They walked down the road until they reached the open gates of the Cauldron and went inside. The high, towering walls looked like liquid that had been frozen in the midst of its movement—which it was.

The heavy gates closed behind them. A sprawling stone building took up most of the area, but she could see smaller buildings to the side, probably for the caretakers. She wondered if Sojee's house was there.

With every step she took, Kaley felt heavier. *This is it*, she thought. *This is where my life will be decided. Do I go home or become an apprentice?* She didn't have any hope of any other choices being offered.

They halted at a pair of heavy doors and two muscular women opened one. The hall she entered wasn't nearly as spectacular as what she'd seen in King Aramus's sprawling palace, but then this island didn't seem to be as rich.

The two women guards motioned toward her heavy robe and she took it off, exposing her everyday trousers and shirt. Another door was opened and she entered a rather plain room. Standing in the center was Sojee. Beside him, Mekos was helping his father out of his silver robe.

Kaley's first thought was joy at seeing her men. But then she reminded herself that they were no longer "her" men. They glanced at her but said nothing. It was extremely annoying that they didn't seem in the least perturbed at what was going on.

When they continued to be silent, she said, "Well?" then glared at Tanek. "You have nothing to say?"

Tanek moved his shoulders about to loosen them. "I got Mekos back and I might be king. I'm happy."

Kaley grit her teeth. "That girl is half your age."

All three men looked at her as though to say, *What's bad about that?*

Tanek said, "I want children and a home. It's all I've ever wanted. She can give me that."

"Without *love*?!" Kaley gasped.

Tanek shrugged. "If I must sacrifice myself, I will."

Kaley said, "You're disgusting."

Tanek gave a shrug of not caring, said, "I'm going to take a bath," then left the room.

Kaley stood there for a moment, not sure whether she wanted to cry or scream.

Sojee looked at her. "He's taunting you. The solution to all of this is that if he's already married to someone else, he can't marry the princess."

Kaley grimaced. "You mean to one of your beautiful daughters?"

Sojee stared at her, shaking his head in disbelief, and Mekos laughed.

Sojee's voice changed to sound like he was talking to a not-very-intelligent child. "Do you have a king-in-waiting on Earth?"

"Oh yes. Drop-dead gorgeous Prince William."

"Think about what he does and what Tanek cares about. If he were king, he'd have to deal with crowds and meetings and greeting strangers. There would be no time for swimming with swans."

"He'd hate it," Kaley said softly. "He wouldn't live through it."

"You are right," Sojee said as he opened the bathroom door. "Now go and save him."

She went into the bathroom and the door closed behind her. Tanek was sitting in a huge stone bathtub, the upper half of his body glistening with water and soap. He was the most beautiful—and desirable—man she'd ever seen. She couldn't help moving to stand close to him. "It's difficult to talk to you when you're like this."

"I hope the princess approves of me."

"You're being a jerk."

"That word doesn't translate. Is it an endearment?"

She knew he was making fun of her. "This is serious! I'm trying to decide what to do with my whole *life.* There's my home on Earth and I've been offered—"

Tanek cut her off. "Go back to your Earth. You have so much waiting for you there, or the witch's son can give you all that you want. It's your choice."

His sarcasm didn't help. "I don't understand what's going on."

His arm came out fast, took hers, and pulled her into the tub with him, soaking her, clothes and all. But then, he began kissing her. There had been so much between them, but kissing was rare. "I can't make a logical decision when you're holding me."

"Remember when we were at the cave?" he asked as he nuzzled her neck.

"Which one?"

He kissed her earlobe. "The good one."

"Oh yes, sunshine and swans."

"I asked you then to live with me. To share my life. Forever."

"Like the swans." His lips were moving down the front of her.

"Yes. The blue swans."

"Meaning you." She'd learned that the blue swans were the humans who were descended from swans. She closed her eyes, enjoying his touches, but when he abruptly stopped, she looked at him. "You're trying to tell me something, aren't you?" When he didn't answer, she tried to remember what he'd told her about marriage on his planet. "You said that clasping—marriage—is between two people. It's private."

"Yes. It's an agreement. I think you said you liked the idea of living with me. Then later, when we spent the night in the cold cave, you still seemed to approve."

She was piecing together what he was telling her. Her eyes widened. "Are you saying that you and I are already married? Therefore you can't join with the princess?"

"Ah, at last you understand me."

She pulled back from him, got out of the tub, and stood up, dripping wet, and didn't speak.

He looked up at her. "Are you afraid?"

"Yes."

"Of this world or of me?"

"Both. Marriage is serious. We've known each other a very short time."

He slid down in the tub to rest his head on the back. "What hardship, what emotions, have we not experienced together?"

So much went through her mind: danger, fear, tears, laughter, grief, anger. They'd done it all.

"I've known what I wanted since Indienne wrapped herself around your neck."

"Are you saying that you let a swan choose your wife for you?"

"Yes." His look was serious. "I'm sorry that if you stay here you will lose your family. All I can offer you is a new family. Children and a home, with people and animals who depend on you—and love you." He smiled. "And if my son marries one of Sojee's beautiful daughters, he'll make you a grandmother very soon."

"A what?! I'm not even thirty. How can I—?" She cut herself off. Yet again, he'd taken away her fear. He'd done the same thing when he'd seen her chained in a dungeon and wearing a glass slipper. "So that's it? There's no big gala American wedding?"

"A what?"

"An Earth-type wedding with a three-foot cake and a white dress. For me. You would wear a black tux." She was trying to take in what he'd said. And she was trying to not collapse at the relief she was feeling, but she couldn't yet comprehend all of it. "I guess I'm staying." Suddenly, she remembered the look on Princess Aradella's face. "But wait! If the princess doesn't marry *you*, then . . ."

His smile disappeared. "Then she's back to marrying Nessa," he said sadly. "That poor girl. But the marriage will unite old and new royals. It'll bring us all closer to being united." He grimaced. "In front of her, that nasty kid said that being crowned king was worth putting up with Aradella."

Kaley cocked her head at him. "You want to unite the islands so much that you were willing to marry her."

"Yes, but it wouldn't have worked. I'd be in the public all the time. I wouldn't be able to unite anyone, certainly not while I'm under the queen's eye."

She picked up a cloth, he leaned forward, and she began to wash his back. His wide, warm, muscular back. There were thick ridges along his shoulder blades, an inheritance from when his ancestors had wings. Kaley found them quite erotic. Her body seemed to have an electrical charge running through it. She couldn't quite grasp the fact that they were united, as Tanek said, "Forever." "Fahir said that if you married the princess that would help you." There was alarm in her voice. "He knows what you're after."

"Of course the king's sleazy advisor knows. The man wants to rule the planet. He tried to get you to help put me in a place where he could watch my every movement."

Kaley smiled, glad she wasn't taking away his goal in life. "So who will help you? Your mother?"

"Perhaps. Sojee said Olina is very glad that Nessa is back as the future king. I'm sure she doesn't want *me* watching what she does. Anyway, Sojee wants you and me to go away while he handles the celebration for the wedding of the two young royals. I know he doesn't want me or Mekos to interfere."

Kaley's eyes sparkled. "You mean he doesn't want two ferms hanging around and distracting the women while they work."

Tanek laughed. "I see you're learning our language."

"So what are we going to do? Go back to Eren?" Her eyes lit up. "To the Homestead? We could start restoring it. I get dibs on the big bedroom."

"No, not yet. The queen is giving us a gift. Do you know what a 'sweetsun' is? I think it's an Earth trip for after the clasping."

Kaley tried to figure out what he meant. "After . . . ? Not sun, the moon. A honeymoon?"

"Yes! That's it. Queen Olina is sending the four of us to the

Lair for three days. It's to be a honeymoon for you and me. I've been told that the place is extraordinarily beautiful. There'll be a guide and—"

"Four of us?"

"You, me, Mekos, and Princess Aradella." His voice lowered. "It's to be a last holiday for her."

Kaley shook her head. "Something nice before she's condemned to a life with hideous little Nessa. In fairy tales, the man the princess has to marry nearly always turns out to be wonderful."

There was sympathy in his voice. "Not this time."

"No, definitely not this time."

It was later that night that Tanek used his chip to contact Jobi. He didn't give the man time to talk. "I don't know what you're up to, but Kaley wants something called an 'American wedding.' Do you know what it is?"

"Yes," Jobi said. "It's—"

"I don't need a description," Tanek said. "Queen Olina is sending us to the Lair for three days. I'm taking weapons as I don't believe this is from her good will. When we return, I want you to have arranged what Kaley wants. Am I clear?"

"More than you know." Jobi didn't seem the least intimidated by the threatening tone of Tanek's voice. "When she returns, she'll be very pleased by what I have arranged. And for that matter, so will you."

"She's the one who's been stolen from her home, so she needs it."

"Is Arit going with you?"

"Of course." Tanek's tone said that was a stupid question. "Why are you asking that?"

"No reason. I must go. The king is calling me." Smiling broadly, Jobi broke the contact.

Tanek frowned. He could tell that Jobi was up to something. The question was if it was good or bad.

# 1

Aradella was waiting to get into the elegant carriage Queen Olina had sent to take them to the Lair. She remembered when her father had presented the coach to his wife as a gift. As young as Aradella was, she knew it was an "I'm sorry" present for his younger brother having married a dreadful woman. She yelled at everyone, complained without stop, and she looked at her sister-in-law with such hatred that people stepped back, afraid they'd be burned.

The carriage was now owned by that awful woman. The king and queen were dead, and their daughter was . . . Aradella couldn't imagine what her fate was going to be.

Olina had tried to hide her jubilance at the announcement that Aradella was *not* to marry Tanek, but she wasn't a good actress. She tried to disguise her glee with lies. "You deserve better than a filthy swan herder," she'd said. "Your dear parents would haunt me if I allowed that to happen to you so I fought them. I know the man's mother is a Seven, but why should *you* be punished for that woman's indiscretion with a . . . a . . . ?" She swallowed, seeming to be unable to say the words of Tanek's low birth.

In the corner sat her wrinkly old mother, pretending to be

sewing, but she was actually staring hard at Aradella. Did the woman never blink?

Through it all, Aradella had sat absolutely still, showing no emotion. If she made any protest, she was sure Olina would punish her by taking away something she had. Would it be Hale? Her library would be found and destroyed? Her cousins? At the thought that those two lovingly "caring" sisters would be removed from her life almost made her smile.

Olina went on to say that Aradella was going to be given a fabulous gift.

*A pet snake?* she thought. *Cockroaches in my pillow?* Actually, she'd prefer bugs to Nessa sleeping beside her.

"I am sending you to the Lair for three days."

At that, Aradella did show some expression. No one went to the Lair. Or left it. Three women were allowed to participate in trade but no one else. Her cousins used to tell her the gossip of terrible things that happened in the Lair, but there was no proof of any of it.

As Aradella waited for the carriage, she sneaked looks at the Earth woman. She had exotic eyes of a deep brown and her hair had a bit of red in it. She had on a blue shirt, black trousers, and brown boots. She didn't look very different from other people, but when she arrived at the carriage, the horses had tried to go to her. They wouldn't get into harness until the Earth woman had touched and talked to them. It was quite odd.

Tanek's son, standing behind Aradella, said in great understatement, "Animals like her."

He was named Mekos and he was as tall as his father, but he didn't have the heavy muscle that Tanek did. Mekos was lighter and more agile. And with his sharp nose and chin, he was handsome to the point of being almost pretty.

It was Mekos who helped Aradella into the carriage. It wasn't easy as she was wider than the door. She had to turn sideways to get through.

When she was seated, Tanek got in from the other side and

he smiled at her in a warm, friendly way. Between them was the memory of the dance they'd shared.

"Are you all right?" he asked.

She gave a slight smile in return and nodded.

"About the, uh . . ." He didn't seem to know what to say.

But she understood. She'd been told she was to marry this man, but a day later, she was told no, he was already married. How the cousins had bewailed that! Shay said if it was done to her, she'd protest.

"I'd send Papá to the queen to say I refused to let him out of the agreement. Married to an *Earth* woman? Their children will be freaks."

Bree had been quiet, but she'd squeezed Aradella's hand and whispered, "I'm sorry."

Whether she was sorry that Aradella had lost Tanek or that she was being forced to marry Prince Nessa, Aradella didn't know.

Mekos got into the coach and took the seat next to Aradella. Last to get in was the Earth woman. She sat down, then looked at Aradella with a mixture of sadness and fear. *She's afraid I'm angry,* Aradella thought with surprise. When the carriage started forward, she said, "Do *all* animals like you or just horses?"

As she'd hoped, that started a flood of talk. Tanek and his son spoke over each other, telling stories of some clumsy bird called a dodo, a little elephant, and swans that loved her. "And Tibby," Tanek said.

Kaley spoke for the first time. "Oh, how I miss him! But he's staying with his daughter."

"She's speaking of a tabor," Tanek said to Aradella and her eyes widened. It was a small, fierce animal that people stayed away from. "Our hope is that he doesn't kill anyone."

"Tell the story about the glass shoe," Mekos said. "About what you did when you left me behind." He sounded hurt at being excluded, but also teasing.

What followed was an incomprehensible story about women

trying on a slipper made of glass, with lots of blood involved. There was talk of someone named Garen, then a prince who wanted to marry Kaley. At that, Aradella lifted her pale eyebrows.

"It wasn't *me* he loved," Kaley said. "He just thought he did. Tell her about Sojee. You're related, aren't you?"

"He was married to my father's late sister," Aradella said.

"Tell her how Sojee threw you across the roof," Mekos said to Kaley.

Aradella leaned back against the cushion, soaking up the camaraderie of them. They were a family—a real and true *family*. How she'd missed that over the years!

When the carriage finally made it up the steep hill and stopped at the entrance to the Lair, she sighed. She didn't want the ride to end.

Two women wearing stylish brown uniforms opened the carriage doors and the passengers got out. Tanek held his hands up to help Aradella down the pullout steps.

Their first sight of the Lair took their breath away. It was warm but not hot. The air was moist but not humid. Tall trees, gently swaying in the breeze, and brightly colored flowers were everywhere. It was stunningly beautiful.

The older of the guards said, "Valona is generously lending you a house. Food will be delivered to you, but you may attend the markets. There will be no charge for anything as you are the guests of Valona."

"Thank you!" Kaley said as she stood beside Tanek.

"Of course you won't see her as she's much too busy with official matters, but you can occupy yourselves."

*Too busy for a princess?* Kaley wanted to ask but didn't. Mekos moved closer to Aradella. "I'd like to explore this place," he said, but Aradella didn't comment. Freedom was not something she knew about.

They followed the guards down a wide path. Unlike in other

craters, it was well-kept and very clean. It was almost as though the grass had been manicured.

"Looks like they don't have a queen who steals the tax money," Mekos said so only Aradella could hear.

She felt the hair on her neck rise. Didn't he know that Olina had spies everywhere? "I have no idea what you mean," she said haughtily, then moved away from him.

They came to a bend and saw a dozen females, ranging from children to grandmothers. Two young women were staring at Tanek as though he was an exhibit on display. They appeared to be fascinated and repulsed at the same time.

The others were staring at Aradella. Their eyes were glazed, as though they couldn't believe what they were seeing.

Kaley looked back at her. "They know you're a real live royal princess."

Aradella didn't smile. She didn't like the way the women were looking at her.

"Stay close to me." Mekos was frowning. He didn't seem to like their stares either.

The guards shouted something in a language the chips didn't translate and the gawking females hurried away.

Minutes later, they reached the house. It was one story and quite long. The center was open on both sides to the beautiful scenery. The big, breezy room held couches and chairs, with a kitchen on one side.

"There are two bedrooms and a bath on each end," a guard said. She looked at Kaley, her eyes not so much as glancing at Tanek. "You may stay with him or not."

Kaley suppressed a laugh. "With him." She stepped back against Tanek.

The guard turned to Aradella. "If this place does not suit you, you may stay in another of Valona's houses." She cut her eyes at Mekos as though he was something vile.

"I'll stay here," Aradella said.

"Then come." The two guards moved so one was on each side of the princess as they walked her toward the enclosed rooms on the far end.

Mekos was left standing with his father and Kaley, and they looked at him in question.

"I'm with her!" Mekos ran after Aradella and the guards.

Kaley and Tanek went to the rooms at the other end of the house. Inside were two bedrooms with a luxurious bath in the middle. When Kaley finished looking about, she found Tanek standing by the doorway. He was looking across the open-air living space to the closed door on the other side.

She went to him and he put his arm around her, but he kept looking at the other bedrooms. "Are you worried about them? Two teens alone? Are you wondering if they can be trusted?"

"Yes," he said simply.

She pulled back to look at him and there was passion in her voice. "What if they do roll about? Aradella *should* take all the happiness she can get before her hideous marriage. That poor girl! You know what? I hope Aradella gets pregnant and the baby has pointed ears. Better that than inheriting genes from Nasty Nessa." When she looked at him, his brow was furrowed. "You don't like this idea, do you?"

"My son has never been with a woman. He'd be able to soar higher if he had been. Once he finds a life mate, he may be able to touch the sun. But if . . ." He didn't finish.

She knew what he meant. They were Order of Swans and swans mated for life. They might have a tryst here and there—as Tanek had with Mekos's mother—but a love commitment was forever. If later, a male swan's mate was taken from him or died, he stayed alone for the rest of his life. If Mekos fell in love and that woman married another . . . Kaley didn't want to think of what the consequences would be to Mekos. An entire life without his chosen partner?

Tanek turned her in his arms. "We must not think of that

now." He ran his hands up and down her back. "Unless you want to change rooms. Mekos and I could be together and you can stay with the princess."

"Nope!" she said firmly.

Tanek smiled. "Speaking of babies, my ears are fine but my next son may have ridges."

"Oh? And what if it's a girl? Maybe she'll have wings like a Never."

"I guess we'll have to wait and see what we can produce," he said as he began kissing her.

"This place is great!" Mekos said from Aradella's bedroom doorway. "The house, the outside. I've never seen anything like it."

In Aradella's life, she was rarely allowed privacy, but even so, she wasn't used to males being in her room. Or in her house. Or for that matter, on her island.

He was eating an orange and had another one in his hand. "Here!" He tossed it to her.

Aradella had to stretch, but she caught it.

"Good catch." He sauntered into her room and looked out the big window. "Where do you want to go first? Wonder if the markets are held every day? It's nice to think everything is free. I could get Grandpapá something. Or we could go see where the steam from the volcano comes out. I heard they have festivals there." He turned back to look at her. "Which one do you like? Or do you know of something else?"

On the bed was a big cloth bag and she'd pulled out a few dresses.

"Is that all you have to wear? You need pants like Kaley wears."

She had no idea what to reply. The idea of being free to walk wherever she wanted was beyond her comprehension.

"What are you doing here?!" came a shout and the two young people looked at the doorway. Standing there was a large woman with crinkly gray hair pulled tightly back. Her dark eyes were full of anger. "You!" She sneered at Mekos. "Get out! How dare you put yourself near the Honored Girl? You cannot—"

Aradella was so used to attacks from people that she reacted quickly. "Queen Olina has ordered that he is to stay with me. For my protection."

"You need no protection here. Valona is all the security anyone needs." She was obviously insulted.

"I'm sure that's true," Aradella said calmly. "However, I must send word to Queen Olina that you will not comply with what she has arranged for me." She raised her left arm where the chip was. "I will tell her now. What is your name?"

It took the big woman a moment to recover, then she lowered her voice. "Valona said that you are to stay with me."

Aradella had her fingertips on the chip that was buried under her skin. "I understand. I'll tell my aunt, the queen, that Valona's orders supersede hers. And your name is?"

The woman seemed to recover enough that she stood up straighter, then gave another sneering look at Mekos. "He is to stay away from *me*." She stomped out of the room.

Mekos went to Aradella. "That was wonderful! You were so very clever!"

Aradella felt her face turn red at the compliment. She wasn't sure what to say. "But I wasn't good enough for your father" came out of her mouth.

Mekos took a step back, looking as though he'd been slapped. "He and Kaley . . ." He didn't finish.

Aradella was embarrassed at what she'd said, but she didn't tell him that. Instead, she followed the big woman into the open living area. Mekos was behind her.

"I am the guide. You need to know nothing more," the woman said. "Come! I will lead you to see this place."

What followed was thirty minutes of the guide raving about what a spectacular place the Lair was—and all of it was due to the magnificent, glorious leadership of Valona. They were told of her beauty, her wisdom, her kindness. "She is generous to a fault. She gifts us with holidays and ceremonies that others can only dream about. Whatever we have, it is due to Valona."

Aradella's eyes seemed to grow wider with every word. Olina ruled by fear, but Valona seemed to rule by love and kindness. How was that done? When she looked at Mekos, he gave a gesture of vomiting. Aradella clamped her lips together to keep from laughing.

When they entered the village, they saw that it was perfectly kept. There wasn't a weed in a flower box, a pebble in the trimmed grass, an unwashed window. As for the women, they were all clean and tidy—and they abruptly halted and stared at Aradella. "Good Day of the Moon to you," one woman said softly. "Is that her?" asked a very pretty girl. When the woman nodded, the girl mouthed *thank you* to Aradella.

Mekos stepped closer to Aradella. "There's something not right here."

Aradella nodded in agreement, but she didn't know what was making her feel that way.

They left the village and entered the lovely countryside. Tropical forest surrounded them. "We will now see the stupendous home where Valona lives," the guide said in a voice full of awe.

"Maybe it's made of gingerbread," Mekos said, but Aradella didn't get his meaning.

It was on the path to the great and wondrous Valona's house that they saw a little girl step out of the greenery at the edge of the road. When she turned, they saw that she had a human face but with dark circles around her eyes, and a little nose. She looked like a raccoon.

"Get out of here!" the guide shouted, then hissed like a snake. "Go!"

The frightened child ran back into the forest.

The guide's face was red with anger. "You should not have seen that. They're filthy creatures! But the women will not stop—" She didn't finish.

"She is a Lely," Mekos said quietly. "Are there many here?"

"There are too many of those things and they should be destroyed! Monkeys and a wolf. There's even a bear!" She was almost shouting. "Those things go against all that is good. They—" She broke off at the sound of a horse close by. "Hurry! We might see her."

The guide ran as fast as she could, Aradella and Mekos behind her, and they came to a crossroads. Not far away, a woman on a horse came into view. She was elegantly beautiful, with long black hair, and a dark dress that showed off her hourglass figure. She was almost out of sight when she abruptly pulled the reins back. The horse reared but the woman didn't lose her balance. She turned and looked at the three of them standing there. Her eyes were on Aradella—and she frowned. But then she seemed to decide that whatever she didn't like was all right, and she nodded at Aradella in greeting. In the next instant, she kicked the big horse and was out of sight.

"That was Valona," the guide said breathlessly. "You are fortunate to have seen her. She is the most beautiful woman on the planet."

Aradella shrugged. "Actually, I have some cousins who are better looking than—" At the guide's fierce look, the princess closed her mouth.

The woman angrily walked ahead of them, while Aradella and Mekos stayed behind. "I don't like her," she said.

"Nor do I," he replied, then pulled his long hair back to show his ears. They were pointed. "I am a Lely." He seemed to expect Aradella to be shocked.

"I know," she said. "Your mother is half fox, and you were born to your father when he was sixteen. That he could get a fox with child shows his extraordinary strength."

Mekos blinked at her, then laughed. "It did take strength with my mother. She has claws." The guide had turned and was frowning at them to come on. "I can't stand this. Will you be all right if I leave?"

"Perfectly fine," Aradella said, but her heart sank at the thought of spending time alone with the awful woman.

Dutifully, they followed her down the road that Valona had been on and heard more about the glory of her. Goddesses had fewer good attributes than Valona did.

Aradella slowed with Mekos so they were well behind the woman. "Should we pick up rocks and make a shrine to her?" she asked.

"All hail Valona," Mekos said. "We can offer prayers to her."

"And food and flowers."

Mekos plucked some white flowers from a row of bushes growing by the side of the road. "I'll offer this and say that it pales beside her beauty."

"You better say more than that. That's oleander and it's deadly poisonous."

He tossed the flower away. "How do you know that?"

Aradella shrugged. "Just something I heard. Come on, she's waiting for us."

"What's next? We get to kiss the droppings of Valona's horse?"

She tried to suppress a laugh since the woman was glaring at them, but Aradella's only thought was that she didn't want to be left alone with the guide.

The road led alongside a steep drop-off. It was as though the long-ago lava flow had created a gully. There might be a river running at the bottom of it, but there were so many trees with hanging vines and tall bushes that they couldn't see down.

"What's that?" Mekos asked loudly. He was moving about to see through the trees.

"There's a waterfall on one wall." The guide frowned at him.

"Could we go to see that?"

The woman glared. "Absolutely not! Valona does not allow anyone to go there!"

Mekos looked at Aradella and gave a slight jerk to his head. She didn't know what he meant. In the next second, he grabbed a vine dangling from a tree and swung out on it. He disappeared into the forest.

Again, the guide's face turned red with anger. Through clenched teeth, she said, "Come! We must return to your house and you will stay there until he can be found. No man is allowed to wander about freely. There are women here! They have to be protected from male abuse. From their incessant violence. We have to—"

Aradella didn't think about what she was doing. She reached up, grabbed a vine near the one Mekos had used, and swung out over the abyss. Behind her, she heard a scream of terror, but it felt so good to move that she ignored it.

Mekos was standing at the bottom, seeming to be waiting for her. "I hoped you'd come." He reached up and caught her, set her on the ground, then looked at her in surprise. "You don't weigh very much. You—"

There was a rustle near them. Mekos took her hand and they ran down a narrow trail that had probably been made by animals.

Minutes later, he said, "We're almost there."

"I hope so," she murmured, her voice a bit shaky.

He stopped and turned to her. "Is something frightening you?"

"Of course not." She kept her shoulders back.

He seemed to be studying her as though trying to figure out the problem. "Is it this trail that's so far from people?" When she just looked at him, he began to walk backward and said, "You needn't worry. I can smell things. It's something I inherited from my grandfather. According to my mother, he was pure fox, a big, beautiful creature. I can assure you that only rabbits have been on this trail in the last two days. No bears of any kind have been here. If there is anything dangerous near us, I can smell it, hear it, and see it." He smiled at her. "You are safe with me."

"But they can smell, hear, and see just as well as you can."

Mekos laughed. "True, but none of them can soar. If something shows up, I'll take you up into the trees."

"Like your father did," she said dreamily.

Mekos looked shocked. "My father soared with you?"

"Yes. At the dance years ago. He whirled me about the floor. It was pure heaven." He was blinking at her. "You were there. After the swan show? King Aramus?"

"Oh yes! That was you? I saw you two but I was so hungry! The food was wonderful. Salty little meat pies, fruit I'd never seen before. And cider!" Abruptly, he stopped and held out his arm. "We are here."

Turning, she saw the waterfall. The path had led them downward, making the lava wall that surrounded the Lair very tall. The water cascaded from the top and rushed down to the bottom. It was beautiful!

"I hear slow-moving water so there must be a river nearby," Mekos said. "Let's go—" He broke off at what they both saw.

Halfway up the waterfall, emerged a human head with dark hair.

"It's Papá," Mekos said and took a step forward. But then he halted.

Tanek came out of the water, his back to them. He was shirtless, with his curved wing ridges exposed. When his waist came into view, they saw two bare legs clasped about him. He was nude and Kaley, also bare, was wrapped around him.

"We should go," Aradella whispered, but neither of them moved. They didn't even blink.

Tanek and Kaley soared up the waterfall, joined as man and woman. At the top, just below land, they disappeared inside the water.

Aradella and Mekos stayed frozen, watching and waiting, but the couple didn't emerge.

Mekos took a breath. "There must be a cave. They like caves."

"Do they?" Aradella asked, her eyebrows so high they nearly disappeared into her hairline.

"I guess we shouldn't get any closer."

"Could be dangerous," Aradella said, but she meant "embarrassing."

"Very." They followed the path that led away from the waterfall.

It was an awkward silence between them and Aradella wanted to break it—and get rid of the unsettling images in her mind. "What can you see or hear or smell now?"

Again, he walked backward, seeming to be grateful for a change of subject. "There are two red birds nesting in that tree. They're watching us."

"Do you mean the tree with the purple flowers? The *Jacaranda mimosifolia*?"

He stopped. "My grandfather has one of those trees. He brought seeds back from his trip to Earth. How do *you* know that tree?"

She was afraid to tell him the whole truth. "I have some Earth books."

He stared at her. "Who gave you those books?"

"I'm a princess," she said. "I receive many gifts." She started walking but he wouldn't let her pass. After several of his back-and-forth steps blocking her, she sighed. "Your father sends me books, and a man named Jobi does. He—"

"I know Jobi well. He trained me with a sword." Mekos picked up a long stick off the ground and made movements like a sword fight.

Aradella grabbed another stick. "Like this?" She lunged toward him and countered his thrusts. She was as fast as he was and as accurate.

He was staring at her in astonishment. "Where did you—?" he began but then stopped. "Someone is near." He held his hand out to her and they ran down the narrow path.

When they reached a tall tree, Mekos opened his arms to her.

It took her a moment to know what he meant. "The dance," she said and he nodded. She went to him, he pulled her close, and they floated upward. He stopped at a tree branch and let go of her to sit down. He went to a branch across from her.

They sat in silence for a few minutes, then Mekos relaxed and leaned back. "It's gone. I don't know what it was. I've never smelled it before." He looked at her. "Who trained you with a sword?"

She hesitated. "Hale, my guard."

"Who knows that you can do that?"

"Just Hale and me." Her lips were tight as though refusing to tell more.

"I'm not royal but I do know about loyalty. I won't betray anything you tell me. To prove it, I'll share a secret about me. I've not even told my father this." He paused. "I am the Reaver."

"The Reaver? Ah yes, the menace jumping about on rooftops. The Head of Government was quite annoyed. You stole from her."

"I did," Mekos said proudly. "I gave the credits to the farmers and I unlocked a steel door so they could get seeds."

"So I heard," she said. "Hale told me some gossip. Everyone assumed the Reaver was female, but then the Reaver kissed a girl, and she . . ." Aradella rubbed her hand over her chin. "She found out that *he* had whiskers."

"Oh?" Mekos said. "She told that? I thought it was between just us." He changed to a faraway look. "It was a wonderful kiss. The best I've ever—" He caught himself. "I mean, it was all right, but I've been with many women."

"I'm sure your father has, but then he's a truly gorgeous man. All women want him."

"He can't see as well as I can or hear. Or smell things." He sniffed the air. "You had eggs this morning, and—" He stopped. "You're right. I'm no competition for my father." He jumped down from the tree, his feet landing lightly, and held up his arms to her. "Jump and I'll catch you."

Aradella hesitated only a second, then she fell forward. He easily caught her and set her down.

"Let's follow this path and see where it leads. Maybe there's another waterfall."

"One that's not occupied," she said.

Laughing, they ran ahead.

When they heard the gurgle of water, Mekos parted the bushes so they could go through. As soon as he reached a clear area and looked ahead, he stopped. "We should go back."

His tone made Aradella push past him to see what was stopping him.

In front of them, there was a wide stream with crystal clear water. On the far side, lying on the ground, was Tanek. He was partially hidden by plants, but they could see that his upper half was bare.

Kaley, wearing Tanek's shirt that hung halfway down her thighs stepped out of the bushes. She was holding what looked like a glass of red wine.

Mekos and Aradella were about to turn away when they saw Kaley pour the wine onto Tanek's bare chest.

"They've had an argument," Aradella said and looked away.

"No," Mekos said in an odd voice. "They have not."

Aradella looked back. Kaley had dropped to her knees and was licking the wine off Tanek's chest. "Oh," Aradella said. "That's . . ."

Mekos took her hand and tightened his grip until it hurt, but she didn't protest.

When Kaley's mouth moved down to below Tanek's navel, Mekos and Aradella hastily and awkwardly hurried back into the bushes.

"We should go the other way."

"Yes," Aradella agreed. "Do you think people are looking for us?"

"I've heard voices but not many and not close. We're only here for a few days so maybe they're giving us peace. I smell fruit. Let's find it." He hurried down another path, this one more narrow than the other one. They didn't say so but they didn't want to encounter his father and Kaley again.

They found a tall tree filled with little red rambutan hanging in clusters. Aradella watched as Mekos lifted himself off the ground and tossed down a pile of the fruit. She tried to split the little bulbs with their soft spines with her thumbnail. Mekos pulled a knife out of his boot and handed it to her. She slit the skin, removed the translucent fruit, and showed him how to eat it around the seed. He smiled warmly at her.

They sat side by side under the pretty tree, eating and listening to the sounds around them. Mekos could pinpoint where every critter was, even the big beetle that was lumbering through the grass.

Suddenly, he moved faster than she'd ever seen anyone move. In one swift action, he pushed her to the ground and rolled on top of her. When she started to protest, he put his hand over her mouth.

With his other hand, he pushed back his hair and she saw his pointed ears twitch, then stop. They seemed to home in on a sound.

He was lying fully on top of her, his body tense, as though he was preparing to leap up. His face was a study in concentration as he listened. His breath was so slow, his body didn't move.

Aradella heard nothing. She just looked up at Mekos, his face inches from hers, his hand still on the bottom half of her face.

After minutes, his body went limp—but he didn't get off of her. "I think it was Bear Boy. This is my fault! I wasn't paying attention and he got too close."

Aradella's heart was beating hard. When Hale had explained to her about men and women and procreation, Aradella said it sounded awful. "The man is larger. He'll crush you." Hale had smiled. "No, he doesn't," she said, her eyes seeming faraway. "Not heavy."

With Mekos on top of her, Aradella understood. He didn't feel heavy at all.

He was looking at her face. "Your lashes and brows are dark near your skin, but lighter at the top."

"I dye them to make myself as plain as possible. It's not good to make a queen jealous."

He looked at her for a moment longer then rolled off of her. "I didn't mean to startle you, but I had to cover your scent with mine."

Aradella sat up. Her whole body was vibrating. "You couldn't just talk to him?"

"I doubt it. That boy is half bear. His father is a full bear, which is dominant. I don't know how he'd react to finding humans out here alone and I don't want to risk it." Mekos sighed. "There are more Lelys here than I've ever seen before."

"Women are here with no men, so I guess they get lonely."

Mekos made a swipe at his hair, exposing a pointed ear. "I know about being lonely."

"I don't," Aradella said. "My life as a princess is a joy. Utterly without problems."

He laughed. "Let's see more of this place. I think there are houses and people this way."

"Then let's go that way." She pointed in the opposite direction.

"You are speaking to my heart. There are ducks not far way. And more fruit."

"I'm with you!" she said.

He looked at her. "You are, aren't you?" he said softly. He seemed reluctant to turn away, but he did.

They reached a wide pond, formed by the stream, and floating in it were ducks with green and purple iridescent feathers. "Would you like to go swimming?" he asked. "We can go under and I'll show you their feet."

Aradella took a step back. The way she was dressed was a

hindrance to swimming. "I—" She said no more because Mekos gave a look of alarm.

"No!" He grabbed her hand and pulled her with him behind a stand of reeds. When he parted the stalks, they saw Tanek and Kaley coming up from under the water. "Starken-el!" Mekos muttered.

This time, they didn't stay to watch. Mekos quickly stepped away, Aradella close behind him. But then he stopped so abruptly that she almost ran into him. He didn't look back at the water, but pointed upward. He'd heard something.

She looked up, over the reeds, just in time to see Kaley and Tanek rising into the air. They were nude and kissing.

Aradella quickly turned her back to them. "Do they ever wear clothes?" He started rapidly walking away, Aradella struggling to keep up with him. "Do they not stop for meals? Or sleep?"

"It doesn't seem so," Mekos said tightly, then he halted and looked at her. "My guess is they've been told that you and I are with the guide, seeing the town, and we know this area is off-limits, so they believe they're alone. My father is soaring to move from one place to another so quickly."

Aradella shrugged. "It's their wedding trip and obviously, they are creative people. And perhaps they have repressed themselves for a while."

The tension seemed to leave Mekos. "Yes, they have." He smiled at her. "You are a good peacemaker." Abruptly, he tilted his head in a way that was becoming familiar to her.

"What do you hear?" she asked.

"Swans just landed. The western variety."

Aradella suppressed a laugh. "I guess we know where *they* are going."

Mekos looked at her, then he too laughed. "I think I'll tell Grandpapá about this. My father acting like this when he's a guest isn't right."

"Is it fair to tell on him?"

"He's ruining my day with a beautiful girl so he deserves it. Let's find that fruit."

Aradella stood still as she watched him go down the narrow trail. *Beautiful?*

"Come on!" he said impatiently. "I'm hungry." He led them to a papaya tree. He gathered and she peeled.

"It's odd that rambutan and papaya are ripe at the same time," she said.

"*Everything* about this place is strange." He looked around. "It's getting dark. We should go back."

Neither of them moved. Aradella did not want the day to end.

Mekos seemed to understand. "We have tomorrow. I don't think my father will notice that you and I are missing."

"Surely, they'll want to sleep tomorrow."

They looked at each other and laughed.

He stood up, then held out his hand to pull her up. The light was quickly growing dimmer.

"Do you know the way?" she asked.

"We're very close to the house that the kind and generous Valona is lending us. See?"

Through the trees was a pale yellow light. "We can meet in the morning and go—" He broke off, then gave a sound of exasperation. "She is there! I can smell her. That woman is waiting for us." He pulled back a shrub and there, right in front of their end of the house, sat the guide—and her face showed her fury.

Mekos let the shrub go back in place.

"We can go in through the other side and tiptoe past her."

He grimaced. "There's someone else there. A guard, maybe. They'd hear you."

"But not *you*?" she snapped.

"No." He looked thoughtful. "I can stay out here all night, but you need to go inside."

"Because I'm a princess? I'm too delicate to stay?" He didn't seem to hear her and she knew he was thinking about what to do with her. Aradella thought how she'd had a lifetime of people wondering what to do with her. "I'm going to stay here," she said firmly.

"You can't do that," he said, but then he looked into her eyes. "All right, but it's going to get cold. I'll get some covers."

She was pleased that he wasn't sending her away, and also excited and a little frightened at spending the night outside. "Are you going to sneak through a window?"

He smiled. "I'm a fox, remember? I'll walk right past her."

"Ha! I'd like to see that."

"Then sit here and watch." He cleared a small area among the shrubs. "Look through there."

She could see the open area of the house and the guide sitting there, arms crossed. "Yes, I can—" She cut off because Mekos was gone. She looked back at the house, straining to see in the growing darkness. There was a shadow but it could have been a night bird flying past. She tried hard to hear but it was only night sounds.

As she waited, she began to grow concerned. What if he didn't return? She told herself it would be fine. She'd just walk to the house and—

When she felt something touch her she made a squeak.

Mekos sat down beside her. In silence, they watched as the guide looked around. She'd heard the sound.

After a few minutes, he stood, held his hand out to her, then led her through the forest. It was too dark for her to see but she trusted him.

When he stopped at the foot of a big tree, she saw a pile of bedding. He'd not only been to the house and retrieved the things, but had put them by a tree. He picked up a blanket and wrapped it about her. She knew it was made of swan cloth, that fabric that the Order of Swans had been making for centuries.

"You move in silence," she said.

"I can. I brought food. Sorry we can't have a fire."

She sat down on one blanket, her back against the tree, and he spread a second one over her.

He opened a bag. "I brought bread and cheese and a jug of some kind of juice. Do you mind?" He meant that he would get under the blanket beside her.

In answer, she lifted the cover, he sat beside her, and they began to eat.

"We've talked too much about me today. Tell me about you."

"My life has been simple. My parents were king and queen. It was lovely, but then my uncle married Olina. Not long after the wedding, my parents died. It was said to be an accident."

"And you were locked away," he said.

"I have my cousins," she said solemnly. "They are a delight."

He laughed. "Sojee's daughters are not like him. They stand there and stare at me. Try this bread. It has some spice that I've not tasted before."

Smiling, she ate the buttered bread he held out to her. For a while, they sat together, not speaking, just listening to the sounds around them.

"Papá told me that Kaley read Nessa a story to get him to go to sleep."

She knew he was hinting. "I know that we've been told a lot of good about Valona, but there's another story that goes around the island. It's very secret and Hale wasn't supposed to tell me, but she did. I asked my cousins about it, but they knew nothing—as usual. Anyway, it's said that Valona is very, very old. Ancient even. But to keep her youth and beauty, every year, she must sacrifice a beautiful young woman."

He waited, but she said no more. "That's it? No blood and horror?"

"Sorry. That's all I was told." She gave a little snort. "I remember what my cousin Shay said. I'd just bested her on a test, and she said, 'If it's beauty Valona wants, then you're safe.'"

"What did you say?"

"That if *brains* were wanted, then *she* was safe."

Mekos laughed. "I think it's easier to be male. I would hit anyone who said something like that to me."

"You?" She was astonished, disbelieving. "Why would anyone say something derogatory to *you*?"

"Did you forget my ears?"

"Your ears are quite useful and I think they're pretty."

"That's what my mother tells me."

"And what did your beautiful father say about them?" she asked.

"He has big ridges on his back so he can't say anything about me. Besides, it's his fault that I have them."

They laughed together and Mekos handed her the jug of juice.

They were quiet for a while, both of them drowsy, then Mekos said, "I'm sorry that you have to marry Nessa. I've known him all my life and he is a vile, selfish person."

"I know," she said. "I've been on the receiving end of his venom since the day I met him."

"Do you know that he has a dragon?"

"I've heard that but I've never seen it."

"Neither has he. At least not for a while. Would it help if I tell you that I know where his dragon is? It's with my grandfather Roal. That big green dragon has swans crawling all over him and he's very happy."

"When I'm married to Nessa, it'll be good that he doesn't have a fire-breathing dragon that he can command."

"Then I shall keep him hidden forever."

"Thank you," she said and closed her eyes. Mekos had now revealed two secrets to her, that he was the Reaver and that he held a lost dragon. That he'd confided in her made Aradella feel good, but at the same time she was aware that she'd revealed very little about herself.

# 2

A loud buzzing woke Aradella. It wasn't daylight yet, but she knew she was in a bed inside the house. She was also fully dressed, sweaty, and quite uncomfortable. *Who brought me inside?* she wondered. *Since I didn't wake up, was I carried? Who could do that? Tanek? Bear Boy?* She knew in her heart that it was Mekos and that thought made her smile deeply.

Suddenly, a voice said, "Mekos has been up for hours, and he should not be alone. He always gets into trouble!"

Aradella was used to people being in her room, but when she looked around, she saw no one. But then, a light appeared and it was surrounding a tiny woman with silvery wings. The pretty little creature was wearing a yellow dress that seemed to glow. She had to be a Never. Jobi had told Aradella of them, but she'd not seen one. He'd said that no one knew the full extent of what a Never could do, but they could make themselves understood if they wanted to be. It appeared that this one wanted Aradella to understand her.

"I am Arit and I'm bonded to Tanek." She spoke as though she was annoyed that she had to do this. "Mekos is waiting for you."

Aradella could only stare at her. "You are extraordinarily beautiful," she whispered.

Arit's expression changed, and her tone became more gentle. "Thank you. Now, you must get up. Tanek's son is—" She looked toward the open doorway. Aradella wondered who had left it open, but then, the climate was divine so it was good to let the air in. Before Aradella could say anything, Arit vanished, and in the next second, Mekos was at the door. He was leaning against the jamb in that slack, easy way that only men could do.

"Do you mean to sleep all day?"

Aradella's padding had slipped and one of the ties was loose. She thought maybe if she stood up, the lower pad would fall to the floor. She put on her most autocratic attitude. "I must bathe and change my clothes."

"Why?"

"Because I'm a girl," she snapped. "Did you forget that?" She started toward the bathroom.

"I did." He yawned. "I suppose I should look for someone who isn't weak and afraid. Perhaps Bear Boy can help me explore the garden I found."

That word make her halt. "A what?"

He looked uninterested. "Nothing. It's just a tall stone wall with some plants inside. I'm sure they're ordinary ones. Although, some of the birds were chirping quite loudly. There seems to be something, uh, special about the garden. I have no idea what it is." He stood up straighter. "I'll go by myself to see it, then I'll come back and tell you all about it." He gave her a look up and down. "You probably couldn't get over the wall anyway."

Aradella gave him a look meant to singe his hair. "Try me."

He gave a false look of surprise. "But you need to . . ." He waved his hand up and down, meaning to reclothe herself.

"Stay! Wait," she ordered, then ran to the privacy of the bathroom. She took no bath, didn't change her clothes; just a toilet run, then a quick tightening to her padding. She ran out, but he was already about ten steps down the path. She hurried after him.

He gave a smile of welcome. "I think it may be a secret garden that probably belongs to—" He cut off as they heard a giggle coming from the other side of a tall hedge. It was Kaley. It was followed by a crash of what sounded to be branches hitting the ground, then something heavy fell. An entire tree? "I think they're up." Mekos looked at Aradella with wide eyes.

She couldn't help laughing at his double entendre.

With sparkling eyes, he began running down the path, Aradella close behind him.

They skirted the village, then hid behind a shed as they waited for two women to pass.

"It's nearly the Day of the Moon," they heard a woman say.

When they were gone, Mekos said, "Is that a holiday?"

"I have no idea. We should ask the Reaver."

He gave a laugh, then led them down a narrow trail. Twice, they went over fences.

"How did you find this place?" she asked.

"A flock of green birds, a kind I've never seen before, woke me and wanted me to follow them."

"I bet your father could have asked them where they were going. I believe there's a special language he knows."

Mekos stopped and looked at her, then he leaned forward, his lips close to her ear. He said something in an incomprehensible language that was liquid cream, soft as a cloud, and oh so very enticing.

Aradella felt her knees weaken. She felt like saying, *I am yours.*

Mekos stepped back, his expression smug. "*That* language?"

Aradella was *not* going to show him how she was affected. "I assume it is, but with Tanek's deep voice it would be much more—"

Mekos made a groan mixed with laughter. "I cannot win! Come on, we're almost there."

When he turned away, Aradella wiped the sweat off her brow. "Where did you sleep? How did I get in my bed?"

"Eagles carried you. It took six of them," he said.

"Tanek could have—"

He turned and gave her a look to stop it.

Aradella smiled sweetly, then closed her mouth.

Minutes later, Mekos pushed tall branches aside to show a stone wall. "It goes down quite a way. I didn't go all the way around but I think it's attached to Valona's big house and it encloses a garden. See the leaves?" He pointed upward to some large, spiked leaves hanging over the stone. "Know what plant that is?"

"I'm not sure," she said, but she had an idea, and it wasn't good. "How do we get inside?"

"We must return to get my father—if Kaley can spare him, that is—then he'll take you over by soaring."

She gave him a look to cut it out.

"Unless you think *I* can take you over. No! That's not possible."

Aradella stepped close to him and put her arms up for him to take her.

He gave a chuckle, embraced her, then they soared up and over the wall. He took his time landing. "You smell good," he said. "Like earth and water and rather strongly of fox."

She rested her head on his shoulder. "It's the smelly company I've been keeping."

Smiling, he floated down with her and they broke apart.

Aradella began walking and looking at the plants. When she realized what they were, her face became solemn. *This is what Jobi foresaw*, she thought. *He knew that someday I'd see this and I'd need to know what these plants are.*

She became more alarmed with every step she took. It was a garden of poisonous plants. Every tree, bush, and flower could kill. There was one plant that she looked for. She'd seen pictures and drawings of it, had read about it, but had certainly never seen one. At the back, against the stone wall, she saw three little plants inside a short barbed fence. For a moment, she just stared, knowing that even touching the leaves could cause death. She should get away from them! But then, some instinct told her she might need some of the noxious poison of these plants. Cautiously, she stepped inside. Hale had sewn a deep pocket inside Aradella's voluminous skirt. With her hand covered, she gathered a dozen leaves and concealed them in the pocket.

She left the enclosure, then looked for Mekos, but she didn't see him.

A large bird was sitting on the tall wall. "I wish Jobi had sent me some bird books," she muttered. The bird started rapidly moving back and forth, then it gave a squawk that sounded like an alarm—a warning.

Aradella grabbed her big skirt and ran toward the bird. Standing just below it was Mekos—and he was about to bite into a big green fruit. She didn't take time to yell a warning. She just went into a running jump and hit Mekos with all the force she had.

The hit was unexpected and he staggered back. "What the fark are you doing?" he demanded.

She struck out with her fist and knocked the fruit out of his hand. The bird on the wall flew down and put itself between the fruit on the ground and Mekos. "That is a sea mango. It's the suicide plant. It's *deadly*." She stepped back, trying to calm her shaking body. "That bird was warning you. Why didn't you *listen* to it? If *I* hadn't understood it, you might be dead now."

Mekos was watching her intently, then he pulled her into his arms. "I'm sorry. It was stupid of me. I should have listened but I was hungry." He was stroking her hair. "It's all right," he whispered. "I'm safe. You saved me."

They stood together for minutes and she was gradually able to get herself under control. Hale had taught her how to slow her breath to quiet her heartbeat.

Mekos held her at arm's length and looked into her eyes. "Are you all right now?"

She nodded.

"Will you tell me about this garden?"

Again, she nodded, then looked at the bird, still guarding the poisonous piece of fruit. "He saved you."

Mekos stepped away and held out his arm. The bird landed on his forearm. "Thank you, my friend," he said. "I am indebted to you."

The bird did a little bow then flew away.

"Do *all* birds come to you?"

"If I ask them to, yes." His eyes sparkled. "They go to my father without asking."

Aradella's eyes showed her laughter. "But then, Tanek is—"

Mekos groaned. "You've recovered too much! Show me this place."

Turning, Aradella looked around her. Her voice was solemn, serious. "This is a garden of death." He followed her as she pointed out the plants. "Sea mango, gympie-gympie, wolfsbane, snakeroot, belladonna, oleander, hemlock, foxglove. They're all poisonous plants. Every one of them."

Abruptly, Mekos jerked his head upward and looked toward the far side of the garden. The hair over his ears twitched. "Someone comes," he whispered.

Aradella stepped toward the near wall, meaning to get out of there, but Mekos didn't move. "This is who I've been smelling," he said softly. "Following and watching us."

He looked at her, silently asking if she wanted to leave or to stay with him. There was no doubt that he was going to investigate what he was hearing.

She gave a firm nod. She was staying with him. When she took a step and a twig broke, he put his arm around her waist and they moved forward, her feet barely touching the ground. Together, they weren't as silent as Mekos would have been alone, but they made less noise than a human would.

When they reached the wall, Mekos soared upward with her so they were sitting on the top. They were so engulfed by tree leaves that they couldn't be seen.

Below them were two women, one of them the beautiful Valona.

Aradella, her back against Mekos's front, looked at him and he nodded. Yes, *she* was who he'd known was near them.

He swiped his hair back to expose his ears and listened.

With Valona was a very old woman. She walked slowly, bent over, and she was holding a silver pot.

They watched Valona sit down on a wooden stool, then turn her face to the sun.

The old woman, who seemed to be the maid, opened the pot and began to spread a thick pink lotion on Valona's lovely face.

"The cream is almost gone," the maid said.

"I'll make a new batch from that princess Olina sent me. She's big so there'll be a lot of it."

The maid frowned, which deepened the creases on her face. "She's not pretty so maybe it won't work. To keep your looks, you must take true beauty."

"She's royal. That's a different kind of radiance."

The maid paused, seeming to be worried. "Her status will make people miss her."

"Olina arranged that. There'll be proof that the two men killed the bland princess."

"What men?" The maid sounded alarmed, then calmed. "Oh. You mean the swansman and his son. That's good. They have no worth or importance, so no one will notice that they're gone." She nodded in approval. "Yes, that is a very good plan."

When Mekos tightened his grip on Aradella, she knew he was warning her. Of Valona? But no, he nudged her to see a huge green lizard silently and stealthily walking toward them on top of the wall. It was the size of a bear cub, heavy and strong—and she knew it could spit fire. They had been exterminated on the rest of the island since they tended to kill livestock—and a few humans.

Aradella held her breath, waiting for the creature to come for them. Of course Mekos would take them to safety. But he didn't move, and the lizard stopped to just above where Valona was sitting. Did it mean to jump on her?

Mekos kept holding Aradella tightly and she thought maybe it was his scent of fox that made them uninteresting to the creature.

Because her attention was on the lizard—or "little dragon" as some people called them—she didn't see the light that appeared near Valona.

"Yes! I know she's here," Valona said angrily. "Does Olina think I'm as stupid as she is? Must she remind me of what I'm to do?"

Aradella slid her eyes to the side, too afraid to move her body and alert the lizard. The light near Valona surrounded a little man with wings of gold and red. He was a handsome Never in his green trousers and sleeveless brown top. As small as he was, he was quite muscular.

Valona swiped her hand at him. "I don't want to hear any more."

To escape her hand, the little man flew backward toward the wall. In a lightning movement, the lizard's long tongue shot out. It hit the man and made him tumble through the air.

"Borel! No!" Valona snapped, then made a grab for the Never. She caught it, but then she sneered. "It's ruined! Now it's ugly." In disgust, she threw the Never over the wall.

He went flying past Aradella and Mekos, but they didn't dare move from their hiding place.

Valona held up her hand. "It got blood on me! Filthy creature."

"That thing was useful to Queen Olina," the maid said. "She won't like losing it, and you know how she likes to give punishment."

"This is bad." Valona sounded exasperated. "Where can I get another one to replace it?"

"I believe that swansman has one, a female. I'll get her for you."

Valona smiled. "I'll miss you when you die." As the two of them went inside, the lizard slid down their side of the wall and followed them into the house.

Immediately, Mekos held Aradella and they soared to the ground.

"We have to find him," Aradella said.

"Yes." Mekos's ears twitched, he breathed deeply, and he squinted his eyes as he looked about.

Aradella saw three birds in a tree. "Help us find him. Please," she said urgently.

The birds swooped down, went under low-hanging leaves, then to the ground.

Mekos pulled the plants aside to expose a thick spider's web. In the center was the tiny, unconscious man. The lower half of his left leg was gone and the stump was thickly coated in webbing silk. The bleeding had been stopped. To the side was a large black spider, hiding and watching.

"Thank you," Aradella said to the spider, then she reached down and carefully lifted the little man.

"He's a Never," Mekos said. "He—"

"I know. We must tell Arit. She'll know what to do."

"How do you know—?" he began but stopped, then said, "Arit! I need you." There was no response. He grit his teeth. "She is bonded to my father and she thinks I'm useless, so she rarely obeys me." He spoke more urgently. "I know you're not needed by my father right now, and I've found a Never who needs help." They waited but nothing happened.

Aradella said, "He's a *male* Never."

Instantly, the air fluttered and tiny Arit appeared. This time, she had on a pink dress, her long hair glistening. She stared at the man lying on Aradella's open palm as though seeing something she didn't believe existed.

"Is there something that can heal him?" Mekos asked. "If it's here, Aradella can find it."

"Toris berries," Arit said.

"I saw them!" Aradella slipped the man into Mekos's hand, then ran deeper into the garden. In seconds, she returned with a handful of the black berries.

"Are they poisonous?" he asked.

"Not to touch, but for humans to eat, yes." She looked at Arit, who was standing on a foxglove flower with its bell shape.

"Would you mash them?" Arit asked.

Aradella didn't trust any plant in that garden not to kill whatever it touched. Her dress had been repeatedly snagged so she tore away a strip and rolled the berries inside it.

"Put him on the cloth." Arit looked at Mekos. "Can you call the birds?" She sounded doubtful.

Mekos gave a quick eye roll. "I'm not my father but I believe I can manage that. Come," he said as he gently placed the man on the big berries on the fabric. Four birds arrived. He and Aradella watched as Arit mounted a bird and the other three carried away the wounded Never in the package.

When they were alone, Mekos looked at Aradella. They didn't need to speak to know that they wanted to get out of that garden. He clasped her to him and they soared over the wall.

They'd barely touched the ground when Mekos said, "She wants to make a magic cream out of you."

Aradella shrugged. "The very definition of a princess is that someone is always trying to kill us. But it's usually *after* we marry them."

Mekos frowned. "This is not a joke. We need to stop this. We have to tell people what's going on."

"Tell them that the old legend is true? That Valona is making a beauty cream that keeps her young forever? You don't know women. They'd probably offer their daughters in exchange for a pot of that cream." She turned away, walking rapidly, and Mekos followed her.

"Kaley might know about this," he said. "She knows stories that happen here. I think maybe they've already happened on Earth, but I'm not sure. Get down!"

The two of them flattened themselves on the ground. Aradella heard nothing, but Mekos's ears were alert.

"It's that lizard," he said. "He's searching for the Never and he smells it on us." They wiped their hands on the grass but they knew it wouldn't be enough. "That thing will stalk us. I'd like to catch it, but those claws are too much to deal with. Oh, for a bow and arrow. If only I had something to throw over it, I could get it."

They watched as the lizard turned away, then Aradella sat up. She reached under her skirt.

"What are you doing?" he asked, eyes wide.

She untied the lower pad around her waist and handed it to him. It was big since it had been made to cover her from waist to knees. "Will this work?" She took a breath. "That feels wonderful!"

Mekos was looking at her in speculation. "Is this like your eyebrows? To protect you from the queen's wrath?"

"Yes." She smiled at his perception.

He nodded to the large upper half of her. "Is that more?"

It was harder to remove the upper pad and pull it out of the big dress.

Mekos gave a crooked smile. "I didn't mind that part of you being large. It—"

"Get that lizard!" she ordered, her face turning red. She stayed back and watched as Mekos wrestled the lizard, deftly escaping the claws. *He can certainly move well,* she thought. Finally, he wrapped the pads around it. Once the creature was encased, it stopped moving about.

Looking like a cave dweller who'd just conquered a marauding beast, Mekos went back to her, all fifty pounds of the mini dragon held by one arm on his hip. "We need to tell Kaley this story," he said. "Maybe she'll know a solution."

"But if we tell your parents what we heard, won't they take us away?"

"Definitely! They'll get us out of here so fast we'll disappear. But then you'd be in danger from Valona for the rest of your life. I don't think that woman will let distance stop her."

"So how can an earthling help?" She sounded as bewildered as she felt.

"I don't know, but I have this monster to use as a bribe. If we can get Kaley to, uh, stop with my father long enough, she might tell us what to do about this woman's murders. Maybe there's some ancient spell or potion." He looked into the distance. "I wonder where the woman does it?"

"And your earthling stepmother might know this? And she would *like* that thing?" She nodded to the lizard.

He pushed in a foot of the lizard. "Yes. Kaley walks up to the most dangerous animals and they become tame. She might trade my father for this creature. She—" He broke off, seeming to be waiting for Aradella to make a joke, but she was silent. "Go on," he said, "you can say it."

"I wouldn't trade your father for all the dragons on Earth."

"That's mild. You can do better."

Aradella thought. "I'd trade it for one night of ecstasy with him? I would let him rule Pithan if I could be his queen?"

"That's better."

Aradella laughed, then gasped. The lizard had just burned a hole in the padded wraps. "It might hurt her."

"Not Kaley. Wait until you see what she does."

"I've already seen too much of what she does." Her sarcasm was heavy. "The question is, how do we find them? Search every waterfall and cave? Swim the rivers and look at duck feet?"

"Good point." Mekos gave a low whistle and the large black bird that had given warning about the fruit flew to a tree branch.

"Find Papá and tell him I have a special animal to show Kaley. Alone." He gave the bird a warning look. "Don't even hint at poisonous plants or the evil plans of Valona. Understand?"

The bird gave a body dip, then flew off.

"It's convenient that they can talk to your father that way."

"Ha!" Mekos said. "When I was a kid, the birds told on me wherever I was. I'd fall asleep with my cousins and Papá would come and get me and carry me home."

"He doesn't like your relatives?"

"They're foxes and there are predators after them."

Aradella nodded in understanding. A little boy curled up with a litter of kits was a sweet vision, but dangerous.

The bird returned and gave chirping noises that made Mekos smile. "Kaley is at the house and Papá is going to take a nap. He seems to be very tired."

Mekos and Aradella looked at each other, then burst into laughter.

# 3

As they approached the house, they saw Kaley sitting at the big table in the open area. She was eating from a plate of food that looked like it could feed a dozen people.

"Don't tell her so much that she'll guess the truth," Mekos said.

"Lie, then cover it with more lies?"

"Exactly."

"That's what I've been doing my whole life," she said.

"Hello," Kaley said when she saw them. "I don't know why I'm so hungry but I could clear a Thanksgiving table by myself. I guess it's all the hiking Tanek and I have been doing."

"I'm sure that's it," Mekos said.

Kaley looked at Aradella. "Sorry. I'm forgetting my manners. There's a lot of food here. I'll get plates and you two can—" When she stood up, she saw that Mekos was holding a big white bundle that was moving. "What's that?"

"A gift for you." He lifted the cover—which wasn't easy considering that it was trying to get out by clawing him to death. "We saw it and I knew you'd like it, and . . ." He paused for drama. "We thought maybe you'd tell us one of your Earth stories. I told Aradella how great they are."

"How nice of you." Kaley put her empty plate on the counter so the big table was clear. "Let's have a look."

Mekos, with Aradella behind him, put the animal on the table but kept a firm hand on its back.

Kaley lifted the padding to the lizard's face. "How pretty you are," she said.

Aradella gasped when Kaley reached out and touched the lizard's nose.

But Kaley was smiling. "Come on, let me see all of you." While she untied the padding, the lizard was very still. When it was free, it leaped onto Kaley.

"No!" Aradella yelled, but Mekos just smiled.

The lizard hugged Kaley like it was a human infant.

"His name is Borel and today he ate something that tasted very, very good and he wants more of it. He's set himself a quest to find it." She looked at them in question.

"No idea what that is." Mekos and Aradella shrugged, looking innocent.

Kaley sat down, holding the big lizard to her. "What kind of story do you want to hear?"

Mekos and Aradella sat down across from her and he looked at the princess.

"An old woman kills a girl then takes her youth and beauty," Aradella said.

Kaley was stroking the lizard who looked so content it was falling asleep. "That's the basis for many fairy tales. There's usually a beautiful, but evil, queen who will do anything to keep her beauty. Often, she has a stepdaughter, probably a princess, who is more beautiful than she is. The queen believes that if she, well . . . takes the girl's heart, she'll get the girl's beauty. Is that what you mean?"

"Maybe it's not just a princess but a beautiful girl every year," Mekos said.

"That's a popular variation."

"Could she make a kind of youth cream from the sacrifice?" Aradella asked.

Kaley shifted the lizard on her shoulder. "Whatever he ate, he's dreaming of it. Do you know what it was?"

"No!" Mekos and Aradella said in unison.

"The cream?" Mekos asked.

"Oh yes. It sounds somewhat like 'Snow White.'" She was looking at Aradella's pale lashes and brows. "The evil queen put Snow to sleep with a poisoned apple."

"Then what happened?"

"There are variations on that. Some stories say her casket fell over and the apple fell out or she was awakened by True Love's kiss." Kaley was thoughtful. "True Love's kiss often does it. Unless you're poor Sleeping Beauty. Her rescuer 'gathered the first fruits of love,' meaning that nine months later the unconscious girl gave birth to twins."

Mekos was frowning. "If the girl is put to sleep, is there no other way to wake her up other than . . . ?"

"Rape?" Aradella asked.

"We broke the gingerbread witch's spell by killing her," Kaley said.

"Death," Mekos said. Under the table, he took Aradella's hand and squeezed it.

Kaley was looking at them hard. "Is something going on that your dad and I should be told about?"

"No, nothing. Not at all," Mekos said quickly. Kaley's tone reinforced their decision to not tell what they'd heard Valona say. If Olina had sent Aradella to them once, she'd do it again. They needed to find a way to stop Valona!

"I haven't heard any stories here on this island," Kaley said.

Without a hint of humor, Aradella said, "I would imagine that you've been busy. It's a pretty island and there's much to see."

Mekos gave a cough to keep from laughing. "Does a person of royal birth have more value?"

"Oh yes," Kaley said. "All the stories agree on that. Royalty has special powers. Some say royals can heal people or that the ability to rule is transferred. There's always something evil people are trying to achieve."

Aradella said, "Have you ever heard of the sea mango?"

Kaley looked surprised. "Yes. It's one of several plants called a suicide fruit. Have you seen such a tree?"

"Jobi gave her Earth books about plants, so Aradella knows a lot. We've been identifying them." Mekos knew he was talking too fast.

Kaley was looking from one to the other. "I think you need to talk to your father. He—"

At that moment, a sleepy-looking Tanek entered the room.

Instantly, Mekos stood up. Talking faster than an Empyrean ship could go, he said, "I've been explaining Lelys to the princess. She thought they were bad but I said we're just people. We have to go." He grabbed Aradella's hand and they ran down the stairs and were quickly hidden by the forest.

She jerked out of his grasp. "You made me look like an idiot, and what you said had nothing to do with anything."

Mekos smiled. "That was a good save, wasn't it? We can fool Kaley but Papá knows when I'm hiding something. If he thought something was wrong, he'd have us out of here before you could put on clothes that fit you."

Aradella grimaced. "But it was at my expense in front of *him*! I never thought Lelys were bad!" She sighed. "But yes, it was a good diversion."

Coming from the direction of the house, they heard Tanek say, "We have to get rid of that thing."

"But he's so cute!" Kaley replied.

"He just set fire to a chair. Out! Now!"

They heard doors shut, then voices came from the other side of the trees. Tanek said, "I'm not carrying it and you can't release it here. It might go after the kids." Their footsteps faded away.

Aradella said, "He's kind of bossy, isn't he?"

"The worst," Mekos answered. "I don't think Kaley is going to be able to stand him."

"Then maybe I could still make him a king."

"You won't get *that* wish," he said. "Come on, we have things to do."

She turned away, but when Mekos went back to the house, she followed him. "What's your plan?"

He looked her up and down. "You can't wear that. It looks like a ship's sail on a rowboat. It's good that Kaley had the lizard to distract her or she would have started asking questions."

She sat down on the edge of the bed. "Maybe I can repair the pads."

"That lizard ripped them apart. You need to—" At the look on her face, he stopped talking, then sat down beside her. "Are you afraid Olina will hear the truth about how you look?"

She nodded.

He reached out and took her hand. "I can't imagine what it's like to live in fear every day. But we do have things to do. Did you forget that Valona wants to make you into a pot of face grease?"

She grimaced. "I'd rather be made into beauty cream than spend my life as Nessa's wife."

Mekos squeezed her hand. "I would feel the same way if I had to live with someone I didn't like." He stood up. "Wait here. I have an idea." He left the room and a few minutes later, he returned with some of Kaley's clothes over his arm. "I can't tell under that tent you have on, but I think you two are the same size."

"I can't take Kaley's clothes. She needs them. She—"

He raised an eyebrow.

"You're right. The last thing she needs is clothing. But then, she's with Tanek." Aradella gave an exaggerated sigh.

"That's better." He tossed the clothes to her. "Get dressed, then let's eat. I want you to tell me all about what training you've had and who helped you."

It took her a moment to realize what he was saying. Reveal her secrets? Tell someone the *truth* about her life? "I don't . . ." she said softly.

Mekos seemed to understand her reluctance. "I'm a swansman, remember? Valona and her maid said I'm worthless, therefore I'm completely trustworthy."

"Worthless? Trustworthy? How do those two go together?"

"Who knows? Get dressed. I'm starving."

Aradella clutched the clothes to her. "You always are. Like the night of the dance. You never looked up from the table. You—" At his look of impatience, she ran to the bathroom. She was taller than Kaley, so the pants were ankle length and the top wasn't long enough to hide much. But they were certainly better than the big dress. The Earth clothes were strange to her but she liked them very much. When she walked, she didn't have a big skirt against her legs. *Wouldn't my cousins be jealous*, she thought.

When she stepped into the bedroom, her breath was held. *What would he think of her dressed like this?*

Mekos was looking out the window and when he turned and saw her, he gasped, his eyes wide. But he made no comment.

After a moment, he got himself under control. "Food!" He led the way to the kitchen.

It looked as though the kitchen had recently been restocked. There was bread, butter, eggs, fruit, and little bowls of food they didn't recognize.

Mekos was the chef. He told her to sit on a stool on the other side of the high island as he began assembling everything. He expertly lit the little wood-fed grill and began cooking meat and a concoction of batter that he poured out of a bowl.

As he worked, Aradella told how Hale came into her life. "She was my punishment and I hated her at first, but . . ."

"You had no one else except Sojee's daughters for friendship," he said. "I thought one of them was going to attack me when we were on the platform."

"That's Shay. She's only interested in beauty and which man her father is going to get for her."

"What about the other one?"

"Hale said Bree sneaks out of the Cauldron but she couldn't find out where Bree goes."

He pulled little flatbreads off the grill. "What else did Hale do for you?"

Aradella told how the only food given to her by the queen were cakes and pies. "They kept me big, but when I offered them to Hale, she said she didn't eat them. That made me curious about what she did eat. And at night I heard noises in the courtyard. I wondered what caused them."

"She was training. And she changed your diet."

"Yes." Aradella ate one of the grilled breads he put on her plate. "These are delicious."

"My grandpapá learned how to make them while he was on Earth."

When she told him how she and Hale often sneaked out at night to train, she didn't look at him. There were some secrets she wasn't ready to reveal. But when she looked up, Mekos was staring at her hard, as though he was figuring out something.

"Did you—" he began.

Suddenly, Arit appeared, her light shining.

Aradella's face lit up as bright as the light. "You have a new dress. It's beautiful!"

Arit was pleased by the compliment. "Kaley drew it and Daln's daughter made it."

"Hard to believe that Kaley had time for anything besides—"

Aradella cut him off by loudly clearing her throat. "I'm rather good with a needle. I'll make a dress for you."

"And I'll have Grandpapá send me the best swan cloth," Mekos said.

"How kind." Arit sat down on a little pot that Mekos overturned for her. She looked Aradella up and down. "And you look very good. Doesn't she, Son of Tanek?"

"Now I'm merely a son?" he asked.

The two females stared at him, waiting for his reply.

Mekos smiled. "Yes, she looks good. *Very* good!"

"I have news. Ian said—" Arit twirled around but saw no one. "Ian!" she said loudly. It was an order.

One of the things Nevers didn't tell was how they appeared and disappeared so suddenly. Nor did they tell where they were when they weren't with humans.

As he was told to, Ian appeared. The light that surrounded him was blue and dull compared to Arit's. He had on the same clothes he'd been wearing, but below his left knee, there was nothing. They could see fresh spider's web glistening, and there were dark stains on his clothing.

"Are you all right?" Aradella asked.

"I'm fine as long as I don't try to walk."

He was obviously trying to make a joke but his pale complexion told another story.

"Maybe you should lie down," Aradella said. "You—"

Mekos cut her off. "I didn't know Nevers could walk. Arit rides around on my father's shoulder or hides in his beard."

Arit said, "Ian can ride on *your* shoulder. Too bad you don't have a beard."

"Yes!" Aradella said. "That's an excellent idea. Mekos's shoulders are very wide so you'll have lots of room. And his hair will cover you as it's quite thick. You can't even see sunlight through it. He has—"

The three of them looked at her in a way that made Aradella's face turn red. "Just an idea," she murmured.

Mekos put his shoulder forward and Ian flew to sit on it. It had only been a few hours since the lizard had bitten off part of his leg. That he was there with them showed how important his mission was.

Arit waited until the two men were settled then said, "Ian knows the truth about the Lair, about Valona. She plans to kill Aradella tomorrow, and she'll make it look like—"

Aradella interrupted. "We know this. Everything Valona does is backed by my aunt-queen. She wants me dead, and Tanek and Mekos are to be blamed. Her purpose is to stop the men from coming to Pithan."

"Does she think the men will start a war?" Arit asked.

"Worse," Aradella said. "She's terrified that they'll stay and create families. Children will have both a mother and father. Wouldn't that be horrible? She knows that men won't put up with her treachery. They'll storm the palace and—" Aradella took a breath.

"But if you're alive," Mekos said, "then the men *will* arrive, and maybe your island will change." His voice got louder. "But only if you're still *alive*."

"But you'll be married to Nessa," Arit said sadly. "I traveled with him. We had days and days of hearing him complain. He's a coward and thinks only of himself. He'd sell other people if he could, and—"

"You're not helping," Mekos said. "We have only a few hours to figure out how to keep this from happening. Then we have to *do* it."

Arit said, "If Tanek were told he'd—"

"Start a war," Mekos shot back. "If I were threatened, Papá would go in with blades drawn. And Kaley has an Earth gun. The worst part is that whatever the result of that battle, win or lose, Olina would use the violence as an excuse to stop the men from coming. And even if we take Aradella away now, today, I'm sure this evil woman, Valona, will pursue her."

They were quiet for a moment, filled with the helplessness of how to solve this. Should they try to hide forever?

"The ceremony is tomorrow morning," Ian said. "At sunrise. They call it the Day of the Moon."

Mekos and Aradella looked at him in shock. "We heard of this. Does everyone in the Lair know about it?"

"Oh yes. Every person will be there. It's mandatory. This year they're pleased that all their pretty daughters will be safe.

Valona only tells who the Honored Girl is on that morning. She likes the loud tears of relief for the girls not chosen—and the screams of grief for the one who is. One minute the girl is alive and the next she's lying on the stone altar and Valona is holding her beating heart up high. Afterward is feasting and celebration, but I can tell you that no one is genuinely joyous."

For minutes, they couldn't speak as they envisioned the horrific scene.

Mekos said, "Do they know that this year it's Princess Aradella who is to be sacrificed?"

"Yes," Ian said. "Everyone knows and they're grateful to her."

"That's why the girl said 'thank you' to me," Aradella said softly. "Do they think I know what's to happen?"

"Yes," Ian said. "Valona told them you volunteered. She said that you believe it's the duty of a princess to serve her people."

"That is sick!" Mekos said.

Ian looked weaker, as though telling this had taken even more of his blood.

"Why do you stay?" Aradella asked him.

"Queen Olina holds my sister in an iron cage. I obey or she dies."

Arit's gasp made her fly backward. "But that's not . . ." She couldn't finish.

"Honorable?" Ian said through clenched teeth. "It goes against codes of decency and fair play? We are small and they are large, so we are at their mercy? Yes. All of it."

"Zeon's mask," Arit said. "We might be able to use it to fool Valona. Maybe it could give us time."

Mekos's eyes widened. "I forgot about that! Kaley has a mask. She told me she has a whole box full of magic things, but the mask is special. It can make people look different. Let's go find it."

"Wait!" Arit said. "They may be in their bedroom. We can't intrude on them."

"They are anywhere on this island except their bedroom," Mekos said. "Waterfalls, lakes, meadows." He looked at Aradella.

"In trees, and don't forget caves. They love caves," Aradella said. "I can guarantee that they're not in their own bed."

As tiny as Arit was, she gave them a prim-and-proper look. "And how do you two know that? Spying is a disgusting trait!"

"Like you don't watch Papá every minute of the day," Mekos snapped at her. "Let's find that mask."

When they got to Kaley and Tanek's bedroom, it did indeed appear to have never been used. There was a tall cabinet and the door was locked.

"I bet Papá has the key." Mekos sounded defeated.

"Allow me," Ian said. He flew to the cabinet, put his face down to the hole and made the light of his body go very bright. He reached in, moved something, and they heard a clunk sound. Then he put his head into the lock and his body followed. By the third move, he was halfway inside the keyhole, his wings flattened against him. He did a wiggling back out and the door opened.

"Very handy talent," Mekos said as looked inside. There were two boxes on the shelf. One was metal. Beside them was a necklace.

"That's Kaley's Truth Necklace," Mekos said. "I guess that right now she doesn't want to know if anything isn't true."

"Or she's with someone she trusts completely," Aradella said as she looked at Mekos.

Arit frowned, seeming annoyed at their banter. "Get that box," she said.

Mekos removed the metal box and opened it. Inside was a transparent half mask. "It doesn't look like much."

"It is," Arit said. "You can change yourself or make another person into something different." She glanced at Aradella. "Tanek and Kaley changed themselves and each other."

"I like that idea," Mekos said to Aradella. "We'll try it. You can change me then change yourself. No one will be able to find us."

When they got back to Aradella's bedroom, Ian flew off Mekos's shoulder and sat on a bedpost to watch.

Mekos handed the mask to Aradella. "You first. Change me into a ferocious beast so I can do away with Valona."

"There is only one way to kill her," Ian said under his breath, almost too quiet for anyone to hear.

Aradella put the mask to her face and it seemed to meld into her skin. She certainly wasn't going to change Mekos into a fierce creature so he could risk being killed. Instead, with all her might, she wished to be as beautiful as a princess should be. In other words, she wanted to look like one of her cousins. Instantly, she felt different, and she looked down at herself. She was wearing a pale lavender dress, the color a mix of the pink and blue her cousins wore. When she turned to the others, their astonishment showed that it had worked. There was a mirror on the wall and she looked in it. She looked exactly like her beautiful cousins. Her hair was thick and glossy, her skin perfect, her eyes blue and her cheekbones high. Aradella turned around. "Well?" she said proudly.

To her surprise, Mekos was frowning. "I don't like it." His voice was almost angry. "Take it off!"

She was puzzled by his response. What man didn't like beauty? The mask was easy to remove and she held it out to him.

Still frowning so deep his eyebrows met in the middle, he took the mask and put it on.

They watched as Mekos changed to look like his father. He was heavier, had a black beard, and he wore the skeptical expression that was always on Tanek's face. Mekos turned to Aradella. "And now?"

She shook her head no. "It's not right," she said quietly. "Remove that thing."

Mekos took the mask off and tossed it onto the bed like it was something dirty.

Arit looked at them. "I think you like each other as you are."

Ian gave a snort of laughter. "You think so?"

Mekos ignored their comments. "We must think about what we need to do." He paused. "Actually, it's simple. Tomorrow,

I'll put on the mask and hide, then I'll jump out at Valona and kill her."

There was a long silence, then Aradella spoke. "Have you ever killed anyone before?"

"No," Mekos said.

"And certainly not a woman," Arit added.

"Of course not!" Mekos said. "But she must be stopped, and death is the only way."

Aradella looked at him. "We're an army of a Lely, a princess, and two Nevers. I can't see that we're going to strike fear in anyone, even if you make yourself look scary. Besides, if Valona is powerful enough that she can make a youth cream out of a person, she'll probably be able to see past some magic mask." When no one replied, she said, "I'm going to take a bath and wash my hair. I want to look my best for tomorrow. After all, I'm the Honored Girl."

When Aradella was gone, Mekos looked at Arit. "Stay with her. She's more scared than she lets on."

Nodding, Arit flew away.

He turned to Ian. "I need to do some thinking. Want to go with me or stay here?"

In answer, Ian flew to Mekos's shoulder.

"I don't have my father's beard so you must hold on tightly." Mekos casually left the house, but when he was out of sight, he bent forward and moved very quickly. His steps were light and utterly silent. Ian held on to Mekos's shirt but twice he was thrown off and had to fly back. A couple of times pain shot through him, but he kept going. Mekos would stop to sniff the air, then he'd turn sharply. At last, he halted and sat down under a tree.

Ian flew upward to a low-hanging branch. "I've not been near a Lely before." He was trying to catch his breath. "Does Aradella know you can move like that?"

"She's seen hints of it." Mekos sat very still. "Stay where you are. Don't come down." In the next moment, three little fox kits came tumbling through the forest. They stopped beside Mekos and looked up at him. "Did Mamá send you to check on me?" he asked as the cute little creatures climbed onto his lap. "They aren't answering," he said over his shoulder to Ian. "This is just like her. She sent kits that are too young to tell me what she's up to." He stroked their fur as they curled up and went to sleep. "But it's good to know that she's nearby." He turned his head to look at Ian. "You said there's only one way to kill Valona. What is it?"

Ian looked surprised that he'd been heard, but then he hesitated, seemingly trying to figure out what to say. It was dangerous to reveal what he knew.

"There's no use trying to make me believe you're a Never who doesn't listen at doors," Mekos said. "I grew up with my father and Arit. I often saw her skulking around him with her light off. What do you know about Valona?"

"She can only be killed with a special knife. She keeps it where she sleeps."

"Then I must go get it."

"How can you? That room is under an enchantment. The only person allowed in there besides Valona is her maid."

"Then I shall be her maid."

"You think that mask will protect you?" Ian asked. "You didn't listen to the princess. She's right that Valona is very powerful. She's over a hundred years old and she's taken the life of a pretty girl every year since she was twenty. I've heard her laugh about how many people have tried to get that knife. She's killed them all." He took a breath. "There's a woman named Reena who might be able to help you. She can—"

"I know Reena and there's no time to contact her," Mekos said calmly, being careful not to disturb the kits. "I know that Valona spends hours riding her horse so I'll go when she's away." He looked at Ian. "I would imagine that such a knife is under lock and key."

"Yes." Ian knew what he was asking. "If I go with you, will you help me free my sister?"

"Of course. I'll do that even if you don't go with me. If I live, that is."

Ian gave a small smile. "No pressure on me, then, is there?"

"On neither of us." Mekos glanced at the missing half of Ian's leg. "How are you doing?"

"All right. The spider's web stopped the bleeding, and Arit gave me something to eat that makes me almost not feel the pain. I think that if I were still, I might feel rather awful. What about you?"

"A big part of me wants to go to my father and ask him to take over all of this. I can see myself crying to him. He would tell me to stay with the women, then he would go fix it."

"He'd have to fight against magic so he'd probably end up dead," Ian said. "Then the essence of Aradella would be put in a silver pot, the Selkan men will not be allowed to come to Pithan, and next year another girl would be murdered. But Valona and Queen Olina would be very happy."

"That's my biggest fear," Mekos said, "that evil will win. Come, we must go and watch."

Mekos was on his stomach in the tall grass, so flattened and still that he could hardly be seen. He watched Valona mount her horse and ride away.

Ian flew to land near him, but Mekos didn't move. "How are they?"

"Arit gave the princess a drink that calmed her. They're planning dresses for both of them."

"Good," Mekos said. "I don't want Aradella worrying. She—" He became alert. "There she goes!" The maid was leaving for her daily trip to the market. "Are you ready?"

"I've said my prayers and written a note of apology to my sister. Yes, I'm ready."

Mekos gave a half smile. "Kaley told me that in her stories, Nevers are always happy."

"My sister is a prisoner, I work for two evil women, and a lizard found my leg so delicious that he's stalking me so he can get more. My apologizes for not being full of joy."

"Kaley would love to hear your story." Mekos rolled to his back and slipped on the mask. He closed his eyes and concentrated on looking like the maid. When he opened them, he looked at Ian. "Did I do it?"

"You are extraordinarily ugly."

Mekos lifted his hand to feel the wrinkled skin. "Indeed, I am." He got up and in spite of how he looked, he fluidly moved toward the big house. That Valona had no human guards stationed about showed her true power. No one dared threaten her. But he was sure that if he tried to enter as himself, it would be the last thing he ever did.

Once inside the house, Ian led them through the rooms. There was little furniture and almost no decoration. It seemed that Valona didn't allow competition from a painting or a pretty cabinet. The only glory allowed was Valona.

The bedroom was at the back of the house and the door opened easily. It was an austere room, just a narrow bed and a table. No pictures were on the walls. There weren't even any windows.

Ian flew to the far wall. Hanging there was the only other furniture. It was a small cabinet with a locked door. It looked so insignificant that no one would guess it was of any importance.

Ian landed on top of it and Mekos nodded to him. *Yes, open it,* he was silently saying.

The little man flew down and looked in the keyhole, then pulled back. He held up six fingers to show that there were six tumblers in the lock. He waved his hand toward the door. *Was anyone there?*

In spite of how he looked to others, when Mekos pulled his hair back, his pointed ears moved in a circle as he listened. He shook his head. They were alone.

Ian quickly moved two tumblers, but the third one gave him trouble. It was an old lock and hard to turn. When it finally moved, he backed out. There was blood on his hands from all the pulling and pushing. He took a few deep breaths, wiped his hands on his bloodstained trousers, then went back in.

When the fourth tumbler moved, he felt Mekos's fingertip on his remaining foot. He backed out.

Mekos pointed toward the doorway and put his finger to his lips. Someone was coming.

Arit was looking at Aradella as she yawned for the third time. Mekos had told her to keep the princess quiet while he and Ian . . . Annoyingly, they'd refused to say where they were going or what they planned to do. But she knew where and that it was dangerous. "Dumb, dumb, dumb," she muttered.

"What?" Aradella murmured. "Where's Mekos?"

"Practicing his bow and arrow," Arit said quickly.

Aradella smiled sleepily. "For the Reaver. He's very good with a bow and he's beautiful in his black costume. Don't you think he's beautiful?"

"He's a poor copy of his father," Arit said. "But he's all right. Why don't you sleep and I'll look for them?"

"Good idea," Aradella said. "Then the Reaver will come and I'll kiss him again. One more kiss before I die."

Arit rolled her eyes skyward, then back. She was glad she wasn't a princess!

Aradella went to sleep as soon as she closed her eyes, and Arit flew out the door. She had no doubt where the two stupid men had gone, alone and unprotected. She didn't know Ian very well, but she'd known Mekos all his life. He'd always believed he could do *anything.* She'd seen Tanek pull his son out of a well, release him from a trap, and twice he'd caught him as he fell out of a tree. One time, Tanek ran into a building on fire. He came out carrying his limp five-year-old son over his arm.

So now, Mekos was no doubt yet again in a mess. She was tempted to tell Tanek what was going on, but she didn't want to see him up against a nasty creature like Valona either. Tanek could handle any weapon, but magic was something different.

Arit got to the big house just as the old maid was entering it. Since her shopping basket was empty, she'd probably forgotten something and had returned for it. Arit was sure the men were inside, so she needed to distract the woman. The maid was just inside the door when Arit began buzzing around her head. Round and round and as loud as she could make herself vibrate.

The old woman swatted at her, but Arit easily avoided her. The maid kept walking—and Arit heard a clunk sound. She knew it was Ian slithering inside some lock to find . . . She didn't know what.

The maid kept walking toward the room at the back.

Arit knew how to annoy humans. She'd learned how when Tanek was a boy and she wanted his attention. Buzzing loudly, she flew past the woman's eyes, her feet grazing her lashes.

The woman shook her head to get away from the pest.

Arit went to her ear and let her wings flutter against it. The woman hit at her, almost striking Arit. She encircled the woman's head, entangling her feet in her hair.

With a screech, the woman ran back up the hall, away from where the men were. But the second Arit quit buzzing, the maid started back down the hall.

"What the fark?" Arit muttered. She knew what she had to do.

With a sigh of resignation, Arit got in front of the woman's face and let herself be seen.

"You!" the maid gasped. "You dirty little creature. Valona needs you."

When Arit flew backward, the woman followed her out of the hallway.

"I'll get you!" the maid said.

Arit wanted to fly at the woman and put her feet on an eyeball. Instead, she landed on a table—and stood there waiting. The old woman took what seemed like hours, but she finally put a glass goblet down over Arit.

"Now I have you!"

Arit obligingly pretended to be helpless and afraid as she put her hands against the glass.

The woman tipped the goblet to the side and slid her hand under it, seeming to trap the little Never inside.

Arit disliked standing on the woman's hand. "Mekos!" she muttered. "And Ian! You two owe me in a very big way."

The woman was smiling, proud of herself, and Arit had to endure the humiliation of being carried through the rooms. At least she'd done what she meant to. She'd distracted the woman from whatever Mekos and Ian were doing.

Mekos waved his hand to let Ian know that the woman was gone. A minute later, the sixth tumbler moved into place and Ian scooted back out of the keyhole. He sat on Mekos's shoulders while he opened the cabinet.

Inside was just one item. It was a beautiful knife. The blade was crystal and the handle was gold set with blue stones.

They didn't take time for more than a cursory look. Mekos shoved the knife into the band of his trousers and left the room.

When they heard someone in the distance cackling in triumph, Mekos stepped back into a doorway. The sound faded as the person moved away.

"What's that?" Mekos whispered.

Hanging on the wall was a framed piece of old and stained paper. At the bottom were smears as though someone had dragged two bloody fingertips across it. The gold writing on it was clear.

*Double royals. Fair by day. Dark by night.*

"What does that mean?"

"I don't know," Ian said, "but it scares her. I've seen her shiver at the sight of it."

Mekos took the document, frame and all, off the wall and put it inside his shirt. "If it says royal, I'm sure it means Aradella." A minute later, they were outside the house and Mekos said, "Hold tight to me." He moved swiftly through the trees until they reached the house where the women were.

As soon as Mekos stopped, Ian said, "Arit isn't here."

Mekos snorted. "My father probably called her to scratch one of the ridges on his back." He looked at Ian. "You should know that if he calls her, she'll walk into a volcano for him."

Ian sighed. "She won't ask *my* opinion. She has little use for *me*."

Mekos cocked his head as he looked at him. "Arit is pretty, isn't she?"

"She's like the stars and moon had a child, then they put sunlight in her eyes." Ian looked embarrassed at that, but then he said, "And what do you think of the princess?"

"Completely different," Mekos said. "The sun is in her hair, and the moon in her eyes." He shrugged. "But the rest is the same."

Ian's mouth twitched to keep from laughing. "Will you go to her wedding?"

"I do plan to be there, yes."

Again, the men exchanged smiles of understanding, then Mekos said, "I have a plan that I think will work. Can you get me something to put Aradella to sleep? I want to take her to safety, then I'll—" He didn't finish telling his plan. That would come later. First priority was getting Aradella away from danger.

Aradella was dreaming. She could smell the fresh air around her and snuggled by her were little furry animals. They smelled a bit like Mekos so that made her smile.

"You must wake up!" said a female voice. "We have to *do* something."

Aradella snuggled deeper in her bed. Whatever was near her was so warm and cuddly.

"Wake her!" the woman ordered.

In Aradella's dream, the little creatures around her came alert and began nudging her. "Go away," she murmured. But one of them sank its tiny teeth into her arm. "Ow!" she said and opened her eyes.

It was dark but she could see the most extraordinary creature standing over her. It had the face of a woman, but it also had the look of a . . . Aradella blinked. *A fox?*

"Get up. We have to go to my son."

Aradella managed to sit up. She was still wearing Kaley's clothes—which was bad. She needed to keep herself covered. A bit of a breeze made her realize that she truly was in the forest. She looked down at a movement by her leg. There were four little foxes staring up at her with big eyes.

Aradella looked back at the woman who was glaring at her. "You are . . . ?"

"I am Toki, the mother of Mekos, and we must go to him. That magic woman is going to *kill* him!"

At that, Aradella came fully awake. She realized the dark wasn't full night, but it was just before dawn—and it was the day she was supposed to be sacrificed. "Tell me what's happened." She brushed away the babies and stood up. The terror in the woman's eyes sent chills down her spine.

"The kits said Mekos and that little man sneaked into that woman's house. They stole a knife because only it will kill her. Now they're saying that Mekos hid the knife in his big clothes and he's you and he's asleep and she's going to murder him. I don't understand."

"I do," Aradella said. "He used the mask to make himself into me, but that knife is new to me. If Mekos is asleep, something went wrong." She looked around. "How did I get here and how can I reach him?"

"My son carried you here, and you are a long way from the steam."

Aradella knew she meant the steam from the volcano, where the sacrifice was to happen. When the woman turned, Aradella saw that she had a tail.

"I tried to get to him, but they—"

"The guards won't let you past. They don't like Lelys," Aradella said.

"I will give my life for my son."

Aradella didn't have time for politeness. "If you're dead, you won't be able to help at all," she snapped. "Get me to Mekos immediately! It's *me* Valona wants."

Toki's eyes changed from fear to resolution. "Can you ride?"

"For this, I can ride anything you have."

"My friend will take you there swiftly." Out of the darkness came a huge gray wolf. It looked like it could destroy a human in one bite. "Starken-el," Aradella whispered. When the animal bent down, she saw it had on a leather collar. Aradella swallowed her fear, threw a leg over the wolf, and grabbed the collar with both hands.

It ran so swiftly that Aradella could hardly breathe. Beside them, Toki was running on all fours. She was more fox than human.

They reached the pinnacle of the Lair just as the sun was rising.

As they'd been told, every woman who lived in the crater of the Lair was there. Young and old, they were standing, their faces filled with grief and fear. They were slowly swaying back and forth and making a low, mournful, rhythmic sound. Behind them, steam billowed up out of the ground, the last remnant of the volcano that had created the crater.

The great wolf abruptly stopped, Aradella slid to the ground, then ran forward. Four fierce-looking female guards flanked her, each one holding a long spear aimed at Aradella's throat.

"It's her," a woman said. Then another said louder, "The princess is *there*!"

As the words spread, the forlorn singing stopped, and the women stared in silence.

The guards stepped back and let the princess go through.

What Aradella saw sickened her. She saw herself lying on a long, flattened stone, her body engulfed by her big dress. Her face was calm and her eyes were closed in a peaceful sleep.

Standing at one end of the altar was Valona. She was dressed all in black and gold and looked magnificent. Her eyes were alight as though in ecstasy. Her arms were raised and in her hand was an old knife with a half moon blade.

"I am here!" Aradella shouted as she swiftly walked forward.

Even Valona was shocked into silence and she lowered her arms.

In the silence, Aradella, her back straight, her chin up, walked to Mekos lying on the stone. She leaned forward and put her left hand on the invisible mask on Mekos's face. At the same time, she put her right hand to where she knew was one of the pockets in the dress, and slipped it inside. As she'd hoped, the knife was there. It was small enough that she could conceal it in her hand.

With her other hand, she peeled the mask off Mekos's face. When his face was revealed, wearing his own clothes, everyone gasped.

"A man!" Valona said in disgust, her face filling with rage. "Do you know what his essence would have done to me?" She glared at Aradella. "I'll teach you to try to fool me," she screamed at Aradella and lunged for her. She raised her arms, her hands holding the old blade in a striking position.

In her training, Aradella had been taught that if someone leaves a body part unprotected, you can take advantage of it. The middle of Valona was open, completely uncovered. With all the strength Aradella possessed, she plunged the jeweled knife into Valona's stomach.

Valona looked astonished. She put her hands on the knife and staggered back. Everyone watched in shocked silence as her beautiful face began to age, showing the many years of her evil life. She gave a keening cry of disbelief, then the sound changed as though she was begging for mercy.

It took only minutes before Valona was a withered carcass. Her last breath escaped and she was dead.

Aradella looked at the crowd of women. They were all staring at her, too stunned to react.

Then someone said in astonishment, "She is dead."

In the next second, the women started rushing toward Aradella—and she felt faint. She'd just stabbed someone! That the woman was evil was beside the point. Her knees wobbled, she felt dizzy, and she knew she was sliding down. She almost smiled at the irony that she was about to be trampled to death by the happy, grateful women.

But she didn't hit the ground. Mekos was there, and he put his strong arms around her. He lifted Aradella up into the air and soared above the joyous women. He took her away, out of sight of them all.

# 5

"You are the stupidest man on this planet. No! On *all* the planets! Including Earth. I should tell Kaley what you did, then she'd tell your father, and he'd tell your grandfather. I can't imagine what they'll do to you. Something with swans. Can they drown you?"

"No," Mekos said.

They were at the waterfall, he was stretched out on the sweet grass, and he didn't stop smiling in a contented, pleased-with-himself way. "Papá would be angry, but he's always glad when I come out alive. Grandpapá would be slapping me on the back in pride."

Aradella gave him a look that should have singed his hair, but he didn't seem to notice. "You drugged me! You left me out of all of it! If it hadn't been for your *mother* you'd be dead now."

"Actually, it was the kits. They understand more than I thought they could. I shouldn't have underestimated them. It was clever of you to guess where I put the knife. If you hadn't covered it, Valona would have seen it when the dress disappeared."

"It was *my* dress! Of course I knew where the pocket was. I'm the one who sewed it in the skirt. And as to finding it, even I know that men love pockets!" She ran her hand over her forehead, then looked back at him. "You're missing the point. You shouldn't have excluded me. You should have told me what you were going to do. You should have . . ." She trailed off and sat down on a rock.

"The oddest thing was that when I looked like you, inside I was still myself. I could see and hear as well as always." He took a breath. "The real mistake in all this was that neither Ian nor I guessed that they'd poison your bedroom. We thought that Valona would want me awake through it all so they'd come and get me, I mean you. But they blew gas in on us and we were paralyzed."

Her voice lowered. "Where was I when you were in *my* bedroom?"

Mekos shrugged. "I took you to a safe place. You were meant to stay there while Ian and I took care of Valona."

"But thankfully, your mother found me," she said angrily. "It was stupid of you to try to do it all alone."

"The problem was that the gas smelled like flowers. I thought it was your perfume."

"You think Olina allows me to have perfume?" she shot at him.

"So what I smell is your natural scent? It's like you're made of flowers. Next you'll tell me that little space behind your left ear is also natural to you, that you use nothing to make it as soft as the down of a newly hatched swan."

She was looking at him in disbelief. "What are you saying?"

"Nothing that others haven't heard. Ian and I argue about whether your eyes are like the moon or the sun."

"Ian?" she asked. "A Never spoke of me?"

"Well, he talked about Arit, but I meant you. But we did agree about our women."

She was looking at him with her eyes wide. He was lying on the grass, so relaxed that it was hard to believe he'd been close to death. The good thing was that her anger had filled the void inside her—which had been emptied by jamming a knife into a person and seeing her turn to dust.

Mekos was smiling in contentment. "I think you should kiss me again," he said.

"Kiss? Again?" Her face turned red.

He smiled in a knowing way. "Do you think I didn't know it was you who kissed me?"

"I don't know what you mean." She was flat out lying but after what he'd done, she felt no guilt.

"I think it's time to clear up some things between us." His smile left him. "If you want to hear what my next plan is, I need you to tell me the truth."

"*What* are you planning next?" Her mouth was set in a hard line. "Will your mother have to summon wolves? Will I have to use a knife to . . ." She couldn't speak of what she'd done. "I'm still not sure the town won't come for us."

"To thank us? That isn't what I mean. It seems that the first time you and I met was at a dance."

"We didn't actually meet. I'd seen you and your divine father cavorting about with swans. He was truly magnificent. He was—" She stopped because Mekos got up, and she could see that he was serious.

"If you aren't going to tell me the truth, there's no reason to continue. We can go back to the house and . . ." He shrugged. "And go our separate ways."

The last thing Aradella wanted to do was separate from him. They were scheduled to leave the Lair tomorrow morning, that is if there was no firestorm over Valona's death.

He looked at her with those eyes that could see more than a full human could. "Since we met, you've kept secrets from me. I'm now asking you to tell me the truth." He took a breath. "I know it was you who kissed me that night I fell off the roof. That wasn't a kiss with no meaning, there was something behind it. I want to know what it was." His eyes grew serious. "I must know what you feel." He paused. "About me. The truth. All of it."

Aradella had lived a life of hiding, of keeping life-or-death secrets, so it wasn't easy for her to bare her soul. When Mekos took a step away from her, she knew she had to reveal herself. "It wasn't your father from the show, it was *you*."

He turned back to her. "Tell me," he said softly as he sat back down.

It wasn't easy for her, but she told him the whole story of that dance.

*Aradella was sitting in the shadows and looking around the room. She was careful not to pause as her eyes passed Tanek's tall, beautiful son, Mekos, but she was memorizing everything about him. His long hair was still damp from the water of the show. She wondered if he always kept his ears covered. During the swan show, she'd seen that they were pointed and she found them exotic and enticing. He wore a white shirt with a black leather vest, black trousers, and tall black boots. When he picked up a cherry by the stem, then let it dangle over his mouth before pulling at it with his teeth, Aradella felt quite dizzy.*

*Mekos was walking around the table, looking at the food. She'd watched him devour one plateful and he was filling a second one. It made her think that no one was feeding him, which made her fantasize about learning how to cook. She wasn't like her glorious cousins who could lure men to them merely by being there, so she'd need some talent or knowledge. But what did she know? She could read the English of Earth. She could identify plants. What possible use were they compared to a girl with a big bosom, a tiny waist, and a face like an angel?*

*Later, after her dance with Tanek, he asked if she'd like to meet his son. Aradella had stepped back, trying to keep control so her shock didn't show. "Perhaps another time," she'd managed to say. She knew she'd make a fool of herself if she came face-to-face with the beautiful Mekos. He was for girls like her cousins, not for her.*

When Aradella finished, Mekos didn't smile or even comment. "And the Reaver? What happened that night?"

Aradella tried to keep her voice from shaking. She couldn't tell what he was thinking. "Hale always did the market runs and she kept me up-to-date on the gossip on the island, of which guild was angry at another guild, that sort of thing. We usually laughed—except when she told of Telma. I guess you know that she's the head of Olina's government."

Mekos gave a brief nod but said nothing.

"She's a greedy, bad-tempered woman who sets herself above everyone. We all knew she stole from us and it was rumored that she shared the profits with Olina. Then suddenly, the Reaver showed up. Everyone said that a woman dressed in black was fighting back against the corruption of the government. We all knew that if she was caught, she'd be executed publicly and horrifically."

Aradella took a breath. "Hale and I stayed out of it. We had our own secrets and couldn't risk becoming involved in any more. One of our secrets was that on some evenings we'd leave the Cauldron and go to farmland where we didn't have to be silent. We could clash swords and not worry that someone would hear us." She looked at Mekos. His face was unreadable; his usual laughter wasn't there. He waited in silence for her to continue.

"I did take precautions by wearing a mask over the top half of my face." Aradella closed her eyes, remembering that night that came to be so important to her.

*It was close to dawn when Aradella and Hale left the field. "Look!" Hale said. There was just enough light to see the shadow of a person leaping from one roof to another. "That must be the Reaver."*

*Aradella was staring. "I don't think that's a woman," she whispered.*

*Hale hissed, "Get down!"*

*Coming out of the shadows was the Queen's Guard, an elite troop of women who protected Olina. They'd been hiding and waiting to catch the Reaver.*

*Aradella thought fast. "Distract them!"*

*Hale pulled her hood up, outstretched her cape, then gave a cry like an animal in pain. The noise seemed to echo across the fields. Instantly, the guards ran after her.*

*With all of them rushing toward her, swords drawn, Aradella ran toward the trees. She stayed hidden, her eyes searching for the person on the rooftops. She saw a shadow heading toward her. When there was a loud cry from the forest, the figure tripped and fell. She watched in shock as the Reaver tumbled off the roof.*

*Forgetting about keeping herself hidden, Aradella ran forward. Lying on the ground was a figure all in black, face half covered, and appearing to be unconscious. She bent down and removed the black mask. With a gasp, she recognized Mekos from the swan show of years before—and he was still the most beautiful human she'd ever seen. She smoothed his hair back and saw his pointed ears. When they twitched, she drew back, startled. He was awake! When he tried to sit up, he seemed to be dizzy. "You are an angel," he said. He had a beautiful voice!*

*As though it was a natural thing to do, he put his palm on her cheek, his fingers in her hair, then leaned toward her. She met him halfway and experienced her first kiss. It was sweet and lovely and it stirred things in her that she didn't know existed. When he pulled away, his eyes were wide, as though he too was surprised. "Who are you?"*

*She didn't dare tell him! When he reached up to remove her mask, she quickly stood up, then turned toward a noise coming from the forest.*

*When she looked back, Mekos was gone. Silently, with grace and ease, he had disappeared into the early morning light.*

*When Hale reached her, Aradella was silent, her mind on what had happened. When they got back to the little apartment, Hale took a nap, but Aradella didn't sleep for two days. She was afraid she'd awaken to find that the kiss was her imagination and not real.*

When she finished her story, Mekos was looking at her in a way that she thought might melt her.

He stretched out on the grass. "Now I understand. Since that night I've wanted no other woman. The cousins you worry so much about? They bore me. I've dreamed of that kiss. At the dance, my only memory—besides the food—is that my father was with a very pretty girl. I knew he liked her since he was soaring with her." He looked at her. "You and I need to make plans about our future."

"*We* have no future."

He smiled. "Do you intend to have a life without *me*?"

"I must," she whispered. "I am a princess and I am bound by centuries of duty."

"And I'm part fox. We all have burdens in life. I've known for a long time what I want to do, but I wasn't sure about you." He paused. "Can you possibly overlook your great and noble destiny of being a princess?"

She smiled at his sarcasm. "I wish I could."

"There is a way," he said.

"Do you have another one of your plans?"

He smiled at her tone of disbelief. "Yes, but this one includes you." He looked up at the waterfall. "But first, I think you and I should try everything we've seen my parents do. We'll need some wine."

Her eyes widened. "But . . ." She didn't know what to say.

"What was it Kaley said? 'Gathered the first fruits of love.'" He held out his hand to her. "I lied about having many women. I've waited for the woman I kissed on that moonless night. She risked her life to save me." He smiled. "Shall we remove our clothing and see what happens?"

The only thing Aradella could manage to say was "Yes."

# 6

"I never want to leave here," Kaley said as she followed Tanek down the path through the pretty tropical forest. "It's been so peaceful." It was evening twilight and early tomorrow the carriage was coming to take them away. "This place is perfect. There are no evil queens or cannibalistic witches. No fairy-tale puzzles that need to be solved. We can tell people that there's nothing bad about the Lair. I only wish we could have met the beautiful Valona."

"This place is too peaceful to be believed. Sometimes I get the feeling it's all one of your Earth stories. I'd like to know how the kids found that lizard you liked."

"I don't know and I don't want to look a gift horse in the mouth."

Tanek looked at her with an eyebrow raised. It was his silent question about her sayings.

Kaley didn't explain. "How do you think Sojee is doing in arranging for the men to arrive? Do you think they'll behave themselves?"

"If they want to live, they must," Tanek said over his shoulder. "I'm sure I'll be put on guard duty."

"I don't like that."

"It'll be all right," he said. "There'll be enough of us to keep the peace. Your magic man will probably help. Think he knows which end of a sword to hold?"

"Be careful! Garen might turn you into a frog."

He snorted. "You and kissing frogs! It hasn't worked so far. I'm still not a prince."

"From the ones I've met, that's good," she mumbled, then looked up. "We're going to the waterfall, aren't we?" She sighed. "That was the first place we made love. It will always be in my heart and now we can re-create it."

"Actually, I'm going to the top to see if I can find my son. His mother is here so maybe he's with her."

"Toki?" Kaley smiled. Her love of animals extended to the Lelys. "I'd like to see her again."

"Not me!" Tanek said emphatically. Their love of their son was all they shared. "I'm sure she knows where Mekos is."

"With the princess," Kaley replied. "How do you think they got along these last days?" She sounded hopeful.

"Don't forget that she's to marry Prince Nessa."

"Who calls Aradella 'Princess Bitchy,'" Kaley said. "Maybe we can—"

Tanek halted and looked at her. "It's enough that men are being allowed on this island. You cannot interfere in this marriage."

She gave him an innocent look. "You mean like *you* interfered in it? You declared that you and I made vows while we were alone in a cave. What I remember is that you went to sleep while Arit and Tibby and I—" She didn't want to remind him of what they'd seen that night. When she'd told him about it, it had been hard for him to hear.

Tanek let out his breath. "I don't think wives are supposed to—" He broke off.

"Contradict the wisdom of men?" She batted her lashes at him. "I would *never* do that."

Tanek shook his head. "Come on, let's find the children." They could hear the waterfall. "I hope Mekos got a gift for my father. He—" Tanek had parted the tall reeds and when he saw the waterfall, he froze.

"What is it?" She moved to stand beside him. "Oh my goodness."

Soaring very high up in the water were Mekos and Aradella. They were both nude, her legs wrapped around him.

Tanek stepped back behind the tall reeds and looked at Kaley. There were tears in his eyes.

She put her arms around him.

"My son has become a man," he said.

She held him, feeling his strong heartbeat. She said nothing but waited for him to pull away and they started to walk back the way they'd come.

"She's so small—I almost didn't recognize her." Kaley's head came up. "After this, she could be pregnant!" She'd said that before, but if the child was obviously not Nessa's, there could be repercussions.

"No," Tanek said. "Not unless he allows it."

"You mean withdrawal?"

"I don't know what that is. He must choose to release what is necessary."

Kaley was trying to figure that out. "You mean a man can choose when he impregnates a woman?"

"Yes, of course."

"What about me? Us?"

He glanced back at her. "Not yet. I want to make sure you want to stay here. If you don't like me, you may leave."

"Wait a minute!" she said. "That means you *chose* to get Toki pregnant when you were just a teenager."

"I had a dream, a very vivid dream, and I saw what would come of that union. Could you have resisted creating a son like Mekos?"

"No, I could not." She paused. "Have you had any dreams about you and me and what we'd produce?"

"None at all." He was walking so fast she was having trouble keeping up with him.

"Should we tell them that we know what they've been up to?"

"What do you think?" he said.

"Absolutely not. We should let them think they've kept it a secret from everyone."

"I agree."

She started to say that they were going to be heartbroken when Aradella had to marry someone else, but she didn't. She was sure that Tanek was already thinking of that. Swans mate for life. For Mekos not to get the woman he wanted would hurt him. Forever.

When they reached the house, she had a thought. "Have your father and your mother seen each other since you were created?"

"Not that I know of."

"What did he tell you about your mother?"

"That it was one night, she was one of the Seven, and I was to keep my mouth shut about who she was." He went into the house.

"A good, long, boy talk," she muttered, then followed him inside.

Early the next morning, the four of them were staring at the beat-up old flatbed wagon that had been sent for them. The woman who drove it tied the reins to the seat, then nodded to Tanek, letting him know that he was to be the driver. The back of the wagon was full of lumpy bags of coconuts and pineapples.

Tanek and Kaley were standing close together, watching what was going on around them. Both of them wore expressions of surprise. While Mekos and Aradella, wearing one of her big dresses, looked at home, as if they knew everyone in the Lair, the older couple were outsiders. Their focus had been on each other and they had met no one.

"Something happened here besides what we saw at the waterfall," Tanek said softly. "Something much bigger. I'd like to know what my son was up to."

"I think Aradella can hold her own. Whatever it was, I think they did it together."

Frowning, Tanek was looking at the dilapidated wagon. "We, meaning my son, appears to have displeased someone."

"Maybe they need the pretty carriage for dignitaries from Selkan." Kaley wanted to remove the worried look from her husband's face. "Maybe Prince Bront will be there."

"He won't like your shoes," Tanek replied, referring to the glass slipper that the prince had found. He turned to Mekos. "You two will have to ride back there. If you're friends enough, that is."

"We'll manage," Mekos said without meeting his father's eyes. He stepped forward, then stopped and listened. "They're coming."

"Who is?" Tanek asked.

Mekos didn't answer him. He went to Aradella and put his hands on her waist. In a half soar, half leap, he put her on the back of the wagon, her legs hanging down, then he got on to sit beside her.

When Tanek looked down the road, he saw nothing, but he was used to his son's keen hearing. He helped Kaley up to sit on the hard narrow seat, then got up beside her and untied the reins.

"We don't leave yet," Mekos said in a tone he didn't usually use.

With eyes widened in disbelief, Tanek leaned over to Kaley. "My son just gave me an order."

"I think that's good," Kaley said. "He's—" She didn't say any more because they heard the happy voices of women. Lots of women. And *very* happy.

When she and Tanek turned around to look, they saw what appeared to be every female in the Lair coming toward them. The women were talking, some of them singing, and all of them were smiling.

When the crowd got closer to the wagon, they began tossing flowers. Mekos and Aradella were laughing as they twisted about to catch the blossoms.

"We will come to your celebration," the women were saying. "We will bring gifts."

Hobbling at the side was a very old woman with three women helping her to reach them. She was Valona's maid. When she got close, the woman held out an extraordinary flower to Aradella. It was dark gold and yellow, with tall spikes at the top. "Thank you," the old woman said. "I am free. I don't have to lie and pretend anymore. Thank you." Tears were running down her face.

Aradella took the flower and bowed her head to her.

The women led the maid away.

"What is it?" Mekos asked.

"An oncidium," Aradella answered. "Also called the butterfly orchid."

He nodded in satisfaction that she knew.

Six women stepped forward. Their arms were tightly wrapped around their pretty daughters—who had soot on their faces and clothes. "Our daughters are safe," the women called to Aradella. "Thank you."

Aradella said loudly, "We'll send the most beautiful men from Selkan to you."

The women gave a cheer so loud that Mekos's ears flattened against his head. "You can't promise them that," he said.

"These women have been fornicating with *animals*. The ugliest men will look good to them."

"Hey!" he said. "My mother is half fox."

"Yes, but the other half of you is from Tanek, who is the best-looking man on the planet."

Mekos gave a sound of half groan, half laughter. "Wait! Since he's my father, does that make me second best? On the entire *planet*?"

"With those ears? Not possible," she replied. They turned back toward the women.

On the seat behind them, Tanek and Kaley looked at each other in shock. "Even if I hadn't seen what we did, I'd know now," he said. "They are *together*." He smiled. "I am the most handsome man on the planet?"

"Ha! There's Prince Bront and Garen and I'm still looking for that guy who has wings. You have lots of competition."

Tanek gave a scoffing laugh, then snapped the reins and they started moving. He said over his shoulder to his son, "What did you do to win this much favor from them?"

"I sang to them," Mekos said quickly. "They love my voice."

"And he put on a display of soaring. All the women were in awe of him." Aradella caught more flowers and waved to the women who were standing still. She put her finger to her lips, meaning that they were to keep the secret, and they nodded in understanding.

"They loved me so much," Mekos said to his father, "that there may be a few pointy-eared babies."

Aradella scoffed. "If you'd touched one of them, Valona would have made you into a girl."

Tanek and Kaley blinked at each other at this banter.

"Where is Valona?" Kaley asked. "We only saw her from a distance."

Mekos leaned back against a bag of coconuts. "I heard there was a fire and every plant in her private garden was burned to the ground."

"We were told that the six prettiest girls in the Lair set it," Aradella said. "They even danced."

"There was nothing left," Mekos said. "So maybe Valona is dealing with that."

Aradella leaned against a bag of pineapples across from Mekos. Their outstretched legs were so intertwined, they were like latticework.

Kaley turned around to Tanek as he guided the horses down the long road back to the Cauldron. "I'm afraid you're right. Something happened that we know nothing about."

"Yes." He lowered his voice. "And under no circumstances do I *ever* want to know what my son was up to."

Kaley reached into her pocket and pulled the Truth Necklace halfway out. "I don't think I should put it on, do you?"

"Not unless you want a burn to go all the way through you," Tanek said, then snapped the reins.

Behind them, Mekos and Aradella held hands under the cover of her big dress. Early this morning, women had come to them and told them about their lives. For generations, everyone in the crater, from guards to children, had lived under the dictatorship of one woman. There were no prisons. The punishment for breaking any of Valona's rules was death. Even the women who pretended to love her were glad she was finally gone. Their talk buzzed of going to other craters, of meeting people. Some were talking of visiting other islands. They smiled at each other, feeling good at what they had accomplished, but minutes later, they passed a woman riding a horse. Tanek and Kaley paid no attention to her, but Aradella and Mekos knew she was the guide they'd run away from. The look she gave them was full of hate.

"Someone's not glad Valona is gone," Aradella said.

"Now she has no one to worship." Mekos replied.

Aradella frowned. "My aunt-queen will not be happy to see that I'm still alive."

He squeezed her hand. "By the time she makes another plan, ours will be done."

They looked at each other. They couldn't speak of what they were going to do, but they were thinking about it so hard they could read each other's minds. They were confident that their plan would work.

When they got close to the Cauldron, where Aradella was to marry Prince Nessa, they could feel the excitement of the women. Tomorrow the men would arrive! Their anticipation was a vibration, a sort of buzzing that seemed to electrify the air. They could see that an effort had been made to clean up the town, and even hide the more damaged areas of the houses. Everything looked better, even if it was superficial. And the women were looking great! Clothes had been washed and pressed, and their hair was so shiny it glistened.

"All done for the men." Aradella wasn't smiling. It was hitting her that now she'd have to face her aunt Olina. Of course the queen would have somehow found out what had been done to Valona. If no human told her, her mother could conjure a vision in a pot of something unspeakable. There would be no anguish about that, but *Aradella was still alive.* She had no doubt that her aunt would go into a rage—then punish her niece. *What will she do to me this time?* Aradella wondered.

Mekos moved to sit on the edge of the wagon and Aradella got beside him. Under her big dress was her patched padding. She and Arit had done their best to repair it, but it was still scratching her. At least the fabric covered that she and Mekos were tightly holding hands. "I'll have to go to my . . ." She didn't know what to call where she lived. *Home* certainly didn't describe it.

"I think you should stay with me," he said.

"That's not possible."

He squeezed her hand. "Just two more days, then . . ." He smiled at her.

"You have it?"

He knew she meant the mask. "Yes. I just hope Kaley doesn't see that the box she keeps so close is empty." He twisted around to look ahead. "Sojee is waiting for us."

Aradella groaned. "I do hope he brought my beautiful cousins."

Mekos laughed. "When you're queen will you have them executed?"

"Better. I'll have them clean all the toilets in the palace."

Smiling, he leaned forward to kiss her but he stopped himself. *Not yet.*

When the wagon halted in front of the gate to the Cauldron, Sojee spoke to Tanek and Kaley on the seat. "You're to go to the Sanction Room in the palace. Now."

"Uh-oh," Kaley said. "I bet we're going to find out why this old wagon was sent to us. Is the queen angry about something?"

Sojee swung Kaley down. "That would imply that there are times when she is *not* angry. It's never happened and never will."

Kaley laughed. "What's waiting for us?"

Sojee looked over her head to Tanek. "It's what you asked for."

Tanek smiled broadly. "All of it? Everything?"

Sojee's eyes sparkled. "There is more than you imagined."

In the back, Mekos got down, then swung Aradella to the ground. Her face was solemn. She'd not seen the big, beautiful Sanction Room since she was a child. It was where her father listened to the problems of the people of Pithan and where he greeted important visitors. As far as Aradella knew, Olina had never used the room. "I'll see you later," she said to Mekos, her eyes conveying her hope for the days to come. Turning away, she headed toward the gate and her solitary apartment. It was going to feel small and confined after the freedom of the Lair.

"You too," Sojee said, but when Aradella kept walking, he caught up with her. He was so tall that he bent to speak to her in a low voice. "You're invited to a great surprise for Kaley. Jobi has done it all."

Aradella's eyes lit up at the mention of her friend. "He's here?"

"Yes, but don't tell Kaley. They've had a bit of a falling-out." Sojee looked over her head. "Come and see what it is."

"But the queen—"

Sojee put his hand on her upper arm. "Don't worry about her. Right now she's pretending that she's a kind and loving person." He gave a snort of laughter. "Let's take advantage of it for as long as it lasts. Come have some cake." His hand was still on her arm. "Unless you'd rather eat something that will keep your arms as strong as Hale has made them."

Aradella's eyes widened. "I, uh . . . I . . ."

He let go of her arm. "Young Mekos is waiting for you." He saw her face change, then he looked from one to the other, and his eyebrows raised. "Did you two enjoy your time at the Lair?"

"Oh yes, we did." Every feeling Aradella had was in those words.

Sojee gave a great, loud belly laugh. "I am very glad! Now go!"

Aradella held her skirt away from her legs, ran to Mekos, and they entered the palace.

The others were ahead of them and Aradella had to think about how to get through the labyrinth of halls to find the Sanction Room. Her heart was beating fast as she was afraid that any minute Queen Olina would leap out at them. She'd shout, "Arrest her! She killed my beloved friend Valona." Aradella knew there would be no trial. There'd just be death.

But the halls were empty. Was even the Queen's Guard getting ready for tomorrow?

"This way." Aradella paused. "No, this way."

Mekos pulled her into an alcove, their bodies pressed together, and kissed her. "Just two more days," he whispered, his lips against hers. "You haven't changed your mind?"

"Never." She looked around. "If someone sees us—"

He kissed her again. "There are two women three hallways to the left, but no one else." He cocked his head. "I just heard Kaley laugh. She's very happy about something." He stepped back and sniffed the air. "I smell food." He held out his hand. "Shall we go see?"

She took his hand and they ran through three hallways then stopped at big double doors.

Mekos pulled one open and they stepped inside—then they stopped as they looked about in awe.

There were two wide rows of pretty chairs flanking a long white rug. At the end was a wooden arch covered in flowers of white, pink, and lavender. To the side was a long table covered in a white cloth and great pots of food. In the center was a cake.

Mekos and Aradella stared at the cake in open-mouthed astonishment. They'd never seen anything like it. It was a hill of round, terraced layers. Pink sugar roses ran in a spiral down the sides.

"What is all this for?" Aradella whispered.

Mekos shrugged. He had no idea.

A far door opened in the big, decorated room and in came Kaley, Tanek, and Sojee. Kaley looked like she'd been crying. "It's perfect. It's the most beautiful wedding I've ever seen. The cake, the decorations, it's all . . ." Her eyes were so full of tears she couldn't speak.

Tanek gathered her in his arms, and he looked very pleased with himself.

Sojee also had his shoulders back and his chest out. "There's more," he said.

Behind Aradella and Mekos, the big doors opened and they stepped to the side. In came a man. He was older, handsome, and he had on an unusual black suit that could only have come from Earth. He stopped and looked across the room at Tanek and Kaley, who were still holding each other.

Tanek was facing the man and when he saw him, he had an expression that Mekos rarely saw. It was of shock, of relief—and especially of love. It was the way Tanek looked at Mekos every time he pulled his son from one of his near-death escapades.

Tanek dropped his arms from Kaley, then took a step toward the man at the door. But after only one step, he began to soar. He moved quickly across the big room, his feet touching only air.

Wide-eyed, Mekos looked at the older man by the door. His face was a smile of welcome—and also of love. He seemed to know about soaring as he opened his arms wide.

Tanek enveloped the man and went up and up with him. Had they not been in a room, they might have reached the clouds.

"I remember," Mekos heard his father say. "I remember it all. Fishing. The truck. The jars. The birds. I remember everything."

Aradella saw that Mekos had tears on his face and she moved closer to him. "Who is he?"

"Someone my father loves," he said.

*This is true love*, Aradella thought. *To be glad when someone you love is given happiness.* In her life, she'd seen little but jealousy.

They were just coming down when a woman entered. She was older, slim, with gray hair that curled about her head. "And me?" she asked softly.

Tanek turned to her, his face showing surprise, then pleasure. He put an arm around her waist and the three of them went upward. Not as high as with just two but they were far off the floor. They came down slowly.

"I had no idea that could be done," Aradella said. "Lifting two people at once."

"Me neither!" Mekos said. "Let's find out who they are." He stepped forward, Aradella close beside him.

"You've grown into a fine young man," the woman said, her hand on Tanek's shoulder in a motherly way.

"He always was a big kid," the man said proudly. "Remember when he drove my pickup? And the chickens landed on him? I thought they were going to nest in his hair."

The woman smiled. "I remember how he got the birds to pick the blackberries that were way in the back. They filled buckets of them, then young Tanek helped me make jam."

"I remember the jars," Tanek said. "They were so pretty. I haven't been able to remember any of that until now. I—"

"I'm Mekos," he said loudly.

Tanek put his arm around his son's shoulders. "This is my son."

"Aren't you a beautiful boy," the woman said. "And who is this?"

"Princess Aradella," Mekos said.

The woman's eyes lit up. "A princess? Kaley must love that. Has she told you any of the thousands of stories that she knows?"

"She's lived a few of them." Tanek turned to look across the room at his wife. Kaley had her back to them as she was talking to and hugging a younger man who wore the same kind of suit the other one did. "Cars!" he said. "I remember changing tires and carber-something."

"Carburetors," the man said. "That's Jeff, my son. You worked in the garage with him."

"He's Kaley's father." Tanek looked at Mekos and Aradella. "This is . . . What do I call you?"

"Frank and Rita," the man said. "Or Grandpapá, as you used to. You can't have too many grandparents." Frank looked at Aradella. "You probably have your own grandparents but—"

"No," Aradella said. "None at all. I do have an aunt who's a queen and her mother is a witch."

Frank and Rita blinked a couple of times, then smiled. "Kaley must truly *love* this place! Let's go tell her we're here."

The five of them walked across the room to where Kaley was talking to her father.

"So we blackmailed him," Jeff was saying. "If they wanted the Solium that Dad and I'd grown, we were going with them. It was the plan your mother and I made before Jobi took her away. I'm sorry we couldn't tell you the truth for your whole life, but Graceen made us promise. And—" He broke off when he saw Tanek.

"I can still drive a manual shift," Tanek said, and they began hugging.

Jeff said, "When I yelled at you for not holding the flashlight right, you . . ."

"I had the birds grab fireflies and hold them so you could see. I think you said some bad words in shock, but I didn't know it was strange."

Smiling at the men laughing together, Kaley looked away, then froze when she saw her grandparents.

Aradella and Mekos stepped back as there was a flurry of hugs and tears, and proclamations of everyone missing everyone else. Tanek pulled the young ones forward and introduced them to Jeff. "And this is Aradella. She's a princess."

"Are we allowed to hug a princess?" Rita asked.

"Yes." To her joy, Aradella was swept up into everyone's warm embrace.

"So when do we get to eat that cake?" Mekos asked and they all laughed.

Frank said, "You're just like your father. He could eat his weight in beef and fish."

"But not chicken," Rita said. "Remember when I served fried chicken and Tanek threw up?"

"Oh yeah," Jeff said. "Then he floated out to the coop and wouldn't come out for hours. Mom had to promise him that there would be no birds of any kind served ever again."

"He hasn't changed," Kaley said. "He still gets sick if a bird is hurt. I guess I was a baby during all this."

"You weren't yet born," Jeff said. "Tanek used to talk to you in some language that we couldn't understand. He gave you a white feather."

Kaley gasped. "It's in one of my books."

"We brought all of them with us," Rita said. "Jobi bellyached about the load, but we insisted."

Through all this, Sojee had been standing near the far wall, but he stepped forward. He looked at Kaley. "You asked for a wedding."

Kaley stepped back. "I take it you've met Sojee."

"Oh yes," Frank said. "Right from the first." He looked at

Tanek. "We were told that somebody made a penguin suit for you."

"A what?" Tanek asked.

"He means a tuxedo," Kaley said. "Like they have on." She looked down at herself. "I'm not dressed for this," she said softly. "I need—"

Sojee clapped her hard on the shoulder. "Think we forgot that? Reena did a little magic and the Beauty Guild put together something they hope you'll like. There's a room over there."

Kaley turned to Aradella. "Would you like to join me? You can be my maid of honor."

Aradella's eyes widened. "I would like—"

Mekos cut her off. "We have to go see the Third Crater. They have books there and Aradella really wants to see them."

Sojee looked amused. "That's the Fourth Crater. The Third has music and magic."

Mekos was backing up, Aradella beside him. "That sounds good too. When should we be back here for the uh . . . ?" He wasn't sure what to call it.

"Four hours," Sojee said. "I'll send someone to find you." He was giving Mekos a look that said he'd better be where he could be found.

"Great! We'll be here then." He and Aradella ran out of the room.

Frank looked at Tanek. "I think your son is in love."

Tanek grimaced. "She's to marry a prince who is a snake of a human. Not even his dragon wants to live with him."

"Dragon?" Frank whispered.

Kaley sighed. "It's true. Aradella was to marry Tanek, but . . ." She shrugged. "I better get dressed." She looked at Sojee. "Please tell me you have hair and makeup people to help me."

"They sent a lot of women." Sojee nodded toward a door. "They're waiting for you in there."

Kaley ran from the room and closed the door behind her.

Frank, Rita, and Jeff were looking at Tanek.

"Young Aradella was to marry *you* but she's being forced to marry someone else?" Rita asked. "How did that happen?"

Sojee put his hand on Rita's back. "Why don't you help Tanek dress while he explains everything? I have to see to my women." He left the room in a few long strides.

"Does he have multiple wives?" Rita asked.

Tanek smiled. "Worse. He's head of security for this whole island full of women, and tomorrow the men will come here."

"Men?" Frank asked. "Come from where?"

Tanek raised an eyebrow. "If you were on the ship with Kaley, where have you been all this time?"

Jeff grimaced. "Isolated. Some officer told us that we couldn't see you or Kaley or we'd destroy many years of work, so we were hidden away. It was beautiful and the food was good, but we were told hardly anything. It was maddening!"

Rita smiled. "I think you and Kaley were to be given time to reacquaint yourselves." Her eyes sparkled. "It does seem to have worked."

Tanek laughed. "It did. Come on, I have a lot to tell you."

# 8

Kaley was glad the room she entered was empty. She needed time to grasp the fact that her family was really there. She wanted to hear a more complete version of what her father and grandparents had done to be allowed to come here. Her mother had told them everything? And they believed she was from a different planet? But then, there was Tanek, just a boy, floating around the place and having chickens land on him. Did they see him talking to the birds in the trees? Probably.

She hadn't yet digested that they'd known about this all her life, but they'd told her none of it. While she was growing up, they'd been cultivating some algae by the stream on their property. All of it was done in preparation for when Jobi returned to take Kaley away—to another planet. She remembered being on the plane and seeing her father. But Jobi put his little blue light on the chip in her arm and Kaley went to sleep. When she woke up, it was three years later, and she was on Bellis.

She—

"There you are," came a female voice. "We've been waiting for you."

Kaley looked up to see the woman Garen had pointed out as his aunt. Her name was Reena and she was one of the four witch sisters. She was tall, gorgeous, and dressed head to foot in red. All the fairy tales in Kaley's head took over. "Can you cast a spell?" she whispered.

Reena laughed. "Better than my nephew can. Now, come on, you have to get ready for Tanek. Your hair is a disgrace and what you're wearing isn't fit for the stables."

Kaley looked apologetic. "I've been traveling with men."

Reena nodded. "You poor thing. But wait until you see what the Beauty Girls can do, even with someone in your condition."

*Ah, the comforting, bitchy familiarity of women*, she thought. "I am yours. Do with me what you will." She smiled broadly.

"Sit still," Reena ordered. "You still have an hour to go, so don't move. And above all, stay away from men. Knowing Tanek, he'll want you to wrestle some of those birds that trail after him." She waited for Kaley to answer.

"I won't move. I promise."

"You better not! I have to go. The women in my guild are in a frenzy. Half of them are terrified of the men coming and the other half are planning to rip their clothes off and leap on them. Then they'll . . ." She waved her hand. "They need me."

"Understandable. I've seen the men from Selkan and—" Kaley didn't finish. The men played what they called "Cutting Games," which left their faces scarred. "Go on, I'll be fine. And thank you very, very much. If there's anything I can do for you, please let me know."

Reena looked like she was about to say something but didn't. She just nodded, then left the room.

When she was alone, Kaley looked around the empty room. There was a little couch and a few hard chairs. To one side was a wood-framed mirror and she looked in it. The white wedding dress the women had put on her was beyond beautiful. She knew that if she'd chosen one, it would be this one. The whole top was lace that looked like it had been handmade. It left her shoulders bare, but was modest across the front, with long sleeves, then down to a fitted waist and a full skirt. There was more lace at the hem. A veil was pinned to her hair. Reena told her that making the dress had been under the charge of a young woman who said to tell Kaley that she was "Daln's daughter." Kaley said to tell her thank you and that she'd love to tell her about her father. That the father and daughter hadn't seen each other in years made her glad of the coming reunion.

Besides the dress, Kaley knew she looked the best she ever had. When the four young women, Beauty Girls, had seen Kaley, they'd shaken their heads in despair. Sweat, underwater dives, sleeping in caves, soaring in waterfalls, had taken a toll on her appearance.

But the women had repaired the damage. Herbs, lotions, heat and cold had been put on Kaley. There'd been a lot of pain but she was a woman so she could stand it. Her face had been treated with four colors of concoctions that hardened or peeled off. One of them burned like acid.

The result was that she was now glowing. Her skin and hair were like a mix of cream and starlight.

She sat down on an ottoman and didn't move. When her nose itched, she was afraid to scratch it. Very carefully, she used just the tip of her nail, not daring to dislodge the thick layer of makeup on her face.

She was so absorbed in remaining still that she didn't hear the door open.

"Oh, sorry," said a woman. "I didn't mean to interrupt you. I was just going to leave this for you." She held out a little canvas-wrapped package. "It's the photos you left at the museum."

Kaley didn't know what the woman was talking about, but then Kaley was having a strong feeling of having seen her before. She was quite pretty, probably in her forties, and she kept herself in shape. She had on a beautiful blue dress, so Kaley thought she'd probably been invited to the wedding.

"I'm Neta and I'm the curator of Museum of Earth. It's the photos you took of the men on Selkan. We got the printer to work."

"Yes, of course." Kaley took the bag and peered inside. They were of the men she and Tanek and Sojee had met. They wanted the photos given to the females of their families who were on Pithan. She opened the package and flipped through the photos. Considering that they'd been printed on a home machine—one Jobi had supplied, and maybe the only one on the planet—they looked good. She made a silent vow that she'd find out where electricity was available on the islands. Was it being kept from the people?

She looked up at Neta. "These men will be here tomorrow. I apologize for stealing your Jeep, but we needed it."

"That's all right. I was glad someone knew how to drive it."

"I do and so does Tanek. But then, he seems to know how to do most anything."

When she smiled, Kaley again felt that she'd seen the woman before.

"You're happy here? You want to stay and not return to Earth?"

"Yes." She wasn't going to say any more, but the woman seemed to be waiting to hear. "I was offered a folklorist's dream job that includes a castle and lots of magic. I was going to take it, but I couldn't imagine a life without Tanek and Mekos and Sojee and all the people who've become my friends. And now my family is here. I guess I've always had faith that my own personal fairy tale was going to work out." She paused. "Sorry, I'm blathering on."

The woman's smile seemed wide enough to split her face. "Sojee is my father. My mother was his first wife and she wasn't a princess, so I'm quite ordinary." She reached out and straightened Kaley's veil. "I am—" she began but the buzz that was Arit came between them. Both women leaned back, trying to focus on her.

"It's too busy out there," Arit said. "I like it better in here."

"It does feel nice," the woman said.

Arit stared at her. "You must be a Recorder. Only they can understand me—unless I allow it."

"And us earthlings," Kaley said.

"There are people out there and I can't show myself or I'll be swatted at like a fly. Or stared at like an oddity." She hovered, looking from one woman to the other, seeming to be waiting for something.

"What's happening?" Neta asked.

"Yes, tell us all." Kaley knew how much Arit loved gossip.

The little woman landed on the back of the couch and gave a sigh of relief. She'd been holding in her news for too long. "Something strange is going on. Two important-looking young men, carrying a huge bag with gold embroidery on it, met with Queen Olina. In private! When they left, all three of them were smiling!"

Kaley didn't think that sounded particularly mysterious, but Neta said, "Where did they go?"

"Well . . ." Arit said, drawing her story out. "The men walked across the big courtyard and waiting for them were Aradella's three maids. You know, those lying, sneaking spies that Olina put on the princess? They seemed to know each other, and one of those women pointed to Sojee's house."

Neta's eyes widened. "I wonder if my father knows them."

"Maybe, but those men weren't there to see *him*." Arit lowered her voice. "The maids gave one of the men some pink mushrooms that looked like candy."

With all the fairy tales Kaley knew and what she'd experienced on this planet, the hair on her neck stood up. "Is that some delicacy here?"

"I've never heard of them." Neta was frowning. "Then what happened?"

"The maids left and they were laughing so hard that I was suspicious. They've never wished any good on anyone. The men went to Sojee's house and the twins let them inside, but I wasn't invited, so of course I didn't go."

Both women gave her a look that said, *Right. And we believe that.*

Arit tried to look innocent. "Maybe I did slip through a window that was a little bit open and maybe I did hear a few words."

Kaley and Neta waited in silence.

"First of all, those men gave the girls the candied mushrooms. Then one of the men said they'd brought two dresses from Empyrea and the fabric is the best ever made. I don't know how it can be better than swan fabric, but he swore it was. He said that everyone on the planet had heard of the beauty of the girls, so dresses had been made just for them. He said they'd be honored if the girls would wear them to the ceremony today."

"That's very kind of them," Kaley said.

"My sisters will be radiant." Neta was frowning. "I just hope that man also brought a gown for Queen Olina. She won't like it if my sisters outshine her."

"What do the dresses look like?" Kaley asked.

"I don't know," Arit said. "I didn't see them."

"Come on," Kaley said. "Don't try to make us believe that you left before seeing those fabulous dresses."

"No, of course I didn't. I mean that I *couldn't* see them. The men were gushing over them, saying they were exquisitely beautiful. They held them up to the light and said only the twins were beautiful enough to wear them."

"But you saw nothing?" Neta asked.

"Not a thing. To me, it looked like they were holding up air."

"'The Emperor's New Clothes,'" Kaley and Neta said in unison.

Neta's face showed her horror. "If my sisters arrive naked, my father will go into a rage. He might kill people."

"If anything bad happens, Olina will use it as an excuse to keep the men from coming tomorrow."

"I have to go. I must stop my sisters."

"You're not going without me!" Kaley stood up. When Arit fluttered her wings very fast, she added, "And Arit."

"Your dress," Neta said. "You can't—"

"This is urgent." Kaley grabbed her skirt and lifted it. "Lead the way!"

It wasn't easy to make it through the big palace but Neta knew the way down deserted corridors, and out a door into a courtyard. Neta slowed down twice for Kaley, who was burdened by high heels and the heavy dress, to catch up. When they reached a house, Neta stood still, caught her breath, then threw open the door. Arit went in with them, then sat down on a window ledge to watch the show.

Standing in the middle of the room, stark naked, were the two beautiful twin sisters. From the hazy, dreamy look in their eyes, they'd been drugged. Both of them turned slowly around. "How do you like our dresses?" Shay asked. She reached down to her naked leg, seemed to grab a handful of skirt, then held it out. "Aren't they beautiful?"

Bree smiled in a faraway look. "I hope we don't outshine you, Kaley. It is your day."

"*Shine* is the right word." Kaley looked at Neta. "Will a blue pen work on drugs?"

"I hope so. I'll get it." Neta ran out of the room.

"No!" Shay said. "She's just jealous because we're younger and she never got a husband. This dress will get us the attention of all the men."

"That is very true," Kaley said. "Every man will look at you and all the women will too." She took a big scarf off a chair. "This would look good on the dresses."

"Absolutely not!" Shay said. "You're not going to cover up this beauty."

Behind them came Neta holding out a little metal pen with a blue light on the tip. She reached out, grabbed Bree's left arm, and put the pen to it before the girl could object.

Bree stood still, dazed.

"Not me!" Shay said and headed toward the door. "I'll show everyone my dress and tell them how jealous you've always been."

Kaley tackled the girl before she could get out the door, and they landed on the couch. Her big white dress billowed around them, her skirt catching on a table edge. She had to hold Shay down while Neta fought to put the pen to her flailing arm.

On the other side of the room, Bree gave a scream, then grabbed a scarf from a chair. "Shay," she shouted. "Let them do it. We are naked!"

"We're not," Shay said, but her sister's words made her hesitate long enough that Neta could put the pen on the chip in her arm.

Bree, wrapped in the scarf, sat down on the couch. Her face was bloodless. "We almost went out like that," she said softly. "It would have . . . We could not . . ." She looked at Kaley and Neta. "Thank you."

Kaley let go of Shay but she was still waving her arms about and she was still angry. When Kaley moved, she felt her skirt tear, but she couldn't deal with that now.

When Shay screeched in shock of realization, she grabbed the big covering her sister threw to her.

"How can we repay you?" Bree asked.

"We don't need anything," Neta said. "Just get dressed."

"You'll tell everyone, won't you?" Shay's bottom lip was stuck out. "We'll be laughed at by the entire island."

"If people find out, it won't be from us," Neta said firmly. "But Aradella's nasty maids were in on this and I've never known them to keep a secret."

"I know how you can repay us," Kaley said. "You could be nice to Aradella. I mean genuinely nice. No sideways punches shot at her."

Shay gave an ugly sneer. "She came back on the arm of the

most beautiful man we've ever seen. She doesn't deserve more than that."

Kaley's eyebrows raised. Since she agreed about Mekos, they had a point.

Neta put her hand on Kaley's arm. "You're going to be late."

"Right." A sense of panic ran through Kaley. "My hair! My dress!"

"You're still perfect," Neta said. "Let's go back." She turned to her two half sisters. "Meet us at the wedding and be nice to Aradella. Understand?!" She did indeed sound like the older sister.

The girls nodded, Bree looking grateful, but Shay was still sulking.

As soon as they were outside, Neta said, "If Aradella's maids were in on this . . ."

"That means Olina was behind it."

Neta picked up her pace. "If we tell the men about this, swords will be drawn."

Kaley started running. "In my case, it'll be a pistol and shots fired."

"Especially since I doubt Tanek has calmed down since finding out what his son did at the Lair."

"What did he do?"

Neta had a frantic look. "I think we need to keep our mouths shut. About everything."

"Agreed." Kaley hesitated. "I don't mean to be impolite, but those girls don't look alike." She was referring to the fact that, when dressed, the young women looked the same, but undressed, they were very different. Shay's body looked as soft as a feather pillow, while Bree was lean, even muscular.

"Bree and I take after our father. Shay is like her royal mother."

Kaley couldn't help a quick up-and-down look at Neta. "Good to know."

When they reached the palace, Neta flung open a heavy door. "Let's go get you remarried."

They ran through the hallways until they reached the Sanction Room. Jobi was standing outside the closed doors. Kaley hadn't seen him since he'd put her, unconscious, on a ship headed to another planet. She wasn't sure whether she should be glad to see him or smash him in the face.

"What have you done to yourself?" He sounded horrified. "You look as bad as when you met King Aramus."

"That was because I'd been running with—"

Neta stepped between them. "She is beautiful." She smoothed a long strand of Kaley's hair behind her ears.

Jobi grimaced. "Of course a mother would think that. Graceen! How could you let her run around the streets in her wedding dress?"

Kaley's eyes widened.

"I'm sorry," Graceen whispered to Kaley. "I should have told you. I wouldn't have left you behind on Earth if . . . if . . ."

After all that Kaley had experienced, nothing could surprise her. "Let me guess. You were drugged to the point of death then carried back to a spaceship. Been there, had that done to me." She held up her hand for a fist bump.

Since Graceen had spent time on Earth, she knew how to respond. She bumped back.

Jobi groaned. "We should put some swan feathers in your hair, then Tanek won't notice the mess you're in."

"I'm marrying a blue swan," Kaley said, "so I need pink feathers. Are there pink swans?"

"Ssssh!" Jobi hissed, then opened the door.

Kaley's father was standing just inside, ready to walk her down the aisle. Jobi left them to go to the front where he stood under the arch.

A musical instrument started playing an odd version of "Here Comes the Bride." Graceen lowered her daughter's veil, and

Kaley took her father's arm. But then she stopped and looked at Graceen. "Is Sojee really your father?" Kaley was wearing the Truth Necklace, and it was cool so she knew she wasn't being lied to, but she wanted to hear it.

"Yes, he is."

"Then he's my grandfather?"

"He most certainly is. He wasn't about to leave you alone among strangers when you first arrived."

"And he needed me to pull him out of the mud."

"What?" Graceen asked, then smiled. "You'll have to tell me. I love stories."

"Me too," Kaley said. "We can—"

Pointedly, the music got louder, meaning she needed to go. A glance at her father showed that his eyes were on his wife, who he hadn't seen in years. Kaley looked ahead to Tanek and Mekos waiting for her at the end of the aisle. They had on Earth-style tuxedos and she'd never seen anything as beautiful as they were. On the other side was Aradella in one of her big, elaborate robes.

Kaley tightened her grip on her father's arm and they started the slow walk down the aisle.

"Happy?" he asked.

"Completely. To my soul."

Jeff laughed. "Spoken like a lover of fairy tales. We begged Jobi to let us see you but he said that if we got to you before you'd bonded with Tanek, you'd leave him and go with us."

"And that would prevent the overtaking of Empyrea," Kaley said. "I'm learning that everything leads up to that. Are you glad to see Mom?"

"To my soul." They were at the arch. He kissed her forehead, then took his seat.

Tanek was looking at her in curious pleasure. Her dress, her veiled face, all of it was strange to him.

"Sorry I'm such a mess," she said, "but I had something to do with my . . . with my mother."

Tanek smiled. "They told me she was still alive and here. She was hiding when we were at the Museum of Earth. As for beauty, you look like *my* Kaley."

From the back came Jobi. It looked like he was the officiant and he was ready to say the Earth words. But then, Tanek saw Kaley's skirt. "Your dress is torn. What have you been doing?" His voice was alarmed.

She did *not* want to tell him about the naked women. She needed to deflect his attention. "I think you should ask your son what he did while we were at the Lair."

Mekos, standing next to his father, gave a startled look. "What do *I* have to do with your dress being torn?"

Jobi looked at Mekos. "On Earth, we'd say you just got thrown under the bus."

Kaley kept looking at Mekos. "Why did you two bring that little dragon to me? Was that part of something you shouldn't have been doing?"

Mekos looked ahead. "I have no idea what you mean."

Suddenly, Kaley's Truth Necklace got hot, then hotter. "Ow!"

Tanek jerked it off her neck. When it burned his hand, he dropped it to the floor. They watched as the little half round pendant burned a hole through the white rug. It lay on the stone floor, steam coming off the heat.

They looked at Mekos. "That was one powerful lie," Kaley said.

Tanek narrowed his eyes at his son. "What have you done?"

Jobi, frowning so hard his eyebrows met in the middle, said, "Do you two want to get married or not?"

Mekos grimaced. "They're only interested in the honeymoon," he muttered.

"What does that mean?" Kaley asked, eyes wide.

It was Sojee and Frank, sitting behind them, who bellowed, "Get on with this!"

Kaley looked at Tanek. "They're my two grandfathers."

"Sojee is?" he asked.

Kaley said, "Yes," then Tanek looked back at the big man, who smiled and nodded.

Jobi spoke loud enough to hurt Mekos's ears. "Dearly beloved, we are gathered here today to—"

Tanek looked at Kaley through her veil. "That means you're related to Aradella. Are you a princess?"

Kaley smiled. "No, but you'll always be my prince." She turned to Jobi. "Please continue."

"Are you sure? Or should we wait for a dodo bird to appear? You have no fairy tales to destroy? Maybe you want to introduce us to Rumpelstiltskin."

Kaley gave him her sweetest smile. "I'll save all that for later."

There were no more interruptions for the rest of the ceremony. They were a happy group, full of stories, and they loved the cream-filled cake. Mekos ate three sugar roses and stayed far away from Kaley and her questions.

# 9

Early the next morning, Hale opened the door to Mekos, but she frowned hard, letting him know that if anything went wrong she'd be after him.

With a solemn nod of thanks, he took a step toward Aradella's room. But then he turned back and kissed Hale's cheek. "Thank you for taking care of her," he said.

Her face turned red and she pushed him away. Her strength was such that Mekos almost fell, but he kept his balance.

Smiling, he went to Aradella's room. It wasn't daylight yet, but he could see perfectly well in the dark. It was a barren space, more like a cell than a bedroom.

Aradella was asleep, her breathing soft and quiet. As always, he marveled at how much he loved her. His grandfather had told him this would happen. "Basically, our family are still swans," Roal said. "You'll love once and it will be forever." Mekos had laughed. There were so many pretty girls! He knew he could never choose just one.

But then he saw Aradella. She was sitting on that platform, securely fastened inside that outlandish garment, and staring at the crowd. All his senses went on high alert. It was as though he could *feel* her sense of resignation.

He saw her look up at Kaley in the window of a derelict house. Kaley always bonded with suffering animals and in this case, a human. Tanek said that Kaley attracted so many animals there was no room to walk. Sojee had said, "Are you afraid they'll step on one of those noisy birds that follow *you*?" Now that they knew Sojee was Kaley's grandfather, Mekos smiled in memory. And when he looked at Aradella that first time, he'd thought of those lost animals.

Quietly, soundless even to his own ears, Mekos stretched out beside Aradella on the narrow bed. A thin blanket was between them. He didn't dare get too close to her or they'd be there until sunset.

He kissed the soft skin of her cheek.

"Mmm," she murmured and turned to him.

He rubbed his face against hers.

She didn't open her eyes. "You have whiskers."

"They'd grow as long as my forearm if I didn't cut them. I'd look like my mother's father."

She sleepily smiled. "Why don't you have a tail like her?"

"My blood was corrupted by my father."

"Ah, Tanek the Great." She pulled on the cover to lift it, but he didn't move.

"You have to get up," he said.

"That's what I'm to say to *you*."

He chuckled. "You need to get dressed in your disguise. The commanders of the men from Selkan have arrived and Sojee's going to go over their orders. It's in a room with a balcony and you and I are to hide and listen."

Aradella opened her eyes and leaned away, but it was too dark to see him clearly. "I'd like to hear what he has to say."

"I thought you would."

Aradella flipped the cover away on the opposite side. Since her bed was against the wall, she stood up and stepped over Mekos. As she passed, he deftly ran his hand up her leg.

"I don't have your eyesight. I need light."

Mekos lit the little lantern, then put his hands behind his head and watched her get dressed. She tied on the pads, then put on one of her hideous dresses.

"Are you ready?" she asked.

Smoothly, he got out of bed, quickly kissed her lips, then opened the door.

Aradella wasn't surprised to see Hale waiting for them. What did surprise her was the look of affection on Hale's face. When they were outside in the cool night air, Aradella said, "What did you do to my guard?"

"Wild fox sex," Mekos said over his shoulder as he hurried toward the palace.

"At least it wasn't the slow swan kind," she said. "They're my favorite."

He laughed. "Your place is attached to the palace. Why isn't there a door into it?"

"Someday I'll show you why." He was holding open a narrow door. "Will Sojee be angry if he finds out we're here?"

"He invited us. He wants me to listen for anyone coming. He doesn't want Olina to hear what he's planning. He said she's too busy making her own plans to bother with us." He glanced at her.

"Think she's plotting other ways to get rid of me?"

Mekos didn't want to answer that. "At least my father doesn't know I'm involved. He still thinks I'm five years old and need protection from the world."

Aradella looked at him. "At the wedding, I was afraid he was going to find out about Valona."

"Me too. If he knew that, he'd yell at me for days, then he'd lock me in a swan pen."

"He'll certainly be angry when he sees what happens tomorrow."

Mekos grinned happily. "I'm sure he will be."

Smiling in conspiracy, they went into the palace. Mekos had to listen hard to figure out where Sojee and the men were.

They entered the room through a small door that opened to a circular staircase and they hurried up it. Mekos moved silently while Aradella tried to. Her big garments were a hindrance to movement.

They stepped onto a railed balcony that looked down at a big room with a dozen chairs set up.

"It's my birthday room," Aradella whispered. "Or that's what I called it. It's where my parents held my . . ." She didn't finish as the memory of her lost family hurt too much.

"We'll hold birthdays for our children here," he said.

That image made Aradella's knees weak, but she made herself stop that. "Please tell me you don't give a woman a litter of kits."

Mekos suppressed a laugh. "I guess we'll see what happens."

They smiled at each other in mutual anticipation.

Below them, a door opened and the room filled with the noise of men arriving.

Aradella and Mekos stretched out on their stomachs and watched.

There were twelve men, each of them huge. They were muscular, heavy, and scarred. Several of them had scars that distorted their faces. One had a piece of his nose missing.

"Are they the winners or the losers?" Aradella whispered.

"They won. The losers have missing body parts."

"This isn't going to work," Aradella said. "These men will hurt the women. They'll—"

When she started to get up, Mekos put his hand on her shoulder. "You don't trust Sojee?"

Aradella lay back down but she was frowning.

Sojee, taller than any of the men and as heavy as they were, strode to the front of the room, and the men quickly took seats. Whether they respected Sojee or were afraid of him wasn't clear.

The men waited in silence.

Sojee began. "What you and your men are to do today is more difficult than any Cutting Game. It requires extreme effort and discipline. Do you think you can restrain yourselves?" He glared at his audience. "More importantly, can you control your men?" He almost shouted the last, then looked at the huge men one by one, waiting for their curt nods. "All right, then, I will go over all of it again. You are to make these women *care* about you. And how are you to do that?"

There was a soft, incoherent rumble of voices.

"How do you make the women *like* you?" Sojee shouted.

"Tools!" the men yelled in unison.

Aradella and Mekos looked at each other in horror, silently asking, *Do what with the tools?* They looked back to Sojee.

"That's right. You are to entice the women by using tools. You are to repair whatever needs it. If you see a broken wagon, fix it. Build her a grape arbor. And above all, do *not* ask, 'What do you want me to do next?' Just *do* it. Unasked." He paused. "What is rule number two?"

Several of the men looked at each other blankly.

"Listen!" one of the deeply scarred men said.

"Yes," Sojee said. "Listen to whatever the women want to tell you. Imagine that they're explaining the rules to a game that could cost you your right hand. Believe me when I say that your life depends on hearing what she's saying. Rule three?"

A man in the back said, "No teaching."

"That's right," Sojee said. "Don't try to teach them anything. I don't care if a woman tells you to hang a door over a window, keep your mouth shut. Do you understand me? Do it correctly, but don't puff your chest out and tell her how dumb she is and how smart you are."

"But what if she—?"

Sojee didn't let the man finish his question. "If you can't get your men to do this, let me know now and we'll send the lot of you home. You are on a team. Act like it!"

The man nodded and leaned back in his chair.

"No fighting!" Sojee said. "No matter what dishonorable

thing is said to you or disparaging remark is made, there is to be *no fighting*. Understood?"

Again, the men nodded.

"Now," Sojee said, "the big one."

In unison, every man gave a sigh so hard, so deep, that the curtains swayed.

A man in front mumbled something.

Sojee glared at him. "I can't hear you."

"No se . . ." He didn't seem able to say the word.

"What?" Sojee shouted.

"No sex!" the men yelled back.

"That's right," Sojee said. "No sex. If a woman strips off naked in front of you and says, 'I'm yours,' what do you do?"

The men looked like they might cry.

"Do not touch her," a man in front said, his voice full of grief.

"Exactly," Sojee said. "The chips in your arms will tell us who does what. If even *one* of you is a weak, cowardly excuse for a man who can't control himself, all of us will know. Then what will happen?" He didn't wait for an answer. "Queen Olina will use it as a reason to send all of you away *forever*. Those of you with wives and children here won't see them again in your lifetime."

"But we can have sex with our wives, right?" a man asked.

"No!" Sojee said fiercely. "Do *not* give the women cause to say, 'Is that all you want from me?' Fix her roof, repair the plumbing, and listen to your teenage daughter tell you how some girl said a really mean thing to her. Respect! That's what you're to give to these women."

The men looked as though they'd lost a war. Miserable, sad, defeated.

"Now, let's go over what you *can* do," Sojee said.

"Meat!" a man said. "My men have been slaughtering for days. We've got so much meat it's the ship's ballast."

"Right," Sojee said. "These women make pets out of the animals. Most of the girls have never tasted a steak. They don't know what a pork sausage is. The grills that were left behind when—" Sojee swallowed, dampening down an anger that never left him. "The grills from before the men and women were separated are still here. They need cleaning but they work. I want this island smelling of beef. And chicken." When he added the last, his eyes flicked up toward the balcony, an apology to Mekos of the Order of Swans.

The men were silent as they digested what he'd said.

"Cutting Games are easier," a man muttered.

When Sojee said no more, they started to get up.

"There is one more thing," Sojee said and they sat back down. He hesitated as though what he was about to say was embarrassing. "Shirts are optional."

Their faces showed astonishment—and puzzlement.

Sojee shrugged. "Don't ask me to explain women to you. Go naked and the women will run away. Go shirtless and they'll nearly faint with lust."

"But if we're not to touch them, what use is that?" a man asked.

"None whatever," Sojee said, "but it won't hurt to remind them of what they'd get if you *did* touch them."

The men still looked confused. That "logic" was beyond their comprehension.

One of the men laughed. "Tools and listen, no fighting, no sex. All on top of a shipload of beef and all done shirtless."

Another man laughed. "We'll be blistered by the sun."

"And *lust*?" a man said. "I like that word."

They looked at Sojee. "You really think this will work?"

"It has to. Queen Olina has full power and I want no excuses for this to fail." He took a breath. "Don't forget that tomorrow you'll be free to impregnate any woman on the island who'll have you." He narrowed his eyes. "*Only* women who want you!"

The men stared at him. "You didn't tell us about the second day."

"Didn't I?" Sojee asked with fake innocence. "Must have

slipped my mind. Just know that what happens tomorrow depends on if you can keep it in your pants today. Any more questions?"

The men looked at each other and shook their heads no.

"Good!" Sojee said. "The next ship will be arriving soon. I suggest you again go over the rules with your men. You know who the troublemakers are and who can't follow rules. If you have to, chain those idiots to a rudder." He paused and looked at them. "Above all, remember this—you are in a battle to the death with a queen who is used to ultimate power. It's your choice whether you win this war or lose it."

The men nodded in understanding. They weren't going to mess this up.

Minutes later, Aradella and Mekos were downstairs. As they approached the exit door, he pulled her into a dark corner. "I hear people standing outside. I think they want you."

"I'm sure it's Olina." Aradella stepped into his arms. "I've had too much freedom and no doubt she's angry that I'm not dead."

He held her close. "She's going to be furious if the men last until tomorrow."

"She gave the promise of having an orgy on the second day so she'd be praised—and loved. She only did it because she's absolutely sure that today the men will erupt into violence. Then she'll send them away. The lack of intimacy won't be *her* fault."

Mekos stroked her hair. "Let's see if the men can hold to Sojee's plan." He moved his head sharply to one side. "There are guards waiting for you, as well as those women."

She knew he meant the three odious maids. "The queen's spies." She held him tighter. "I want to stay with you."

He kissed the top of her head. "I don't mind knowing that you'll be safe today. Sojee has more faith in the men than I do. Some of them look on women as wild, exotic creatures. I don't know if they can restrain themselves." Bending, he kissed her, then held her at arm's length. "Your jailers are getting impatient. Think of tomorrow."

"Everything is ready?"

"Grandpapá is bringing the dragon. It'll keep Nessa busy while you and I . . ." He didn't finish, just kissed her again. "Go!"

Reluctantly, Aradella went to the door. She took a deep breath to give herself courage, then looked back at Mekos, but he was already gone. She opened the door to see that waiting for her were the three spy-maids with four of the Queen's Guard. With Aradella in the front, they started walking toward her prison.

"The queen has ordered that you're to be protected," a maid said, her lips held tightly, primly. "The Cauldron has been locked against those . . . those . . ." She could hardly say the word. "Men. Those barbarians from Selkan."

"*We* will be spared what will happen, unlike our beloved friends who are in the other guilds. They don't have the safety of the Cauldron." The second maid was wiping at her fake tears of sorrow that she supposedly felt for the unfortunate women.

Aradella grit her teeth, then turned and began to walk backward. "You're right to stay here in safety. I heard that the men brought special food that will give them the potency of gods. It's said to be so delicious that it makes women's bodies quiver with desire. And their ship is loaded with tools that have been specially made to give pleasure to women. However, only the men know how to use them. And . . ." She lowered her voice. "*All* of the men will be half naked. All those sweaty muscles will be exposed." She shivered in disgust.

The spy-maids looked faint and even the well-trained guards' faces showed shocked interest.

Aradella smiled sweetly. "It's good that we'll miss all that. I think we should play cards today. All day. Perhaps we can get a court musician to perform so we can drown out those nasty screams of pleasure from those poor women. I heard that the men's tools pound *very* hard. I'm sure the whole island will echo with the cries of the women." She gave an even stronger shudder of revulsion. "How truly dreadful!"

One of the maids stopped walking. "I believe the queen needs our help."

"Yes! We are very loyal to her and if she needs us, we must go."

"We have to . . ." The third maid didn't finish, just hurried away with the others, heading toward the front gate. Each step they took got faster.

"What about our card game?" Aradella called after them.

One spy-maid waved her hand but the others didn't bother.

Aradella looked at the four guards. "I'm sure that two guards at a time will be enough to protect me. If you'd like to have some time off, please take it." She didn't wait for an answer, but turned her back to them. She smiled all the way to her little apartment. Once inside, she went straight to her library.

At the wedding, Jobi had given her a new stack of books and she very much wanted to see them. He'd said they were from the stash that Rita, Kaley's grandmother, had brought from Earth. "You may recognize some of the stories in this one," he'd said. The book was titled *The Greatest Fairy Tales Ever Told.* She began reading—and yes, some of the stories were of things she'd seen or had been told about.

It was hours later that a divine smell reached her. She looked up to see Hale standing in the open doorway. In her hands was a great earthenware bowl full of . . . "What is that?"

Hale rolled her eyes in what looked to be ecstasy. "Beef, but this is like nothing we've ever tasted. The men are cooking great piles of it."

Aradella closed her book and followed Hale into the sitting room. There was a big jug of beer on the table. "Tell me what's going on. How many guards are still here?"

"One, and she's on the roof looking for her companions to return so she can leave." Hale dished out a huge serving of beef. "I don't think they'll come back." She took a deep drink of her beer. "Out there, it's wonderful. The men are putting this place back together. I know we have carpenters and plumbers, but the men . . . Oh! But they are fast. It's like they're full of some wild energy and they're trying to use it up. Hammers, saws, I've never seen such workmen!"

"So they're keeping their lovemaking quiet, then?"

"There is none!" Hale grinned. "You should see the women. They're wearing so little clothing they may as well have on nothing. They bend over buckets and tables and toolboxes. They walk with their legs so far apart, you'd think they just got off a horse. But the men barely look at the women. Yet when a scantily clad woman shows up, the men seem overcome with enormous strength. They pick up . . ." Hale shook her head. "Three of the Beauty Girls walked by and I saw a man pick up a wagon—horse and all. It was extraordinary!"

Knowing what she did, Aradella couldn't keep her laughter in. Between the beef and beer and the images conjured, she laughed hard.

"I'm glad you find some humor," came a familiar voice. They looked up to see Arit buzzing into the room. "It's awful out there. I was afraid one of those men would swat me all the way to the lake. May I have some of that?"

Aradella got up, took her silver thimble out of her sewing basket, washed it, then filled it with beer. She turned over a teacup, showing the ridged pedestal on the bottom, and filled it with beef. Her big needle for leatherwork was the best she could do for a fork. She put everything on the low table, with a soft pincushion serving as a chair. "Tell us everything."

Arit said thank you, then sat down on the cushion and started on the beef and beer. "The women are working to get the attention of the men but they're being ignored."

"I bet Olina is angry about that," Aradella said.

Arit took a drink of beer and smiled. "Yes, she is. She's riding around on her horse and frowning at everything."

"Where's Ian?" Aradella asked. "You two have hardly been apart since you met."

Arit's face stiffened as though she was trying not to show her feelings. She shrugged. "I have no idea. It's none of my business where he is or what he does or who he sees." She drank more beer.

"If it were any of your business, where would he be?" Aradella persisted.

Arit grimaced. "My sister is here with King Aramus. She is beautiful beyond belief. It's said that the moon asks her for beauty advice. Any male who sees her, no matter his size, declares his eternal love for her. It's a love that can never be broken since she's so . . . so . . ."

"Glamorous?" Aradella said. "Dazzling? She enters a room and everyone runs to her? No one even sees *you* after she appears?"

"Yes, exactly," Arit said.

Aradella refilled the thimble. "Did Ian actually run off with her or are you assuming—based on past experience—that he's fallen for your beautiful princess cousins?"

Arit and Hale looked at her.

"What did I say?" Aradella asked, then remembered. "I was just pointing out that I understand due to my own life experience. Is your sister why you've always been a bit cool to Ian?"

"I refuse to have my heart broken. I know he'll leave me as soon as he sees—"

The familiar sound of a Never buzzing came through the window, but this was a lower, deeper vibration. It was Ian. In place of the half of his leg that he'd lost, was a beautifully carved piece of wood. Aradella had seen it before. In a room where Olina held meetings was an elegant clock that had belonged to the former king. On one side was a carving of an old man with a cane. That cane was now strapped to Ian's leg.

Aradella couldn't resist saying, "Does your leg tell time?"

Ian gave a chuckle of understanding, then lit on the table to stand across from Arit. "Peace at last." He picked up her thimble of beer, drained it, then grabbed a handful of beef and ate it in one bite. "It's bad out there. Sawdust is flying everywhere—and all the men are half naked. The dust is sticking to their sweaty skin and it itches them, but they will *not* put their shirts on. It's very strange."

The three women looked at each other.

"Sweaty men," Aradella said. "Half naked."

"Covered in sawdust," Arit added.

"I could scratch a few backs," Hale said.

Ian looked at the women in chastisement.

Aradella cleared her throat. "But the men aren't touching the women, are they?"

Ian drank more beer and ate more of Arit's beef. "No! No matter what the women do to get their attention, the men don't touch them." He looked at Arit. "Four of your sisters are here." He said it as though it was an accusation.

"Oh." Instantly, Arit looked sad.

Ian clamped his teeth together. "Those women rolled dice to decide who . . ." He didn't finish.

Hale and Aradella leaned forward. "To decide what?"

"Who would get me as a . . ." He took a breath. "As a prize."

Aradella and Hale closed their lips to keep from laughing.

Arit, with no hint of humor in her eyes, said, "Who won you?"

Ian drained another thimble of beer. "The oldest one, I think. I'm not sure."

Arit looked like she might cry. "Tink is beautiful, don't you think?"

Ian wiped his mouth on his sleeve and scratched his leg above the peg. "She certainly thinks she is. She even told me that she is." He looked up at Aradella. "Mekos's grandfather arrived on a dragon. That creature glistens. I'd like to have one of his scales for a shield. That giant was very glad to see Mekos."

It was Aradella's turn to look sad. "Is he with the sawdust boys?"

Ian grinned, then went to the pincushion and stretched out

on it, his hands behind his head. Arit remained sitting close by him. He looked extremely pleased about something. "Mekos and I sneaked into the palace and rescued my sister."

The women looked at him in surprise.

"Tell us," Aradella whispered.

He shook his head in memory. "Mekos moves so fast even I can hardly keep up with him. He only stopped to listen. I don't know what he heard, but then he'd sprint through the halls. We had to go down two flights of stone stairs. Did you know there are underground rooms in that old palace?"

"Yes," Aradella said. "I used to play in them when I was a child."

Ian nodded. "We had to go through four locks to get to the room where my sister was kept."

"And you opened them all." Arit sounded proud.

"I did. And there she was, my dear sister, Laylit." He smiled for a moment. "The good part was that her guard was an old woman, and they'd become friends. Laylit was given the freedom to fly about the room and they talked. The woman used fabric scraps from Olina's clothes to make dresses and a little bedchamber for my sister. Mekos had a piece of swan cloth with him and he gave that to her."

Aradella said, "Mekos is very kind, and he thinks about other people. He can move silently and he hears everything, and he—" She broke off as they were staring at her. "Where is your sister now?"

"Home, I hope. I sent the woman to the Lair. I think she'll like Valona's old maid." His eyes sparkled. "You and Mekos are heroes to those women. They'd do anything for you."

Aradella smiled in memory. She knew that whatever happened, she'd always remember those days at the Lair as the best of her life.

# 10

When Aradella woke the next day, it wasn't yet dawn. *After to-day,* she thought, *everything will change.*

She listened carefully but she heard no sounds. But then, with yesterday's free-flowing beer and that divine beef, people were probably sleeping it off.

Not long after the arrival of Arit and Ian, Olina had sent more guards. Aradella knew it was a symbol of her anger. The visit of the men wasn't going as she'd planned. Maybe she was afraid that the princess would somehow join with the men. Then what would happen? Aradella would lead an army to reclaim the throne? Or maybe Prince Nessa would get angry and refuse to marry her.

*I should be so lucky,* Aradella thought as she put her arms up, her head on her clasped hands. How wonderful yesterday had been!

There was Mekos in bed with her in the early morning, then sneaking into the palace to hear Sojee give orders to the men. The memory of the men's looks of defeat made her laugh.

The rest of the day had been full of visitors, all of them bursting with news.

Three women from the sewing school came by to measure Aradella for what would be her marriage gown. Of course the robe had been made months before, but the idea of seeing the reclusive princess was too much to forego. They'd made up excuses to visit. The women felt the pads under Aradella's big dress but they made no comment about them. Instead, at Aradella's encouragement, they excitedly told her what was going on outside.

"Men are seeing their daughters for the first time," one gushed.

"No one is talking about how those conceptions occurred," another one said.

They all knew the husbands sneaked across the water to get to their wives. And the women risked their lives to spend a few hours in the secret meeting. Afterward, when the warning came that Olina or one of her suck-ups was coming, the pregnant women were hidden away.

But on this day, families were openly together. Girls who'd never been around men in their lives were seeing their fathers and brothers for the first time.

"And mothers are seeing their sons," they told Aradella.

The whole island experienced the tears and horror of a boy's seventh birthday. That's when he was taken away and sent to Selkan to be with the men. The wails of the women were so deep, so loud, that the birds left the trees to seek the safety of the ground.

Those boys had returned to their mothers, many of them now grown men.

"But you wouldn't know they were men from the way their mothers tend to them," one of the women said. "They treat them as though they're toddlers!"

"The women have been baking for weeks and they ply the men, young and old, with breads and cakes and pies of every flavor."

"Don't forget the wounds on the men! If a man so much as scratches his shoulder, a woman will insist on applying salve to his back. His *bare* back."

"And his front," a woman added and they laughed together.

"My favorite was the men teaching their daughters how to fight."

"I heard, 'Just punch her in the nose,' a dozen times."

Aradella listened to it all, smiling deeply. "I heard that the women are wearing very little clothing."

"Well . . ." they said hesitantly. "They're trying to entice the men away from working on the houses."

"But they've failed." Aradella's eyes were sparkling.

None of the women had ever viewed Aradella as one of them, someone they could share with, but when she laughed, they loosened.

"Today, my friend couldn't lift a basket of carded wool, so one of the men carried it for her," said one woman. "Yesterday, I saw her go up a two-story ladder with a barrel strapped to her back. That woman has thighs like that dragon we saw, but around the men, she is helpless!"

"Ferms!" one of the women said and her eyes nearly rolled back into her head. "Fertile men. Has there ever been a more grand sight on this planet?"

"No," the other women—including Aradella—agreed.

All day had been like that. At one point, Aradella realized the women were coming to say goodbye to her—and she knew why. It was the day before she was to be married to a slime like Nessa. There were many subtle remarks made that showed they knew him. She asked a few questions, and yes, he'd visited the island several times.

"Let's just say that he's not the Reaver," one said.

"I thought the Reaver was a woman," Aradella said innocently.

At that, the women laughed, then they enlarged the rare sightings of a person running across rooftops into stories of the Reaver leaping from one crater to another. There were hints that he could fly. *Soar, not fly,* Aradella thought.

The women brought food and drink and as much laughter as they could create. And best of all, her beautiful cousins were nowhere to be seen. It was wonderful not to be looked on with pity, then see their sad eyes. *Poor Aradella* seemed to be written across their foreheads.

The rare treat of being with the happy women made Aradella think about how life could change in an instant. For years, she'd been the treasured only child of a king and queen. She'd freely gone places, talked to people. When she went to the craters on her pony, people ran forward to give her gifts of food and hand-made objects. Of course they were hoping to sell them to the palace, but still, it was nice.

In one day, Aradella's life changed. On the day that her parents died, Aradella had been put into insolation and fed sugary cakes. Her only "companions" were her two cousins, who she despised.

Now, years later, everything had again abruptly changed. Tanek had brought Mekos and eventually, he had given her love.

Aradella came out of her reverie. Morning light was coming into the room, and when she heard a sound in the next room, fear seemed to engulf her. If they didn't succeed today, she didn't want to think of the consequences.

She knew Mekos had the mask, and he had Prince Nessa's beloved dragon. The plan was for Mekos to use the animal to entice Nessa away from the ceremony, then Mekos would . . .

Aradella closed her eyes in prayer. Then Mekos would stand beside her for the marriage ceremony—and they'd leave the big hall as one, united forever.

She didn't want to think about what could happen after that. Olina might declare war. But with the men on the island, she wouldn't win it. But then, what did the men care about who the princess of another island married? It wasn't any of their business.

Like all the women on Pithan, Aradella had had a lifetime of hearing how "evil" men were. All of them. No exceptions. It was said that men cared about only one thing and once they got that, they discarded the women.

These complaints were what had originally separated the men and women. The Empyreans had decreed that the sexes would be happier if they lived apart. So a separation was ordered.

Women stayed on Pithan in their pretty, well-kept houses, while the men, and boys over seven, were sent to the sparsely populated island of Selkan. Over the years, as their homes deteriorated, the women began to learn how to restore them, but there was too much too fast. The women made themselves feel better by spreading rumors that the men were building fortresses and violently attacking each other. The women's roofs may be leaking but at least they were *safe*!

As Aradella grew up, she remembered her fear that her beloved father would be sent away to live with the men.

"I am fortunate that I'm the king," he'd said, but he didn't sound "fortunate."

She remembered the talk of rebellion that went on after the separation was first enforced. There was a hero, a man named Haver Beyhan, who'd fought to take the islands out from under the control of the Empyreans. Aradella remembered her father crying over Haver's "disappearance."

"He didn't 'vanish,'" her father shouted. "He was *killed*. Murdered!" He'd broken down into tears, holding on to his wife as she too cried. "Haver was our last hope."

It wasn't until years later that Aradella found out Tanek was the grandson of that glorious man.

"And Mekos is his great-grandson," Aradella said aloud. That knowledge made her wonder if she and Mekos were about to start another revolution. She hadn't yet come to terms with having killed a person. Yes, Valona had been evil, but she was still human. So far, there didn't seem to be public knowledge of her death. What would happen when people did know? Would it become part of what Mekos's great-grandfather started?

*And look what happened to him*, she thought. He had "disappeared" and later it was found that he'd been killed. Would the Empyreans be so enraged at what she and Mekos did that they'd do what they'd done to Haver's big Homestead? They dropped bombs from machines that no one on the islands had ever seen. In a matter of hours, the once thriving business of the people of the Order of Swans had been destroyed. Afterward, Haver had gone undercover. He'd led the revolution in secret.

But ultimately, it had failed. Had she and Mekos restarted it?

As she remembered all this, Aradella's heart began to race. *What will Mekos and I cause to happen?* echoed through her mind.

Hale opened Aradella's door. "It's time," she said, then left the room.

Sometimes Aradella thought her friend knew what was planned, but she didn't say so. If it worked out, this could be their last day together in such close companionship.

Aradella got out of bed. Was this her last day to wear the hated pads? Or was it her last day of being *alive*?

Aradella was hidden away at the end of the big room where her union to Nessa was to take place. She hadn't been allowed any rehearsal for the ceremony. Nor were the Beauty Girls allowed to use their talents on her as they'd done with Kaley. Aradella's lashes and brows were very light and with her nervousness, her face looked as though it had been erased. Her robe was so thick and heavy that if it weren't for her years of training with Hale, she wouldn't have been able to carry it. This seemed to have been anticipated as a wheeled chair was waiting for her.

Aradella's only experience of a royal wedding was when Olina married her uncle. It had been a serious affair of signing contracts and valuable gifts being presented to the couple. Young Aradella hadn't been allowed to participate, and she'd only seen a bit of it. Olina, in her golden gown, had seen the child and ordered her to be taken away.

But now, the reproduction of an Earth wedding that was done for Kaley seemed to have made an impression. Aradella was to walk—or be pushed—down an aisle. She was alone, no male escort, but she hadn't expected Olina to be that generous.

Out of sight of everyone, Aradella stood at the back of the huge room and peeped through the curtains. She wanted to see what was waiting for her.

In the front, seated on the right side, was King Aramus and his entourage. There were several beautiful young women with him. *Does he have multiple wives?* she wondered.

On the left side of the aisle was Queen Olina and her ancient mother. They were dressed in robes that flashed and sparkled so much, it hurt to look at them. There were rumors that missing jewels from Earth were owned by Olina and her witch mother.

The rest of the room was full of couples, men and women sitting side by side, nearly all of them holding hands. To Aradella, raised with mostly women, and being constantly told of the uncontrollable violence of men, it was a jarring sight. The plan was for the men to leave Pithan by midnight, but she wondered if they would.

Tanek and Kaley, with her family, were halfway down, sitting by the aisle. They looked very serious. *They think I'm marrying Nessa*, she thought. *They think*— Her eyes widened. Kaley was holding Tanek's hand and she raised it to her cheek as though in reassurance. Since Aradella had spent much of her life trying to figure out what was happening around her, she'd become rather good at lip reading.

Kaley said, "Mekos can do this. Have faith in him."

Aradella stepped away from the curtain and leaned against the wall. *They know!* she thought. *They know our plan.* She took several deep breaths. Kaley was reassuring Tanek that his son could handle being king. Considering that Tanek's grandfather had "disappeared" when he went against Olina and the Empyreans, Kaley was asking a lot of her husband.

"It's time for you to go," a woman Aradella didn't know said in the tone of an order. She wasn't in uniform, but she was obviously a guard, a woman fully prepared to stop Aradella if she tried to run away.

Aradella put her shoulders back and started to walk down the wide, lonely aisle. When she reached Kaley and Tanek, she almost stopped. Both of them looked so serious, grim really.

They seemed to be asking, *What will happen when it's revealed that you've married Mekos?*

It took Aradella's years of discipline to continue walking. Waiting at the end was what appeared to be Nessa. He looked so real that Aradella had to remind herself that he was actually Mekos, and that he was wearing the mask. She remembered how realistic he'd looked when she saw herself lying on Valona's sacrificial altar.

Mekos was so good at imitation that he was wearing Nessa's sulky, pouty look, as though he was too good to be doing this. He looked Aradella up and down, sneering at her wide girth.

She gave him a tiny, reassuring smile to let him know he was doing an excellent impersonation.

When he scowled at her, Aradella couldn't help frowning. She quickly erased it but she still felt uneasy.

When she got to the end and took her place next to Mekos, a tall man stepped before them. She drew in her breath. He was Fahir, King Aramus's advisor, bully, co-ruler, servant, executioner. His job description depended on the person speaking. Aradella had always disliked him as he looked at her as something to be bought and sold—and he'd always found her lacking.

She leaned toward Mekos. "I didn't expect *him* to be here," she whispered.

He stepped back, looking repulsed at her nearness.

Aradella straightened. *Mekos was certainly staying in character!*

"We are here to unite the kingdoms," Fahir said in his booming voice. "Through this union—"

Suddenly, they heard voices coming from the back. They were low and strong. It was like the whispers of a hundred people.

Fahir's voice rose. "Through this union, the islands will unite. Old royals and new will come together in equality. There will be no division between the two thrones."

*Olina is going to share her authority?* Aradella thought. *Never!*

The whispers from the back grew stronger but Aradella couldn't understand what they were saying. She didn't dare turn toward them and risk Fahir's anger. His great, jeweled staff leaned against a post. She'd been told that he could use that thing to turn people into snakes. Again, she leaned toward Mekos. "What are they saying?"

He bent backward, away from her, his lips curved in revulsion. "How the fark do I know? Get away from me!"

It was then that Aradella knew. Mekos would be able to hear what was being said, and he'd *never* speak to her that way.

Without a thought of what she was doing, Aradella's hand shot out. She grabbed at the mask and pulled to remove it. But he wasn't wearing a mask! Her nails dug into his skin, leaving bloody streaks.

Nessa screamed, his hand to his face over the bleeding claw marks.

Aradella stood there, staring, unable to move. All she could think of was, *What have you done to Mekos?* She managed to look at Fahir. His smirk twisted his mouth and eyes into a look of triumph. He had won!

"You know!" Aradella said in horror.

In the next second, the room seemed to erupt into chaos. In the back, shouts went up—and Fahir made a lunge to grab his staff. The jewel on top flashed as though in happy anticipation of causing evil.

Aradella was frozen. The heavy garment seemed to double in weight and she stood there awaiting whatever Fahir was about to do to her.

In the next second, Tanek swooped down to her. He was a big man and in his black suit he looked like an enormous bird of prey. He grabbed Aradella about the waist and soared up with her almost to the ceiling. He carried her over the top of the guests, then went down and out the door.

When they were outside, Tanek set Aradella down, then hurried to the others who were waiting in the big courtyard of the palace.

So much had happened that Aradella couldn't comprehend

it all. *How? Why?* She saw Sojee standing at the closed doors to the palace with the commanders he'd lectured that morning. Up close, the men were even bigger than they'd seemed when she'd seen them from above. They were holding the doors closed so no one could get out.

An unholy noise made her look up. A huge machine was coming down to the ground, and it was creating a wind so fierce that Aradella was pushed back several steps. The flying machine had an oval body and giant blades going round and round on top.

Aradella raised her arm against the wind. Before it got to the ground, Kaley's grandfather Frank bent and ran to the big machine and jerked open the door. A small man was inside and shaking his head no. Frank grabbed the man by the shirt, pulled him out, and tossed him to the side like he was a child's toy. Frank got into the machine and began flipping switches.

Kaley's grandmother, Rita, directed people to the machine, then helped them get into the seats. First came Tanek's parents, Vian and Roal, then Kaley and Rita. Tanek was last. He held back as he constantly watched the sky. At last, Tanek nodded in relief, then turned to the machine. He looked like he'd rather jump into a volcano than get on the thing. But at last he climbed inside.

Frank pulled the curved, transparent door closed, and the machine rose up.

They were barely off the ground when Sojee took Aradella's arm and turned her around. Coming out of the sky, like some great winged god, its green scales glistening in the sunlight, was a dragon. She assumed it belonged to Nessa.

On its back was Mekos.

In spite of its size, the dragon deftly landed on its toes. Its eyes were on the loud, windy machine that was still rising, seeming to try to decide if the thing was a friend or foe.

Bending, Mekos held out his hand to Aradella. She started to run toward him, but then Sojee grabbed her by the waist. He couldn't soar but his long strides covered the ground quickly. Sojee picked up Aradella and dropped her into the saddle behind

Mekos. She wanted Sojee to join them, but he wouldn't. He made a gesture toward his men. He would stay with them.

With the flying machine high in the air, the sound of the people being held inside the palace reached them. Women of Olina's Queen's Guard came out from both sides of the palace, their bows drawn.

Mekos gave a whistle to the dragon and it rose from the ground.

"A spell," Mekos said over his shoulder, and she knew it was explanation for what had kept him from the ceremony. The unasked question was, *Who cast the spell?*

The guards raised their bows and shot them. The arrows sailed through the air, and three of them struck Aradella.

Mekos twisted his body to shield her from the arrows, but she pushed him away. Between her heavy robe and all the padding she wore, the arrows hadn't touched her body. She ripped at the ties down the front of the robe, then wrapped it around Mekos so they were both covered.

As the dragon rose higher, the range of the arrows grew weaker. Even so, there were at least a dozen sticking out of the hated robe, some of them reaching the padding beneath.

"This is Perus," Mekos said, then he pulled the reins and they turned sharply north. Pithan was a long island that ran east to west, so they were soon away from land and over the quiet calm of the sea.

She held on to Mekos, her head nestling against his back. Seabirds that she'd never seen before came toward them and they were drawn to Mekos. One pretty blue-green bird landed on Perus's broad head and looked at Mekos as though to ask who and what he was.

He leaned to the side so she could see the quizzical creature. In the next moment a flock of tiny, iridescent birds encircled them. Then all of them flew away in a dazzle of colors.

"Arit and Ian could ride them," Aradella said.

"Perhaps they do." He nudged Perus to go down, closer to the water. "Take it off. Now. Forever."

She knew he meant her wedding robe. She had no idea what the future held, but it was for sure that what had been was now gone. There was no going back.

It was a joy to slip out of the heavy robe. She started to drop it, but then she remembered that Hale had sewn a leather purse inside the garment. It contained the poisonous plants that Aradella had collected from Valona's garden. "I don't need that!" she'd said, but Hale had ignored her. "You don't know what you'll need."

Aradella pulled the purse loose and shoved it between the blankets on Perus's saddle. When Mekos tilted the dragon, she dropped the robe. They watched it fall down toward the water—but then three enormous eagles swooped down and caught it. They latched on to it with their talons and carried it up and up. They saw the birds fly into the distance where they could barely see what looked to be the top of a mountain.

"They'll use that thing for their nests." Mekos nodded toward the mountain. "That's Selkan and the Homestead."

"Is that where we're going?"

"Yes." He twisted about and grabbed a handful of one of her pads. "You have anything on under that?"

"My training garb. I thought you'd be the one to see it." She meant their wedding night, after Mekos had been revealed as her husband.

"Someone told Olina what we were planning."

"But who? We told no one." They hadn't even confided in people who could help them.

Mekos's answer was to shrug. He had no idea. "There's that thing."

They could see the machine in the distance. "What is it?"

"My grandmamá travels in it," he said. "It's called a hell."

"It's well named." She tightened her arms around him. "What now?" she asked softly, knowing that he'd hear her.

"You will be disinherited, the men will be sent away, and Olina will rule forever. *Nothing* will change."

She didn't comment. It wasn't the revolution they'd hoped for, but at least they'd come out alive. For Aradella, she was relieved that she'd realized who she was marrying before the vows were said. She was glad she wasn't clasped to Prince Nessa. The question was, Would Olina be satisfied with her win or would she demand punishment? Unfortunately, she knew the answer. They would *never* be safe.

They said no more as she removed the hated pads and dropped them into the water below. No birds came after them.

They rode in silence. Aradella, with her cheek against Mekos's back, looked ahead to see the place where his family had once lived. Her father had told her about the heroic Haver Beyhan's place. It was sealed off and private. "Not even I am allowed to visit," her father had said, laughing at the idea.

"Who'd want us when they have swans?" her mother asked.

"It's the *blue* swans that you like," her father teased.

"Young Roal is indeed a sight to behold."

Aradella had adored hearing her parents' loving wordplay.

She and Mekos watched the hell machine land. He held Perus back, hovering above as the passengers got out. Aradella looked down at what had once been a magnificent place before the bombing by the Empyreans had forced them to abandon it.

To the left, down a wide road, was what had once been a village. She knew it was where the workers, the swansmen, lived. There were open areas with covered pavilions where the valuable swan feathers were processed. The feathers were made into cloth and medicine. There were even lotions that were said to slow the signs of aging.

To the right, at the top of a low hill, was what had been the home of the Beyhans. Most of the roof of the sprawling estate was missing, but it was obvious that it had once been beautiful. She saw flashes of blue tiles in what was left of the walls. There was a crystal clear lake for the swans, empty fountains, and broken stone structures.

"Look!" Mekos was excited. Below them, too far away for

her to see clearly, were two men. "It's Daln and one of Collan's sons. They're returning!" His voice rose. "And there!"

She didn't know what he was seeing, but then she saw a little shadow that was moving quickly.

Mekos dipped Perus down so sharply that Aradella almost fell off. When they got closer to the ground, he let out a high-pitched call that she'd never heard before—at least not from a human.

Tanek heard it and looked up at his son. Mekos pointed and his father turned toward the village.

"Is that a—?" Aradella's eyes widened in fear. Hurrying down the path was a tabor, a small animal that could kill a bull. They were very dangerous creatures!

Tanek yelled, "Kaley!" then stepped out of the way of the animal.

"It will hurt her!" Aradella cried, but then she remembered Valona's lizard.

Kaley opened her arms and the fierce little creature leaped into them. They snuggled and caressed, both of them looking like they were crying.

"Your stepmother is strange," Aradella said.

"Said the princess to the fox," Mekos replied.

"I bet Kaley already has a story about us."

"I hope it has a happy ending." He'd meant it as a joke, but it was too real for them to laugh. "Let's go down and talk to my grandpapá. He'll know what to do now."

"I'm afraid of what they'll say," she said honestly.

He reached back and took her hand. "It will be all right. The worst is over now. We've escaped. We're free. There is nothing but good in front of us."

"I doubt that my aunt agrees with that," Aradella mumbled as the dragon headed toward land.

Everyone was waiting for them in the big, open courtyard, the ruins of the house curving around it. Aradella could see fresh signs of restoration and she wondered if that was what the swansmen were doing there.

Roal, who she hadn't seen since the swan show when she was young, was talking to Vian. Aradella was curious about her. She was Tanek's mother, but she was also an Empyrean. Those people were spoken of often, but rarely seen. There were rumors of what they looked like. The talk ranged from their being giants to having snakelike tails and two heads. The more beer that was drunk, the wilder were the descriptions.

But Vian looked like the women on Pithan, tall, handsome, slim.

Still holding the tabor, Kaley and her grandparents were standing in front of the silent flying machine. Kaley's parents were absent and she hadn't seen them at the wedding. But then, they hadn't seen each other in many years. *Is it waterfall time for them?* Aradella wondered as she smiled in happy memory.

Far from the others, Tanek and Mekos were in deep discussion about something. *Are they discussing what Mekos and I tried to do at the wedding? What we failed at?* Aradella asked herself. *Will I be forced to marry Nessa? Or can we find a place to hide—and for how long?* She knew the four islands that were under the control of the Empyreans, but the planet of Bellis had more islands, large and small. Were they also controlled by the Empyreans? Would she and Mekos be sent away to one of them? To forever live in exile?

As though he knew what she was thinking, Mekos gave her a smile of reassurance. Then Perus lowered his big head and nudged her. She put her arms around his head and her face against his cheek. "I know I've caused problems. But what was I to do? Marry Nessa? If I had, would everyone have been pleased? Except for Mekos and me, that is."

Perus nuzzled against her as she watched Roal go to Tanek and say something. Tanek nodded, then Mekos returned to Aradella.

"We're meeting in the egret room. My grandmamá wants to talk to the four of us."

She knew he was excluding Frank and Rita. "Is this going to be good or bad?"

"I have no idea. I don't know what she's like, but I hope she's going to thank us."

Aradella liked his positive attitude and hoped he was right.

They held hands as they walked through a hallway that was half destroyed. "Kaley wants to put this place back together," Mekos said in an attempt at small talk.

"It would be a big job," she murmured.

They stopped in a room that still had most of the ceiling. Through the missing part they could see a roofless, second-story room above. The walls were tiled with pictures of egrets. Their long legs and plumed heads were striking. Four chairs had been set in a row, and standing in front of them was Vian, with Roal a few steps behind her.

Aradella couldn't help being awestruck. Vian was one of the Seven, the rulers, the lawmakers. She was higher than all the kings and queens of the islands. And she was number one in the Order of Sight.

The only person who didn't look as though she was attending a funeral was Kaley.

"Your father is gorgeous," they heard her say to Tanek. "Think you'll grow up to look like him?"

That Tanek made no response to her joke took away her smile.

They sat down on the chairs, the two women in the center, with father and son on the ends.

Vian began to speak. "I can foresee the future. That this ability was detected early is why I look as I do and not as—" When no one seemed to understand what she was saying, she waved her hand in dismissal. "When I was young, I foresaw that evil people would overtake the islands. Male and female would be separated and they'd come to hate each other. It was a truly horrible sight. As I got older, I asked myself, 'Can this future be changed?' And if so, how could it be done? Gradually, I discovered that I could apply 'What if?' to my visions. If a person was given choices, how would that change the outcome? After much work and trying many, many different pathways, I foresaw that the bad *could* be changed."

She took a breath. "But, to my horror, I saw that to reach the good, it would take thirty-five years and great sacrifices would have to be made. Most shocking was that the biggest sacrifice would have to be made by *me*." She paused, seeming to look back in memory. "I foresaw that if I were impregnated by a ship's officer, a man I'd never even seen, we would produce two descendants who could change the future." She looked at Mekos, her eyes showing her sorrow at having missed sharing his life. "I also saw that it was imperative that *I* not be part of the lives of these children. If they had contact with the world I occupied, none of the good would happen. And if I removed myself from that world, it would not happen."

When she turned to Tanek, the sadness in her eyes deepened. "I worked on the details. I saw that in my son's early years he needed to spend time on Earth. He needed to meet people and learn things. And also, he was to talk to an unborn baby, as his words would greatly influence her life." She glanced at Kaley, then back at Mekos. "When my son returned to Bellis and while he was still quite young, he was to mate with a Lely."

Vian paused for a moment. "It was difficult for me to deal with the fact that I would be a grandmother before I could be part of their lives. But my vision showed me that if I made all the sacrifices, eventually, we would be a family. I would have a life with a man who, in just one splendid night, I would come to love completely and forever."

When she and Roal smiled at each other, it could be seen that their love—and yearning—was mutual.

Kaley looked at Tanek, silently asking if he knew about this. He gave an almost imperceptible shake of his head. No, he didn't know.

Vian paced a bit, then halted. "All those many years ago, I

decided that my sacrifice would be worth it, so I set about making it happen. My son grew up without me. I wasn't there to see my beautiful grandson tumbling about with the fox kits. When the Earth woman arrived, I had more decisions to make. For one, I had to figure out how they were to meet Zeon. He's like me, but with a weaker version of foresight. There were things they needed to find through him."

Kaley looked at Tanek. They knew she meant Haver's skeleton, and he had given them gifts of magic items.

Vian continued. "My family *had* to get that mask from Zeon. That I was forced to risk my beloved grandson's life to obtain it made me ill, but, as always, I focused on the results." She didn't look at her son, knowing that Tanek's face would show his anger.

She paused, and when she drew in her breath, her face changed to what was unmistakably anger, but she kept her voice under control. "The end of my years of sacrifice was to be that Mekos would wear the mask and marry Princess Aradella. My grandson would be king! Evil Olina and Urah would know that the end had come, and they'd flee in terror. And finally, Roal and I could have a life together."

Vian paused for a long moment and a fire seemed to ignite in her dark eyes. "But that didn't happen." Her teeth were clasped together. "Do you know who destroyed my thirty-five years of work?"

The faces of the four showed they had no idea. Aradella and Mekos could be married now, couldn't they?

Vian looked at them slowly, one by one. But when she got to Mekos, she stopped. "Tell them what you did."

Tanek and Kaley bent forward to look at Mekos and Aradella, but they didn't return the gaze.

"My mother told me you did something," Kaley said as she looked at Mekos. "It had to do with that lizard, didn't it? This time, please don't lie." She put her hand on her necklace. "Lies *hurt*."

Tanek looked at his wife. "Your parents are not here. Where are they?"

"Probably in a waterfall," Mekos muttered. "Seems to be a family trait."

Aradella snickered.

His smart-aleck remark didn't have the effect he meant it to. Everyone in the room turned sharply and looked at him, waiting for him to do as his grandmother said and "tell them."

But Mekos and Aradella were silent, their lips tight, their eyes straight ahead.

When Vian spoke again, her voice was so calm it was scary. It made them remember that this woman, as one of the Seven, had the power to give or take life. "Tell me, do you remember the guide Valona assigned to you?"

She waited for an answer, but there was none. "You two, with your I-know-everything attitude, were so contemptuous of that woman that you never even learned her name." She glared at Aradella. "I believe you threatened her."

Aradella kept looking straight ahead.

Vian looked at her grandson. "After what you two did to her beloved Valona, she went to Urah and demanded to be heard. She told Urah and her vicious daughter how you used that mask to dupe Valona. You used it *before* you were supposed to show that you had it! It didn't take Urah much thought to figure out what you two planned for the wedding. They were ready for your clumsy little play!"

"But I kept the mask locked up," Kaley said. "I have the only key. How could they . . . ?" She trailed off.

Vian glared at the two young people. "They stole the mask. They found a Never who seemed to be part snake. He can slide inside locks! A mask, a pretty knife, even a picture on the wall, they took them all." She glared at her grandson. "Tell your parents what you two did with those things."

"We—" Mekos began.

"It was me!" Aradella said loudly. "All of this is my fault. I—"

"No!" Mekos said. "I was the one who breathed the gas. I should have protected you and Ian and—"

Vian put up her hand for silence, then looked at Tanek. "Your son stole a knife out of Valona's house, then he put the mask on so he looked like his royal girlfriend. When Valona was about to kill who she thought was the princess, Aradella arrived on a wolf and stabbed Valona. *To death!*"

"She rode on a wolf?" Kaley whispered in awe.

Mekos straightened his shoulders, looking defiant. "What would have happened if Aradella and I had *not* stopped her?"

Vian narrowed her eyes at him. "What I foresaw was that the princess was to be on the altar, then *you* were to sweep her away to safety. Valona would have been enraged, but she would fear exposure too much to run after you. Your marriage in front of all those armed men—who I worked hard to get there—would have sent Urah and her daughter running to hide at the Lair. Then those three spiteful, arrogant women would have killed one another in a battle of jealousy. It was a perfect plan that took *thirty-five years to set up*!" She shouted the last.

Looking like she was trying to swallow her anger, she turned to Tanek. "Valona's death has increased the power of Olina and her mother. Right now, the people are occupied with the idea of domestic bliss—as was planned. However, without a young king-to-be as a leader, they'll have no desire to overthrow a queen. This will give Urah enough time to create enchantments to subdue the people. She'll fill the water, the very air, with her evil concoctions." Vian looked at Aradella. "I foresee that they'll find the princess wherever she hides. She'll be told that she'll either marry that simpering Nessa or the people she has come to love will be killed. Urah's plan—which will happen when she gains control of the men—is to take over King Aramus's island."

Vian lowered her voice. "My vision also shows that the princess will sacrifice herself in an attempt to save everyone. But it won't work. The truth is that no matter what Aradella does, she and my grandson won't be allowed to live long—nor will the people who have helped them." She looked at Kaley. "Urah hates you for killing her sister at that cake house. Her revenge plan of eradicating you and your family will be successful." She turned to Tanek. "*You* won't live long enough to unite the people. You won't get to Empyrea. You won't . . ." Suddenly, it was as though all energy left Vian. Her eyes rolled back into her head and her knees bent.

Roal caught her in his arms, then soared with her up through the hole in the ceiling and out of sight.

Tanek turned to Kaley. "We need to get the princess out of here. Now."

Kaley was feeling the effects of Vian's words. It was like she'd been stamped on by a herd of wild horses. "Mekos . . . Aradella . . . You . . . All of us . . ." she whispered.

Tanek grabbed her by the shoulders. "Don't give up on me now. Do you know who Ian is?"

Kaley was staring at him. "Didn't you hear what she said? We can't—"

"We have more important matters to deal with. I need to find Sojee." When he looked at Kaley's face, he bent, his nose almost touching hers. "If everything can be turned in a different direction by a single act, it can be turned the other way by another. We just have to figure out how to do it." He straightened and looked at Mekos and Aradella. They were on the far side of the room, their heads together, and talking intensely. "We'll take her to the top of the mountain where you hid, then Papá and I will try to figure out what to do next."

Kaley looked as horrified as she felt. "I do *not* like being *inside* a fairy tale."

"Neither do we." Tanek kissed her forehead then hurried out of the room.

# 11

Aradella woke when she felt Mekos's breath on her cheek. She partially opened her eyes, afraid that even the slight movement would wake the people around them.

They were in a beautiful stone pavilion that was at the top of the mountain above the Beyhan Homestead on Selkan. Earlier, they'd gone through the old village and up the gravel path to the top. Aradella and Mekos were in front, with Tanek, Kaley, and Sojee behind them.

It was a solemn group. The words, *What do we do now?* seemed to hover over them.

With every step, Aradella felt worse. *This is all my fault*, she thought. *If I'd married Nessa, everyone would be safe now. Or if I'd not killed Valona.*

When they came to a break in the neglected path, Mekos took her hand and helped her across. He didn't let go of her hand. He gave her a look that was meant to cheer her up, but that was impossible.

The top of the mountain was extraordinarily beautiful. There was a lake with elegant white swans, and as soon as the birds saw Tanek, they came forward. He walked into the water, fully clothed, and dove under them.

Kaley stood on the shore and watched. They all understood that he needed to be with the birds.

Sojee was at the side, also watching. His usual cheerful demeanor was gone.

At the back was the long stone pavilion with massive stone chairs with arms carved into the shape of swans. Sojee easily moved them, putting two on each side as though he was forming a cage. He put down a blanket filled with swan feathers in the middle. When he stepped back, he looked at Aradella. It was to be her bed. He didn't say so, but Mekos was to be with her as protection.

In the grass, more blankets were spread. Tanek, Kaley, and Sojee were to use them. Lurking near the lake was the tabor. They all formed a barrier around Aradella.

They shared a sparse meal of bread and cheese, with no conversation. Everyone was thinking of what could be done.

When Aradella went up the steps to her bed cover, she thought she'd never sleep, but she did, and she didn't wake until she felt Mekos's breath. As she looked into his eyes, she knew he meant for her to go somewhere with him.

Of course he'd have to take her. As a human, she was much too noisy to slip past the people and animals who were guarding her. And too, Tanek had said that if there was danger, the swans would warn them.

Kaley had muttered something about an "infrared heat search" and "a bomb squad" but at a look from Tanek, she said no more.

Aradella put her arms up and Mekos held her. Silently, they soared across the grass, over part of the lake, then landed beside a swamp.

When she was on the ground, she waited for him to speak. The moonlight was bright but even if it had been full dark, she would have felt his seriousness.

"In the morning, Papá will take you to my mother. She'll keep you safe. The kits will love you."

She knew she was being dismissed and it wasn't easy not to be sarcastic. *Sounds like fun!* she could say. Instead, she said, "Where are you going?"

"To meet Zeon. He's also in the Order of Sight. Maybe he'll have some ideas about how to solve this."

"I'm going with you."

"No, you are not." He sounded like his father issuing a command. "You're going to my mother."

"That's a good idea," she said cheerfully. "I'll get that gray wolf to give me a ride to Zeon. I hope nothing bad happens to me since I'll be *alone*. With no protection from anyone."

"You can *not*—" He broke off. "You will *not*—" Again, he stopped. His eyes were pleading. "Please. I want to know that you're safe."

She looked out at the water. There were tall reeds around them and she could see what looked to be a nest. "I hope you know that *you* are being blamed for all of this. My father said that if something goes wrong and both a man and woman are involved, it is *always* the man's fault. I guess you should have known better than to kill an evil woman who was murdering pretty girls to make them into face cream. Shame on you!"

He gave her a sad look, but there was a tiny bit of a smile under it. "It was you who did the stabbing."

"Men would probably say my nail file slipped."

He did smile and with it came a break in his stoicism. "How am I supposed to fix this?" Frustration filled his voice. "I have ruined lives! I should have asked Papá—"

She cut him off. "Let's do what you said and go to Zeon. He's number two in the Order of Sight, so maybe if he helps repair the damage of this huge problem, he could be pushed up to number one. Is he ambitious?"

"I have no idea."

She went to tiptoe and kissed him. "We're in this together so let's go find out. Can you call Perus?"

"Yes." He groaned. "Arit. She'll follow us then return and tell Papá where we are."

Aradella thought for a moment. "Jobi gave me a book about fairies. That's what earthlings call Nevers. It will occupy her."

"I can't see Arit reading a book that's bigger than she is."

"The book says fairies lay eggs and make dresses out of flower petals." She paused for drama. "It says that fairies can't really talk, that they just make squeaky little sounds."

Mekos gave a snort of disbelief. "That will outrage Arit so much that she'll go to Earth to set people straight. Yes, a book like that might keep her busy." He pulled Aradella into his arms and held her. "Thank you. You've made me feel better."

She held on to him. She wasn't going to tell him that *she* didn't feel any better. But her mother had said that building a man's sense of self was part of a woman's job.

"Maybe Zeon has a magic spell that can send us away."

Aradella didn't smile at that. She didn't want him to have to leave his family because of her. "I should have—"

He kissed her. "Don't finish that. Are you ready to go?"

She blinked a few times in surprise. *Now?* She nodded. Yes, she was ready.

Mekos gave a low whistle.

"Your father will hear that!"

"He has human ears. He'll hear nothing." In the next second, big beautiful Perus landed beside the reeds. One of the swans almost made a sound, but Mekos said, "Quiet!" and the bird silenced.

"I wish I had some magical power," she said as he got into the saddle.

"What would you like?" He pulled her up to sit behind him.

She was feeling too much fear to dare say anything serious. "Great beauty. Like my cousins. Then I could command anyone to do anything and they'd say, 'Oh yes, please may I do that for the beautiful, stunning, gorgeous lady that you are?'"

Smiling, Mekos nudged the dragon forward and they left the ground.

When Kaley turned over, she saw that Tanek was awake and staring at the moonlit sky.

"Mekos is leaving," he said.

She listened but heard nothing. "You're sure?"

"With a child who is a quarter fox, I had to learn to hear him even when he made no sound."

Kaley started to get up, but he caught her arm.

"This is something he has to do on his own. A very heavy burden has been put on him."

"They killed Valona on their own and that was a mistake," she said. "They should have come to us."

"It's what you and I did. We killed your gingerbread witch."

"But they did it on a much bigger scale." She pulled back to look at him. "You're proud of him."

"When I see my son becoming a *man*? Yes, I am very proud."

She snuggled in his arms and they were silent for a moment. "I have a confession to make. I thought maybe *you* might sneak away, so I put that box of magic items that Garen gave me in Perus's saddle."

"You mean the box that you *stole*?"

"Tomato, tomahto." She shrugged.

"More Earth humor." He could tell that she was worried and he wanted to distract her—and himself. "I was thinking that we should tear this whole place down and start fresh. We'll take everything to the ground. Flatten it all."

"What?!" she said too loudly, then quieted. "That's a horrible idea."

"Is it? Tell me why."

Not far from them, Sojee smiled. He was glad that his three children were daughters. Girls tended to stay where he could keep an eye on them. Well, maybe not his eldest, but that was a different matter. At least Shay and Bree were safely tucked away, their minds full of dresses and who their father would choose to be their husbands. Sojee had a couple of good men picked out. Solid, reliable, prosperous. He knew there was a "problem" with Bree since she could probably beat any of them at arm wrestling, but a wise and patient man could overlook that.

Smiling, he rolled over and went back to sleep.

"Do you know the way?" Aradella asked as soon as they were out of sight of the Homestead. They were still over Selkan and heading north.

"Kaley told me about it, including how to get there."

"The Great Storyteller." She looked ahead. "What is that?" It looked like fog but it was so dense it appeared to be solid.

"The Mist."

She could feel his heart beat faster, as though he sensed danger. "Do we go through it?"

"Sometimes it's easy to get through, but sometimes it's a stone wall."

"Can we go above it?"

"That's what I'm going to try to do. Hold on."

She clutched him hard as Perus went straight up. It took all her leg muscles to stay on. It was cowardly of her, but she closed her eyes, too afraid to watch. It seemed as though it would go on forever, but suddenly, they leveled out. She opened her eyes and looked behind them. They were past the Mist and gently going down.

"That was the best!" Mekos said. "Didn't you think so?"

"Delightful," she murmured. "Look at that! Are they real?"

Below them were farms but they were too perfect to be genuine. At home, farms were full of manure, piles of rubbish, and burned areas. But these were perfect, green and fertile. The houses were immaculate and the people were like moving statues.

"Kaley's mother said they're called Obeyers. They're under

some enchantment and they'll do anything you tell them to do. Papá said it was the scariest place he'd ever been."

"Worse than you being tied up and held by some Cutters?" She was referring to when Mekos had been kidnapped.

"I had that under control," Mekos said.

"I'm glad I don't have on the Truth Necklace. It would burn through my bones."

He laughed.

They passed a small house in the woods. "That's where Kaley met with Garen. She has a whole box of magic things from him." As they flew, the land rose higher, with mountains surrounding them. Mekos pointed to what looked like dark holes in the sides of the rock. "My great-grandfather . . ." He didn't finish, but she knew. He'd told her that the skeleton of the famous hero, Haver, had been found in one of those caves.

Finally, they saw a long building. It seemed to wander through the woodland, peeping out here and there. A pointed roof could be seen, then a pretty balcony. There were tall windows and short ones, all with a stone façade.

"It looks like the pictures in Kaley's books."

"She called it 'a storybook castle.'" Mekos reined Perus to the side and he easily settled on the ground. Before them were double doors that opened and two men came out. They wore big trousers and short jackets that glistened with gold embroidery. They were beautiful men!

"Wonder if you could borrow one of those uniforms," Aradella murmured suggestively.

"And here I thought you liked wolves."

She smiled sweetly at him.

The men didn't speak but led them down an ornate hallway to a big room with guards at the corners. The ceiling was painted with pictures of men and women in a garden. The walls were covered with gold-embossed carvings.

"Beats our old palace," Aradella said. "Although, we've heard that Olina has a room covered in jewels."

"All of them stolen, I'm sure." Mekos lifted his head and his nose twitched. "Food."

Aradella had to hurry to keep up with him as he went to the end of the big room. A guard opened a door to a smaller, cozy room that had a table laden with hot food. There were no guards stationed around the walls.

Mekos didn't hesitate in picking up a delicate porcelain plate and filling it.

Aradella stood back, looking at a door at the far end. She wasn't surprised when it opened. In came a man who she instinctively knew was in charge of the place. He had an air of importance and knowledge about him. She sensed that he'd expected them. The question was whether or not he could help them.

"My lady," the man said and gave her a bow from the waist. "I am Zeon and I am at your service."

His courtesy was flattering, especially since she had on clothes meant for skulking about at night. Reaver clothes. She did her best to put on her princess pose. "How do you do? I'm Aradella and this is—"

"Son of Tanek," Mekos said. "As Arit calls me. I believe you've met her. Did she drink your beer cellar dry?"

Zeon smiled. "Nearly. She certainly had all my guards doing her bidding."

When the two men laughed, Aradella felt a wave of pride. Her aunt had disparaged Mekos's family as being uncouth, lowly swansmen, but Mekos was charming—and he was not intimidated by a man who owned a place like this.

Zeon gestured toward the table. "Please help yourselves. If there is any other food you'd like, let me know."

"This is quite lovely." She picked up a plate and began to fill it. "I take it you know why we're here."

"Yes," Zeon said. "I've had some significant revelations in the last hours."

"From Grandmamá?" Mekos asked as he sat down.

"Yes," Zeon said. "Right now, she is . . ." He didn't seem to want to finish his sentence.

"Losing her mind?" Aradella sat across from Mekos.

"Thinking about flying to a mountaintop and never returning?" Mekos asked.

Aradella took a bite, then held out her fork, looking at Mekos. "It's your family, so maybe they've found a waterfall."

"So now *you* don't like waterfalls?"

Smiling, Aradella looked back at Zeon. "I apologize. Our current situation is more than we can comprehend, but we're doing our best to deal with it. Have you foreseen a solution?"

"Yes."

Aradella put down her fork but Mekos kept eating. She waited for Zeon to tell what he knew.

"Have you heard of the island of Abicis?"

The two young people shook their heads no and waited for him to continue.

"I think you need to go there. The Empyreans are . . ."

When he couldn't find the words he needed, Mekos said, "You mean the rulers? The people who have declared they will Right the Ancient Wrongs—as they call it? All done while they continue to honor traditions? But if we don't agree with them, they will bomb our homes and kill the people who stand against them?" His voice was rising, getting deeper. "They call themselves the Peacekeepers." He nearly spit the last.

Zeon was wide-eyed. "You sound like Haver," he said softly. "You *look* like him."

Mekos was trying to regain his composure. He pushed his hair back. "I'm flattered, but with these ears, I don't think so."

Zeon began to blink rapidly as a sight came to him. "You want to see Haver's cave."

"I do," Mekos said.

"His body is no longer there, but the room has been left untouched. I can send a guide with you today."

"And afterward, we're to go to the island you mentioned?"

Aradella didn't wait for him to answer. "What's it like? Why do you seem to be afraid of it?"

Zeon gave his attention to her, looking pleasantly surprised. "You're right, I am afraid of it. In my visions, I saw that your senses had been keenly developed from living under Olina's rule." He seemed proud of her.

"I have managed to stay alive," she said modestly.

"In your circumstances, that is a monumental feat." His eyes narrowed. "This mission carries the possibility of a death."

"Death is always around me." Aradella sounded uninterested in his revelation.

"She's lived most of her life under threat," Mekos said solemnly.

"Tell us about the island," she said. "Do we need weapons? Kaley has an Earth gun. We could—"

"No, no," Zeon said. "Abicis isn't like that. It's full of people who don't fit in."

"Fit in what?" Mekos asked.

"They don't belong with the Empyreans, so they're sent to Abicis. They're misfits."

"You mean criminals?" Aradella asked.

"No, not at all. Or at least not too many of them are. But they are different. Unusual. They're not like the other Empyreans."

"Have you been to this island?" Mekos asked.

"No." He grimaced. "My foresight isn't as clear as your grandmother's. I believe she has the ability to propose different possibilities of action. I cannot. I can foresee what will probably happen, but that future can be changed."

Aradella and Mekos glanced at each other. "We know that too well," Aradella said. "Are you being blocked from that power or was it not born in you?"

Zeon smiled. "That's the question I'd like answered. I think I'm being held back. Or maybe it's my vanity that hopes so. Whatever the cause, I'd like a stronger power of foresight." He pointedly looked at Mekos, as though saying, *Tell your grandmother.*

The door opened, a guard entered, gave a curt nod to Zeon, then left. He turned back to them. "The horses are ready to take you to the cave if you'd like to go now." They nodded yes. "But first, I have a gift for you. A bit of magic."

To Zeon's astonishment, Aradella whispered, "Oh no!" and Mekos gasped as though in terror.

"Sorry," she said. "The mask you gave Kaley and Tanek caused us some problems. Big ones."

Zeon raised an eyebrow. "Did it? I'll have to look into that. But this gift is something you'll need. I can't see clearly enough to know the details—" there was bitterness in his voice "—but I do know that it's necessary." On a table by the wall was a cloth bag made of worn-out tapestry. It certainly didn't look like anything special. Zeon held the bag up. "This holds a lot."

"That's nice." Aradella tried to sound interested, but the bag didn't stir any emotions.

Zeon picked up four metal goblets and dropped them into the bag. It stayed flat. He put in a serving plate, a set of cutlery, then a vase of flowers. The bag didn't expand. He put in a silver tray that was too big and too heavy to go into the bag, but it slid inside, and showed nothing on the exterior.

With an unexpected movement, he tossed the bag to Aradella. She almost sidestepped to miss it as it was bound to be heavy, but she did catch it. It was flat and light.

"Go on," Zeon said, "open it."

One by one, she pulled out the items he'd put in there and set them on the table. She looked at him. "This is the fantasy of every woman who has ever been born."

Zeon laughed. "You're to fill it with plants. I foresaw that you're going to need them. It takes only a sprig of each one, but you're to collect as many different types of plants as you can find. And . . ." His eyes seemed to go blank, as though he was seeing something inside his mind. "And small stones," he said softly. "There will be a need for some very odd things." With a shake of his head, he came back to them. "Sorry. I can't see much more. But take the bag and fill it."

"I can get some plants on the way up the mountain," she said.

"And a bone," Zeon said sharply. "'The bone of a righteous man.' I can hear that." He shook his head, as though coming back to reality. "I'm keeping you here too long. It's a pretty day and you should go out. There was a storm when your parents were here, and they nearly froze to death. I had to go get them. If you'll come with me, I'll give you a map and tell you how to open the hidden door." His face softened and his eyes lit up. "When you return, I have a surprise for you. It's something very good." He looked pointedly at Aradella. "You, especially, will be glad of this. At dinner, I'll tell you about whatever I foresee this afternoon, then early tomorrow, the lot of you can go to Abicis."

"The lot of us?" Mekos said. "How many are there?"

"Only as many as necessary. The arrival of too many people would arouse suspicion." They could see that he was enjoying being secretive.

Mekos took the bag from Aradella and put in bread, cheese, sliced meats, and two bottles of wine. When he held up the bag, it still appeared to be empty. "Can I put a person in it?"

Aradella squinted her eyes at him. "So you can leave me here? Oh no you don't!" She took the bag from him, and turned to Zeon. "Thank you. You've given us hope."

He looked over her to Mekos and his eyes grew serious. "Maybe someday you can introduce me to your grandmother. I should very much like to talk to her."

"Gladly." Mekos turned away and raised his eyebrows at Aradella. It appeared that Zeon was indeed ambitious.

Zeon watched the two young people fly away on their green dragon, then he went back inside to work. What he really wanted to look into was finally being allowed to see that Vian, an Empyrean and one of the Seven no less, was number one of his order. But that information would have to wait. To clear his mind, he thought of the joy he was going to bring to Mekos and Aradella when they saw what he'd done. It hadn't been easy!

When he'd first seen the vison of what could happen, he'd groaned. To make it come about, he knew he'd have to contact Reena. She was a very independent person and it was hard to persuade her to do things. He reminded himself that she didn't like being called a witch, even if she was one. He knew that when she was five years old, she'd turned a playmate she didn't like into a toad. It had taken a lot of threats to get her to change the girl back into a human.

Even though Reena was an adult now, her attitude hadn't changed. She'd embedded the compulsory chip—the device Empyreans required to be implanted in everyone—into her big gray dog instead. When Zeon tried to reach Reena, the dog had been out chasing rabbits. Zeon had seen into that rabbit's future. It would escape the dog and produce more offspring. A *lot* more!

Finally, he'd reached Reena and told her what he needed. She'd been suspicious—and very protective.

Zeon had talked fast and persuasively and, at last, she'd agreed. But she'd made it clear that she didn't like doing what he needed.

"You couldn't use the other one?" she'd asked. "They're twins."

"Ah, so that's why I kept getting a blurred vision. It's the younger one I need. The one connected to *you*."

Reena grimaced. "All right, I'll send her, but you better not let her be harmed."

"I don't think she will be," Zeon said honestly. "How soon can she get here?"

"I'll send her on one of Olina's birds."

Zeon raised his eyebrows. He knew she meant one of the huge creatures that had the head of an eagle and a four-legged body of some unknown Earth animal. "Good," he replied. "I look forward to meeting her, and I'm sure Aradella will be very happy to see her."

Reena seemed to be suppressing a smile. "I'm sure she will be. They've spent their whole lives together." Abruptly, she cut off the connection in a way that made it seem like she was afraid she'd say something she shouldn't.

Now Zeon was smiling. Aradella's cousin, the beautiful Princess Bree, had arrived an hour ago. She was going with Aradella and Mekos to Abicis.

# 12

# PRINCESS BREE VARLON

## SOJEE'S YOUNGEST DAUGHTER

Bree was sitting on a stone bench in the most beautiful garden she'd ever seen. She knew she should be wandering down the pathways, inhaling the fragrance of the flowers, and admiring the sculptures. Enjoying herself.

Most of all, she should be reveling in her freedom. Here she didn't have to sneak around, didn't have to hide.

But right now, death looked better than what she was facing. She glanced skyward. "What horrible thing have I done to deserve this?" she asked. "Who have I angered that I'd get such punishment?"

Of course there was no answer. Her lips tightened. Oh, how Reena had talked! It was still hard to believe that her friend, her mentor, the person she trusted second only to her father, had betrayed her.

Reena, annoyingly speaking through the chip she'd embedded in her dog's hind quarters, had told Bree to pack a bag as she was going on a trip. She was to take the dark clothes she wore when slipping out at night to go to Reena's house, but she was also to pack some dresses that were exquisitely beautiful. "I want you to look your best," Reena said.

Bree had done as she was told, then made the familiar walk to Reena's house. She usually did it at night so it was nice to go in the daylight.

The island, now full of men, had a different feel to it. It seemed to vibrate with new energy. But she knew the cause was more than just the presence of men. After Aradella had fled her own ceremony, leaving the wimpy, sulking Nessa standing by himself, everything happened so fast that it took people a while to realize what had occurred.

Bree hadn't been surprised by Aradella's escape, certainly hadn't been shocked by it. She'd known Aradella all her life and her cousin *always* found a way to get what she wanted. Even being imprisoned by the evil Olina hadn't kept Aradella under control.

Throughout Bree's life, looking after Aradella had been one of the many secrets she and her father kept. Her sister, Shay, hadn't known what was going on, but then, keeping a secret was not something Shay could do.

One of the things Bree and her father did was get the books that were sent to Aradella past the guards. They were Earth books sent by Jobi, then later, someone from the Order of Swans began sending them. There were crude attempts to hide them under pastries, but they were easily found. Sojee, as head of security, had prevented the forbidden books from being confiscated then sent to Olina. It hadn't been easy. More than once, Bree had hidden the books under her clothes.

Aradella never knew she'd nearly caused Sojee and Bree to be subjected to one of Queen Olina's "punishments," meaning torture, if not death.

For all that there was a deep bond between Bree and her father, he didn't know his daughter spent a lot of time with Reena. But then, Reena was one of the four witches who had great power. Her oldest sister was the evil Urah, Olina's nasty, hate-filled mother. Another sister, deceased, was Garen's mother. It was said that two of the sisters were for good and two for evil. Reena worked hard to be known as one of the good ones. But still, fathers didn't want their daughters working for a witch. So Reena had put a spell—number 1A72—around Bree so no one would know where she went at night. No pure human knew, that is. People born with magical powers might know, but there were few of them.

When Bree was told to get ready to leave, she'd been excited. *Is this it?* she wondered. Years ago, Reena had conjured a "future spell," as she called it, to see where Bree's life would lead. When the spell showed itself, Bree remembered the shocked look on Reena's beautiful face. But she'd quickly changed to her usual air of giving nothing away. "You will find a man you love." She hesitated. "And he will love you desperately. Yes, I think that's the right word. Desperate."

"Have I already met him?" Bree asked but Reena didn't answer.

While Bree packed, she thought of Reena's words, and thought that this might be it. Maybe she was to meet "him."

Her sister had already had three proposals of marriage, but then she was brilliant at flirting. Oh, how Shay *loved* the back-and-forth dance of teasing that she did with men! "I'll have to ask my father," she would say demurely, coyly hinting to each man that her answer would be positive.

For all that they were twins, the sisters were very different. This had greatly bothered Bree when she was a child. One time, after an incident at school, her father had held her while she cried. "I'm not like my sister," Bree said.

"No, you're not," Sojee replied. "And your life will be different. Shay will marry some wimp of a man and have twelve children. All of them will depend on her for everything, and she'll rule the household."

"What about my life?"

"You're harder to know. I can't see you with a man you can boss around. What you need is a man who isn't afraid of you."

The word *afraid* made her cry harder. "I picked up the wagon off that boy. He didn't even thank me. I think he was angry at me."

Sojee hugged her. "I know. The truth is, I think you should keep all of this between you and me. Hide it. It would make your sister jealous and it will scare the skin off of most men. And the women will shun you."

"That's not fair," she'd whispered.

"No, it's not, but then, living on this island with so few men isn't fair to anyone. We have to adjust to what *is*."

When Bree got to Reena's house, she saw one of the queen's great beasts waiting for her. She didn't like the look in the creature's eyes. She began to protest but Reena didn't listen. Nor did she answer any questions of where and why. She told Bree to get in the saddle and that she'd contact her soon. Hours later, right after Bree had flown up and over a creepy-looking fog, Reena contacted her on the screen from the chip in Bree's arm.

"After you meet Zeon, you're to go to an island called Abicis," Reena said. "I've never heard of it and I can't find anyone who has been there."

Bree had been told of Zeon and knew he had the ability to foresee the future. It wasn't easy to talk while sitting on the back of a great creature that was flying through the air. "Why? What am I to do there?"

"I have no idea, but Zeon said you *must* go with them."

"With who?"

Reena hesitated—which was out of character for her. She usually had a quick reply for every question. Finally, she said, "With Tanek's son, Mekos."

Bree was startled. "I thought he and Aradella were together."

"Yes," was all Reena replied.

The animal Bree was straddling made a dip, then smoothed

out. Below them were farms of mind-boggling perfection. "So he's leaving her behind. I understand *that*! Aradella is impossible to even tolerate. Her words cut and slash—but she never repairs the damage she causes. I'm glad Mekos found out early."

Through this tirade, Reena was silent, but she was staring at Bree as though she was sending her a message.

"Why are you looking at me like that? Does Mekos need my help?" She gasped. "Is *he* the man I'm to . . . to . . ." She couldn't say the words.

"He won't be alone," Reena murmured.

The creature tipped to one side and Bree held on. "Do I know the person with him?" When Reena didn't answer, Bree finally understood. "No," she said calmly. "Not her. I will go with a murderer, *three* murderers, before I go anywhere with Aradella. I'd rather go with Olina or Urah. I'll face beasts and monsters. I'll—"

"Must go," Reena said cheerfully. "Be safe." The screen disappeared back into Bree's chip.

Bree didn't hesitate. "We're going back," she said to the bird-beast. She pulled on the reins for it to turn, but it kept going straight ahead. "No!" she yelled. "We must return."

When it didn't obey, she leaned forward and put her arms around the neck of the animal and began to squeeze. When the creature started to choke but still didn't change its course, she relented and let go.

"Did Reena put you under a spell?" she demanded. "How did she find the right spell without *me*?" She grit her teeth. "I'm going to mix up something so Reena will never recover. I'll get Urah to ignite it. I know! I'll make Reena ugly. I'll . . ." Bree stopped talking. It was hitting her that this was actually going to happen. Her most dreaded, feared nightmare was coming true. She was going on a trip with Aradella.

Bree had had a lifetime of the horror of dealing with her cousin. No matter what the twins did, Aradella was contemptuous, arrogant, and condescending. Her motto seemed to be

*I am smart and you are stupid.* When they were nice to Aradella, she looked at them with contempt. Talk to her, and Aradella curled her upper lip and didn't reply. Even if they said nothing, Aradella still managed to let them know that she was superior in every way.

Neither Bree nor Shay had ever done anything that pleased Aradella.

Sometimes, Bree got so frustrated that she was tempted to tell her cousin what she knew. There was more besides the illegal Earth books that Bree help deliver to her cousin. At night, Bree and her father often went out together to do some heavy lifting. More than once, they'd flattened themselves behind rocks and watched Aradella and her guard, Hale, practicing with swords.

"Why does she pretend to be so much larger than she is?" Bree had asked the first time.

"To protect her life." Sojee had masses of sympathy for Aradella's circumstances.

Through it all, Shay knew nothing. Bree had heard the term *girly-girl* and that was Shay. Hair and clothes were the highlights of her life. Bree just ordered a copy of whatever garment Shay chose and had it made in blue. It was an easy solution to something that held little interest for her.

When the animal finally slowed down, she saw a long house that was nearly hidden in a dense forest. Bree grimaced. "Just what Aradella wants—to never be near anyone because she's smarter than everybody."

When the animal landed in a big courtyard, she slid off its back. "I guess I should thank you but you're a traitor and I don't want to be here." The bird-head of the creature seemed to smile as it gave a shake and her bag fell to the ground. "I'll get Tanek to tell the top half of you off. Then you'll be sorry."

With a quick bow, the animal rose up and was soon out of sight.

Standing by a set of double doors was a very handsome young man. She was tempted to offer him one of the sapphires she'd brought if he'd get her a horse and point her toward the nearest town. Or to anywhere else on the planet for that matter.

"Zeon is occupied," the man said. "You may wait inside or in the garden."

"Garden," she said quickly. Maybe she could start walking down the mountain. "Are they . . . ?" She waved her hand. "Are the others here?"

"The guests are away. They will return for dinner."

*Hours*, she thought. *I only have a few hours before my life is over forever.*

So now she was sitting in the garden and all she could think about was how to get away from the beautiful place.

She saw a movement of something half hidden by the greenery. It was probably an animal and she paid no attention to it. Her mind was fully occupied with the coming horror of spending time with Aradella.

*No matter what she says, I won't react*, she thought. *She can sneer at me, insinuate that I have no brain, that I know nothing, that I—* She leaned forward. Coming toward her wasn't an animal but a child.

On Pithan, children were so precious that they were never without an adult nearby. But no one was near this one.

It was a boy, about three years old. He had on trousers with a long, embroidered robe that reached to his knees. His black hair was pulled back into a braid. He was so cute that Bree thought her heart might melt.

When the child got closer, he looked up and saw her. He was so startled that he froze in place.

In the next second, several things happened at once. A little animal that Bree had never seen before ran out of a flower bed, and behind it came a big, burly creature, like a bear with dog legs. The boy started laughing.

The sound so enchanted Bree that it took her a moment to see what was happening. The big animal had bumped into a stone statue of a woman pouring water out of a pitcher. It had been dislodged and was now rocking back and forth.

The little boy was standing still and watching the animals roll about together. He was in the direct path of the falling statue!

Bree jumped up, leaped the few feet to the statue, and caught it just before it landed on the child.

When a man shouted in warning, the child looked back, then ran to him and was picked up. He was a tall, handsome young man, his body thick with muscle. He and the child looked very much alike.

"Thank you." The man's voice was full of emotion.

Bree was holding the statue like it was an infant.

He put the boy down. "Here, let me help you with that." He went to Bree, slid his arms under the statue, and took it from her. But it was too heavy for him to hold. When he dropped it, the head broke off and rolled away. He looked at Bree in shock.

"Sorry," she murmured. "I tried to save it."

He was blinking at her in astonishment. "I couldn't hold that thing. It was too heavy. For me, anyway."

Bree could feel her face turning red. "My father . . ." she mumbled. "I'm like him."

The little boy was clutching the man's leg. "Tell this lady thank you for saving your life."

The child looked shy, but then he put his arms out for Bree to pick him up.

"I usually warn people that he's heavy, but you . . ." He didn't finish.

As Bree held the boy, he snuggled his face into her neck.

"He likes you," the man said. "I'm Tam, Zeon's son, and this is my son Pilkellan, Piks for short. Are you the princess?"

"I'm Bree, and I'm one of them." She loved feeling the child in her arms. "The important princess isn't here right now."

"You look important to me," he said. "Have you seen the garden? It's the pride of my father." He held out his arms, Piks went to him, and Tam set him down. "Go home to Mamá and stay away from those two creatures."

The child nodded but from the look in his eyes, he didn't plan to obey. They watched him walk away.

"My wife is carrying our second child and Piks drives her crazy. We never know where he is." Tam looked at Bree. "Again, thank you for this." He gestured to the fallen statue. "I don't want to think what would have happened if you hadn't been here and if you weren't . . . uh, like your father."

"Could you not mention this to anyone? My father and I work hard to keep it secret that I'm like him. Of course he's much stronger than I am, but still . . ."

Tam's eyes sparkled. "I know about hiding talents. Before I married my wife, I had no idea that she's very smart. I thought *I* would be the leader and I would wisely make all the decisions."

Bree gave a one-sided smile. "That's different from a wife who can pick up the man and toss him across the room."

"But that would be one exciting wedding night!"

They both laughed and she was pleased that he didn't make her feel like a freak. He indicated the garden and they began walking.

"I don't mean to be rude," he said, "but why are you here?"

"I'm not sure. I've been told that I'm to go to an island called Abby. Something like that."

"Never heard of it." His head came up. "Could it be Abicis?"

"Yes! That's it."

"Ah," Tam said. "I assume this has to do with what we were told happened on Olina's island."

"She'd like to think she owns it, but she—" Bree broke off. "I guess she does. My cousin Aradella was supposed to be clasped with one of the new royals, but she refused. I don't know what's going on. I was told I *must* come here and I *must* go to some island no one has heard of. Do *you* know anything about this?"

"My father loves to keep secrets, but I listen." He motioned to a bench and they sat down. "If you're to go to Abicis, then it's probably to see Qip. He visited here once and told me about where he lives. It's an island full of people who've been thrown out of Empyrea because they're different. The name Abicis translates as 'Unwanted.'"

"I've never heard that such a place exists."

"I can't imagine that a royal princess would know about it."

Bree felt she needed to defend herself. "We are an island of women and we feed on gossip. And, like you, I listen. I'm very good at sitting so still that people don't realize I'm there. To most people, a pretty face means an empty head."

He smiled warmly at her. "If beauty takes away brains, then your head is totally empty."

She smiled at his compliment. "Where is this island and how can this man help?"

Tam shrugged his big shoulders. "I have no idea, but I don't think it's too far away. I spent time with Qip while my father worked. I don't think he knew that Qip and I got to know each other."

"Did you inherit your father's ability to foresee the future?"

"Not at all." He paused. "But I did get some things from my mother." When he snapped his fingers, a flame appeared at the tips. He broke off a plant and set it on fire from his fingers.

"What a very useful ability to have."

"It's nothing compared to my mother. She can make this house disappear."

"That spell would probably take two days of energy."

"It does," Tam said. "How do you know that?"

"I work for a woman who is a—" Bree hesitated. "A sort of doctor. She can make plants and objects do unusual things."

Tam was looking at her with interest. "And what do you do for her?"

Bree was so used to keeping secrets that she was afraid to tell. "I help mix the plants. Like for a cooking recipe."

Tam got up and picked a flower. "Like this one?"

"I know the names of the plants but not by sight."

"This is ragwort."

"It's good to stop itching," she said, then added, "and for other things."

He sat back down. "I think I understand. My mother had an apprentice. She called her the 'Book.'"

Bree smiled. "Yes, that's what Reena calls me."

"Reena! I've met her. She's scary powerful."

They were quiet for a few moments, then Tam said, "My entire life has been ruled by what my father foresees. He'd say, 'No! Don't pick that flower. It'll make a whole forest die.' He constantly reminds me that everything affects everything else. He arranged my marriage because he foresaw that with the woman he chose, we'd create a son who'd grow up to be important."

"You're unhappy at that?"

"No! I adore my wife, my child, and even the new one who isn't born yet. My point is that if you're here and you're going to Abicis, probably to find Qip, then there's a reason behind it."

"I'm sure there is." Bree's eyes widened. "You have powers. Maybe *you* could go with Aradella. Or your mother's Book could go. I can pay you. I might be persuaded to sell my soul if it gets me out of spending days with Aradella."

He frowned. "I don't mean to 'take over' as my wife accuses me, but it sounds like you need to stand up for yourself."

"No one talks back to Aradella! Even bad-tempered Queen Olina is scared of her. Aradella could make a genius feel stupid." Bree took a breath. "And I can do nothing in retaliation! Someone saved me from an ultimate humiliation and I promised that in return I'd be nice to Aradella. Nice! I'd like to—" Bree made a motion of twisting and snapping a body in half. But then, she sighed. "I'm sure there's a good reason for all of this and that I must endure it. It's as your father said, 'Everything affects everything else.' But being with Aradella is a cosmic punishment."

"And you won't tell her of your strength?"

Bree's face seemed to drain of color. "Tell her I am more than just a face? Her words are stronger than my arms! No, I prefer to keep my privacy."

They heard a bell ring and Bree stood up. "I guess that's dinner." She looked at Tam sitting on the bench. "I apologize for complaining. I'm sure your father has a good reason for bringing me here, and I guess I'll live through it. However . . ." She gave a wicked little grin. "I know fourteen spells that would help me step out of my body and just be an observer. Maybe I'll mix one up and you can ignite it."

"That sounds like fun," Tam said. "I think maybe I should go. Someone needs to protect the brilliant Aradella from Bree, the powerful goddess."

The bell rang again and, laughing, Bree stepped back. "Yes! You are needed to protect me from myself. And by the way, your son is a gift and I envy you." Turning, she ran toward the house.

# 13

Aradella was standing by the bedroom window looking out at the sculpture of a bird in flight. Mekos said it was the room his father and Kaley had stayed in. He also said that later the house had disappeared. *Wonder who the resident witch is?* she thought.

She turned to look at Mekos stretched out on the bed. His hair had fallen back and she could see that his ears were still. While they'd been in the cave, his ears had constantly twitched as he listened to every sound around them.

When they'd arrived at the cave, the two guards had stayed outside with the horses while she and Mekos entered. In the outer room, he told her where Nessa had slept, and where Kaley and Tanek had been with her pet tabor.

"Arit showed Kaley the hidden room," Mekos said as he led Aradella to the back into what appeared to be an area with solid stone walls. If they hadn't been told there was a door, they wouldn't have seen it.

Mekos lit a little stick lamp that Zeon had given them. It had an eerie green light that showed the outline of the doorway. They had a bottle of some chemical that they dabbed along the edges of the door that Zeon had sealed.

When the door opened, they stepped inside. The room was

full of machines such as they'd never seen before. All of them looked as though they'd been beaten with a hammer.

"Kaley said they're computers and they're full of information. My—" Mekos broke off because Aradella had turned on an old lantern hanging on the wall. The light was weak but it showed the whole room.

There was writing on the wall in the ancient swan language. "What does it say?" she asked.

Mekos's voice was so low she could hardly hear him. "R, T, M, I will be with you forever. I will not abandon you, H."

She didn't have to be told what it meant. The *H* was Haver, *R* and *T* were for Roal and Tanek, his son and grandson. The *M* was for Mekos. Aradella put her arms around him and held him.

"I was six years old when he didn't come home. I couldn't understand where he was. He was as close to the swans as my father is. They loved him, and when he didn't return, they cried. The sound was horrible!"

She stroked his hair and waited for the pain to lessen. If there was anything Aradella knew about, it was grief.

After a while, Mekos stepped away, wiped his eyes, and looked about. He told her that his great-grandfather's remains had been found near the far wall. He didn't go there, but she did. Peeping out from under a long black cord was something small and white. Bending, she picked it up. It was a bone, probably the tip of the smallest finger. *The bone of a righteous man.* Zeon had said it would be needed. She put it in her pocket.

They didn't stay in the room for long. Mekos said he wished he had Kaley's camera, and that set him off to telling the story of taking photos.

Aradella was glad to see him remembering good things.

They left not long afterward and rode the horses back to Zeon's house. They were told he was still working and wouldn't be out for a couple of hours.

In their room, they found food and drink. They filled the

tub with hot water, took a bath together, then made love on the big bed.

"Thank you," Mekos said softly as he held her. "I couldn't have survived today without you."

Her mind filled with all that had happened since they'd met, then she thought of the mystery of the task they must complete. As they snuggled together, she held on to him tightly. "You're in this because of *me*. You should go home to your swans and your beautiful family. You should—"

"Please stop." There was no pity in his voice. He pulled back to look at her. "What do you think the people on Abicis look like? Three heads? Six eyes? Are they as big as Sojee?"

"Maybe it's full of tabors, only they're the size of your mother's fox father."

He rolled over on top of her. "You sure liked that wolf you rode on."

"Gorgeous creature. I would have thought his fur was rough but it was silky smooth. Why don't *you* have furry skin?"

He kissed her neck. "I could—" His head came up. "Someone is coming."

"Besides you?"

Laughing, he rolled off her. "It's Zeon's footsteps."

At the knock, Mekos got up to answer the door.

Zeon was there, resplendent in a silver-and-black robe, and he stepped inside. "I apologize for intruding but I've been talking to my son. He's adamant that I tell you something before we meet for dinner." He looked at Aradella. "Your cousin, Sojee's daughter, is involved in this. She—"

Aradella gasped. "Not again! She's to be sacrificed, isn't she? Those two have no other use than to be sacrificed for something. So *that's* what this is all about." She looked at Mekos. "We need the mask. This time you and I will work *together.*" She looked back at Zeon. "Where's she being held? Who sent her there? Olina?"

The two men were staring at her with identical expressions of astonishment. Aradella was talking *very* fast.

"Or did she get on a ship with the men from Selkan? Sojee will be blamed for this! This will keep the islands apart *forever*." She looked back at Mekos. "We need Perus so we can leave this minute. Those girls are idiots! They'll be dead soon." She stopped talking and glared from one man to the other, silently asking why they weren't doing something.

Zeon swallowed. "She's here," he said softly. "Bree is here."

"Of course she's the one," Aradella said. "Shay would be so obnoxious they'd release her."

Mekos looked at Zeon. "Why is her cousin here?"

Zeon was looking bewildered—and a bit afraid. "She's going with you. To Abicis."

At that, Aradella backed up against the bed. "All right," she whispered. "I'll marry Nessa. That will be better than spending even a day with one of my cousins."

Mekos opened the door and Zeon gladly hurried out of the room.

When they were alone, Mekos turned to Aradella, ready to say that things couldn't be as bad as she thought they were. But he saw a princess. Not the woman he loved, but a stranger who had glassy eyes and an unreadable expression.

"I'm sure it'll be all right," he managed to say. "She's Sojee's daughter so surely—"

Aradella stepped past him. "I must get ready for dinner." To his consternation, she went to the wardrobe that held clothes for them. Earlier, she'd happily chosen their robes. For him, she'd pulled out a black garment. "Like your hair." For herself, she chose red with sparkling swirls of rose gold.

But now Aradella ignored the gown on the chair, went to the wardrobe, and removed one of light brown, then she went to the bathroom and shut the door.

Mekos sat down heavily on the bed. Right now, more than

anything in the world, he wanted to talk to his father. Or better yet, to Kaley. He needed someone to explain what was going on.

But contacting them was too risky. In theory, no one knew where they were. If Queen Olina was searching for them, no one should have to lie.

In minutes, Aradella came out of the bathroom—and he was shocked by her appearance. Her hair was pulled back tight against her head, and she had on a thick robe that was huge on her. Was it made for a man? The color was so bland that it seemed to make her disappear. Worse than the clothes was the deadness in her eyes.

"It's how she expects me to look," she muttered. "I am ready."

If he'd heard the voice unseen, he'd say it wasn't Aradella's. In fact, he wasn't sure it was human. Maybe one of the stone statues was speaking.

"I'll be ready soon," he murmured and picked up the robe she'd chosen for him. He didn't go to the bathroom as he didn't dare leave Aradella alone.

They didn't speak as a guard ushered them to the dining room. Zeon and Bree were waiting for them.

Mekos hadn't seen Aradella's cousin often and she was certainly beautiful. She had on a blue dress that clung to her perfectly proportioned body. Her thick dark hair was fastened up on her head and looked like it was about to tumble down to her shoulders. She was totally perfect—and boring, Mekos thought. He couldn't imagine her sitting on top of a wall and watching a giant lizard snap at a Never. Nor could he see her caring for the injured Ian. Or riding a wolf as she ran to save someone's life. She definitely wouldn't sink a knife into an evil woman. And she wouldn't—

He realized that Aradella was watching him as he stared at Bree. He might not know a lot about women, but he could almost read her mind. Aradella thought he was entranced and awed by the beauty of Princess Bree. "She isn't—" he began, but Aradella briskly walked away, her chin up in a defiant position.

The table had been set for six people, but there were only five of them. A pretty guard led Aradella to a chair. Another one sat Bree directly across from her. As was customary, Mekos was put next to Bree, and Zeon took the chair at the head of the table.

Zeon nodded to the empty chair next to Aradella. "My son was to be here tonight but he's with his wife and son."

"Piks is a beautiful child," Bree said.

Zeon's face glowed. "He is. And very smart."

They were served their first course, a type of pâtè.

"You met him?" Mekos asked Bree.

"In the garden, with his father."

"My son . . ." Zeon hesitated. "Tam says he's going with you." It was obvious that he didn't like that idea.

"How wonderful!" Bree said.

Mekos looked at Aradella. She wasn't eating and there was no light in her eyes. He turned to Zeon. "Have you foreseen any more about what we're to do?"

Zeon sighed and his jaw tightened. "I am being blocked!" He worked to calm himself.

"We're to meet Qip, aren't we?" Bree asked.

Everyone looked at her.

"Yes," Zeon said. "How did . . .?" He waved his hand. "Qip will know what to do. He lived on Empyrea for most of his life, and he's the key to everything. I wish I could tell you more, but I can't see past that."

Mekos said, "We'll ask him."

Zeon leaned back as the second course, medallions of meat, was served. "The problem is that Qip is very difficult to find. You must understand that the people on Abicis are . . ." He paused.

"Unwanted, as the name implies?" Bree turned and looked at Aradella. "The word means 'thrown away, discarded.'"

Mekos saw fire flash in Aradella's eyes. He would *not* like that to be aimed at him! But Bree didn't seem to notice.

"Yes," Zeon said. "The people are outcasts from Empyrea

for one reason or another. It could be the way they look or that they lack approved forms of socialization." He turned to Bree. "Anyone who is different is sent there, and that includes pretty people. It seems that on Empyrea, they're considered 'offensive.'"

While Zeon smiled at Bree, Mekos looked at Aradella. Her eyes were so full of rage—or was it hate?—that she looked like an executioner who delighted in her job.

"So!" Mekos said loudly, "your son is going with us. Tell us about him."

Zeon's face showed his love, but before he could speak, Bree said, "He is a lovely man. I'm so glad he'll be with us. I'm sure his friendship with Qip will help us solve this problem.

Zeon's surprise was obvious. "I didn't know Tam knew the man."

"He does." Bree smiled angelically. "But perhaps you can tell us more about him."

"Maybe I should ask *you*," Zeon said.

Bree gave the silent Aradella a look through her lashes. "I do know a few things," she murmured. "Certainly more than people think I do."

The two men looked back and forth between the women. It was like seeing the beginning of a war—and they had no idea how to arm themselves.

It was an hour after they'd left the dinner table, they were in their room, and Aradella was still ranting.

"Did you see the snide look she gave me?"

Mekos was stretched out on the bed while Aradella was pacing back and forth. The big, bland gown had been tossed over a chair and she was in her underwear. He thought she looked very, *very* good!

"She was *telling* me that she knows so much! About what? Dresses? Hair? How long her nails should be? She spends whole days with the Beauty Girls. Hale often saw her slipping around at night, but she wants people to believe her beauty is natural.

Ha!" Aradella stopped, hands on hips. "She couldn't wait to tell everyone that she'd coaxed Zeon's son into blabbing about some man. Qip! Doesn't she understand that he has a *wife*?"

"Qip?" Mekos asked.

"No! Tam! He has a wife and a child, but my cousin can't bear for any man not to lust after her. I should warn Tam's wife. I should—"

"I like what you have on," Mekos said. "Why don't you come to bed?"

"This is not the time for that." She squinted her eyes at him. "You certainly didn't protest when you were told to sit next to her."

"I could better see you from across the table." He smiled, proud of himself for coming up with that.

"It didn't help you defend me when she attacked."

His puzzlement showed. "When did that happen?"

Aradella looked aghast. "Really? You didn't see it? Didn't *hear* it?"

Mekos could see there was no winning this battle. He got up on all fours and stealthily moved to the end of the bed. Like a fox stalking prey.

She'd not seen him do that before and it made her stop talking. In the next second, he pulled her onto the bed and wrapped his body around hers.

"Then she—" Aradella said, but Mekos kissed her and finally, she stopped talking.

# 14

When Aradella woke, it was still dark but Mekos was up and dressed and staring out the window. She knew by his stance what he was thinking. If they didn't find a solution to the problems they'd caused, he'd be letting down his whole family, and maybe even all the people who were under the rule of the Empyreans.

Yesterday, after the burden of taking care of her cousin was dropped onto her, Aradella had overlooked what Mekos was facing.

She got out of bed and put her arms around him, her face against his back. "We'll solve this. We'll find this man Qip and he'll tell us what we need to do."

He lifted her hand and kissed it. "I hope so. Last time we tried to thwart the Empyreans, they destroyed our home and killed my great-uncle. This time—"

She moved in front of him. "Come on, let's finish packing. Do you think my cousin can dress herself?"

He raised an eyebrow. "Are you asking me to go help her?"

Aradella's throat closed so tight she nearly choked. No words came out.

"Tell me," he said, "are you going to be jealous of all women I look at or is it just the beautiful Bree?"

She stepped away from him. "And here I was feeling sorry for you. Did you pack my things too or just your own?"

"I put that big brown coat you wore to dinner in the magic bag. I'm sure you'll want to wear it when another pretty girl shows up."

With an eye roll, Aradella went to the bathroom.

It was barely daylight when they left Zeon's very comfortable home and went to the big courtyard. Coming slowly down to them was Perus. He was saddled and looked well-fed.

When he landed, Aradella put her arms around his neck. "Were you treated well? Ian wants one of your scales. If you shed any, let me know."

Mekos ran his hand down the dragon's neck. "I would imagine that you're glad to get away from Nessa."

"Aren't we all?" Aradella said.

"Good morning."

They turned to see Zeon. He had on a light blue robe embroidered with yellow and pink flowers, and he was holding something wrapped in cloth.

"More gifts?" Aradella asked.

"Yes, but not from me." He flipped back an edge of the cloth. "This was under the saddle of your dragon." It was a small, plain box.

Mekos took it. "This is from Kaley. It belonged to her witch friend." He opened the box to see three items inside. One was a little man made of wood and he was dancing about.

"He's adorable," Aradella said.

"I believe he's meant to be a distraction to anyone who views him," Zeon said. "I think the little bag is rather interesting."

"It contains a bottomless supply of gold coins," Mekos said. "I'm sure we'll be able to use them."

"And the key?" Aradella asked. "What does it open?"

"I have no idea," Zeon said seriously. "I focused on it but I got a blank. It does have the crest of Empyrea so there is a connection." He grimaced. "Perhaps Vian knows."

Mekos gave him a very serious, caring look. "Do you think someone is blocking you from your full powers?"

Zeon laughed. "It appears that I've made my point. Please introduce me to your grandmother."

"I will," Mekos said, then mumbled, "if she ever speaks to me again." He shut the box and nodded toward the cloth. "Anything else?"

Zeon took out an oval case the size of his forearm. It was made of embossed leather and it had several holes in it. He opened it. Inside, it was lavishly lined with silks in colors of blue and purple. "I could not figure out what this is."

Mekos and Aradella looked at each other and smiled, then Mekos looked up at the nearest tree. "Where are you?" he asked, and held out his hand, palm up.

Ian flew down from the tree and landed on his hand.

"Oh, but it's good to see you," Aradella said. "How is your leg? Did Arit like the books? What's going on with everyone?"

Zeon was looking at the little man in astonishment. "They are real," he whispered.

"Very real," Mekos said. "Are you going with us?"

"Of course," Ian said. "I have a lot to atone for." He looked at Aradella. "Arit is outraged by the silly books and the men refuse to leave Pithan. They mixed bacon with jams the women made and put it on the beef. Everyone is in ecstasy." He lowered his voice. "But Olina is trying to incite them to begin to search for you. So far, no one cares."

When Mekos stepped aside with Ian, Zeon went to Aradella and held out a small leather bag. "I believe this is yours."

She reached for it, but he held it back.

"I put an enchantment of protection over this as its contents are toxic. Does Mekos know of this?"

"No. He wouldn't like that I had it." She took it when he handed it to her. "Will I need it?"

"Maybe," he said. "I could not see clearly, but Bree and you—"

Aradella was not interested in hearing about her cousin. She turned away.

Zeon nodded in understanding, then went to Mekos. He withdrew a thin, narrow box from inside his robe. "I had this case made for you," he said softly. "It is made of magnar wood and it will offer some protection."

Mekos spoke in the same low tone. "I take it that's the knife that—"

Zeon held up his hand. "I don't want to hear the details. What I saw when I touched it was more than enough. This knife has seen centuries of violence. Do not clean it as you may need all of its power." Zeon stepped back, then turned to the side and smiled. "My son is here. Come and meet him."

Ian flew to land on Perus's saddle, out of sight. At his size, he knew to be wary of strangers.

Coming out a side door was a handsome young man. He was the same height as Mekos, but while Mekos was lithe, this man was thickly muscled.

Aradella was smiling at the man, but then Bree stepped out from behind him. Like her cousin, she had on wide-legged trousers, a shirt and a jacket. Her hair was in a big braid that hung down her back.

"She's so—" Aradella began.

Mekos gave her a look to stop and stepped forward to greet the man. They exchanged names, then, like all men seemed able to do, they began talking like they'd known each other forever.

"You know this man, Qip?"

"Yes. Smart man. Very interesting. Worked in Empyrea for years. Short guy."

"Think he'll be willing to help us?"

"Sure. You get anything to eat?"

"Not much, what about you?"

Aradella thought they might go on like that forever. "Are we *all* riding on Perus?" she asked loudly.

"Reena sent something," Tam said.

"And here it is." Zeon was looking up at the sky. The beautiful creature, half bird, half four-legged animal, quietly landed near Perus. The dragon looked startled, as though he'd never seen such a being.

Mekos's face softened to love. For all that he was a Lely, his order dealt with birds. "I know you," he said to the eagle head.

It bowed to him. Mekos rubbed his face on the feathers, then spoke to it in the deep-throated language only his order knew.

Through all this, Aradella and Bree stood apart, on opposite sides of the circle of men and beasts. They were enemies sizing each other up.

It was the first time Bree had openly seen Aradella in clothes that fit her. When Bree looked her up and down, Aradella stood straighter. She was feeling every moment of Hale's training. When Bree got back up to Aradella's face, she gave a nod of acknowledgment, as though to say, *Well done!*

Aradella returned the nod.

The men had trained for battle, so they recognized the women's rigid stance and their face-off nods.

Mekos looked at Tam. "It won't be easy. I fear that Aradella might harm her."

Tam gave a snort. "She can try."

Mekos looked at him in question, but Tam wasn't betraying secrets. "You've met her father?"

Mekos smiled. "Sojee. Oh yes. A great man."

"She is his daughter," Tam said pointedly, as though he was sending a message. Turning away, he went to check the saddle on the eagle-beast.

"Again, with her being Sojee's daughter," Mekos mumbled, then he also checked the harness. A good soldier never trusted anyone else to do his job.

Zeon went to Aradella. "The death I foresaw?" he asked quietly.

She gave him her full attention.

"It's a wrongful death and it has to do with you and Princess Bree. Both of you. Together."

Aradella's face showed her skepticism. "I can't imagine that she and I will do anything with each other."

"That's what I thought, but in this you need to be together. You two—" They saw Mekos glance in their direction and they knew he was listening. "Remember this, that's all I ask. It will take both of you to stop the death."

It was hours later when the big animals finally slowed down and began their descent. They were approaching an island. It didn't look very big and like the islands they knew, it had been formed by a volcano. In the distance, they could see a steep-sided mountain with a thin line of steam coming out of the top.

"Like the Lair," Aradella said to Mekos and he nodded. For the whole long trip, she'd had her arms around him, her head against his back.

Tam and Bree, on their eagle creature, had stayed close by, but they didn't ride with Bree's arms around him.

At times, the flight had seemed to be never-ending. At one point, the men broke the monotony by playing catch with the food Zeon had sent with them.

Mekos was better at catching what was thrown toward him, but Tam was better at chasing what he didn't catch.

The first time he sent the eagle straight down toward the water, Aradella gasped. "She'll fall off!"

But Bree held on to the saddle—not to Tam—and stayed on. When a seagull decided to see if they were something to eat, Tam encircled its neck with his hand before it hit them with its beak. The bird tried to attack his face, but Mekos called out to it and the bird settled. When Tam released it, the bird stood on the eagle's head and squawked at Tam.

"You are being told off," Mekos called to him. "He says he's just trying to feed his family."

"But not with my nose!" However, Tam put his hand on his heart and apologized, then tossed him a large chunk of bread. With its chin up, the bird flew away.

All four of them laughed, but when the two women looked at each other, they abruptly stopped.

By the time the animals landed, their riders were glad to be on the ground, and they looked around at where they were. It was a wide, deep ledge made of volcanic rock. Based on the overgrown plant life, it didn't seem to have been used recently.

At the end was what they knew was a volcanic bubble. Centuries before, the erupting volcano had formed a bubble of gas, then surrounded it with molten rock. It had left a deep, round circle that would be good protection from the elements. But the entrance was blocked by three huge boulders.

"We'll get Perus to move those rocks," Mekos said, but as soon as the saddles were removed, the big animals took off into the sky.

"No!" Aradella cried out in panic. "Don't leave us here alone. We need you!" But they were already out of sight.

The four people looked at each other, wondering what to do next.

Mekos said, "I'll get the firewood," then opened Ian's case and he flew out.

Aradella said, "I'll go with you and see what plants I can find."

Tam picked up the old tapestry bag. "I'll see what Papá has sent us for dinner."

Bree said nothing.

Mekos and Aradella found a path that led up the steep hill.

"Sheep's wool," she said as she plucked a fuzzy bit from a bush. "Ian will like this. Oh! That's pellan. And there's oonic. This may be a botanist's dream garden."

After their tasks were completed, they started down the path back to the ledge and felt raindrops.

"I hope there's a cover in that bag," Mekos said. "The fox part of me will melt."

Aradella blinked against the drops. "We'll have a complaining princess on our hands. She's too used to luxury."

He turned to look at her. "*You* are a princess too."

"Yes, but I've been indoctrinated by fox—and wolf."

Mekos gave a one-sided grin. "So now your lust has shifted from my father to a wolf?"

She walked past him. "I'm woman enough for all of them."

"Are you?" He shifted the load of firewood to a free arm and his feet left the ground. As he soared past her, he swooped her up with him.

They sailed down onto the ledge like two birds, then halted at the sight before them. At the end of the ledge was the round, cave-like enclosure, the bubble. The boulders had been rolled away. Inside was a cheerful fire, with food and wine laid out. Tam sat on one side, Bree on the other.

"Come in out of the rain," Tam called, motioning with his arm.

At a crack of thunder, Mekos and Aradella ran into the dry space. He dropped the wood he'd collected, and Aradella spread out the many plant sprigs she'd gathered. She looked at Tam. "How did you move those rocks?"

He glanced at Bree, then mumbled, "Oh, you know, muscle."

# 15

In the morning, the four of them were quiet, occupied with their own thoughts about the island they were on. The Empyreans traveled through space, but the ships were often staffed by people from the islands on Bellis. Everyone knew someone who had visited one of the other planets that had the same atmosphere as Bellis. So what did the Empyreans mean when they declared a person a "misfit?" What kind of people were on this island? The two men quietly armed themselves.

The four of them did their best to clear away any sign that they'd been on the ledge, but they didn't close off the entrance to the opening.

"You can just roll the rocks back into place," Aradella teased Tam. When he didn't reply, she looked away, disappointed. Her attempt at friendship had been turned down. Had Bree poisoned him against her?

Zeon had put backpacks in the tapestry bag and they put them on. Mekos showed them the bag of coins.

Through it all, Bree was silent, standing to the side of the others, just watching.

When they were ready to go, Aradella turned to her. "Stay with us," she said. "We'll protect you if there's any danger.

Mekos can hear anything and we have the advantage of Tam's extraordinary strength. Don't be afraid." She didn't wait for a reply before turning away to follow Mekos to the path leading down.

Tam tightened the strap on his pack and looked at Bree. "My great strength will protect you." He was smiling. "Just so you know, anyone comes after us, I'm getting *behind* you." He winked at her.

Smiling, Bree followed him to the path.

For all their bravado, the unknown they were facing made them tense. The path down was steep. The bits of sheep's wool they saw showed what the trail was used for.

Ian flew ahead, then returned.

"What did you see?" Aradella asked.

"There's no one like me," Ian answered. He looked past them to Bree. "There are many like you."

They turned to look at her, but they weren't sure what that meant.

Ian would say no more but his laughing manner reassured them.

They came to a crossroads and to the left they could see what looked to be a town.

"I hear people." Mekos listened. "They're laughing and talking." He looked at Tam. "There are children."

Their pace increased and their fear left them.

The town they entered was clean, well-kept, and busy. There were two-story buildings with shops below. Stands containing fresh food, meat, fruit, and vegetables were abundant. An elegant fountain was in the center and children were running around it. They'd been expecting monsters but what they saw were normal people. Old, young, little, big, they were all there.

The only thing unusual was, as Ian had said, that many people looked like Bree. That meant pretty. Like Bree, they had perfect skin, lustrous eyes, hair that glistened. On Pithan, the Beauty Girls, with their lavish makeup and hair, stood out. But on Abicis, most of the people were, well, beautiful. Both men and women were exceptionally good-looking. Few of them seemed to have made an effort to look good but appeared to have rolled out of bed looking like that.

"My goodness," Aradella said, her eyes wide from staring at men who, in normal circumstances, would have women gathered around them.

A farrier looked up from a horse's hoof. His dark eyes were like burning coals. The blacksmith was enough to make a woman swoon. Storekeepers had chiseled jaws and shoulders as wide as a broom handle.

Mixed with these male and female demigods were people who, indeed, were "different." There were people with crooked backs, faces with birthmarks, others with obvious mental disabilities. There were people with crutches or in wheeled chairs.

In spite of their differences, they all seemed to be equal—and happy. Smiling, laughing, friendly, they went about their daily business.

As they walked through the town, they asked about Qip, but no one had heard of him—or that was what they said.

The team hadn't gone far when they began to realize that Aradella was the focus of attention. The other three were barely looked at, but everyone looked at Aradella as though she was different—and highly desirable.

Mekos stepped closer to her. When a man so gorgeous he could have been the model for a deity, halted and stared at Aradella, Mekos put his arm around her and sneered at the man.

Aradella had never experienced anything like that and she couldn't resist turning his own question back on him. "Tell me," she said, "are you going to be jealous of *all* the men who look at me?"

Mekos gave her a look that said this was no joke, but Tam laughed.

As for Bree, her steps slowed and the distance between her and "them" increased. That they didn't notice her absence was new to her. All her life, her physical appearance had garnered attention, but now she was being ignored. She saw a woman better looking than her standing over a tub of water. Not one man had so much as glanced at Bree.

The experience was quite liberating.

Bree stopped walking. Aradella, between Mekos and Tam, was far ahead of her—and they'd not noticed she wasn't with them. *Is this how the world has seen me?* she wondered. *The most desirable woman commands everyone's attention? No wonder Aradella hates me!*

"Is it two boros of moringa or one?" she heard a man say. The voice came from behind a curtain hanging across a doorway.

"It's one and a half," she said without thinking.

There was a pause, then the voice said, "Get in here!"

She pushed aside the curtain and saw a room that made her feel comfortable. There were pots, vials, glass jars, and bunches of herbs hanging everywhere. Just like Reena's house.

Behind a long, stone-topped table set close to a wall was a man. She was relieved to see that he wasn't heaven-sent beautiful. He was short, his head barely reaching Bree's shoulders, with a long gray mustache, and one arm was longer than the other. On the table was a tall stone mortar surrounded by bowls of ingredients. On the side was a cloth doll of a woman with babies sewn all around her.

"I assume you're making a fertility potion," Bree said.

The man frowned at her. "Who are you?"

She was hesitant to tell him her name. "A Book."

"Ah. For Reena?" When she nodded, his smile filled his round face. "Brilliant woman but very lazy."

"True. She doesn't want to deal with all those volumes."

"She still have a spell on her books that burns the hands of anyone who touches them?"

"Oh yes! It's easier to put some bored, useless girl under a forever spell than to try to memorize them herself."

He raised his bushy eyebrows. "Do you know *all* of the books? Even the ones she stole from her father?"

"Yes." Bree was surprised that he knew about those dusty old volumes. "I sneezed all the way through them." She looked at the bowls. "Do you have wild rose? Hibiscus? Any dirt?"

"Taken from the grave of a woman who had twelve children."

"What about a snakeskin? It helps the man last from how this excites the woman." She watched as he opened a box that looked ancient and pulled out four snakeskins, each a different color. "Just a tiny bit is all that's needed."

He used his thumbnail to snip off a piece, put it in the mortar, then picked up the pestle to begin mashing. The table was tall and the mortar made it taller. The man had to stretch to reach the top of it.

"Let me do it." She started to go behind the table.

"There's not enough room," he said.

Bree picked up one end of the heavy table and moved it a few inches farther from the wall. Then she moved the other side. She went behind the table and began to crush the ingredients.

The man was staring at her in awe. "It takes two of my big male assistants to move that table."

Bree shrugged. "I inherited a bit of strength from my father. He's a giant and very strong."

"Do you always explain what you can do by giving the credit to your father?"

"I guess I do."

"I'm called Cappie. It's for Copernicus. Ridiculous name, but everything from the Empyreans is absurd."

"I'm Bree Varlon from Pithan. We're trying to find a man named Qip." She began stuffing the doll full of the contents of the mortar.

"Qip doesn't like to be found. Why do you want him?"

There was so much to that answer that Bree didn't know where to begin. "Have you ever heard of Queen Olina?"

"I've had some dealings with her mother," Cappie said.

"Yes. Urah. She—"

Cappie held up his hand. "That's more than enough for me to understand. Qip is my friend." He handed Bree a sewing kit, watched her thread a needle, then she began to sew the fertility doll closed. "If you want to stay here on Abicis, I need a Book."

She smiled at him. "You're very kind, but I'm here with others and we have something to do. We must—" She broke off at the sound of a familiar voice on the other side of the curtain. It was Aradella—and of course she sounded angry.

"Where is she? I know she hasn't the brains to find her way around, so why did she wander away?"

Cappie looked at Bree. "Does the owner of that voice mean *you*?"

"Yes."

His eyes twinkled. "We can mix something that'll change her attitude. I'll ignite it for you."

Bree laughed. "How kind you are! But I promised someone that I'd be nice to Aradella. It wasn't added, 'Unless she's such a bitch that you want to tear her head off.'"

Cappie didn't laugh.

"This is my fault," said a man's voice from outside. "I should have been watching."

"Your lover?" Cappie asked.

"Oh no! That's Tam. He has a wife and child."

"And who do you have?"

"I—"

Aradella's voice came to them. "How can we accomplish anything if she gets lost every few minutes? We'll never find this man Qip if we have to deal with *her*."

"I better go." Bree sighed. "I wish my cousin could see that my life isn't the perfection that she believes it is."

"I might be able to arrange that."

Bree smiled. "Not even Urah's magic can defeat Aradella. She is an unstoppable force."

As she went toward the curtain, she turned back and kissed his forehead. "I hope I get to see you again."

"So do I," he said. "If it gets too bad, you know where I live."

Bree took a breath and opened the curtain. She saw Tam first. He was standing apart from Aradella and Mekos and seemed to be looking for her.

Aradella was talking. "If we don't find her, we'll have to—"

Bree moved away from Cappie's curtained doorway, then said loudly, "I'm here."

Aradella gave her cousin her usual look of anger. "We've had to backtrack to find you. We should be going ahead. If we move too quickly for you, just tell us." By the end, Aradella's teeth were clenched.

"I didn't mean to—" Bree began.

Tam stepped forward, slightly in front of Bree in a protective way. "This is my fault. I should have stayed with her. Why don't you two go that way and Bree and I go this way? This town is small. If we spread it around that we're looking for Qip, maybe he'll be told."

Mekos looked over Aradella's head and gave Tam a nod of thanks. Neither man wanted to deal with the animosity between the women. "Excellent idea." Mekos put a firm grip on Aradella's arm. He took out the little bag of endless coins and handed several to Tam.

The men looked at each other in understanding and the couples went in opposite directions.

"Thank you," Bree said when she and Tam were alone.

"I saw you come out of the doorway. Who did you meet? Did you wheedle out any secrets like you did from me?"

"You make me sound like a spy."

"I told you more in one conversation than I've told anyone in years."

"I can say the same about you," she said. "I work hard to keep my involvement with Reena a secret, but I told you."

"And you showed me that you're as strong as a yoke of oxen."

"That's not a nice thing to say about a princess!" She was smiling.

"So tell me all. Who or what was behind that curtain that you tried to keep us from seeing?"

She laughed. "I am exposed! I met Cappie." As they walked, she told him about the meeting.

"Friends with Qip, is he?" Tam said thoughtfully.

They'd left the town behind and were now on the outskirts. Tall trees surrounded them.

"I think we should stop and wait," Tam said.

"For what?"

"For Qip to find us. My guess is that your man Cappie will reward you for helping him by sending Qip."

"And here I was hoping for a fire-breathing dragon to kiss Aradella."

Tam groaned. "You *must* stand up to her. And do not tell me of your promise. Aradella thinks you're stupid."

"And useless." Her eyes widened. "Isn't that pretty?"

In front of them was a crystal-clear blue lake. Behind it was a sloping hillside with a flower-covered meadow. There were no people. "Reena would love this place. She'd want a sample of every plant."

Tam was pulling his shirt off over his head. "I'm going for a swim, then afterward, I'll pick them for you. We'll put them in Papá's magic bag that I'm sure he wheedled someone into selling to him. For a good price, of course."

Smiling, Bree tried to be polite and not look, but the sight of Tam's nearly naked body was too good to resist. As a woman with strength, she did love muscles. "Did he pay for items by telling fortunes?"

Tam looked surprised, then smiled. "I think Aradella should be afraid of how clever you are." He was down to a small garment about his hips. He stepped toward the water, then turned to look at her. "Join me?"

"I don't think—" She stopped speaking. That phrase that got so many women in trouble came to her: *Why not?* She was out of her clothes and down to her two pieces of underwear in seconds.

Tam was in the water and he wasn't shy in appraising her body. "I can see it now."

She knew what he meant. Clothed, she looked like her sister. Unclothed, they were different. Bree was sleek, with defined muscles. At the sight of her unclad sister, Shay would sneer and say, "You look like a boy."

"Can you swim?" he asked.

"Bet I can go faster than you," she said.

"You're on!"

They raced and Tam won four out of the five races.

"Sure you're not Order of Swans?" she asked as they got out of the water.

"Order of Sight, second class. I can't foresee anything."

"You could take your wife's order."

"She's from another island. They have no orders."

His tone made her look at him. "Do you have cultural differences?"

"Oh yes! Many of them. My wife and I—" He broke off as they heard laughter.

They turned to see three boys and a girl, ten or eleven years old, coming toward them.

"We heard you two were ugly but you're worse than they said," the largest boy said.

"And fat." The girl was looking at Tam.

"Is this what I have to look forward to with my son?" Tam mumbled. He picked up his trousers and withdrew four coins. "Are these worth anything?"

The way their eyes lit up was the answer.

"These are yours if you'll pick a sprig of every plant on that hillside."

Bree, still in her underwear, stepped forward. "We want as much variety of the plants as you can find, but no duplicates." When the kids didn't move, she said, "Like Cappie needs."

At that, the children's faces turned solemn. "He can turn you into a bug."

"Or a lizard."

"He made me into a bat," the smallest boy said. "I liked it, but my mother didn't. She put me in a jar and screamed at Cappie."

Bree and Tam worked not to laugh.

"We can do the same thing," Tam said fiercely. "And I can guarantee that you will *not* like it. Now go!"

The children scurried off and Tam and Bree went to the bottom of the hill. He lay down on the ground, turned his face up to the sun, and looked up at Bree. "My son will never be a brat like them."

Bree lay down a few feet from him. It felt good to be near someone who knew her secrets. "I'm sure you're right. Piks will be kind and considerate. He'll never call anyone ugly or too soft."

They looked at each other and laughed at that absurdity. Piks had already shown that he had a mind of his own.

The sun was drying them off and the children were on the hill behind them, arguing about who already had what plant. Bree and Tam were so drowsy they didn't hear the wagon on the hard-packed dirt road.

"Still being lazy, I see," they heard a voice say.

Bree opened her eyes to see a man sitting on the wagon seat. He was shorter than Cappie and had an ageless appearance. He could be an old thirty or a young eighty. Like Cappie, he had a remarkable mustache, but his was gray. He wore a flat cap that covered what appeared to be a bald head.

"Qip!" Tam shouted, joy in his voice. "How good to see you." He grabbed his clothes, pulling them on as he hurried to the wagon.

Qip somehow managed to frown and smile at the same time. "Everyone in town has told me that you're looking for me. Does your father need help?" He looked at Bree. "I hear you know Reena."

Bree was scrambling into her clothes. "I think maybe all of Bellis knows her." The children made a great noise as they ran down the hill. As they passed Bree, they tossed heaps of plants at her. She agilely twisted about as she caught them. The children ran to Qip, looking up at him expectantly.

"You're going to run me out of my home." He was trying to look grumpy as he reached into a bag and tossed out handfuls of what could only be candy.

After Tam gave each child a coin, they took their prizes and ran off. Qip was watching Bree intently. "You're Sojee's daughter?"

She smiled. "Do you know my father?"

"Only by reputation. And Vian's grandson is here?"

"Mekos," Tam said. "His mother is a Lely. She's half fox."

"How very interesting. Are you ready to go to my home? I'd like to hear why you've sought me out."

"We want to know more about Abicis," Bree said. "Where are the misfits here? We've seen no one unusual."

Qip smiled, showing straight white teeth. "Everything is perspective, my dear. Reality depends on how you see it. Come up here and sit by me. Tam, get in the back. We must find your lost friends."

As Bree climbed up, she looked at Qip. "Please call Aradella that to her face. I dare you."

"Ah, yes. The princess who fights Olina and Urah," Qip said. "I look forward to meeting her. Cappie says you're a Book and you can lift mountains." He looked at Tam sitting on the back of the wagon. "It seems that you're the only one who has no talents."

Tam laughed but Bree didn't. "If I put together a spell, Tam can ignite it, and he is an excellent father, and a—" She broke off as the two men were staring at her.

When Qip looked at Tam, the young man wouldn't meet his eyes.

Qip drove them back to the town and halted in front of Cappie's place. He was standing outside. "Where are they?" Qip asked.

Cappie tilted his head to indicate straight ahead. "They're alerting the whole town." He leaned to the side to see Bree. "Vomiting all night."

"You?" Qip asked, alarmed

Bree knew what he meant. "Try dittany of Crete. Is his wife going to have a baby?"

Cappie grinned. "Yes. First one."

"Give him whiskey. It'll help with his fear." She and Cappie laughed.

Qip flipped the reins to go. "He doesn't like many people."

"Can't imagine why. He's a darling man."

Qip turned to Tam and, again, they exchanged looks.

Aradella and Mekos were easy to find, and as soon as they came into sight, Bree stiffened into steel. Qip looked at her in surprise, but said nothing.

Tam reached down to get Aradella's hand and pulled her up into the back of the wagon. Mekos soared upward, then slowly lowered himself into the wagon. He was so graceful that his feet didn't move.

Qip leaned toward Bree. "Every time I see one of them do that, it gives me chills. They are a strange order."

"Better than being a useless Order of Royals," she said. There was no humor in her tone and she stared straight ahead.

It took a while to reach Qip's house. They went past a few nice houses, then the dwellings became farther apart until there was only dense forest, broken by a narrow dirt road.

The three in the back were so busy talking to each other that Bree felt free to speak. "Do you have neighbors?"

"No. This is all mine and I've hidden charged wiring to keep people out. I don't like uninvited visitors."

"I live in a volcanic crater with houses smashed together. This is divine."

"Tell me about you and Zeon and Tam."

She smiled. "Don't forget Piks, Tam's little son."

"Do I detect envy?"

"Of course. A home and family. What more could a person want?"

"And what does Princess Aradella want?"

Bree's jaw clenched. "To rule the world? I have no idea what would please her."

Frowning, Qip looked ahead and they were silent for the rest of the journey.

He drove through a stone-pillared gate and they saw his house. It was beautiful! It had a columned porch across the front and a steep roof with a long row of dormer windows. He halted the wagon in front of it.

Mekos spoke up. "It's another of Kaley's fairy-tale cottages."

No one said any more because from the side of the building came a . . . They weren't sure what it was. It looked like a tall man but it was made entirely of metal.

In awed silence, the four of them watched it come forward and go around the wagon. It put articulated hands on Qip's waist and swung him down.

"This is Darr." Qip's voice was full of affection. "He is my friend and my helpmate." He puffed out his chest a bit in pride. "I created him."

Darr turned to the three of them, still sitting on the wagon. His head was shaped like a human's, with metal ears and big green eyes. However, the green was where a human's eyes were white. The irises were black. He had no mouth.

Qip said, "Darr can hear, think, listen, and understand, but he doesn't speak. He is a perfect person. Come inside and get settled. You have a lot to tell me." He entered the house.

Tam was the first to get out of the wagon. He went to the side and put his hands up to Bree to lift her down.

She gave a sigh of disappointment. "I was hoping for Darr."

Tam grinned. "If you stage a fight with him, let me know. I want to make a wager."

As they walked toward the house, she said, "And who would you bet on?"

"You!" he said.

"Smart man."

Laughing, they entered the house.

Behind them, Aradella and Mekos were staring at the couple that were so close together. They seemed very familiar with each other. "What the fark?" she muttered.

Only Mekos could hear what they'd said. "She would fight the metal man? What do you think they did when they weren't with us?"

Aradella wasn't smiling. "If anything happens between those two it will cause problems. Zeon needs to stay our friend. He won't be if his married son . . ." She tried to shake off the idea. "If we tell Qip our story do you think he'll help us? Or will he say that what we did was so awful that we're doomed?"

"I don't know, but I hope he has food."

"If he does, do you think it'll be made of metal?"

Mekos smiled. "With creepy green eyes on all of it?"

Clasping arms, they entered the house.

The interior was as lovely as the outside. It was furnished with soft chairs and couches covered in well-worn upholstery. Tables and a wall of shelving held interesting artifacts. They ranged from woven items to an intricately carved stone to a bird's nest. There were several metal objects with wind-up keys at the back. It appeared to be the lifetime work of an inventor-collector.

The whole back of the house was glass doors that looked out onto acres of garden.

"My father would be envious," Tam said.

At one end, in front of the doors, was a table laden with food.

"Help yourselves," Qip said. "Then come to my library."

When their plates were full, they weren't sure if they were to eat first or go to the library with food in hand.

Qip stuck his head out of a doorway. "Come on!" he said impatiently.

The four young people settled themselves in a room that was

floor-to-ceiling books. There was a wide glass door that showed a small walled garden with pink-flowered trees.

"This is divine," Aradella said in awe, with her eyes on the books.

"They're Earth books," Qip said. "Forbidden and unreadable."

"Aradella can read them," Bree said. When they looked at her, she had no idea how to explain how she knew that fact, so she said nothing.

When Darr walked into the room, their attention went to him. He stood to the side, motionless.

Qip withdrew a book and handed it to Aradella.

"It's a novel," she said. "I haven't seen many of them. *Northanger Abbey* by Jane Austen. I'd love to read this."

"It's yours," he said. "What do you usually read?"

"Mostly about plants."

"She knew Valona's garden was all poisonous plants," Mekos said. "If it hadn't been for Aradella, we wouldn't have . . ." He trailed off. "Sorry. That's what got us into trouble."

Darr, who was half a head taller than the young men, stepped forward to stand close in front of Mekos. If he were human, it would have been an aggressive move.

On instinct, Mekos leaned back and his hand went to the knife at his belt.

"It's all right," Qip said. "You have something that's bothering Darr. He sees and hears things that we don't."

"So does Mekos!" Aradella's voice held much love and pride. "Maybe he senses Ian."

Mekos opened his jacket and looked inside. "You want to come out?"

Ian flew out, then up, so he was hovering inches in front of Darr's face.

They watched Darr's green eyes get brighter.

Qip laughed. "He hasn't seen a Never."

"His eyes are kind," Ian said.

Both Qip and Darr stared at the little man.

"I've heard of them," Qip whispered, "but I didn't know they could talk."

"Ian loves beer," Aradella said. "And I bet he's hungry."

"Starved," Ian said.

"Why don't you—" Qip began but stopped when he saw Darr lift a shoulder. Ian flew to it, held onto the metal ear, then said, "Go." They left the room.

They all stared at the empty doorway. "I think Darr has found a friend." Qip sounded shocked.

"Misfits," Bree said. "That's what we were told was on this island. Is Darr what they meant?"

"Oh no!" Qip said. "Far from it. But Darr is unique. Very few people have seen him. I made a few like him when I lived on Empyrea, but they didn't come close to the perfection of Darr. Vian told me—"

"You know her?" Mekos asked quickly.

"Quite well. She fought against my being tossed off the island—but she failed." When they started to ask questions, he held up his hand. "That's for later."

Aradella said, "If you're here now, when we need you, maybe she knew this would happen. Maybe your being here now is part of her long-term plan."

There was such hope in the four sets of young eyes, that Qip didn't want to take it away. "Perhaps," he said then looked at Mekos. "Tell me why your grandmother isn't pleased with you."

"She's angry at both of us," Aradella said. "And it's all my fault. I shouldn't have—" Her throat closed so she couldn't speak, and Mekos put his arm around her.

Qip looked at Bree and Tam, who were sitting close together on a small sofa. Tam shrugged, indicating that he knew nothing.

Bree spoke quietly. "She was supposed to marry Prince Nessa but she didn't."

"You don't know the truth!" Aradella snapped at her cousin.

"I was *supposed* to marry Mekos, but Olina found out and—" She stopped talking, too angry to continue.

It was Mekos who told the story.

For the most part, Qip listened in silence, but at the mention of Valona's name, he interrupted. "The country she was born in threw her out. They feared her power too much to kill her."

"Country?" Aradella asked. "Like on Earth?"

"Yes," Qip said. "Exactly like that."

Mekos told what Vian said would happen—if he and Aradella hadn't interfered, that is.

"Humph!" Qip said. "Maybe those three evil women would have killed each other. Or maybe they would have formed an alliance and destroyed us all. Urah, Olina, and Valona united." He shivered at the image.

At the mere idea that Vian might be wrong, Mekos and Aradella smiled broadly.

Tam was looking at Aradella. "You rode a wolf? You stabbed that woman?"

"I did what I had to." Aradella kept her chin up.

Bree mumbled, "I have no doubt she made a wolf obey her. Poor creature was probably terrified."

Her voice was so low that only Mekos heard her and he choked down a laugh.

Qip said, "Vian knows what *could* happen. But we've seen that her visions are not set in eternity."

"How do we change the future?" Mekos asked. "We're to the point where we'll do anything."

"I don't know," Qip said honestly. "I need to think and to consult with some people." Their eyes were wide as they looked to him for answers. "Go to the garden. Occupy yourselves while I figure this out. I will see you at dinner."

His expression showed that he was done talking. They picked up their empty plates and glasses and left the room.

# 16

Qip stood back as Darr opened the heavy door at the end of the house. The door had been designed to discourage entry so it was well concealed. Darr went up the circular staircase first as he needed to raise the trap door in the roof. When it was safe, he motioned to Qip to come up. At the top was a camouflaged lookout. It was so well hidden that people below could look at it but not see it. From the high vantage point, Qip could see his entire garden. More importantly, he could see his visitors.

"Look at them," he said as he scanned the garden. "They're separate, as far apart as they can be. What Cappie told me was awful. How can *they* do anything? They barely speak to each other." Mekos had found the archery court and was shooting arrows into the target, landing them on top of each other. For the most part, he had his arms around Aradella and was giving her lessons on the use of a bow. From the way they acted, there was no doubt that they'd soon go into the forest to be alone.

On the opposite side of the big garden were Tam and Bree. It was easy to see that his desire for her was so strong it's a wonder the trees didn't burst into flame. Bree seemed to be unused to male attention so she stepped away, but her eyes never left Tam. The two of them were taking turns lifting heavy stone statues of cherubs. Their laughter was so inordinately loud that it could be heard in the tower.

"What do I do with them?" Qip looked at Darr. "And where is your friend?"

The metal man pointed toward a flower bed.

"Ah yes, I heard that Nevers love flowers. Did he tell you about his life?"

Darr nodded, then shook his head. The light behind his eyes dulled to the point that it was almost dark.

"That bad, huh? I guess that means Olina? Or was it Valona? Urah?"

Darr held up three fingers.

Qip groaned. "All three. That poor man." He looked back at the couples. "Why was this dumped on *me*? Am I to tell them how to get into Empyrea? What would they do if they did get in? Snip at each other?"

He looked to the left. Aradella and Mekos were holding hands and running into the trees. "Aradella's hatred and resentment is like a crap-colored fog surrounding them. If she directed that hate in the right direction, she could conquer the planet, but she seems trapped inside it."

Darr made a motion of shooting an arrow from a bow.

"Yes, Mekos is good with that weapon. I heard he used it against Olina's money-stealing officers. But Mekos is under the rule of his father, his grandfather, and especially Haver, his great-grandfather. It's a wonder the boy can breathe."

Darr pointed toward Tam and Bree.

"That girl has no confidence. She's intimidated by everyone, but Cappie told me of her abilities. She knows so much and that strength of hers would be useful." Bree was laughing and Tam was acting hurt that she'd yet again defeated him in lifting.

"Tam. Zeon's son has a wife and child. But he's falling in love with Bree." Qip gave a sigh so strong that it swayed the tree leaves. "Vian wanted Aradella and Mekos to marry then be enthroned on Pithan. But are those two ready to take over ruling an island? There's so much anger in that girl that if she were queen and had power, what would she do with it? I could believe that her anger would make her become like Olina."

He took a breath. "And Bree needs a backbone. She certainly needs to stop being afraid of Aradella!" He waved his hand, unable to voice all that he was feeling. "Why were these four put together? It doesn't take magical foresight to see that as they are now, they can accomplish absolutely nothing. Aradella will give Bree some hate-filled look and she'll run away. Yet this 'team' is supposed to help destroy Empyrea." He gave a snort of laughter. "They don't even know what the place is like. They seem to believe it's full of warriors. If they only knew the truth!"

He looked to Darr to answer. Wisdom was something he hadn't specifically added when he'd created him, so when it appeared it had been a wondrous surprise. Cappie, annoyed at how long it took to get an answer from Darr, had asked, "Don't you regret not giving him a mouth?" Qip had replied honestly, "Never. Not even for one second."

Darr reached up and broke a leaf off an overhanging branch, then held it to the place where his nose should have been. This was odd since Qip had put the olfactory nerves in his ears. Obviously, Darr was mimicking human senses.

"They smell the flowers? Probably."

The light in Darr's eyes got brighter. He repeated his action of smelling the leaf, then he clasped his hands together, fingers entwined tightly. Qip knew he was trying to send a message, but he didn't know what it was. Darr pointed to the sides of the garden, to the far-apart couples, then he again clasped his hands.

"To get them together? Great idea. How do I do that? Act as their mother and tell them they should get along with each other? Be nice? Play pretty?" He grit his teeth. "Right now I'm afraid Aradella will snap at Bree for the thousandth time, then Bree will pick up a horse and throw it at her. Or maybe she'll just break the girl in half."

Darr's eyelights began blinking. This meant "listen and think." Again, he broke a branch and sniffed it.

It took all Qip's concentration before he finally understood. "The Rose of Vaheal," he said softly. "Oh! but I've wanted that for a long time! I know where it is but the bastards won't give it to me."

Darr raised his shoulders.

"Of course I've asked them, but they laugh at me. If these four got it, they'd have to . . . I don't know what they'd have to do, but—" When Darr put his hands back together, Qip smiled. "Yes. Together. Whatever they do, they'd have to do it *together.*"

Darr put his hand on his chest as though clutching something.

This time, Qip understood. "The medallion? Are you crazy? They could be killed! Sheean would—"

Darr pointed to the flower bed.

Qip's eyesight wasn't good enough to see the tiny Never, but he understood what was meant. "Like your new friend. Not what he seems. Yes, that's what Sheean is like. Something other than what he seems."

Darr nodded in agreement, his eyelights showing he was pleased that Qip understood.

But Qip shook his head no. "That's too much. They're too young for something like that. And how am I to know it'll work?" Qip closed his eyes for a moment. "Why did Vian dump this on *me*? Of course she injected me into Zeon's mind, then he obediently sent them here. For *me* to solve it all. What did I do to become thought of as a wise old man?"

When Darr shrugged his shoulders to show he didn't understand either, Qip laughed.

"Let me think about all this. Let's go back down. I'll talk to some people and you need to cook dinner. I forgot how much young people eat."

The light in Darr's eyes changed to a soft blue. It meant he was pleased.

"Thank you," Qip said, then he went down the stairs.

It was nearly sundown when the two couples gathered at the dining table. They hadn't been together since they were in Qip's library, and they'd managed to explore the garden without bypassing each other. They were like explorers among wild beasts, talking loud enough that they wouldn't surprise one another.

The big table was covered with many dishes of food, some of it that they'd never seen before. There were two place settings on each side, and one at the end.

What drew their attention was the other end. A miniature dining area had been set up. It looked like items had been taken from the many artifacts in the house and put together. There was an elegant inlaid table with platters of fruit that had been cut into tiny portions. Pretty porcelain bowls were filled with food from the big table, all of it cut very small. A brown ceramic jug held beer and there was a pewter mug next to an exquisite porcelain service. A carved chair held a tapestry-covered pillow.

"It's beautiful," Bree said.

They looked at Qip. "I have a friend who brings me items from Earth. These are called dollhouse miniatures." He looked embarrassed. "I am a bit of a collector."

"Bit" was an understatement. Unusual artifacts, most of them quite small, were on every available surface.

"Is it Jobi?" Mekos asked.

Qip smiled. "Yes, Jobi is my benefactor."

"And mine." Aradella motioned to the miniature furniture. "Ian will love this."

At his name, the small man flew into the room and went directly to stand on Darr's shoulder. The metal man nodded toward the setup.

They watched Ian fly to it. He ran his hand over the table,

then the plates. He picked up a fork and admired it. Ian seemed to know who had done it. He looked at Darr. "Thank you."

Darr bent his head in a bow of acknowledgment.

"Shall we?" Qip said as he sat down. "Please begin." He watched the young people heap their plates full, and waited to start talking.

"Did you find out anything?" Mekos asked. He was already on his second plate of food.

"Yes," Qip said. He was trying to keep his face expressionless. He had no intention of telling them what he'd been through in the last hours. He was able to reach Zeon, but Vian didn't answer any calls. Zeon had gone into one of his trances, then returned, and said, "It might work." That caused an explosion from Qip. "That's all you can say? It *might* work?" Zeon had been so annoyingly unperturbed by the anger that Qip blurted, "Your son is falling in love with Bree."

"I know," Zeon said. "They were destined to be together, but Reena made some very unpleasant threats if I allowed it." He hesitated. "She said that Bree is desperately needed elsewhere and *not* with my son."

Qip made a sound that was anger and exasperation mixed. "You sacrificed those two for . . . for what?"

"I don't know!" Zeon half shouted. "I do not have free will in this. I want the best for my son but he can't have Princess Bree. And you farken well better keep them apart!" At that, Zeon cut the connection.

Yet again, Qip muttered, "Why *me*?"

The five of them were looking at Qip, waiting to hear what he had to say. He took a breath. "As you have guessed, you were sent here for a reason." He looked back at the trusting young faces. "Vian has set a great and mighty task onto your shoulders. The truth is that I don't know if you can accomplish it."

Like all young people, their expressions said, *Yes we can! Try us!*

In other circumstances, Qip would have smiled, but these people—with their families—were talking of overthrowing Empyrea. "Before you can go forward, tomorrow you must procure two objects." He couldn't help glancing at Darr. His left eyelight blinked three times. Yes, they both knew it was a lie. Obtaining the objects was *not* the goal.

"We have some magic things," Aradella said. "We could—"

Qip raised his hand. "What you will obtain is fundamental to your success." He did not look at Darr. He knew he'd again see the blinking eyelights. But Darr was programed to send messages subtly. He sent a little flashing light that landed on the table next to Qip's hand. It could as well have formed the words *ridiculous rhetoric.* But they both knew there was no way Qip could tell them the truth.

Qip did his best to ignore the censure. "The first item you must obtain is the Rose of Vaheal. It's a simple object and it's being held in plain sight." He looked from one to the other. "The rose is used as a prop at our little playhouse. I've seen it there for years."

"You couldn't slip in and take it?" Mekos asked.

Qip leaned forward. "If it could be stolen, I would have done it years ago. It must be *given* to a person." He paused long enough to see the questions they were forming—but he had no intention of answering them. "It's a purple rose in a little white vase. It's hardly noticeable. Somehow, you must get someone in authority to give it to you."

Aradella made a sound of derision. "Bree can get it. All she has to do is look at a person and they capitulate. I've heard several men say, 'What is mine is yours.'"

Qip tried to conceal a frown at the jab. He looked at Bree. She said nothing but he saw her pick up a steel fork and conceal it on her lap. To his amazement, she folded it in half—with one hand. Seconds later, she straightened it and put it back on the table.

As he tried to not show his shock, Qip cleared his throat,

and looked at the others. "The second thing you're to get is a medallion." He shrugged. "However, I doubt if you can do that—and stay alive, that is. The ancient medallion is worn by the Monster of Sheean."

"What kind of monster?" Tam asked.

Qip took his time answering. "You asked about misfits. Sheean is one of them. His DNA was changed. In other words, he is like me and we are what we are."

"Like you?" Tam asked. "I think I speak for all of us in saying that we don't understand what you mean."

Qip put down his fork, Darr took his plate away, and the older man leaned back in his chair. "All of us here in this room are misfits."

"I am for sure," Mekos said. "I am a Lely, but the others are quite ordinary."

They smiled at his jest.

"No, no," Qip said. "Being *different* makes you a misfit." His voice began to rise. "I was cast out of the world I was born into."

Aradella put her hand over Mekos's. "We saw that in the Lair. The guide we had hated the Lelys. We don't want to offend anyone."

Qip put his hands over his ears. "Do not say that word!" he shouted.

They were shocked at his vehemence.

"Which word? *Lair*? *Lelys*?" Tam asked.

"No! The other one." Darr quickly handed Qip a dark red liquid in a little glass. It seemed to have been prepared beforehand and kept at the ready. Qip drank it in one gulp.

"You mean the word *offend*?" Aradella asked.

They waited while Qip regained his composure. "I apologize. I lived on Empyrea for many years, but I was hidden away for fear that my looks would—" he swallowed "—offend some people. Worse, they might feel sorry for me and that would hurt them. Hurt does not equal happiness or pleasure. And 'equal' is everything."

All five of them were looking at him without a hint of understanding. Yes, he was quite short, bald, and wrinkled, and his nose was rather wide and stubby, but there was nothing about him that would make anyone feel bad. He certainly wouldn't scare anyone!

"I was deemed to not belong, so I was sent here to Abicis with the other offensive people. All of us are too ugly or too beautiful, too strong or weak, too talented or too . . ." He waved his hand. "We are too *different*, so we were sent away."

"But you are magnificent at creating." Bree glanced at Darr.

Qip took a moment to calm himself. "Empyreans are not stupid. In spite of our physical oddities, they know how to use whatever talents we have." He looked at Mekos. "Your grandfather was brilliant with machines so he was put on a spaceship. My friend Cappie is often used. And I have a room full of machines that help me achieve what they need. My work is not offensive, just my physical appearance."

For a moment, they were quiet, then Mekos said, "If we live through this, you can have a home with us Beyhans. Or in Aradella's kingdom. You could get a wife, maybe."

Bree said, "On Pithan, we have women who will take anything male." Instantly, she realized how bad that sounded. "I didn't mean—"

Aradella cut her off. "Fox ladies will even take on humans and look what they get." She reached up to Mekos's hair and exposed one of his pointed ears.

Her joke broke the tension and they all laughed, even Bree. Darr's eyes twinkled with blue and green lights.

"So tell us what we need to know," Mekos said. "Can we do it all in a day?"

"I hope so," Qip said. "I don't believe Olina will stop her search for you. Her army is bound to show up here. We are in luck as tomorrow is our Play Day, with no work to be done. In the early morning, you and Tam will train with Darr. He's seen fights with Sheean so he knows what's needed."

"The fights are a regular occurrence?" Tam asked.

"Every week. The play is in the morning and the fight is later. Nearly everyone on the island goes to watch the play, then they stay to see the fight."

"What happens if a person loses?" Aradella asked.

Qip looked at her hard. "At worst, death. But sometimes it's merely the loss of a limb or an eye." Qip looked at Tam. "You two young men can go in together."

"Are women allowed to participate in the battle?" Bree asked.

Aradella gave a little laugh, then said, "Sorry. It was just an amusing image." She looked back at Qip. "This monster has the medallion?"

"It's around his neck. When you defeat him, you can take it."

"And everyone who has tried has failed to take it?" Bree asked.

"Oh no," Qip said. "People fight to get the prize money that's given based on how long he can survive in the ring. No one cares about the necklace Sheean wears. I doubt if anyone knows of its power."

Ian said, "You sound as though you know this person."

Qip smiled at his perception. "I knew him before he was labeled a monster. He was a scamp but—" Qip broke off. "That doesn't matter now. You will *need* the medallion. Do whatever you must to get it." He pushed his chair back and stood up. "I have to rest now. Tomorrow while the men train, the women will go after the rose."

Aradella gave a sound like a squeak. "My cousin and I *cannot*—" Mekos put his hand over hers and squeezed. With a sigh, she stopped talking. Personal feelings weren't going to be considered in this.

# 17

At breakfast the next morning it seemed that the pretty little house vibrated with the grumbling of the two women. The couples left the three bedrooms and started down the hall, the women with their heads held high. The men trailed behind them.

"Bad night?" Tam asked Mekos.

He rolled his eyes. "How can a person complain so much?"

"The same here," Tam said. "I left her room just hours ago. There is so much anger that I worry for the safety of the two of them together."

"I agree," Mekos said.

Breakfast was set out for them and they ate in silence. The men had their heads propped on their hands but the women were fueled by a lifetime of anger so they moved about quickly. "Ian is going with you," Mekos said. "If anything goes wrong, he'll tell us, and Tam and I will come."

"But . . ." Aradella started but Mekos's look made her stop talking.

It wasn't until midmorning that Qip showed up. Darr lifted him onto the big wagon and he drove the silent women to the arena. It was a huge half circle of stone seats facing an open area.

In the midst of it was a long building that had three rooms with curtains front and back, then a closed-in area on each end.

Aradella was looking at the barren area around the building. "Are the battles held here too?"

"Yes." Qip nodded to the long stage. "Go through there, use whatever feminine wiles you have, and persuade someone to give you the rose." He looked at Ian as he sat on Aradella's shoulder. "You should stay out of sight. Even here, you're too much of a curiosity. You might not be safe as someone might want to put you in a cage."

Ian rubbed his leg above the carved, wooden prosthetic. He knew not to take chances.

Aradella got down from the wagon, then looked at Bree to see if she needed help. With a defiant look, Bree jumped out of the back, landing firmly on the ground. "Please don't break any body parts," Aradella said. "We don't have time to nurse you."

Bree grit her teeth, said nothing, and the two of them walked to the end of the long building. When they turned the corner, they heard voices. At the far end, they saw people and activity, all accompanied by a lot of yelling.

"No! No! You stupid girl," a man shouted. "You're supposed to be a princess. Act like one! Where is she going? What do you mean she quit? And where the farken-el is that Never puppet?"

At that, Aradella and Bree halted and looked at Ian. "You must hide."

There were two more of what they assumed were stages that had curtains drawn across them. One of the men at the end glanced down at them and seemed startled by their appearance.

Bree tossed back a corner of a curtain. "Get in here!"

Quickly, Aradella ran onto the stage, with Bree behind her. They tried to look around but it was too dark to see much. Ian flew up, hovered, then made his entire body light up.

"You are a very useful man," Aradella said.

"Wish Arit thought so," Ian mumbled.

As they looked around, Aradella and Bree saw it at the same time. On the mantel of the fake fireplace was a purple rose in a plain white vase. As Qip had said, it didn't look like much.

"We could just take it and go," Aradella said as she extended her hand.

Ian blocked her. "If this thing is magic, I better test it first." There were other ornaments on the mantel and they were dusty. Ian ran his hands over them until he had a ball of dust, then he tossed it at the rose. It went up in a sizzle. "I guess it won't let us steal it."

"We should—" Aradella began but suddenly the heavy curtain was thrown back and light filled the room.

Standing there was a tall, bearded man wearing lots of makeup and a red dress. He glared at them. "You two don't know where you're supposed to be? You didn't have a clue when you saw all of us at the other end?"

Aradella looked like she was about to make a retort, but Bree stepped forward.

"We're so sorry," she said in her sweetest voice. "We're new here and we don't know how things work."

"It works, sweetie, by you two getting into costume. They're ready to open the gates and the ravenous hoard will soon be filling the seats. Can't you hear them?"

Aradella stepped in front of Bree. "We're not players. We just want—" She pointed to the rose.

The man groaned. "Let me guess, a little old man sent you here and we're to *give* it to you."

"Well, uh . . ." Aradella said.

"The owner always says no. Oh look! There's that Never puppet they've been looking for."

Ian was still on the mantel and he'd frozen into a stance so rigid that he didn't look real.

"This one is missing a leg but I guess it'll do." The man looked toward the end of the building and opened his mouth as though to shout.

"Wait!" Bree said. "What if we do an exchange?"

He looked back at her. "Honey, I'm sure you have nothing *I* want."

"You need players, right?" Bree said.

"We can't—" Aradella began, but then she changed her course. "What play is it?"

"The same as always," he said in disgust. "They don't have the brains to understand anything else."

The women waited for him to answer the question.

"It's *The Beautiful Princess and Her Jealous Maid.* Again."

"Does the maid try to steal the prince?" Bree asked.

"Of course. *They* never get tired of seeing it, but I'm sick of it."

"But the beautiful princess wins." Aradella's tone was so heavy with sarcasm it could have been weighed on a scale.

"Of course she does!" the man snapped. He looked them both up and down in an insolent way. "If you have no experience, how can you do this?"

"For my whole life, I've been acting as part of a lie," Aradella said.

He looked at Bree as though for verification.

"Both of us have done that."

Aradella said, "We'll do it if you'll give us the rose."

"For free," Bree added. "I mean, we won't charge anything to be in the play."

The man looked from them to the rose then back again. "What is the use of that thing?"

"It's for a collector," Bree said quickly.

"He's obsessed," Aradella added.

"All right, let me ask the owner."

They expected him to leave but he didn't. Instead he shouted, "They'll do it if you give them that ratty old purple flower."

A male voice, filled with amusement, yelled back. "If they make the audience stand up and clap, they got it."

The man turned back to them. "Better kiss it goodbye. Those

morons don't appreciate anything. Your collector is going to be disappointed again. We better get you suited."

"I guess she'll wear a crown," Aradella said. "And some divine dress. Do I scrub the floors?"

The man looked at Aradella like she was crazy. "Her?! Are you mad? She's too ordinary looking to be a princess. What color do you want your crown?"

"What?" Aradella asked.

Bree said, "Remind us of the story."

Again, the man groaned. "*She* isn't too bright, is she?" He nodded at Aradella. "But then, with a face like hers, she doesn't need to be, right? The plot is that you, the maid, are so jealous of the princess's great beauty and the man she's to get that you want to kill her."

Aradella was still trying to understand. "But *I* am the ugly one."

The man rolled his eyes. "It looks like the casting is perfect." He spoke to Aradella slowly and clearly. "You're beautiful but dumb. That won't be too difficult for you, will it, sweetie?" He nodded toward Bree. "As you can see, *she* is ugly, but she's very smart. Got it?"

Aradella still didn't fully comprehend. "But she's the beautiful one."

"Not here, baby. Here we like unique, not something that looks like an Empyrean robot. We—" He didn't finish because he was pushed aside by a large woman who was followed by two young women carrying heavy dresses.

The woman looked Aradella and Bree up and down, then gestured for the other two women to remove their outer clothes. Since they were both princesses, they were used to this and didn't fight it. With the speed of lightning, the young women were corseted into dresses that had very low-cut tops. While the cousins didn't resemble one another in any other way, they were both well-endowed.

"My goodness," Bree said. She was popping above the neckline like bread on its second rise.

"You got it, flaunt it, honey," the wardrobe woman said.

One of the young women rapidly put makeup on Aradella. "You should let them grow out." She meant Aradella's pale eyebrows and lashes.

The older woman looked at Bree and sighed. "She's hopeless. There's nothing you can do with her." No makeup was applied.

Bree did her best to ignore the little smirk that Aradella gave her, but didn't succeed. She wondered how much she could take before she betrayed her promise to Kaley and let Aradella have it.

Outside, the audience was arriving.

The man on the auditorium seats was frowning. "Ethel, if I see this play one more time, my eyes will fall out."

"They said they have new girls so it's bound to be different," his wife said.

"Is it still two girls fighting over the same man?"

Ethel gave a heavy sigh. "Bart Ollen. Oh yes. He is perfection in a man."

Under his wife's direction, he put the cushions down on the hard stone seats. She knew he hated the play so she'd brought his favorite cheese and beer. By the end of the performance, he'd be smiling—and she'd get to fantasize about Bart.

Behind the stage, out of sight of the audience, Bart Ollen waited for his cue to enter. He had on a loose white shirt and trousers so tight his bulge could be seen. So what if it was a tiny bit padded? The women loved it.

The stage manager—Bart could never remember his name—was listening to the play that had started. The princess and her maid were talking. Whatever was being said made the stage manager have an odd look on his heavily painted face.

Bart straightened his costume. He liked that he had a bit of time before stepping onto the stage. The two women were to argue about how the beautiful princess was to get the fabulous man—meaning Bart—while the maid would get nothing. The jealous maid was so angry that she would try to kill the princess. That's when Bart was to enter. The audience would gasp at his rugged manliness, then Bart would save the princess. He liked to surprise the people who went to see him regularly by changing the script a bit. Sometimes he'd murder the maid and sometimes he'd just banish her. It depended on if he was sleeping with the actress playing the maid. One way he got the women was to hint that he was thinking of completely changing the ending. He'd murder the princess then run away with the maid. Of course that was a lie, but sometimes it was necessary to say to get what he wanted.

But today seemed different. "What's going on?"

The manager's made-up eyes were wide. "I have no idea. Both of these girls are new, but I gave them a script. I think I did, but then who doesn't know the plot of this play? But they've gone so far off it, I don't know what they're doing."

"It's the audience that matters. What're they saying?"

"Nothing. They're silent. I can't tell if they hate it or love it." He pulled back a corner of the curtain. "See if you understand what's going on."

A woman's voice loudly said, "You're about to have an affair with a married man!"

"That's the girl playing the princess," the manager said.

The other woman, the maid, spoke, her voice angry. "I am not! But why shouldn't I since I'm missing out on all those men in Selkan? But *I* am not the problem. You put the entire island in jeopardy, but then, you've always done what *you* want."

"I have no idea what they're talking about," the manager said.

Bart shrugged his wide shoulders. "Oh well, it'll change when I get there." He flipped back the heavy curtain, stepped into the light, then waited for the usual applause.

But there was none. The light made it difficult to see the audience clearly, but over the years—too many, some said—he'd developed the ability to see them. The audience was almost in a trance, their eyes wide, mouths open. In shock. Bart frowned. *This is why plots shouldn't be changed*, he thought. *Changes take away from the main attraction.* By that, he meant *him. He* was the star and those girls better not forget it!

The princess—who was indeed a knockout—screeched, "I was to marry *Nessa*! He is a whining wimp of a—"

The maid said, "You think you're the only one to have a mate forced upon her? My father has chosen a man for me. He is forty-two years old, but his finances are stable and he has a nice house, so that makes him a fine match."

The princess set her jaw. "You sneered at me for my whole life. You ridiculed me."

The maid snapped back. "And you never missed an opportunity to let us know you thought we were stupid! You took your anger at Olina out on *us. We* didn't lock you up!"

*This has to stop!* Bart thought, so he stepped closer to the women. He expected them to halt. To draw in their breaths and go into a state of awe. On an island with many beautiful people, Bart stood above them all.

When the women turned to look at him, he gave his most endearing smile. Dazzling but with a hint of humility.

The princess said, "Not as good as Mekos."

The maid snorted. "Nor Tanek or even Roal. Certainly not Tam."

The women looked at each other. "At last we agree on something," the princess said.

When the women immediately went back to their argument about who'd had the worst life, Bart was quite agitated. He walked to the side of the stage and artfully posed himself against the fireplace. He knew from experience that it was a stance guaranteed to get the attention of the women. He very much liked their little squeals of lust. He even liked the scowls of the men. Bart adjusted his shirt to show off the inflated pecs he'd worked so hard to get. It was all perfect—except that the two women on stage didn't look at him. This was extremely annoying as the plot of the play was that they were *both* supposed to want him. Covet him. Fight each other to the death to get him.

The beautiful princess yelled, "You have no idea what I went through. I had private things—*dangerous* things—going on in my life."

The girl playing the maid gave her a look of contempt. It was so good that Bart thought he should practice re-creating it in front of a mirror. The girl's disdain was so realistic that she didn't even raise her voice. *Good acting*, Bart thought.

The maid said, "Do you mean your books or your training with Hale?"

*Who wrote this script?* Bart wondered. He'd never heard anything like it.

The princess looked so angry that steam seemed to come out of her ears. "Did Olina pay you to spy on me?"

The maid's anger seemed to reach a peak—and from her expression, it was as though something inside her broke. "You ungrateful bitch! My father distracted the guards while *I* hid your illegal books under my clothes. We risked our *lives* to help you."

The princess looked so shocked that Bart almost believed their dialogue was real. *Where did these girls train? Did someone on Empyrea adjust their chips so they could do this? If so, where do I get it done to me?*

He looked into the darkness at the audience. He'd never seen them so still. Usually, they were fussing over the mass of food they had with them, or telling their kids to shut up. When he was on, the women were lusting over him while the men were frowning. He loved that part! But now, all eyes were staring at the girls. The whole audience was transfixed! They weren't moving, not eating. They didn't even seem to be breathing.

This annoyed Bart so much that he looked around. What could he do to get the attention onto himself—where it should be? When he glanced to the side, he saw the little Never puppet. *Who put that thing there?* he wondered. It wasn't needed for this play. Maybe he'd get some praise if he returned it to where it belonged. *After this fiasco, I* need *praise.* He reached for the puppet. To his shock, the thing moved!

By all that was holy, had he found a *real* Never? Did they actually exist? When his hand started to close about the thing, it made a leap straight up into the air. Bart forgot about how those nothing-nobody girls were stealing all the attention, and made a grab for the creepy little thing. He caught something—he was, after all, a great athlete—but he missed its body. Instead, Bart ended up holding a little carved stick. He stared at it. *What is this?* he wondered.

He was so absorbed in whatever was in his hand that he didn't realize that the girls had abruptly stopped shouting. He looked at them. They were staring at him. *At last*, he thought. The stage thieves were finally giving *him* the attention he deserved.

But then, they yelled. Screeched really. In perfectly timed unison, they shouted, "YOU HURT IAN!"

"Huh?" was the only word Bart had time to get out of his mouth before he was attacked—and that's the only way to describe what they did.

The princess grabbed a steel poker from beside the fireplace.

*That isn't a prop!* he was about to warn, but he wasn't given the courtesy of time to explain. The princess whipped that long poker through the air like she knew how to handle it—and it went very near Bart's chest. He was about to speak out in protest but then he felt something. On his chest, across his perfectly trimmed manly hair, over his perfect chest muscles, was a split line. She had cut his new shirt! Then, with horror, he thought, *She has cut* me*!* Blood was seeping out.

Bart felt dizzy.

In the next second, the maid stepped close. Bart's only thought was that someone was going to take care of him. But to his shock, the maid put her hands on his chest and pushed him. So what? A push from a girl wasn't anything to concern him.

To Bart's horror, he went sailing back through the wall—

and it broke. The mantel of the fake fireplace bent around him like it was trying to hug him. There was a moment when he was in the air, wrapped in the fireplace, then bam! He sailed all the way through to hit the floor of Stage Two. He managed to keep his head up so it didn't hit the floor, but still, he was dazed. He looked up to see the rest of the wall, now with a giant hole in it, teeter then fall around him. The noise made him wince; the dust made him cough. Next, the curtain that had been drawn across the stage came down. When it fell, he knew the audience could see him sitting there surrounded by the layers of fallen wall and thick curtain.

Dazed as he was, Bart didn't dare look at the audience. It was no telling how they were taking this. Would they defend him or be glad of his humiliation?

Bart saw the two women stamp across the rubble of the wall toward him. He was pinned down under the debris and his instinct was to throw his arms over his face and beg them not to further hurt him. But he was too aware of his reputation for being the manliest of men. Bracing himself, he stared up at the women, one on each side of him.

The maid held out her hand.

Bart gave a weak smile. Good! She was sorry for what she'd done—accidently, of course—and was offering help. But when he lifted his hand, she snatched hers back.

On the other side, the princess held out her hand. "Give it to me!"

It took a moment to know what she meant. It was then that Bart realized he was still holding the little piece of carved wood that had been on that puppet. The "puppet" that flew across the room.

He held it up and she rudely grabbed it out of his hand.

"You bastard!" the princess said to him.

The maid said, "Pick on someone your own size, you bully!"

The women stamped back to Stage One.

Bart could only stare at them. He had no idea what was going on. He watched as the princess held up the wooden piece, then the "puppet" flew to her shoulder, and she handed the stick to him. Bart heard a male voice say, "Thank you," then the two—or was it three?—people left the stage. The back curtain closed.

When Aradella and Bree were on the other side of the curtain, they looked at each other in shock, then turned away. They had just seen different viewpoints of their entire lives.

Aradella spoke first. "I think we lost out on being given anything. No rose for us." When Bree didn't reply, Aradella said, "Your push." She was asking a question.

Bree hesitated. "I inherited some of my father's strength."

"And you kept it secret from everyone? Even your sister?"

Bree nodded. "Just Papá knows. We used to sneak out at night to train."

"That's when you saw me with Hale," Aradella said.

Bree nodded. "Yes. We—"

"Starken-el, you two!" the man they'd seen earlier shouted. From his attitude, he was the owner. "Get out there and take your bows. That audience is cheering and screaming. I've never heard anything like it!" He threw back the curtain and they could see through to the stone seats. Everyone, male, female, children, even some weird-looking animals, were shouting and clapping.

"For us?" Aradella asked.

The man rolled his eyes. "Brainless but talented!" He put his hand on Aradella's back to push her forward, started to touch Bree, but then drew back. "I'll give you half of everything I own if you two will do that every week."

"Thanks," Aradella said, "but this was a one-time performance."

The man looked at Bree. "As for you, power baby, anytime you wanta spend the night with me, I'm yours." He stepped away from them. "Go!"

When Aradella and Bree got to the front of the stage, the audience went wild with cheering. The women looked at the flattened wall. Bart was no longer there but the evidence of what they'd done was.

Aradella grabbed Bree's hand and raised her arm like the winner of a contest. Bree looked reluctant, but Aradella nodded to the other arm. Bree raised both arms and the crowd yelled even louder.

What they didn't see in the shadows was Tam, Mekos, and Qip. They'd seen the entire play.

Mekos looked at Tam. "Did you know?"

It was easy to figure out that he meant Bree's strength. "Yes," Tam said rather smugly.

They looked back to see the stage manager making his way through the rubble on the nearly demolished Stage Two. He moved debris until he found the purple rose in the vase. He picked it up, walked across the fallen wall, then made a flamboyant gesture of presenting it to Aradella and Bree like it was a trophy.

Each woman put a hand on the vase and raised it in triumph. There was wild cheering.

Hidden at the side of the audience, Qip looked at Mekos and Tam. "Think you two can live up to that?"

"No," Mekos said. "Not even close." His voice told of his pride in the woman he loved.

"Definitely not," Tam said. "However, I was wondering about the affair part. I could—"

"Touch my relative and you die," Mekos said amicably. "I'll call the fox world on you. And the birds."

"Since when are you related to Princess Bree?"

"Since—"

They bickered all the way back to the wagon. Behind them, Qip nodded toward the young men and thought, *I just want those two to stay alive.*

# 18

Hours later, Aradella was riding bareback on Qip's gray horse. It wasn't easy to hold on, but the wolf had given her some confidence in her ability to ride anything. She still had on the corseted, low-cut costume she'd worn in the play.

She and Bree had— At that thought, she almost halted. The concept that she and her cousin had done something *together* was more than her mind could comprehend.

After the play, they saw Qip and the men arriving in the wagon. As before, Bree sat on the seat beside Qip while Aradella got in the back.

"That's some dress," Mekos said. His tone didn't agree with the look on his face. He took off his jacket and put it around her.

"Tell us what happened," Tam said.

Bree twisted around to glance at Aradella, then turned back. By silent agreement, they weren't going to tell the whole story.

"Nothing really," Aradella said. "We did a play and as payment they gave us the rose."

"And the dresses?" Tam was smiling.

"We, ah, left quickly," Bree said. "We should return them."

"Some woman put your clothes in the back," Qip said. "Was the play easy to do?"

"Too easy." Aradella closed her mouth and answered no more questions. She tightened Mekos's jacket around her. As they rode back to Qip's house, Mekos and Tam talked about training with Darr, about how quick he was and that he could fence with both of them at the same time.

Aradella's mind was too full to think clearly. What she'd learned about Bree, about the secrets her cousin had kept, had destroyed what Aradella thought to be true.

When they got back to the house, food was waiting. Qip proudly displayed the rose in the middle of the table. Later, there would be more training before . . . before the battle.

"The entertainment goes on all day," Qip told them. "After the play, the stages are moved to the back and it becomes an arena."

Maybe it was the reality of the play that was making Aradella realize the seriousness of the coming contest. Like her, Bree was quiet, saying little, but the two men were excited, even looking forward to what they were facing.

*I must stop this*, Aradella thought. *As Bree said, all of this is my fault. If I'd married Nessa, none of this would be happening. Or if I'd not killed Valona they'd be safe. If I'd not—*

She knew she had to stop regretting what had happened. It was time to go forward.

The others went to the garden, but Aradella said she wanted to rest.

"And change clothes," Mekos said as he left the house.

She'd given him a half smile, then went to the room they shared. It was as cute as the rest of the house. There were four shelves holding replicas of animals. Each was about the size of a hand, but they were made of different materials.

"Were we right when we joked that the rose and the medallion are for Qip's collection?" she whispered. "Is that all they are?"

Qip said that no one knew the medallion was worth anything. Maybe it was a cheap metal but held magic, which people couldn't see. The window was open and she heard the clash of swords. Would one of the men die today? Lose a limb? A hand? An eye?

There was a mirror on the wall and Aradella paused to look in it. She still wore the stage makeup, still had on the dress. She'd spent years of her life making herself as unattractive as possible. But here she was on an island where they thought she was beautiful. "Aunt Olina wouldn't even recognize me now."

She turned away from the mirror but then looked back at it. *Beauty!* How may hundreds of times had she seen the beauty of her cousins turn people into doddering idiots?

When she walked with her cousins, people fell over themselves asking to do things for the beautiful twins. Aradella remembered a handsome young man getting water from a well and presenting it to the twins. After they'd had a drink, he handed the bucket to Aradella and said, "Put it back." She'd experienced that kind of thing over and over.

"What can beauty do?" she asked her reflection.

The answer, based on a lifetime of observation, came to her. *Anything!*

On the bottom shelf beside a tortoise carved out of green stone, was the little bag that produced an unlimited number of gold coins.

"Between gold and beauty, I can *do* something," she said. "I can change things."

She didn't allow herself to think too much, but ran from the house. She'd heard Qip's horses but hadn't been to his stables. It was easy to find. Like everything else, it was clean and tidy. She walked along the stalls and the big gray horse nudged her affectionately. "Like to go for a ride?"

Minutes later, she was on its back and riding toward town. She was going to stop this fight!

# 19

"Where is she?" Mekos asked again. "Is she safe? She took a horse. Why didn't she take Ian? Her chip has gone dead. Where is she?"

*I wish someone would love me that much*, Bree thought. She was sitting on the wagon beside Qip, wearing her trousers and shirt, the magic bag hanging cross-body on her. Zeon said the contents would be needed so maybe now was the time. Qip was frowning so hard his forehead was deeply wrinkled. Earlier, he'd voiced his worry. "I don't know where Aradella is. This is not part of the plan. She shouldn't have left here. She . . ." He didn't finish his sentence.

Tam suggested sending Darr to look for her, but Qip shook his head at that. "He frightens people." And Ian was to stay with Darr. In the play, they'd seen what the sight of him caused so they didn't want to risk that again.

When they got to the arena, it had been cleared. The long, three-stage building was now far to the side. There was a big dirt-covered area, and the stone seats were filled to capacity. Word was that the play had been so good that everyone on the island wanted to see this afternoon's match. The people were talking excitedly about what they were going to see.

"This isn't good," Qip mumbled. "Something is wrong." He drove the wagon to the back of the arena. The thick, enclosing wall was stone, with several hollowed out areas that had iron bars for doors. Men were working in the area, preparing for the coming show. They were all smiling. "These people are too happy. They're up to something."

"Are those cages?" Tam was unloading weapons from the back: swords, knives, even Mekos's bow. The seriousness of what they were facing was beginning to hit the young men. "Maybe Aradella didn't want to see this."

Mekos snapped, "She rode a wolf and stabbed a woman. Aradella isn't afraid of anything."

"I never meant—" Tam didn't continue.

Bree had been silent since they'd found that Aradella wasn't there. She wasn't sure but she had an idea that her cousin's disappearance had something to do with what had been said that morning. *You put the entire island in jeopardy*, Bree had shouted. She'd blamed Aradella for *all* of it!

A young man saw Bree and stopped. "It's *you*! You're the ugly maid." He turned to a couple of men who were tying ropes down. "Now we have both of you."

Bree was about to ask him what that meant when Qip said, "I don't like the attention being on you. Here!" He grabbed a smelly old blanket off a hay bale and tossed it to her. "Stay covered and out of sight."

She put the blanket over her head and stepped back into one of the cages. Minutes later, Tam joined her.

"I don't know what will happen today," he said softly. "My father warned of a death that is wrong, so maybe . . ."

As she looked at him, so much went through her mind. From the moment they met, she'd felt close to him. It was as though she *knew* him. The hours they'd spent in Qip's garden had been divine. For the first time in her life, she'd been *free*. She could display her strength and talk about her time with Reena—things she'd had to keep secret. Later, in Zeon's garden, he'd laughed at her stories about preparing concoctions for lovesick girls, and of sharing joy with women who—thanks to Reena—were now expecting children. She told Tam of the "forget everything" spell they'd used more than once on Olina's overzealous guards. Talking to him made Bree aware that she'd had so much bottled inside her.

Now, looking at him, she knew it would soon be over. Whether they succeeded or failed today, they'd separate. Tam would go back to his family and Bree would go . . . Tears came to her eyes. Back to her life of secrecy, of always pretending she wasn't what she was.

For the first time, she slipped her arms around him and put her head on his chest. "Don't say that. You are needed. You and I are . . ." The tears were coming stronger.

He held her tightly. "I know. I've felt it too. If I live through this, you and I must talk. Maybe we can—"

"Tam!" they heard Mekos call.

Reluctantly, he released her and stepped away. "Something is wrong. I can feel it. Maybe I did inherit some foresight from my father."

"I will stay close by and if you need help, I'm here."

In other circumstances, with any other woman, he would have said no, but not with Bree. "If a wall falls on me, come and save me."

She knew he was joking, but she didn't laugh. "I will."

He left the shadows to go to Mekos.

Bree heard a man with a powerful voice announcing the coming match. He said the Monster of Sheean was "undefeated." No one had ever beaten him. He could take on a dozen men at once. He could—

She couldn't stand to hear more. She wanted to see the "monster," to see what the men were about to face. With her upper half covered, she walked along the wall, looking in each of the cages. They were empty, but inside the cage at the end was a creature like she'd never seen. It wasn't very tall or even muscular, but its skin was a glistening brown metal-like substance under long, sparse fur. Its head was long, sticking out past its back. About its neck was an old chain with an oval medallion at the end. As Qip had said, it didn't look valuable. When she looked up, the creature was staring at her. For a moment, its eyes seemed almost human. But in the next second, they turned a deep red and looked like flames.

Bree turned away. She instinctively knew that it would take more than just strength to conquer something like that thing.

When horns were blown, the audience began stamping their feet. Bree saw Mekos and Tam, both heavily armed, standing at the entrance to the arena.

Behind them, four men cautiously opened the cage door. Calmly, the creature walked out. It stood on its two back feet, but its arms were long enough to be legs. Its feet were sharp hooves and in its right claw was a heavy blade. Whatever it was, it was enough human that it could use a weapon.

The men stepped back, as though ready to flee, as the creature got onto a wheeled platform. Obviously, it knew the drill.

As the men started to pull the platform forward, the creature abruptly turned and looked straight at Bree. Yet again, she saw its eyes. For a flash, they were human, then they changed. He sneered at her, showing rows of sharp, jagged teeth. His gesture was threatening.

*I can't watch this,* Bree thought. *I'm going to be like Aradella and run away.*

There was the roar of the crowd, then came the horrible sound of steel on steel. *It has begun.* She leaned against the stone wall, listening to the battle, but not wanting to see it. When there was a collective shout, she knew someone had been wounded.

She didn't know how long it went on, but it seemed like an eternity when suddenly, everything went silent. *Death!* she thought. *Someone has been killed.*

She ran to the big doorway so she could see into the arena.

Tam's left arm had blood running down it. Mekos's leg was bloody. Facing them, unscathed, was the monster, its eyes glowing like balls of fire.

Bree's instinct was to run into the arena. She didn't know what she could do, but there had to be something. *What would Papá do?* she wondered. *He'd grab the creature from behind and break it in half.* Bree knew she didn't have that much strength.

But she could try! She took a few steps forward, then realized that the audience and the fighters were staring at the far end of the arena. There was utter silence. Even the children were quiet.

Bree turned to look. She didn't believe what she was seeing. Men were rolling out a big, heavy sheet of metal. It was tall and wide and leaning against a two-wheel handcart. There were two holes in the big slab and a heavy chain had been threaded through them.

The chain was around . . . Bree shook her head to clear it. Leaning against the sheet of steel was Aradella. She had on her costume from the play and around her waist was a thick chain. She was being held as a prisoner, offered as a sacrifice, to the battle. If Tam and Mekos lost, Aradella would be at the mercy of the monster.

Bree didn't think, she just ran to Aradella. At the sight of her, the crowd erupted. There were cries of, "It's the ugly maid." "With the beautiful princess." "Together!"

Behind Bree, she heard the clash of steel. The men and the monster were back to fighting. She grabbed the chain with both hands. With all her might, she tried to pull it apart but it didn't budge.

Aradella stared at her in silence.

Bree went to the back. There was an old lock on the chain. "If only Ian were here!

"They'd probably rush down here to capture him," Aradella said.

Not even Bree's strength could break the chain. "Why did

you try to do this alone?" she shouted to Aradella over the noise of the crowd.

"They think I'm beautiful so I thought they'd *give* me the medallion. I wanted to stop the fight."

There was a metal stake in the ground. Bree pulled it up—to the cheers of the crowd—and used it as a wedge on the lock. "You think that having a pretty face gets you anything you want?"

"Yes! The men on Pithan leap to do things for you."

"That's because of my *father*!" Bree yelled as she wrenched at the lock. "They hope I'll say something good to him. They know Olina hates you so they're afraid. That's why they ignore *you*." She took a breath to gather all her strength and again tried to tear the lock away.

"Is your sister strong?" Aradella's voice was wobbly as she used her questions to cover her fear.

Bree's arms ached but the lock didn't give way. She went to the other side to look at Aradella. "No, and if she knew I'd inherited Papá's strength and she didn't, she would—" She didn't finish.

"Kill you in your sleep?"

"You *do* know my sister!" She looked Aradella in the eyes. Behind them came the sound of an animal in pain. Had they struck the creature? She didn't look. "There's a spell I can do." She took the bag off. "I'll mix it."

"How do you know how to—?"

"I work for Reena. In secret," Bree snapped. Her mind was on deciding on a spell and remembering it.

Bree's revelation so stunned Aradella that she said no more.

When Bree opened the bag and removed a bowl, there was a rumble from the crowd.

"What's the ugly maid doing?" someone shouted.

Bree held the bowl and gave the bag to Aradella. "I need datura, valerian, penup, and aleenic."

Aradella rummaged through the plants in the bag, took out the ones Bree needed, and threw them into the bowl.

"Karua," Bree said. "Give me as much as you can find. I have to try to make an oil."

Aradella pulled out a short branch of a tree.

The audience gasped that something so big could be in the bag, then they grew silent as they watched Bree break the branch into pieces. She put the pieces between her palms, then used every muscle in her body to squeeze.

Someone in the crowd yelled, "One!" People joined for, "Two! Three!" They got to five before a sunlight-bright drop of oil dripped from Bree's hands into the bowl.

The crowd let out a deafening cheer.

"Tam has to ignite this," Bree yelled to Aradella over the noise.

"What does it do?"

"It will paralyze the monster."

When another roar came from the crowd, both women looked at the men and the monster, fearful of what they'd see. But the men and the monster weren't moving. They were staring at something behind the princess on the board.

"What is it?" Aradella tried to twist about, but the heavy chain around her waist was too tight.

When Bree saw the man entering the arena, her eyes widened in shock. "It's that man, the actor."

Entering the arena, dressed in a shiny black outfit, with a flashy red-lined black cape, was Bart Ollen. He waited for the people to give him their full attention, then he dramatically held up his arm. With a broad gesture, he opened his hand. Dangling from his fingers was a great big key.

Playing his role of savior, he walked to the back of the steel stand and unlocked the chain around Aradella.

The roar of the crowd was deafening. They were glad that Bart was back to being their hero.

"Thank you!" Bree and Aradella said in unison.

"We need to—" Bree began, but then she saw a most welcome sight. Cappie was standing in the shade against the wall.

"Need some help?" He was so calm he sounded like he was offering her an umbrella.

Bree nearly lost it in her gratitude. "Fire it up!" She thrust the bowl at him. "It's the 7K18 spell. Paralyze from the neck down."

He took the bowl, then began mumbling some words. "Hecubus, momalon—"

Bree looked back at the fighters. Mekos soared behind the creature, sword drawn, but it seemed to anticipate the movement. Mekos was barely able to dodge the monster's claws.

"I made it into a ball," Cappie said. "When it hits him and explodes, it will work. Can you throw it?"

Aradella was beside her. "Let me. I have good aim."

The two women went to the men. Tam started to block them, but Bree yelled, "No!"

Aradella grabbed the ball from the bowl. "Head? Heart? Where?"

"Heart!" Bree said.

With perfect accuracy, Aradella threw the ball of the plant mixture and hit the creature on the left side of its chest. It burst with a little plume of dark smoke.

The monster looked down in surprise, then crumpled to the ground.

Mekos and Tam, their swords held out, stepped toward the fallen creature. It was clear that they meant to kill it.

Aradella and Bree looked at each other and they seemed to exchange thoughts. Zeon had said, "The death is wrong. It shouldn't happen." Was *this* what he was talking about? "No!" the women yelled in unison, then knelt down by the creature.

Aradella nodded to the chain around its neck. Bree broke it, and took the medallion. It wasn't very big and she put it in her pocket.

The audience had gone deathly silent as they watched the two women kneeling on each side of the fallen creature. Nearby were the two young warriors, swords ready to strike.

Bree and Aradella looked at each other across the creature. From the neck up, it was awake and alert.

"Keess," it said.

"We're not going to hurt you." Aradella looked at Bree in question. *What now?* her eyes asked.

Bree's eyes widened. "I think he's saying, 'Kiss.'"

"Kaley's Earth stories tell of kissing people to save them."

Bree shrugged as though to say, *Why not?*

The women bent forward and simultaneously kissed the cheeks of the creature.

The audience didn't know whether to boo or cheer, so they were silent.

Suddenly, smoke came from the creature's stomach. Aradella and Bree quickly stood up and stepped away. More smoke came from the body.

"We've killed him," Aradella said.

The men went to them, their arms engulfing the women.

Every eye in the arena was on the creature on the ground. There were no flames, just smoke that grew in density until no one could see what was inside it.

When the smoke began to clear, they saw something standing there.

Mekos was holding Aradella, her back to his front. Near them, Tam was holding Bree in the same way.

When the smoke blew away, they saw a different creature. The upper half was a man with little horns striking out of brown curly hair. The bottom half of him was furry. His feet were cloven.

"Goat," Tam said. "He's half goat."

"He's a Lely," Mekos said.

"I owe you," the goat-man said. His voice was harsh, as though it had been a long time since he spoke.

"Who are you?" Mekos asked.

"Elvin." He swallowed, then coughed and nodded toward the medallion. "Urah. Enchantment. She will want that." In the next second, he ran out of the arena.

The crowd had been stunned into silence but at Elvin's exit, they exploded into cheers. The excited audience rushed down to the arena, meaning to grab the players and lift them, but Mekos soared away with Aradella. Tam lifted Bree in an overhead press and ran with her through the gates.

The only person left for the people to hail was Bart, so they lifted him above their heads and carried him round and round the arena. He was again the island's hero. No one on any planet was happier than Bart Ollen was that day.

# 20

"You're celebrities," Qip said as he drove the wagon toward his house. He didn't sound pleased.

His passengers were silent, recovering from what they'd been through in the long day.

Bree, on the seat beside him, had the medallion and she looked at it. It was oval and made of very old gold. On the outside were nine crudely cut gray jewels, one bigger than the others. When it was opened, painted on a white stone, was the face of a pretty woman with dark curls and pink lips. Bree handed it to Tam.

Tam looked at the picture, then handed it to Mekos and Aradella.

No one mentioned the name the goat-man had said. "Urah." It seemed that all bad began and ended with that woman.

"Of what use are the things we got?" Aradella's voice sounded weak. She hadn't yet recovered her strength. She knew the middle of her was badly bruised.

"Why was he changed into a monster?" Bree was looking at Qip.

Qip sighed. "I'm sure the rose and the medallion have uses but I don't know what they are." His voice was rising, showing his frustration. "As for the Monster of Sheean, it was probably done by magic, but I don't know why."

"It doesn't take much to enrage her," Aradella said softly. They all knew who she meant.

Tam was leaning against the side of the wagon. "Was he transformed by the removal of the medallion or by the kisses?"

Mekos looked serious. "Female kisses have the opposite effect. They turn a quiet, peaceful man into a raging monster."

They looked at him, their faces showing the absurdity of that, then Tam gave a little laugh. "The crowd sure did love the ugly maid."

"And my beautiful princess," Mekos said proudly. "Some man offered me a house and six horses if I'd work for him."

Bree said, "I'm sure it's the same man who wants us to do more plays."

"Ha!" Aradella said. "He wants my cousin for a night of ecstasy."

"I can't blame him for that!" Tam's tone was so truthful, but at the same time so very sad, that they couldn't retain their laughter.

They were exhausted, bruised, and bleeding, but they were *alive.*

For the rest of the way, they were in a better mood. Mekos and Tam argued about who had been injured more.

The two women were silent. When they'd awakened that morning, they'd been lifelong enemies, but now they were . . . Neither of them knew exactly what they were. But they knew that things had changed.

By the time they got to the house, they were all smiling.

"I hope Darr cooked something good," Mekos said.

"I hope he fixed Ian's leg," Bree said. "It was damaged this morning."

"We can—" Aradella began, then broke off. Darr was waiting for them, and the green of his eyes was an ugly color, like pond sludge. Something had made him unhappy.

The young people let out a sigh. *What now?*

Darr lifted Qip down. They couldn't understand Darr's eye-light flashes, but Qip could.

"Why don't you give him a voice?" Aradella sounded annoyed.

"I agree," Bree said and went to stand next to her cousin.

Qip snorted. "He and I do quite well as we are."

Behind them, Mekos and Tam looked at each other with raised eyebrows. *The cousins agreeing on something was certainly a change!*

They heard a noise then turned to see the big eagle-headed creature step out of the forest.

Mekos went to it, stroked its head, and listened. "Your father sent him. Your baby is coming."

Tam immediately got onto the animal. "I must go." He looked at them. "My friends," he began. "I cannot describe . . ." His eyes fastened on Bree's and everyone saw their pain. "I . . ." he began again, but he didn't seem to know what else to say. He nudged the animal forward and up. Minutes later, he was out of sight.

They looked at Bree.

"I'm very tired." Turning, she went into the house.

Aradella looked at Qip. "If whatever that red drink you gave to Qip when he was upset is for calming a person down, I want some of it for my cousin." The way she said it was an order, not a request.

Qip nodded at Darr, and Aradella followed the metal man into the house.

Mekos began removing weapons from the back of the wagon. That Tam hadn't taken time to gather his belongings told that his family meant more to him than anything else.

The absence of Tam left a hole in the group. At dinner, Bree stayed in her bedroom. Aradella prepared a plate for her along with Qip's red drink, and took it to her room. When she returned, she put the empty little glass on the table. "She's asleep." Aradella looked at Qip and nodded thanks.

They told Ian what happened in the arena, but Tam's absence took the life out of the story. They thanked Darr for doing some carving on Ian's wooden leg so it fit better. His eyelights flashed a very pretty shade of blue.

"He's pleased," Qip said.

"Too bad he can't *tell* us that," Aradella muttered. After dinner, she left to take a long, hot bath.

Mekos knew Qip was tired but he wanted him to stay and talk. First, he got the box of magic items that Kaley had tucked under the dragon's saddle.

"We need to find out more about Empyrea," Mekos said.

Qip shook his head. "You can't go there, just the three of you. You'll accomplish nothing."

"Aradella knows plants and Bree knows the recipes. We can use that."

"With Tam gone, you have no one to ignite the spells. Without that, you just have a bowl of salad, probably poisonous."

"Cappie?" Mekos asked.

"He's too old. He'd never live through a trip like that."

Mekos didn't know how to plead his case. He put the box on the table, opened it, and inside the little man began dancing.

But Qip ignored it. He took the key out and looked at it. "This has the crest of Empyrea on it."

"What does it open?"

"I have no idea," Qip said. "But I would imagine that it's important. Where did you get it?"

"Papá says Kaley stole it from the warlock, Garen. He was kidding. Maybe."

Qip was holding it up, twisting it about like it was a jewel of great value. "Yes, that makes sense. Garen is the nephew of Reena, and she is best friends with Vian."

Mekos was shocked. "My grandmamá has a friend?"

"Yes! A very powerful one. When it comes to witchery, Reena is second only to her hideous old sister, Urah."

Mekos considered that. "And Bree is apprenticed to Reena. It's almost like all those women are working together."

Qip snorted. "Are you so young that you think *men* control the world?! Ha! Those women keep all of us in a tight circle, then they lock it down with secrets."

Mekos sighed. "That's probably true, but then, Aradella and I killed Valona, so . . ."

"Yes, you seem to have messed up their plans. Not that any of those women have ever confided in me, but I'd wager they were waiting for Aradella to grow up. Then they'd put whatever their plan was into action."

"And *I* was part of the plan?"

"Sure. If that's what you want to believe."

The men exchanged looks of understanding. They were part of a very large plan and they had no idea what it was—or how it involved them.

Qip put the key back in the box and stood up. "I must rest—and we must trust. There are many people involved in this. You're not alone."

Mekos nodded in agreement. Hope was a good thing.

# 21

## FRANK J. ARENS

### KALEY'S GRANDFATHER

Frank was glad the horse he was on was so well trained. It knew its way down the mountain back to Zeon's warm stall and abundant food. One of Zeon's guards was behind him and another in front, so he knew he didn't have to worry about the horse losing its way.

It wasn't even daylight yet, and he'd just woken up. After days of no sleep, he'd crashed for hours on the cave floor. He knew he wouldn't have had enough energy for what he'd accomplished in Haver's cave if it hadn't been for the three-year trip to Bellis. They had repaired him. Like he was one of Jeff's car engines, they'd overhauled his old body.

Back in Kansas, he hadn't even told Rita about the pain he dealt with every day. He had injuries from Vietnam and the years of hard farmwork had taken a toll on him. But when he woke up inside a pod in a spaceship, all that was gone. Later, he asked the former ship's officer, Roal, about it. He was told that Empyreans had the technology to go back and forth to Earth in just months, but the state of the human bodies they picked up were so badly damaged it took years to repair them. New internal organs were grown, brain and nerve damage repaired. Cells regrown. The result was that when they landed on Bellis, people who'd been in wheelchairs could walk. Diseases were gone. If genetic defects were detected, DNA was reformed.

Frank asked him why people were taken from Earth. Roal said that wasn't his department but the gossip was that each earthling had some talent. "There's something different about each one of them," Roal said. "But who knows what Empyreans think is 'special'?"

Frank thought of his granddaughter, Kaley. There was her connection with animals. When she was a toddler, he'd had to secure her bedroom window or in the morning she'd be gone. They'd find her asleep with whatever wild animal she could find. She never saw a difference between herself and them.

The horse slipped on a rock on the steep downward path. Instantly, Frank came awake. *How good it is to have the reflexes of my younger self,* he thought.

He looked around at the pretty landscape. Yes, Bellis was much like Earth. But the people were very different. He smiled as he remembered Tanek as a boy.

When the family met him, the poor kid was starved for the outdoors and for people. He'd spent his whole life on the ship. He didn't know who his mother was, and his father was too busy running a ship to have much time for him. Between the birds on Earth and the doting honorary grandparents, Tanek opened up. He told them everything. By the time their dear daughter-in-law, Graceen, revealed that she was from another planet, Frank and Rita knew quite a bit about the place. When they were told that Graceen wouldn't be allowed to stay on Earth and raise her daughter, Rita had cried—and Frank wanted to. But they'd put on a brave face for Graceen.

What surprised them—since Tanek knew nothing about it—was the talk of Solium. It seemed that the Empyreans loved the little red plant. Jeff said they were going to grow it. "And when they come back to get Kaley, I'm going to offer it as payment—or blackmail—to go with them." Jeff seemed to be asking his parents if they wanted to join him. Neither Frank nor Rita hesitated. "When do we start?" Frank asked.

He came back to the present and looked around. They'd reached flatter land and were closer to Zeon's big house.

Days ago, when he'd landed the helicopter at Zeon's house, as he'd been told, the man was waiting for him. The idea of someone who could foresee the future was new to Frank, but the locals took it in stride. But then, humans with furry fox tails or a kid whose daddy was a bear didn't phase them either.

He was surprised that they'd never seen a helicopter. After the wedding-that-didn't-happen, Frank thought maybe Sojee was going to pick Tanek up and shove him into the thing. Tanek could control elephant-sized birds with his mind and he could drive a pickup, but a chopper freaked him out.

It was Roal, a master with spaceships, who'd asked, "How?" Frank knew what he meant. How had he learned to fly the noisy machines?

Frank hadn't answered. He and Rita'd had too many years of secrecy to blab to anyone. Their son, Jeff, knew his parents' background, and Kaley knew some, but outsiders didn't.

He and Rita met in Vietnam. She was a nurse and he was a wounded soldier. Classic. After they returned to the US, they were given an opportunity that they took. They got in on the ground floor of the creation of computers. It turned out that they both had that kind of brain. Numbers and logic were easy for them. For years, they lived on caffeine and delivered pizzas.

What none of them foresaw was how lucrative what they were doing would be. Money, and lots of it, came in.

When Rita got pregnant, she set her jaw and faced her husband. "I want *out*." He knew what she meant. She wanted to leave the computer world where working twenty hours straight was normal. There were weeks when they never saw the outdoors. Their lives centered around computer screens.

She wanted to raise their child in a different life. "I don't want a child who thinks eggs come from the grocery store. I want to be there to see the first laugh, the first steps. I want to learn how to bake a pie." Her eyes told Frank she was leaving with or without him.

He was calm. "I hear that Kansas has soil so rich you can plant steel and it'll grow."

Rita, already flooded with six hundred times the normal female hormones, burst into tears.

A month later, they'd packed up what little they owned and bought a farm outside Kansas City. They had an investment account full of stocks that would continue to grow.

Over the years, Rita didn't keep up with the computer world, but Frank did. He'd complained loudly when the system changed from DOS, the disk operating system where the user had to know a lot, to cute little icons that someone with no brain could use.

All that had led him to where he'd spent the last three days. When Kaley told him of a cave full of smashed computers, Frank's ears perked up. She knew her grandfather was a genius with computers.

"Where?" Frank yelled over the sound of the helicopter.

"Zeon!" Kaley shouted back.

Frank got the coordinates of the demolished Homestead from Roal. He dropped his passengers off, then said he was going to get fuel. He knew his daughter-in-law ran the Museum of Earth and that she had cars and gas. She'd know about this man, Zeon.

*It was almost as though someone had foreseen what would be needed,* he thought with a one-sided smirk.

He flew to the museum and refueled. He didn't see his son or daughter-in-law, but then they hadn't seen each other in years. They were "busy." Ha ha.

Again, everything seemed to have been anticipated. Jeff had left a note for his father.

*I know you want to see Haver's computers. Zeon will be expecting you.*

He'd left a map that Frank could follow. He was to go high up over the Mist, then on to Zeon's house.

On the ground, in front of the closed door of the museum, was an old-fashioned, fully charged generator. The islands had spaceships but no electricity to run the computers.

There was also something else Frank was to take. There were three big bales of the Solium that they'd grown. Wisely, they'd given only a portion of what they'd grown to Jobi. Rita's cartons of books had concealed big packages of the dried algae.

It was an easy trip and Zeon was not only waiting for him, but had horses and guards ready to lead Frank up the mountain to Haver's cave.

At his first sight inside the cave, Frank was glad to see that whoever did the bashing of the computers didn't know about them. The motherboards weren't hurt, and the hard drives were intact. It took him just twenty-four hours to get them working. He was thrilled that they were run on the old DOS system. There was not even one cutesy, annoying little icon. He truly believed that smiling faces did *not* belong on a computer!

Zeon sent food and set it outside so Frank could take his time in searching for information.

After he'd found all he could, Frank fell into a deep sleep. When he woke, it was very early morning, but he wasn't surprised to see the horses saddled and the two guards ready to take him down the mountain. Had Zeon told them the schedule before it happened?

When they got to the house, it wasn't Zeon who greeted him, but Tanek and Kaley. Their faces showed their concern. Tanek wanted to go to wherever his son was. Frank had seen that Kaley was with Tanek no matter what happened.

"Think you can stand my whirlybird?" Frank asked. "Or are you going to try to get me on one of your bird-headed lions?"

Kaley kissed her grandfather on the cheek. "He doesn't know what a lion is. They have no cat species here."

"What?" Frank nodded. "Right. Cats eat birds." He looked at Tanek. "You have a map?"

"Yes. Mekos is on an island called Abicis. Aradella is there and it's possible that Sojee's youngest daughter is with them."

"Which means that World War Three has begun," Kaley muttered. "Those girls hate each other." She looked at Frank. "Let's go inside and you can clean up. You stink. We want to hear everything you've been doing, then we can go to the island and save the girls from killing each other."

Frank had no intention of telling them what he'd found out in the cave. At least not yet. "Sounds good." He looked at Tanek to see if he agreed.

"Yes," was all Tanek said. It was obvious that he was worried about his son.

*What the hell has happened on Pithan?* Frank wondered. *With an evil queen and a witch mother, what hideous thing* could *happen?* He almost laughed at his own sarcasm.

They went into Zeon's house.

# 22

It was morning and Bree and Aradella were sitting in Qip's garden. They were on benches facing each other. What they'd been through the day before had changed them, but they didn't know how to begin to repair a lifetime of damage.

Aradella looked at her cousin. "You miss Tam, don't you? I know how it feels to love someone unattainable."

Bree said sadly, "It must have hurt when you didn't get Tanek."

Aradella gasped. "I didn't want him!"

"But he's . . ." By the look on Bree's face, she couldn't understand not wanting that beautiful man.

"Remember when I danced with him? That's when I fell for Mekos, not his father."

Bree's smile showed that she was genuinely pleased. "Shay said you were sick with grief at losing Tanek, so you—" She waved her hand. "Sometimes I think I should *never* listen to my sister." She took a breath. "I'm sorry I laughed at you that night. It was just so . . . intoxicating to be flirted with by a prince—even if he was stupid. And mean." She gave Aradella a heartfelt look. "I'm glad you didn't marry him. He is a despicable person. My father can't stand him! He—"

She broke off because they heard a sound they'd heard before.

"It's that big flying machine," Aradella said, then she and Bree began running back to the house.

It was Kaley who had rushed everyone to go to the island of Abicis. As a female, she knew the depth of anger that could be between women. The men tended to dismiss it, even laugh at it, but Kaley knew it could be serious–especially if what she thought might be true about Bree.

Kaley wanted to tell Sojee about the nakedness of his twin daughters, as she was haunted by the muscular physique of his youngest. But she doubted that her grandfather would confide in her about it. *Family secrets can be very annoying*, she thought.

When she saw Sojee lift a beam that would probably take four men to move, she had an idea of how to open the way. "Bone density," she said to him as though she was just making conversation. "Too bad you didn't have a son. He might have inherited your strength."

Sojee wiped sweat off his forehead. "Bree got a good dose of it." The instant he said it, he looked shocked, then he glared at his granddaughter. "Did you just trick me into telling you that?"

She smiled at him. "I have to go. Tanek needs me." She quickly ran though the rubble of the old Homestead.

So yes, Kaley had a reason to get the men into the chopper to go to what sounded like a very weird island. *As opposed to the others?* she thought.

Zeon gave Frank directions to a landing place that he said belonged to a man named Qip.

"What powers does he have?" Kaley asked.

"The best one of all," Zeon replied. "The ability to survive!"

Kaley asked for details, but Zeon wouldn't tell her more. But then, his mind was elsewhere. His daughter-in-law was going into labor and Tam was to return.

"Baby lust!" Kaley said. "Something like that could set off the girls."

The three men gave her identical looks that said she was being overly dramatic, getting herself into a frenzy for no reason, etc. Kaley grit her teeth. "Different planet, same men."

Minutes later, they were in the helicopter and heading toward Abicis.

Kaley was in the front by her grandfather, with Tanek in the back, headphones in place. It seemed to take forever before they saw the island, but it was actually a short time. "More volcanos," she said as she looked down.

"Wonder where the islands with the active ones are?" Frank asked. He tipped the chopper to the side, circled, and went west.

"There!" Tanek yelled.

Frank and Kaley looked where he was pointing. In an open field, looking up at them, were three people. Well, two anyway. Mekos was standing next to a short man, and the third one was made of metal. The sun was glinting off of him. Or it. *Do metal people have pronouns?* Kaley wondered.

They stepped back into the tree line as Frank landed the chopper.

Tanek didn't wait for the engine to be cut off before he got out.

Kaley put her hand on her grandfather's arm, meaning for him to watch.

The feet of Tanek and his son didn't touch the ground as they hugged and soared. They went higher than the first time she'd seen them do that. Tanek had said that if Mekos found love and lost his virginity, he'd soar higher.

Frank leaned forward to look up through the clear roof. "We don't need *this* bird when we have those two."

Kaley laughed. Tanek and Mekos went quite high. When they began the descent, she got out of the chopper and was waiting when the two of them landed. "We must find the girls," she said urgently. "We have to—"

The sound of laughter made them look toward the garden. Aradella and Bree were walking side by side and . . . laughing.

"Doesn't look like there will be a war," Tanek said smugly.

Kaley just kept staring. "Something really big had to have happened to cause that and I want to know what it was."

# 23

It wasn't long before they sat down at Qip's abundant table.

Aradella looked at Kaley. "We want to know what happened after we left."

Everyone turned to Kaley in expectation.

"Why me?" she mumbled, then sighed. She knew she was the designated storyteller. She looked at Bree. "Your sister . . ." Obviously, she didn't want to tell whatever had happened. "I'd rather hear about your adventures."

"What has Shay done this time?" Bree asked.

"She married Prince Nessa," Tanek said quickly.

Kaley said, "We weren't there, but we were told that immediately after you left, Shay had a private talk with that slimey little weasel."

Tanek nodded. "She told him he should tell everyone that *he* had broken with *you*." He looked at Aradella. "Because—"

Bree said, "Because he's always been passionately in love with my sister. She fantasized about that exact thing happening. And it worked?"

"Yes and no," Kaley said.

"King Aramus—" Tanek looked at Qip "—he's Prince Nessa's father, declared himself as the ruler of Pithan."

"Which means that Fahir, his right hand man, the bully-with-the-magic, is now in charge," Kaley said.

"The men?" Aradella asked. "Do they stay or go?"

Kaley smiled. "They stay."

For a moment they were silent and smiling. It looked like something good had been achieved.

It was Bree who asked, "What about . . . uh, them?"

They knew who she meant: Olina and Urah. The smiles disappeared.

"Gone," Tanek said. "Vanished. No one saw them leave or knows where they went."

"I bet they used the tunnels." Aradella's voice was heavy with guilt.

"No matter how they left, I'm sure they took a big part of the island's wealth." Bree looked at Kaley. "How is my sister doing?"

"Uh—uh," Kaley stammered. "We were told that she's adapted to her new position very well. She seems to like having authority and rank."

Aradella and Bree looked at each other, their eyes lit up, and they grinned wickedly.

"She married a prince so you'll have to curtsy to her," Aradella said.

"I wish it were only that. I'll have to touch my nose to the floor."

Aradella got up, put her shoulders back, and lifted her chin.

Bree stood before her, then went to her knees. "Oh, please, dear sister, do not execute me."

"You deserve it!" Aradella said. "You did not clean *all* my jewels. You left a spot on one of them. You deserve death! Guards, take her away!"

Bree stood up, her elbows bent back as though she was being pulled away. "My dear sister, what of our lifetime of love?"

"Love? I have no time for that!" Aradella said. "I am now the queen-to-be and you are nothing!"

Bree pantomimed jerking away from the guards. "You husband-stealing monster!" She put her hands around Aradella's throat and fake squeezed.

Aradella dramatically and quite flamboyantly went into a death spiral. She landed in a heap on the floor.

Laughing, Mekos and Qip, Frank and Ian applauded, but Tanek and Kaley were staring in stunned silence.

"How . . .? When . . .?" Kaley whispered.

"They are actresses!" Mekos said proudly. "You should have seen them on that stage! The whole island cheered."

"How do you know that?" Aradella asked.

"Well," Mekos said slowly, "we saw you."

Bree gasped. "All of it? Even what I did to poor Bart?"

"We were there for every second of that splendid play," Qip said. "Tam thought you were wonderful."

"And best of all, you conquered the Monster of Sheean." Mekos's eyes were full of admiration.

"We did," Bree said, and she and Aradella looked at each other with smiles.

"But you—" Aradella began.

"Stop!" Kaley said loudly. "Start at the beginning and tell us everything. And please explain the Monster of . . . Whatever he was."

"Monster of Sheean." Mekos looked at the girls.

Frank said, "Yes! Tell it all, and I remind you that I've had a lifetime of good storytelling." He gave an affectionate glance at his granddaughter, then turned back to the others. "What happened when you landed on this island?"

Mekos rolled his eyes. "These two *hated* each other. Tam and I were afraid they'd go into battle. We locked down our weapons."

"Most of it happened because of the bag Zeon gave us." Aradella was looking at her cousin.

"And your knowledge of plants," Bree said.

"And that you know the spells."

Ian said loudly and impatiently, "It was all about my leg! Now stop dawdling and tell the story!"

With much laughter and lots of drama, they told of the play and the fight in the arena. They told of taking the medallion, but by silent mutual agreement, they left out what Elvin said about Urah. They didn't want to ruin the lighthearted moment.

"What did this monster look like when he changed?" Kaley asked.

Their words tumbled over each other as they described the goat parts of him, complete with horns.

"A satyr," Kaley said. "Unfortunately, they are known for sex and booze and truly disgusting orgies. I would imagine that's how he got into trouble that made someone reshape him. Could I see the things you collected?"

They looked at Qip. "I'll get them." He left the room.

Kaley turned to her grandfather. "How's Grandma?"

"Busy. She's setting up a school to teach midwifery. She figures that the whole island is going to be delivering babies at the same time, so they better be prepared."

Kaley gave Tanek a dreamy sort of look. Aradella looked at Mekos with the same expression.

"Sounds like a good plan." Bree's voice was wistful.

"I've been meaning to ask. What is this?" Frank had pulled a sprig of a plant out of his pocket. It was small and red, the leaves firm.

Aradella looked at it. "I don't know. I've never seen this before. Not even a picture of it."

"Do you have a name for it?" Bree asked. "Maybe it's in a spell."

"It's called Solium." Frank held it up. "This is why the Bellis ship landed near us in Kansas. It grows there. We have no known use for it on Earth. Rita made us tea, but it tasted awful."

They hadn't noticed that Qip had come back into the room. "It doesn't work on your bodies." His voice was quiet, almost reverent. When Frank handed him the cutting, Qip's eyes grew brighter. "Do you have much of this?"

"I have a few bales of it in the back of the chopper. My son and I grew quite a lot of it."

Qip looked like he might faint. He sat down. "May I have this?"

"Sure," Frank said. "Would you tell us what it is?"

"To us, it is truly magic. It makes a person forget troubles and pain and all things bad. You become filled with love and wisdom and knowledge." He touched it gently with his fingertips. "Or it lets you know nothing, whichever you prefer." His head came up. "All things good are what it does to us."

"Sounds like LSD," Kaley said. "Or grass. Or whatever the doctor gives you after surgery."

No one laughed. They just stared at the plant in Qip's hand.

"It's useful to know that," Frank said.

"Very," Tanek said in agreement.

# 24

Nearly everyone was gone.

Mekos and Aradella were stretched out on the grass in Qip's garden. They were a foot apart and enjoying the sunshine.

They were also enjoying the silence, the peace. Yesterday had been pure chaos.

Reena was the first to contact them and demand that Bree return to her. "I have no time to trudge through these books."

Bree had been reluctant to leave Qip's house. It was very pleasant there—and she and Aradella had years of catching up to do. But Reena said that Bree was needed on another island. She still hesitated, but then Reena very pointedly said that Bree was "desperately" needed. That word shot through her. She was packed and ready to go in about four minutes.

By that time, Sojee had contacted Tanek, saying his help was needed on Pithan. The first rosy glow of men and women living together was fading and there were problems.

Kaley said to her grandfather, "You don't need me?"

"Not really. Stay there and enjoy yourself," Sojee said. "Did I tell you that I visited the Lair? I had no idea there are so many Lelys there. *We* don't know what to do with them. I sure wish we knew someone who wasn't *afraid* of them."

Kaley mumbled about "dad jokes" then she packed faster than Bree did.

No one asked Frank, but they assumed he'd fly them back to Pithan. He gave a longing look at Darr and Qip. As a fellow engineer, Frank wanted to know more about how Qip had made a living creature. "I'll leave the Solium with you," he told Qip. "Use it to buy anything you need. Maybe I can help on the next one."

They knew he meant building more creatures like Darr, and Qip smiled at the offer.

There was a great flurry of activity, then they got in the helicopter and took off. On the ground were Qip and Darr, Mekos and Aradella. Ian stood on Darr's shoulder. Qip had welded a little handle to Darr's ear so Ian could hold on easier.

When the blast of the chopper was gone, they looked at each other. *Now what?* they seemed to ask.

"We . . ." Mekos said. Since he had no idea what he and Aradella were going to do, he didn't finish.

"Us too," Qip said, then he and Darr and Ian went into the house.

For a day and a half, the young couple were content. They talked some, but mostly they basked in the joy of just being *together.*

On the second afternoon, they were lying on the grass and looking up at the sky.

It was Aradella who broke the silence. "What are we going to do?"

He knew she meant *if* they managed to escape the threat of Olina and her mother. *If* they could repair the damage they'd done to Vian's plan. In a perfect world, where would they live? Where would they fit in? What about a livelihood? The truth was that they were homeless and jobless.

"Should we return to Pithan?" he asked.

"My birthright makes me a threat to King Aramus. Eventually, he'll put Nessa on the throne."

"So he can easily be controlled by Fahir."

"Of course," Aradella said. "I doubt if Fahir would let you and me live in peace in my little rooms. I would always be a threat to them."

"He'd probably seal the doors with us inside. We could go to the Homestead. My father plans to rebuild it to what it was." When she didn't reply, he turned on his side and looked at her. Wherever they went, danger would follow them. "My grandfather lives on Eren. Maybe we could go there."

She didn't look at him. "And will your grandmother, Vian, be living there?"

The memory of being bawled out by her made them both shiver.

Mekos rolled onto his back. It was like a great, ugly cloud was hanging over them. They were the ones who'd destroyed the plan Vian had sacrificed her life to make happen. "Because of us, Evil Olina was exchanged for Evil Fahir."

"In the future, the story of what we did will be embellished," she said. "People will say that our belief that only *we* mattered is what caused us to destroy things."

"And lust," he said. "I'm sure people will talk of that. 'The lust of the Lely swan herder for the high-ranking princess ruined it all' is what they'll say."

"It'll become one of those Earth stories, those fairy tales, that Kaley knows."

"Stories that seem to actually happen here." He shook his head. "I wonder what happened to the goat-man? What did Kaley call him?"

"A satter, or something like that. He said . . ." She looked at Mekos.

"That Urah will want the medallion."

"Then of course we will have to turn it over to someone," he said and she nodded. "So what about *us*?" Mekos sounded frustrated.

"We could join Bree on that island Reena knows about." She was only half joking.

Mekos sighed. "I wish we could do something to erase what happened at the Lair. Something that would make my father forgive me."

"It's not *him*!" Aradella said fiercely. "It's your grandmother! She shows up after years of nothing and shouts at us. If she didn't want Valona killed she should have *told* us."

Mekos couldn't help a laugh. "'Don't kill your hostess.' That should have been her advice. I just hope that when my father at last invades Empyrea, I'll be allowed to go. Or will I be told to stay back with the children?"

"*If* he goes there! None of us have even *seen* the place. Except Vian and she tells us nothing. She—" Aradella looked at him.

It was as though their minds linked and they read each other's thoughts. "Except Qip. He spent most of his life there."

Aradella turned to her side and propped her head on her hand. "Did you hear Frank and Qip talking? Those men want to make more creatures like Darr."

Mekos looked at her. "But they don't have the materials."

Aradella sat up, cross-legged, and looked at him. "Frank left a big package of their treasured Solium so Qip could afford to buy what he needs."

Mekos sat up, also cross-legged. "Qip will need to *go* to Empyrea to get what he needs. To choose it himself."

They looked at each other, blinking rapidly.

"If we went there with him, then we could . . ." Aradella didn't finish.

"We could tell my father what Empyrea is like. What to expect. What he needs to do." He gave a crooked grin. "In the military, it's called a reconnaissance mission."

"But Vian could tell him what he needs to know," Aradella said.

"I don't think Grandmamá can see that island with the same perspective that an outsider would have."

Aradella looked serious. "This time, we should consult with our families before we do this."

They contemplated that for the time it took a hummingbird to take a breath.

"Let's go talk to Qip about how to get there."

"Yes, let's go." They ran.

They had to search for Qip. Through Mekos's keen hearing, they discovered that under his house was a workshop. The door was unlocked and they went down the stairs. The huge room was a bit creepy in that it had lifelike metal body parts on the walls and hanging from the ceiling. At the bottom of the stairs was a full-size metal female. She turned and looked at them with empty eyes.

"Hello," Aradella said, but received no answer. She didn't have the look of life that Darr did.

"She's for Darr?" Mekos asked as he stepped away.

Qip was at a huge steel table in the middle of the room, made low for his height. On it were three heads. One of them was blinking its purple eyes. "Eventually, but she has no soul yet." He studied their young, excited faces. "So what great plan have you two come up with?"

"We want to go to Empyrea," Mekos said.

"We could get the parts you need." Aradella sounded hopeful.

"You mean you want to redeem your behinds after you screwed everything up in the Lair?"

"Yes," Aradella and Mekos said in unison. They were holding hands, as though for protection as they waited for Qip to answer. They couldn't go without his agreement.

"I think that's a good idea."

The two young people looked surprised.

Qip wiped his hands on a greasy rag and turned to them. "I don't want to go and you'll get to see the truth of what Empyrea is."

"Violent," Mekos said. "Warriors. They bombed my home and killed my uncle." His ears were standing up so straight they poked out of his hair.

Aradella held his hand tighter.

"No," Qip said calmly. "That's something that needs to be addressed. Frank wanted to tell Tanek this first but I think you should know." He hesitated. "When Frank searched Haver's computers, he found out that it wasn't the Empyreans who led the bombing of your home and killed your uncle. It was Urah."

Aradella and Mekos looked at him in shock.

Qip continued. "Frank and I think Haver was too close to starting the takeover he'd been planning for years, so someone in Empyrea sent Urah to do the dirty work. Unofficially, of course, but the weapons she used weren't made on Pithan." He shook his head in disgust. "Haver lost his son and his home, but he managed to escape and he hid, but Urah used her magic to find him in the cave. We think she killed Haver and her guardsmen smashed the computers. Then they sealed Haver's body in the cave."

"And because of all this, her daughter was made queen," Mekos said softly.

Aradella was staring at Qip. "Haver disappeared when my parents were still alive. Were their deaths another stepping stone to her goal?"

"Yes," Qip said. "To make her daughter queen was her plan all along."

Mekos put his arm around Aradella's shoulders.

Qip's face brightened. "I think you two should go. I'll contact Davro and he'll send a Spacer to pick you up. You will both need to use Zeon's mask." He looked at Aradella. "You must make yourself less beautiful."

"Oh." Aradella's eyebrows were high. "Uh . . ."

"That will be very difficult for her to do," Mekos said solemnly.

Qip laughed. "Ah, to be young again! Give me today to arrange it all, then—"

"Who is Davro?" Mekos asked.

"Vian's brother. Your granduncle. He's a doctor and he lives on Empyrea, but he sometimes travels to Earth."

"How will we get past the guards?" Aradella asked.

"I know Cutters from Selkan are there," Mekos said. "They are violent, dangerous men. Will we be facing them?"

Qip smiled with a look of amusement. "Empyrea is not what you think it is. It is—" He broke off. "No! I'm not going to tell you. I'm going to let you see for yourselves."

"What do we take?" Aradella asked.

"Which weapons?" Mekos asked.

"Nothing," Qip said. "You won't need anything. Not clothes, not toiletries, nothing at all. Davro will have everything for you. Just take personal items that you think you can't be without." He was teasing them. "I'll tell Davro to program the Spacer to give you a tour of the island before you see him. Now you must go so I can arrange all this. You'll leave early tomorrow morning."

All Mekos and Aradella could do was nod and say thanks, then they ran up the stairs.

Qip looked at Darr, who'd been standing in the shadows, so silently they hadn't seen him among the other robot parts. Sitting on his shoulder was Ian. "Do you have questions for me?"

Ian looked serious. "Urah and her daughter were helped by someone on Empyrea?"

"Yes." Qip was pleased that he'd seen the important part. "A traitor. Not even Vian can see who is backing those evil women."

Darr's eyes blinked red.

"Yes," Qip said. "We believe that whoever or whatever it was sent us away. We were asking too many questions. So will you go or not?"

Ian said, "When I was under the rule of those women, I did things I'm not proud of. Maybe if I go to Empyrea, I can redeem myself by helping in some way. I can make myself unobtrusive."

Qip smiled. "I'm sure you can. Davro will be intrigued by you—as will *all* the Empyreans. Be careful someone doesn't throw a net over you. You could be sold on the underground for great wealth."

"I will be careful and I will look out for them." With that, Ian flew out of the room.

Qip looked skyward. "Haver, your family honors you."

The next morning, before it was full daylight, Mekos went to the dining room, while Aradella stayed in their bedroom. She'd mumbled some excuse for staying, but the truth was that she was curious. She wasn't supposed to have seen it, but she knew Zeon had given something to Mekos before they left. It was a small wooden box and she'd seen Mekos slip it into the magic bag. If he was taking whatever it was to Empyrea with them, it must be important.

When she pulled the box out, she had an idea what was in it. She opened it and, yes, inside was the knife that she'd used to stab Valona. To her disgust, there was dried blood on the crystal blade. Her instinct was to clean it. She could understand why they should keep a magic object but at least keep it clean.

But she didn't remove the knife. Instead, she reached into the bag and withdrew the little leather pouch that contained the leaves of the poisonous plant she'd taken from Valona's garden. She untied the bag, then, being careful not to touch them, she dumped the leaves over the knife. The leaves melded themselves onto the blade until they almost disappeared. "Creepy!" Aradella muttered then quickly closed the lid and latched it. She shoved it back into the bag, then ran down the hall to the dining room. Breakfast was waiting.

"You've got the bag?" Mekos asked, his plate full.

"Yes," Aradella answered. "And I put more plants in it. And I have the mask and the key in case we find a lock to be opened."

"Locks are Ian's job."

"Did I hear my name?" Ian flew into the room and immediately Darr put tiny plates of food on his miniature dining setup.

"You always hear your name," Aradella said. "We're going to Empyrea today."

"I'm going with you," Ian said.

"I don't think that's a good idea," Mekos said. "You could be hurt."

"Because I'm little?" Ian asked belligerently.

"Yes!" Mekos answered in kind. "There will be danger and—"

"Give it up," Aradella said. "He'll sneak into a crevice and go anyway. What do you think Empyrea is like?"

"I'm sure it has a magnificent military," Mekos said. "The soldiers are well trained and fit. And they have spaceships and helicopters and bombs. They are very powerful!"

"I think it's a paradise," Ian said dreamily. "All comfort and luxury." He grinned. "And pleasure. Abundant pleasure!"

They looked at Aradella, waiting for her vision. "I hope it's a place of peace and families. There'll be calm and quiet where people laugh and are friends."

The men blinked a few times, then Mekos turned back to Ian. "What kind of pleasure?"

Aradella groaned. Obviously, they thought her version was boring.

Minutes later, the three of them went outside, then halted, staring at what was before them. It was a little vehicle on two sleek silver runners. The center was a clear bubble, the roof and sides transparent. Inside were two plush seats of a deep blue. In the back was a third seat that was tiny. They looked at Ian on Darr's shoulder.

"I think you were expected," Aradella said.

Darr opened a door that was well concealed.

Qip was standing to the side. When they hesitated, he stepped forward. "It will be safe. Davro is waiting for you. Just remember that Empyrea is not what you think it is. I remind you that they've been involved with Earth for centuries. There will be the offer of uh . . . activities that you won't understand."

Aradella gave a weak smile of not understanding. "I have the mask. Who should I look like?"

"Valona's maid," Ian said loudly.

The thought of her changing to someone so old and wrinkled made them laugh and the tension was broken, but then they looked at Qip.

"Make yourselves look like the first person you see," Qip said.

"Both of us?" Mekos asked. "Shouldn't we choose people to emulate?"

"No," Qip said. "First person, both of you."

They shrugged, not understanding, but agreed to do it.

Aradella kissed Qip's cheek, then she stood on tiptoe and kissed Davro's cheek. His eyes flashed a pinkish-orange. Quite pretty.

"I didn't program him for that color." Qip looked shocked. "Go before you ruin all of us!" He was teasing.

Ian flew into the little vehicle and proudly enthroned himself on his chair.

Aradella and Mekos followed. There were no controls of any kind inside, not even on the doors. They were fully at the mercy of the programming of the machine.

Silently, the Spacer rose into the air. The passengers waved to Qip and Darr until they could no longer be seen.

# 25

They weren't in the air long before they began to see lights. At first, they were just a glow. The Spacer slowed down, as though to give them time to see what they were flying toward.

"Colors!" Aradella said in awe. "Look at them."

For people who spent a life with lanterns, the electric lights were fascinating. Red, blue, green, and mixtures of every color traveled upward until the sky was radiant with them.

They leaned forward in their plush seats to see it all. As they got closer, the lights grew brighter.

"What are those?" Aradella asked.

Against the skyline were buildings many stories high. But they weren't just taller versions of the houses they were used to. These seemed to be separate boxes placed on top of each other.

As they flew closer, they could see them more clearly. The buildings were like a children's game of stacked blocks. Some were long, some short, some tall. They jutted out or were recessed. Some were flat in front and some were three sided. Some of the cubes had dark glass in front, some had solid walls. Size greatly varied.

Besides size, they varied in luxury. A huge building that fairly sparkled with exquisite details would be next to four plain houses stacked on top of each other. Nowhere was actual poverty, but there seemed to be a great variation in wealth.

Especially striking was that each cube was a different color. The buildings were unusual and together, they were beautiful!

The Spacer slowly circled a building. Wide-eyed, they looked at it. The glass was such that they couldn't see inside the cubes.

"They are houses stacked on top of each other, right?" Aradella asked.

"I guess so," Mekos said.

When they reached the far side of the building, they saw a person standing on a balcony. They couldn't tell if it was a man or woman. The person strained so hard to see them inside the Spacer, that they ducked down to the seats.

"Time to put on the mask," Mekos said.

She removed the mask from the bag, put it on and she changed to look like the person they'd seen on the balcony. Then she looked at Mekos and concentrated until he looked just like her.

"This is very strange," she said.

Ian raised an eyebrow. "Now both of you are equally unappealing to men and women no matter what planet they may be from. Good choice."

"Thank you," she said.

When the Spacer circled another building, they saw three people on balconies.

"They look exactly alike," Ian said. "I can't tell one from another."

Mekos and Aradella looked at each other. "And we look just like them," she said.

"I'm beginning to understand why Qip had us do this," Mekos said.

As the Spacer moved ahead, the buildings were closer together. They saw more people, and all of whom looked exactly alike.

"I think we're headed into the center of town," Mekos said.

The lights grew brighter, with more intense colors. On top of the buildings were huge round machines that sent colored lights into the sky.

"Look at that!" Ian said.

The lights showed shapes against the clouds. At first they were animals they recognized, but as the buildings grew more dense, the shapes changed to faces. They didn't know any of the people that were projected.

When they flew around an enormous stack of cubes, what they saw so startled them that they fell back against their seats.

A screen the size of three houses came into view. There was an older man's face on it, and he had a circle of leaves about his head. In brilliantly bright lettering, it said, *Strategize a war with Julius Caesar.*

"Those are laurel leaves but who is that person?" Aradella asked.

"And what does that mean?" Mekos asked. "Are they planning a war?"

"And asking for help to fight it?" Ian asked.

Suddenly, they were surrounded by several of the giant boards, each with pictures and writing.

*Meet Tesla and his pigeon. Autographed beak prints given.*

*Reenact Omaha Beach. Win a 35 mm Leica and 6 rolls of Kodak film.*

*Elvis Live! Hear all your favorites. Free cans of Royal Crown Pomade.*

"What is this?" Aradella asked.

"I think they're announcing plays," Ian said. "Like the ones on Abicis."

They flew past more boards.

*J.R.R. Tolkien talks tonight! Find out if you're a troll or a Ranger.*

*Audition for Shakespeare's new play: King Charles III's Family Tempest*

*Tonight only!! Leonardo da Vinci will paint you smiling.*

"These have to be the Earth things Qip meant," Mekos said.

The Spacer went around three more boards.

*Paul Robeson to sing "Ol' Man River" 206 times.*

*Play "Name the Birds" with Charles Darwin*

*Gunfights at the Not O.K. Corral. Loud revolvers provided.*

"What does all this mean?" Mekos asked.

They saw a huge sign that was very plain. The only thing on it was a symbol.

"I think Qip should have explained more about this place," Aradella said. "He should have—"

She broke off because they went around a building and saw an even bigger board. On it was a picture of Sojee.

*Watch Sojee break a witch in half. Get free gingerbread.*

"This one is *real*," Aradella whispered.

The picture of Sojee began to move and it showed him pantomiming breaking something. Then the picture changed and there was Tanek.

*Watch Tanek, Kaley & Sojee kill the Gingerbread Witch!*

They were too shocked to speak.

When the Spacer was past the Sojee board, they saw a giant picture of Bree's face and she looked like she was about to cry.

*See Princesses Bree & Shay with their magic dresses. Will Kaley & her mother rescue them in time?*

On the other side, they saw a handsome man.

*Is Prince Bront bored with a bride who can do nothing but clean fireplaces?*

"I don't like this," Aradella whispered.

The Spacer kept going. When a transparent shoe was shown on a board, Mekos groaned.

*Watch Kaley try on a glass slipper & end up in a dungeon! Guess who saves her? Prizes given.*

"This is not right," Aradella said. "This is—" Suddenly, she put her hand to her mouth and let out a sound of pure horror.

The Spacer halted in midair. In front of them were two giant, bright boards. The one on the left showed Bree and Aradella in the revealing costumes they'd worn on Abicis.

*See Princesses Aradella & Bree fight it out in a play. Ian loses his leg!*

"At least they got the most important fact right," Ian muttered.

On the right, was a picture of . . . Aradella whimpered. It was her on the wolf.

*Watch Mekos & Aradella kill Valona. See the princess ride a wolf! (Is that* all *she does with it?)*

Mekos put his arms around her and buried her face in his shoulder. "Get us to Davro *now*!" he ordered the Spacer. Instantly, it did an abrupt turn and zoomed through the air so fast they couldn't read more of the brightly lit boards.

For all the speed of the Spacer, inside they felt no difference. The gravity was perfectly controlled. Mekos kept Aradella's face hidden so she didn't see that they were speeding toward a solid wall painted purple. When the Spacer didn't slow down, Mekos and Ian drew back, breaths held.

At the last second, a wide door slid up and the vehicle went in and halted. Doors on both sides opened.

"We're here." Mekos stroked Aradella's hair, then pulled off her mask. "That's better." He kissed her forehead. "Come on. Let's go see what we're facing."

Aradella was still unable to speak, but Mekos kept his arm firmly around her shoulders. The room where they'd landed was plain with a single door open in one wall.

Ian flew to Mekos's shoulder. He was trying to look brave but he hid under Mekos's hair.

They went through the door and entered a room with couches, chairs, and a few glass-topped steel tables. Unlike Qip's place, the furnishings had straight edges, with seating covered in a bland beige fabric. There were no "collections" as Qip called them. The room was clean to the point of being barren.

They stood by the doorway in silence, not sure what to do.

From the opposite side came a person who resembled those they'd seen, but this one was different. For one thing, he gave off a feeling of masculinity. He was tall and slim and had a mass of gray hair. But it didn't age him. He looked somewhere between Tanek and Mekos in age. He had on a long robe of a deep blue, with darker trousers beneath. He was carrying a round tray with three glasses of a green liquid. One of the glasses was tiny.

"Hello," he said in a pleasant voice, then looked at Mekos. "I am Davro, your uncle. Please make yourselves comfortable."

Mekos, still holding Aradella protectively, led her to a couch and they sat down together.

"I take it you were traumatized by seeing yourselves on the playboards." It wasn't a question. He held out the tray. "These will make you feel better." He was staring at Mekos. "I see Vian in you. And Tanek."

"And my half-fox mother?" Mekos took two glasses and handed one to Aradella. Ian was still hiding in his hair.

"I see her in the way you move," he said. "Would your Never like this?"

"Ian?" Mekos asked.

Cautiously, Ian stepped forward.

Davro's eyes widened. "You are . . ." He caught his breath. "Magnificent."

Mekos grinned. "You know how to win his heart." He downed his drink and it immediately relaxed him. As Aradella drank hers, her look of anger lessened. Mekos took the little glass and handed it to Ian.

"You can actually fly?" Davro asked.

Ian had been holding his wings close to his body in what Mekos called his "lock-breaking position." As Ian spread his glistening wings, Davro's wide eyes showed his appreciation. Ian flew to land on the arm of the couch and downed his drink.

"We'd like to know . . ." Mekos said but he wasn't sure where to begin.

"Why do you have *us* on your screens?" Aradella sounded more perplexed than angry. "You spy on us. For what reason?"

Davro's blue eyes grew serious. "For entertainment," he said. "I admit that I'm ashamed of what goes on here. My sister and I are trying to change it, but we are hindered." He withdrew a little round disk from his pocket and put a smaller one in his ear. "Before we get to that, I'd like to analyze your health, if I may. We must be careful that no diseases are brought to us, as we have weak immune systems. We use sound waves for detection and healing. They realign the body."

Mekos nodded and Davro leaned forward, the disk in his hand.

"Ow!" Mekos put his hands over his ears. "That sound! It hurts my ears."

"I apologize." Davro adjusted the disk with his thumb. "I forgot your heightened senses." He swept his arm down the length of his nephew, not touching him. "You have an injured ankle."

"He fell off a roof," Aradella said.

Davro smiled, showing white and even teeth. "As the Reaver. All of Empyrea enjoyed those episodes." When he held the disk over Mekos's left ankle, he winced in pain, then Davro drew back. "There! It is repaired. You are easy. It takes us years to repair those Earth humans we pick up. When we got Kaley's grandfather, he had only weeks to live. Although, as you saw on the playboards, we can bring Earth people back to life after they've died."

When they looked blank, Davro said, "Many of the people on the boards died long ago on Earth, but we revived them. We love talent and creativity and we don't want it to die out." He looked at Ian. "May I?"

Ian shrugged as though to say, *Why not?*

Davro moved his hand before the little man. "Except for the missing half of a leg, you are perfect. If you had the leg here, I could reattach it." His eyes twinkled. "But that lizard is still searching for the rest of you." He turned to Aradella. "Do you mind?"

The drink had relaxed her, but she was impatiently waiting for things to be explained. She opened her arms to give him permission to inspect her body.

Davro held out the little disk before her face. "Good! That mask has caused no damage." He moved downward and when he got to her stomach, he gasped. "I have never heard this sound before," he said softly, then closed his eyes as though in ecstasy. "Our bodies can no longer do this. We . . ." When he looked at Aradella, his eyes were so soft they were like a rain puddle. "You are ovulating."

Aradella pulled back. That was too intimate and way too embarrassing!

Davro put his disk away. "You are in perfect health. No flaws at all. But you . . ." He smiled at Aradella. "Tonight would give you a son. Wait until tomorrow and you'll carry a girl. Males are faster and die quickly. Girls are there for the long wait."

Surreptitiously, Mekos and Aradella touched hands.

Davro stood up. "My sister would chastise me for dawdling. Would you like food? Rest? Bathing?"

"We would like to know why about everything," Aradella said.

"What we have seen is not what we expected," Mekos said. "You people have done terrible things to us. You divided men and women." He held up his left arm. "You put chips inside us. Why?"

Davro walked to the far side of the room, then turned back. "How do I explain that we destroyed ourselves?"

"Does that sign *NOO* have anything to do with this?" Aradella asked.

Davro sat down as though energy had left his body. "It has everything to do with it. It means *No One Offended.*"

"*Offend* is the word that upset Qip," Ian said. "Darr had to give him a drink to calm him down."

"I need to check the medicals on dear Qip. I miss him very much! Did he finish his mechanical man?"

"Darr is my friend," Ian said.

"Friend," Davro said. "Only Qip can put a soul into a machine. *We* cannot do that." He took a moment to gather his thoughts. "Yuzan is the home planet of the people here on the island of Empyrea," he said. "We are intelligent people and our technology is advanced. We can travel through space and visit other planets. We can do remarkable things."

"And you used all that knowledge against *us*!" Thanks to the drink Davro had given her, Aradella was calmer than her words sounded.

"Not at first," Davro said. "Long before we found your planet, we destroyed ourselves. The truth is that our many successes hurt us. We became jealous, competitive, and angry. Technology became overshadowed by what we were *feeling*, and those injured senses began to manifest themselves in violence. Murders were committed, corruption, thievery, burned buildings. We didn't even know we were capable of violence—certainly not against each other."

He paused, obviously not wanting to dredge up the bad history. "Someone came up with the idea of making everyone *equal*. The theory was that if all people were the same, there would be no more hatred and anger. The process of equalizing started generations ago. Babies were created in tubes so the division of the sexes could be eradicated. If the cells were male, they were injected with female hormones and the other way around. Equal. People were neither one nor the other. They—"

"But what about my grandmother?" Mekos asked.

"Ah yes, my sister, Vian. While her cells were developing in the tube, it was seen that she had a special ability. No one was sure what it was, but they knew her brain was different. As I said, we like creativity, so she wasn't changed. After she was born, it was found that she could foresee the future. It's why she was made one of the Seven. And because her body was not changed, she could give birth." He gave a fond look at his nephew, then sighed. "Besides our physical bodies, there were great changes made in the society. People who owned more than others caused hurt, so it was decided that all people would be paid the same. I am a doctor and I earn the same as a street cleaner. Today on Yuzan, we look alike, dress alike, our living areas are the same. There is—"

Aradella interrupted. "And if you aren't the same, you're sent to Abicis."

Davro grimaced. "As hard as it was tried to make everyone alike, there were differences and they offended people. When a person was as pretty as a model or as ugly as a toad, it hurt the feelings of others. Different people tend to get more attention and that caused great anguish."

"So the frogs complained," Ian said.

"Yes, they did," Davro replied. "For years, misfits were sent elsewhere but now it's to Abicis. My sister fought against Qip being sent away, but she couldn't stop it. However, she did manage to protect me before birth and since then. I'm not exactly like others." He gave a slight smile at that.

"If you had a whole planet of people who were exactly alike in looks and income and the misfits were expelled, you must have been happy," Mekos said.

"For many years, we were, but then Bellis, with its similar atmosphere, was found and we . . ." He took a breath. "Your planet and your people were our downfall."

Mekos's face showed his anger. "Are you saying it's our fault that you stole one of our islands, renamed it, then took over control of our lives? How are *we* involved in *your* self-destruction?"

Davro's eyes seemed to agree with his anger. "Your planet was a shock to Yuzans. No one thought such places still existed.

Your healthcare was primitive. Each island spoke a different language. Water and sanitation were bad. I apologize, but we felt great pity for you. With a unanimous vote, the whole planet decided to unite to help you."

"So they inserted the chips," Aradella said.

Mekos drew in his breath. "And they called what they were doing to us the Righting of Ancient Wrongs. And they are 'Peacekeepers.'"

"Yes to all of it," Davro said. "At first, there were only good intentions, but 'helping Bellis' became the main concern of all of Yuzan. People wanted to come here, to see this place, to become involved."

"They wanted to help the poor, pitiful inhabitants of our crude planet," Aradella said tightly. "To help inferior beings who could not take care of themselves."

"That's the way they saw it," Davro said. "And it started with good intentions, but gradually, as they say on Earth, Bellis became our 'vacation paradise.' It was where people could get away from the perfection on Yuzan."

"And stay in your box houses," Aradella said.

Davro gave a small smile. "The houses here—not on Yuzan—are movable. If we go on a ship, either water or space, our houses go with us. It saves having to pack."

"What made you stop 'helping' us and begin ruling us?" Mekos asked. "And spying on us?"

Davro grimaced. "It didn't happen quickly. Yuzans saw that on Bellis people were not alike in wealth or intelligence or personality. By that time, my planet had forgotten about differences—but what they saw made them stop being content with having exactly what everyone else had. People began saying we should follow the Bellis culture, so a different wealth system was set up. Gradually, it became socially acceptable that on Bellis people could have more or less than others. As you've seen by the houses, even colors became a show of independence."

Davro waved his hand. "But wealth was not the biggest problem. There were other things that had been lost."

"Love," Aradella said.

Davro nodded. "Love, passion, hate, anger, grief. They had all been eliminated."

"And the new generation wanted to feel it," Aradella said as she glanced at Mekos.

"That's right," Davro said. "The chips were adjusted so people could *feel* the tears and laughter of the people of Bellis." His lips tightened. "If only that had been enough! They began to want more than just those everyday emotions. They saw that if they manipulated things, they could intensify the anger, hate, and violence."

When Davro looked at them, his eyes showed his sadness and apology. "One thing they saw was that if they separated the sexes, the emotions were stronger. Men were more aggressive if they competed with each other. And women alone deeply yearned for home and family. The Yuzans chose two islands and began a campaign to get the Bellisans to *want* to separate the sexes. Women were told they didn't need men, and the men were made to believe women were holding them back. At first, Bellisans welcomed the split. Both sides wanted to prove they didn't need the other." He took a breath. "You have seen the results."

Aradella had to look away. "And all this was for your planet's entertainment."

Davro's voice was barely a whisper. "I am sorry to say so, but yes. That's what it became. All our great technological knowledge is now being used to give pleasure." His voice was bitter. "Bellis has been made into a place where Yuzans can experience the things our ancestors threw away. They come here to be excited, thrilled, even frightened. Masses of money exchanges hands."

Mekos's face showed his anger. "All while *you* are safe. Your people are untouched by the risks that such strong, violent emotions do to us."

"That is true," Davro said softly. "Even on Yuzan today, anything offensive is immediately taken away. There is still perfect peace and harmony. But on your planet, it is different." He looked at Aradella. "It's no consolation, but everyone cried when your parents were killed by Olina and her mother. I'm ashamed to say that the play for power with King Aramus and you marrying the disgusting Nessa had high ratings. The sponsors made a lot of money."

"How do we stop this?" Mekos asked.

"Unfortunately, it cannot be done through war." Davro sighed. "If it could, your great-grandfather, Haver, would have done it. But change like you want—and need—must be done in stages. It's like a puzzle and you have to find the pieces." He could see that they didn't understand. "There is a practical side to all this. Your utilities go from us to your islands. We give you clean water. We work with your doctors and your food producers. Without us and the chips we created, you wouldn't be able to understand each other. You and Aradella speak different languages." He looked at Ian. "*You* are incomprehensible to all humans." He turned back to them. "And there is the fact that Yuzans truly believe they are balancing the evil with the good." His voice rose, as though in warning. "They will fight change with all the weaponry they can create while they spout mottos that make them feel righteous."

"But my grandmamá has foreseen a future without . . . this." Mekos waved his hand to mean all that was outside.

Davro tried to calm himself. "She has started the first steps." He paused. "For all our knowledge of the universe, there is one thing we cannot comprehend—or conquer." His eyes lit up. "Magic! It makes no logical sense to Yuzans. When Garen's mother and grandfather died, we took their bodies and dissected them. Their brains were put under high-powered microscopes. Every level of sound was used on them, but nothing was found that could explain how they can perform magic." Davro looked at Aradella. "What you and Bree did with those plants in that arena is not logical. That little man . . . What did he do to your mass of weeds?"

"Ignited them," Aradella said. "He made them come alive."

"We cannot understand that. How is it possible? Yuzans could see the difference in the brain of my sister, but they cannot see if magic is in there." Davro lowered his voice. "I will tell you a secret. Yuzans fear your magic. If there is to be an overthrow, it will be through that."

"How do we find the puzzle pieces?" Mekos asked. "How do we unite and stop being your puppets and existing only to entertain you?"

"My sister has dedicated her life to that question. When Kaley and her family were brought here, there were other Earth people who came with them. Each person has something special about them, something he or she can do. They have different levels of magic. What Vian foresaw involves them too. I don't know how."

"Bree was sent to another island," Aradella said. "She was told it was imperative that she go. Will she help undo what your people have imposed on it?"

Davro nodded. "I hope so. One of the earthlings ran away. It's believed she made it to the island where Bree was sent. My sister says that everything is part of a long-term plan."

"Won't your spy cameras see what we're trying to do?" Ian asked.

Davro gave a smirk of a grin. "Thanks to my sister, Yuzans are being told that when you move from one island to another your only purpose is to make friends. So far, they think it's all entertainment."

Aradella curled her lip. "Maybe there are advantages to them thinking we're stupid."

Davro smiled. "That's what my sister says."

"But we are actually uniting the many islands on Bellis," Mekos said, smiling back. "And your language chips are allowing us to do it."

Nodding, Davro looked at his nephew with pride.

Abruptly, Aradella stood up. "It has been a long day."

Mekos stood up beside her, Ian to his shoulder. "Yes, it has. Could we rest?"

"Of course." Davro stood. "Accommodation has been made for you." He led them down a short hall and opened a set of double doors.

What they saw made Aradella gasp. Unlike the rest of the place, the bedroom looked like Qip's cottage. There was pretty striped wallpaper in shades of pink and cream. A wooden bed had soft covers, and fat chairs were upholstered with a print of roses. It was truly beautiful!

"This is what Qip said you'd like." Davro looked as though he hoped he'd pleased them.

"It's lovely," Aradella said.

Davro smiled and looked at Ian. "I have a reproduction of an Earth sultan's palace for you. It is lavishly decadent." To his delight, Ian flew to his shoulder.

"Lead the way," Ian ordered and they left.

Alone, Mekos and Aradella looked about. She went to the window and opened the curtain. Outside were three of the giant playboards.

*Have dinner with Thomas Jefferson.*

*Weaving class with Mahatma Gandhi.*

*See the best of the Cutting Games on Selkan. Feel the pain or not. Your choice.*

She turned away in disgust. "I hate this place."

Mekos fell back onto the bed and the comforter almost encircled him. "This is the finest quality of swan fabric. We save this for our own family. I wonder how they got it."

"Stole it, then enjoyed the tears of whoever they robbed." She dropped down onto a chair.

Mekos looked at her hard. "What's on your mind? Other than solving all this, that is." He waved his hand to mean what they'd been told.

"I understand what he was saying, and it's made me think about my own life. I've always been jealous of my cousins." She looked at him. "What if I had been made queen? What would I have done to my subjects? Would I have hated people based on their looks? Would I have sent pretty people to a place like Abicis? Or worse?"

Mekos smiled at her with love in his eyes. "Maybe learning this makes it all worth it."

"I don't want to stay here. I want to go home."

Mekos turned on his side, his head on his hand. "And where is that? Have we decided where we'll live? With help, we could probably overtake Pithan and you could rule—"

"No!" she said fiercely, then quieted. "Sometimes you can't make up your mind about things, then suddenly you *know* what you want." She looked hard into his eyes. "This—" She waved her hand to mean the whole planet. "This isn't something I want to try to solve alone. That's what you and I did with Valona and we failed. Because of us, Urah and Olina are free to cause more destruction." She paused. "I want us to *help* with whatever Tanek and Vian and all of them are doing. I don't want you and me to ever again think we're alone in this fight." She took a breath. "And I want a home and a family. I want to live at your destroyed Homestead. I want your father and Kaley to be there as we rebuild the place. And I want my friend Hale there. I miss her very much."

She looked at him with great intensity. "What Davro said about my body . . . I want a child."

Mekos raised an eyebrow. "You mean *now*?"

"Yes. *This* child. Don't ask me to explain it but *this* child showed himself to me through your uncle." She paused. "After seeing this place and how much control these people have over every aspect of us, I don't want to think of the future. I want all the happiness I can get right now. This minute. No more postponement!" Her voice was rising.

Mekos was smiling at her, listening.

She smiled back at him. "I want our child to learn about swans, like your family knows. Our son will be of the Order of Swans."

"With you as his mother, we'll make it the Order of Royal Swans."

Aradella raised her eyebrows. "Do you know how to do it? I mean, to make a baby?"

He smiled. "Yes. Papá has only done it once, to make me, but he said it's a pleasure like no other. For both of us." He paused. "You have no doubts?"

"I've never been more sure about anything in my life. What about you?"

"No doubts whatever." He opened his arms to her.

# 26

Aradella heard a noise but she didn't want to respond to it. After the energetic acrobatics of last night, she just wanted to sleep. She vaguely remembered that at daylight, Mekos had left. He'd kissed her lingeringly and said that Davro was offering to give him a tour of the island.

"He says I won't need the mask. Do you mind?"

Aradella was so sleepy all she could do was give a single shake to her head.

Chuckling, he kissed her again, then did his silent-fox act and left the room.

She went back to sleep but now something was trying to wake her up. "No," she mumbled. "Let me sleep."

She heard a crash of something hitting the floor but she buried her face under the covers.

"I will stamp on your eyeballs if you don't wake up."

It was Ian's voice. For someone so little, he could certainly be loud. "Go away." To her great annoyance, the little man slid under the covers and set his body to vibrating. It was like being in the midst of a beehive. "Stop it!" She made a grab at him but didn't come close to catching him.

"Olina and Urah are here."

He was so loud, Aradella winced. Reluctantly, she opened her eyes. Ian was almost standing on her nose. She drew back and flung the cover off her head. "What?!" she demanded.

He flew back but not too far away. "Olina and Urah are here on this island."

Aradella blinked a few times. "Tell Mekos and his uncle that they have to—"

"You think I didn't go to them first?" he shot back. "They're somewhere secret, spying no doubt, and they've disabled their chips."

Aradella was fully awake. "Where are they?"

"In a beauty salon."

"A what?" She sat up.

"Like the Beauty Girls on Pithan have, only a bigger shop. Urah looked twenty years younger."

Aradella's head whirled. "Those farken sound waves! If they can revive dead earthlings, I'm sure they can de-age some old witch." She grit her teeth. "And for what purpose? So these farkwads can send the witch back to Pithan to cause more havoc to give these lazy creeps more feelies?"

Ian blinked at her. "You do not show this side of yourself to Mekos."

"I didn't survive Olina and her mother by being a wimp. Turn around. I'm going to get out of bed and I have no clothes on."

"I've seen—"

"Don't say it!" she ordered.

Ian turned away.

As Aradella rapidly pulled on clothes she asked, "Do you know how to get there?"

"You can't take on those women by yourself."

His words made Aradella think of the reality of facing two extremely powerful witches. She checked that Ian was looking out the window, then she pulled the wooden box out of the bag. She took a heavy cloth off the little table by the chair, then opened the box to look at the knife. She could barely see the poisonous leaves but they were there. Carefully, she placed the knife onto the cloth, rolled it up, and put it deep into the pocket of her loose trousers. A tunic covered the bulge. "No, but I can watch them and follow them, while you go find Mekos. You can turn around now."

When Ian looked back, he saw one of the sexless Empyreans. Aradella had put on the mask and she was camouflaged into being one of "them."

She lifted her hair. "Hide in here and lead me to where they are. Is it far?"

"Not at all. But there are more playboards. There's also a shop selling little gingerbread houses."

She was about to leave, but then she pulled the medallion out of the bag and put it around her neck. *Urah wanted this, did she?* she thought. Maybe she could bargain with it. Or maybe just having it would protect her—or maybe it would turn her into a half goat. She had no idea which.

Minutes later, they were outside Davro's box house, and Ian knew where there was an elevator—something that was new to Aradella.

Once they were on the street, she kept her head down. For all she knew, the people could tell each other apart even with her mask on and she didn't want to risk being exposed. But then, the people around them all seemed very busy—and excited. That was understandable since they were on constant holiday and rushing from one ghastly entertainment to another.

Ian, hidden in her hair, buzzed loudly to be sure she saw the gingerbread store. There was a window display. Some of the little houses had candied flames shooting out of them. There were tiny figures of Tanek, Kaley, and Sojee.

"I wish I could get an image of Arit made out of cake," Ian said into her ear, sounding wistful.

Aradella tried not to look at the brightly lit boards above them. She didn't mind the ones that were about Earth that made no sense to her, but she hated the others—and feared what she hadn't seen. Were there pictures of her and Mekos at the waterfall?

"Here!" Ian said.

The building was glass across the front and there were mannequins of the bland Empyreans—or should she now call them Yuzans?—with promises of soft skin, fragrant perfumes, and rejuvenation.

"No makeup but slash and dice your face is all right?" Aradella mumbled. "Gotta stay young or you'll be sent to Abicis." She started for the door then halted. "How do I find them?"

"Room 6B. I'll distract the others while you slip in there."

She opened the door and went in. It was bustling inside with people in identical tunics of off-white. More of them sat in chairs. For all that their faces were being coated with various colors of creams, the people still looked alike.

"They're too afraid to stand out," Aradella whispered to Ian.

"Could I help you?" a person asked.

Before Aradella could reply, Ian flew to a shelf and began pushing glass containers to the floor. In the resulting chaos, Aradella hurried down the hall, slipped into room 6B, and closed the door behind her.

It was an austere room with cabinets and a sink on one side. In the middle was a tall table. Lying on it was a woman-shaped form covered fully with a white cloth. Aradella knew that it was Olina. The height of her was unmistakable.

Aradella put her hand on the hilt of the knife in her pocket. She hoped the poison of the leaves would not come through the cloth.

"Have you come for me?" Olina asked from under the cloth. She sounded amused.

Aradella said nothing, but she moved a bit closer. Outside, she heard more crashes. Ian was still keeping people busy.

Olina sat up, the cloth falling away. She had on one of the Empyrean tunics, and she looked years younger.

Aradella stared at her. Her newly smoothed face reminded

her of someone she'd seen before but she couldn't remember who or where.

"You think I don't know who you are? Take off that useless mask and show your ugly face." Olina was laughing at her—as she'd done since Aradella was a child.

The crashing outside stopped and Aradella hoped Ian had left to find Mekos and his uncle.

Olina turned to sit on the side of the table. "At least have the courage to face me. Or are you as cowardly as your father was?"

That taunt made Aradella peel the mask from her face, put it in her second pocket, then defiantly look at the woman.

For a second, Olina showed her surprise as she looked her up and down. "You are different. Did you sell your soul for beauty?" She was smirking. "It failed. You'll never be a beauty no matter how hard you try." She got down from the table, obviously unafraid of anything Aradella did.

Olina's hateful words made it difficult for Aradella not to revert to the beaten-down girl she used to be, but she put her shoulders back. "I no longer have to wear big clothes, or hide from your treachery and your evil. Is that what you mean?"

From Olina's expression, she was about to attack. Aradella knew she wouldn't be able to withstand a witch of her power, so she needed to keep her talking—so she could get closer to her. "You took away people I loved. You—"

Olina turned a face of fury to her. "You think *I* was ever loved? My mother despised me. She—"

"Spare me!" Aradella said as she inched closer. "Your mother doesn't love anyone."

"What you don't know could fill one of those books you tried to hide. You think I didn't know about them?" She smiled in a hateful way. "Were they love stories about the life you'd never have? Oh so clever Aradella. You were never half as smart as you thought you were."

Aradella moved a half step. She didn't want to talk about her books. "You tried to marry me off to that whiny little Nessa."

"You think I wanted to marry your uncle?" she half shouted. "With a prince you would have had a glorious future. Better than I've had!"

Aradella wasn't going to allow this evil woman to turn herself into a victim. All she wanted was to distract her and get close enough to use the knife she had her hand on. "You are twisting everything to try to make the horror you did to me seem for the good. I woke up every morning wondering if it would be my last day alive."

"So did I." Olina gave a shrug then raised her hand. "Now you're boring me."

Aradella knew that what was coming was some witchery directed at her. Olina could kill with the stroke of her hand. By reflex, Aradella twisted to the side, her head down, ready to receive the final blow. But nothing happened.

Olina had frozen in place, her hand raised. "Where did you get that?" Her voice was a whisper and she was looking at the medallion around Aradella's neck. Her face might be new but it took on the look of rage and hatred Aradella knew so well. "You're after Haver's soul, aren't you? How did you find that necklace?"

Aradella had no idea what Haver had to do with the medallion, but she wanted as much time as possible. "I got it from the person who stole it."

"That slimy goat?"

"You mean the Monster of Sheean?"

"Whatever he calls himself. Give it to me! It's mine!"

Olina leaned forward, meaning to snatch the necklace—and Aradella saw her opportunity. In one quick motion, she took the knife out of her pocket and slammed it into Olina's stomach.

Olina staggered back against the tall cabinet. She looked more surprised than in pain. She looked down at the knife sticking out of her stomach. With a grunt of pain, she pulled it out, tossed it onto the table, then looked at her hand. There was blood on it. She looked back at Aradella. "You think you have harmed me? That you've ended *me*? This is nothing." Olina put both hands over the wound and muttered some words.

As Aradella watched, the wound closed. No more blood came out.

Olina looked at her. "Now I will do to you what I should have done years ago." She raised her arms into the air and in an instant, a fog came up from the floor and began to fill the room.

*This is the end*, Aradella thought. She stood upright, put her shoulders back, and stiffened her body in preparation. Visions of Mekos came to her and she thought of what could have been—but would not happen now.

But in the next instant, the fog disappeared. There one second, gone the next. Olina put her arms down, her hands over the wound. It was starting to ooze blood. "What have you done to me?" Her face showed her shock.

It took Aradella a moment to realize that maybe this wasn't the end. Not for her, anyway. "You built a wall between me and my home, but I made that space into a library. My *friends* brought me books, not about love but about plants." Aradella paused to look at the blood that was growing under Olina's clasped hands. "That is the knife that I used to kill Valona. It still has her blood on it, and I wrapped it in the leaves of a plant from her garden. She had three of them with a little fence around them."

From the way Olina's eyes widened, she knew about the plants. "Valona said they were her insurance against my mother."

"I immediately recognized that plant. It's from a place on Earth called the Amazon, and it's name is . . ." She waved her hand. "That doesn't matter, but it translates as 'go home.' The theory is that the poison of the leaves allows you enough time to go home before you die." She watched as Olina, still showing her shock, slowly slid down the cabinet to sit on the floor. More blood was coming from the stab wound. And with each second, Olina looked weaker. She might be able to heal the cut but she couldn't survive the poison. Or was Valona's blood on the blade the death knell?

Suddenly, all the hate Aradella had felt for most of her life dissolved. It was over! One of the women who had caused her so much pain was dying. She sat down on the floor beside her enemy, not touching but close, and removed the medallion and held it. "Is there anything you'd like to reveal before you leave this existence?" Aradella raised an eyebrow. "Maybe you know something that could hurt the mother who never loved you. I assume she's alive and safe somewhere."

Olina glared at the medallion. "So you found it. My mother was insane with anger that it was gone."

Aradella opened the case and looked at the picture. "Tell me about it. Who is the beautiful woman?"

"My mother."

It was hard to believe that the pretty woman could age into the old crone that was Urah, but then Aradella looked at the picture. "This looks like you. I saw that it reminded me of someone. Do the stones mean something?"

Olina was getting weaker. "It's a lock. I played with it when I was a child—until my mother caught me and took it away from me. Start with the big one and push 3 7 1."

Aradella pushed the stones in that order and a tiny door opened to show a picture of a man. She instantly recognized him. When he'd disappeared, his picture was everywhere as people searched for him. "This is Haver Beyhan, Tanek's grandfather. Why is his picture with Urah's?"

"She loved him. He was my father."

It took Aradella moments to digest this information. She knew that Haver had not left his wife and family to be with Urah and their child. It must have made Urah furious. "Is *this* why Urah destroyed the Homestead and killed Haver's son?"

"Yes."

"It wasn't an Empyrean conspiracy?"

"No. It was about my father. He wanted nothing to do with us." She gave a half smile at Aradella's look of shock mixed with disbelief. "So you don't know everything as you think you do!

He and my mother were first in love as children. They were to marry but he saw my mother do something he didn't like, so he left her. It was cruel of him as what she did was a small thing. What did a peasant child matter?"

Aradella didn't want to imagine what horrible thing Urah had been caught doing. "But he did impregnate her."

"A few drops of this and that and men are easy. I doubt that he remembered what happened either time."

Aradella's eyes widened. "*Either* time?"

"I have a brother, but my mother sent him away when he was a baby. For his protection."

"Protection from what?"

"From me, of course." Olina's tone said she was proud of that. "I tried hard to kill the brat and I was making progress, so she took him away. I've searched for him but I couldn't find him or the key."

Aradella drew in her breath. "What key?"

"I don't know! But it's something important. She thought it would protect him, but it didn't." Again, Olina gave a weak smile. "The key does something on Empyrea and only he can use it. Without him, it's useless."

Aradella looked at the picture in the medallion. "Haver died in a cave," she whispered.

Olina gave a nod of admiration that she knew that. "My mother only meant to kill *him* but she got one of his sons instead. He tried to hide from her but she found him. To be fair, she offered him their son, Ramil, as a replacement for his other son, but he said no." Olina shrugged. "He forced her to do what she did."

"Meaning that she killed Haver in that cave." Aradella spoke softy as she imagined the horror of the scene.

Olina nodded at the medallion. "That's when she put his soul in there. It's why she was so angry when that goat-man stole it."

With wide eyes, Aradella looked at the medallion. "His soul is in here?" she whispered.

"It's an easy spell. Even a nothing like you could do it—7 7 7 will unlock it. I wanted to put his soul into one of my riding birds but I was kept from it. My mother—"

Olina gave Aradella a wide-eyed look then she said no more. Her head fell forward onto her chest and she was silent. That her lifelong enemy was dead—at her hand—wasn't something Aradella could quite comprehend. With her hand on the edge of the table, she tried to stand, but her legs were wobbly.

Then, suddenly, Mekos was there. She smiled at him in a drunken way. "I did it again." Then the room seemed to start turning around rapidly.

Mekos caught her before she went down. Holding her in his arms, he looked at Davro. At their feet was Olina's body. His eyes were asking, *What do I do about this?*

"I will take care of this," Davro said. With his thumb and a finger, he picked up the knife off the table, dropped it into an empty jar and tightened the lid over it. He ran his disk down Aradella's inert body. When he looked at his nephew, there were tears in his eyes. "I never thought I'd see this. You are going to be a father to—" He swallowed. "To *two* babies."

Mekos nodded, not really taking it in yet. "I want to take her home. May I borrow your little vehicle?"

"Gladly. Ian . . . ?"

"I think he'll be all right." Under Mekos's shirt was Ian's oval case and the little man was inside.

"May I visit you?" Davro asked.

"You are always welcome and we look forward to seeing you again. How do we get back to your house?"

Davro opened a door and they saw that the Spacer was waiting for them. "You don't need to return. Everything you brought with you is in there, plus a few gifts, and all the equipment Qip wants. I will come to you soon."

Mekos placed the unconscious Aradella inside, then put Ian's case near his blue chair.

"Thank you," Mekos said to his uncle, then he got into the Spacer. It quickly rose and started flying away.

When Aradella woke, she wasn't surprised to find herself in the snug little vehicle. Ian was in his chair and Mekos was leaning back, looking at both of them. "Where are we going?" she asked.

"To Qip's. We have some building materials to deliver to him. We put the biggest and heaviest pieces in that bag of yours. Are you hungry?"

"No! In fact my stomach is dancing about, but after what happened, that's understandable." She looked at him. "Are you all right? I didn't want to do that alone but—"

He took her hand in his. "You and Ian are the heroes."

She looked at the little man. "What did you do?"

"It was for my sister."

She turned to Mekos. "Tell me!"

Ian made a gesture that Mekos could tell the story.

"Ian found Urah at a tavern near where her daughter was. He showed himself to her, then he taunted her."

"Buzzing in her face? Wings against her ears?" Aradella asked. "That kind of thing?"

"I spit in her eye," Ian said. "And I called her a few things."

"She ran after him," Mekos said. "Into one of those lifting rooms."

"An elevator," Aradella said.

"Yes. And when she reached the top, Ian was waiting for her."

"She laughed at me," Ian said. "She said she'd foreseen that a *man* would kill her and since I wasn't one, she was safe."

Aradella's eyes widened. "That must have made you angry."

"I laughed and said that no *man* would ever want her, then I flew backward."

"He means," Mekos said, "that she ran after him all the way off the building."

"Oh," Aradella said. "As in *splat*?"

"Exactly like that."

It took Aradella a few moments to ingest all that had happened. "They are gone. Both of those evil women are gone. Now do you think we'll be forgiven?"

"Yes, I do. I think we'll be welcomed home with enthusiasm."

Aradella let out a sigh of relief. "Actually, I think I am hungry. You remember those tiny green fish we had at Qip's?"

"The ones you refused to even try?"

"Yes. Those. Right now I could eat a bucket full of them."

He smiled at her in a way that made her heart hurt. She knew why he was looking at her like that, but now was not the time to talk of it. When they did speak of it, she wanted to be alone with him and far away from the lights of gaudy Empyrea.

She took his hand in hers and held it to her cheek.

"I love you," he said softly. "With all my heart and soul, I love you."

"Yes," was all Aradella could say. "Yes."

Beside them a board flashed.

*See Mekos and Aradella fall in love.*

*What exactly did the lizard eat?*

*Plants hidden by a wall? What could they be? Find out all tonight!*

The three in the Spacer ignored the signs as they held each other. Forever.

*****